PRAISE FOR SAYVILLE TALES

I've sniggered my way through Hell, the train ride—beautifully illustrated—and stories told with such ironic wit, it was almost like watching an American version of a Monty Python show with pot. Nothing is sacred here, American history is told with pictures and conspiracy theories that will blow your mind.

—from *The International Review of Books, July* 2019

Sayville Tales by Lawrence Jay Switzer is an intricately crafted piece of literary fiction. It is a novel of short stories, or tales, and each flows and weaves seamlessly into the next. It is brilliantly written prose with a unique and witty style that pulls you in as if listening to a talented and animated oral storyteller.

It is a satirical masterpiece, with many of humankind's follies and vices on full display. Using derision and caustic wit, the author unveils ugly truths and pulls off a difficult task of personifying the Devil, superbly using the setting of a train ride and its many stops along the way to Hell.

If you are a fan of literary fiction, satire, dark humor, sarcasm, or just plain old-fashioned entertaining storytelling, *Sayville Tales* will not disappoint.

—Amazon reviewer

I was stunned from the first moment by the overall conception of this compilation of short quirky tales strung together. Beautifully conceived and produced, the nuanced use of language, the humor, and the sense of the cosmic brought into the particular with awe and irony, are evident from the first page. The work is seductive, playful and profound—to be savored.

—Amazon reviewer

Come along with me.

Camp Uncas
Legacy
Press

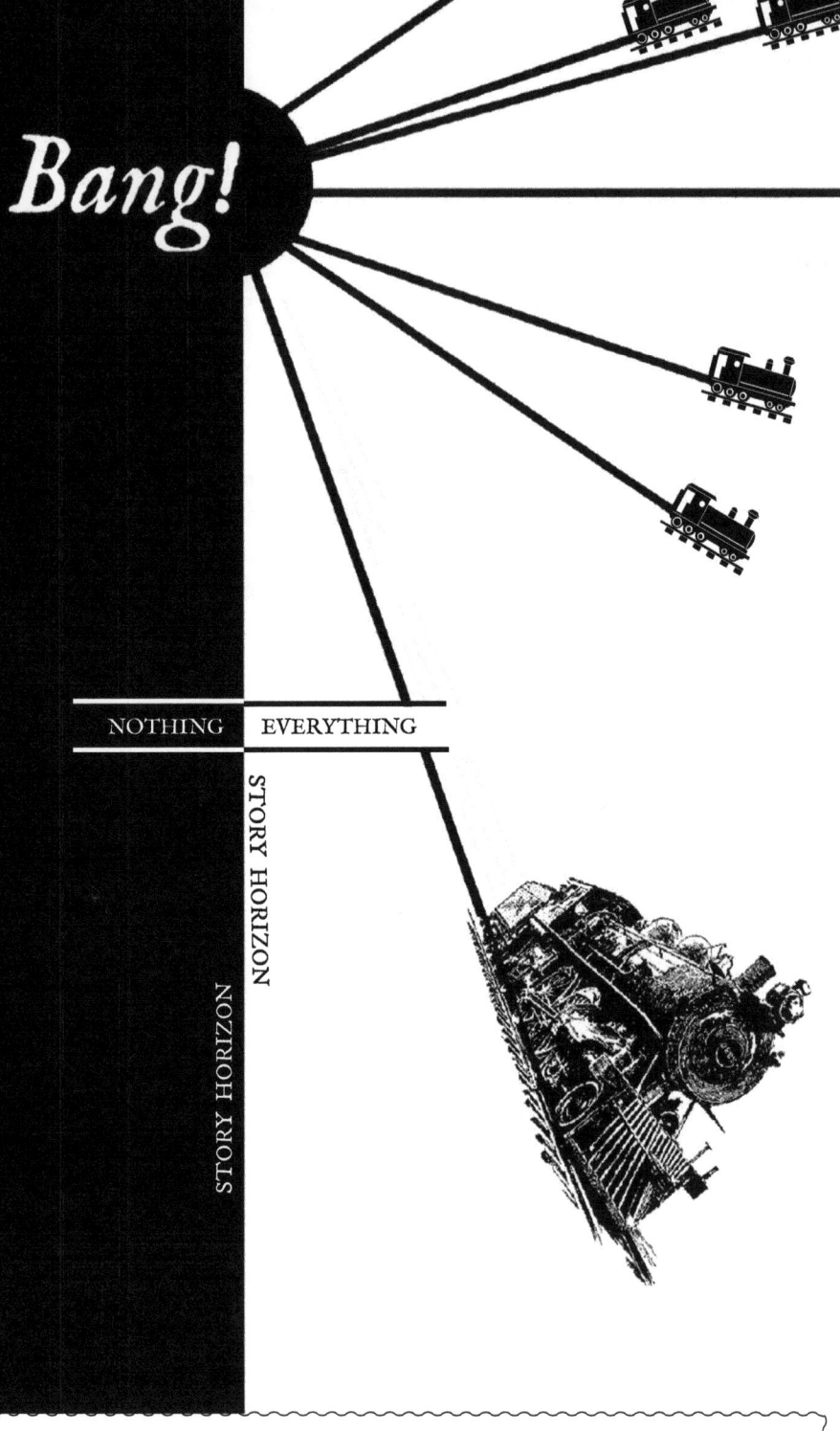

Bang!

NOTHING   EVERYTHING

STORY HORIZON

STORY HORIZON

Illustration from *Mommy, Where Did My Story Come From?*
[M. Zinberg, CUL Press, 1951. Licensed for use by The Zinberg Trust.]

SAYVILL

LAWRENCE · J

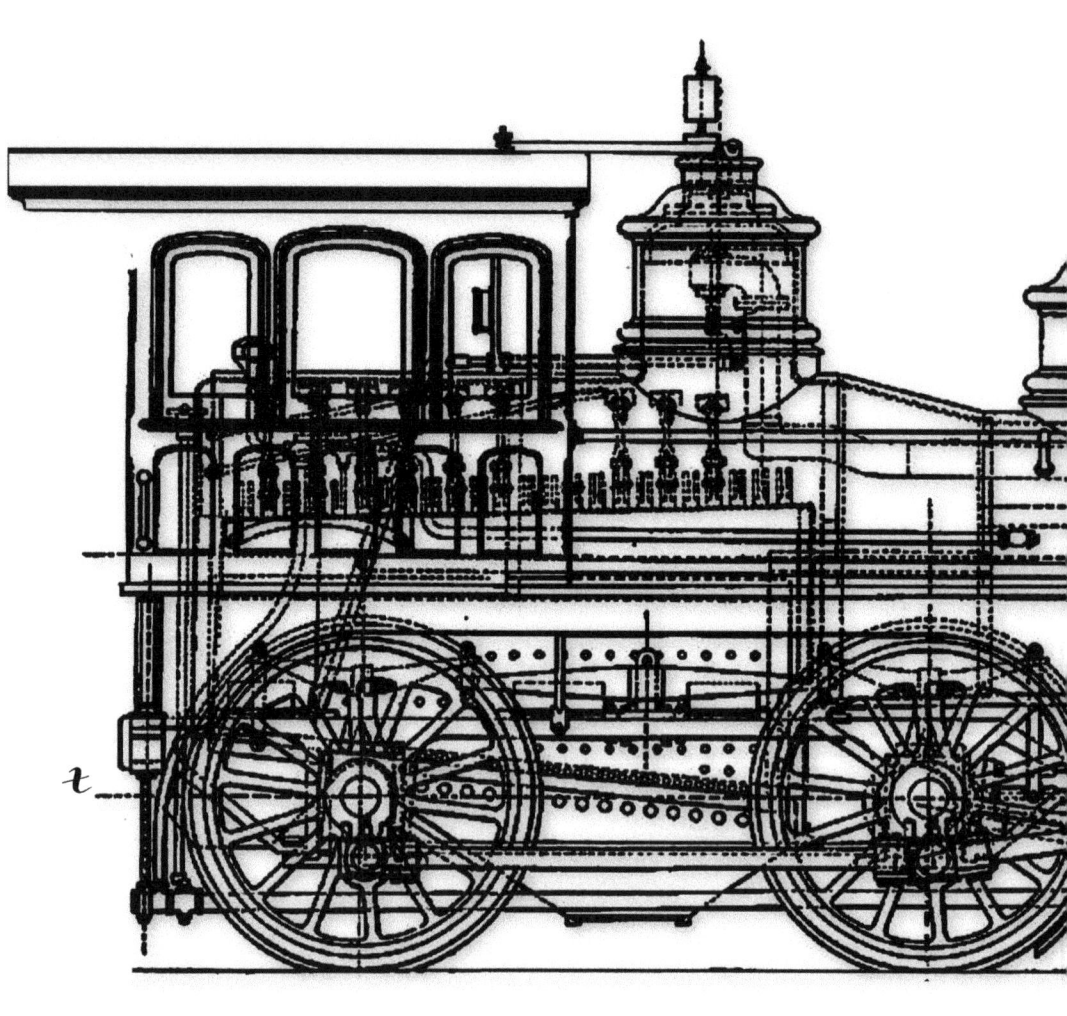

E·TALES

AY · SWITZER

Design for the original Fox locomotive. Courtesy of Fox Ironclad Railroad Ltd.

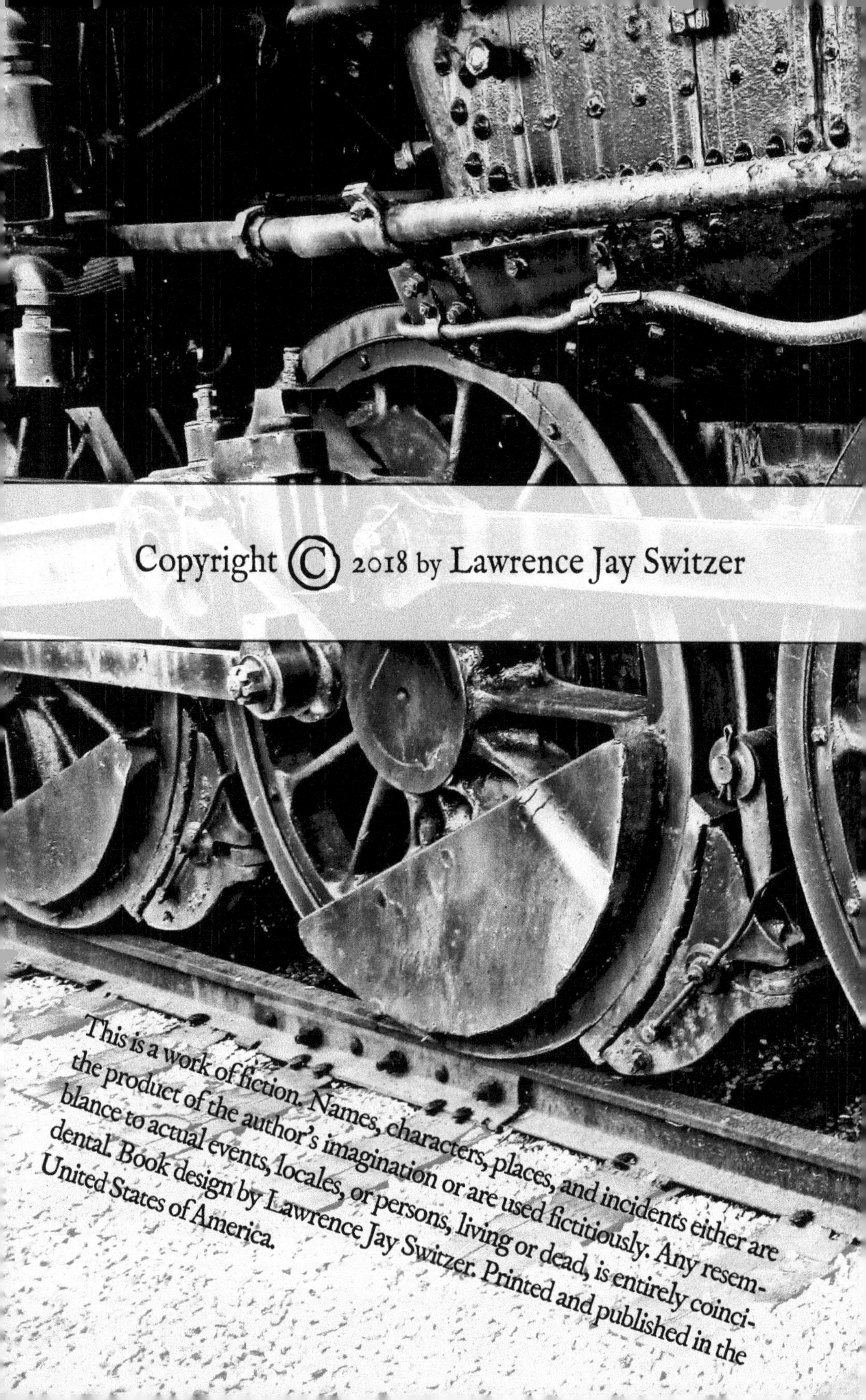

 Book design by Lawrence Jay Switzer. Printed and published in the United States of America.

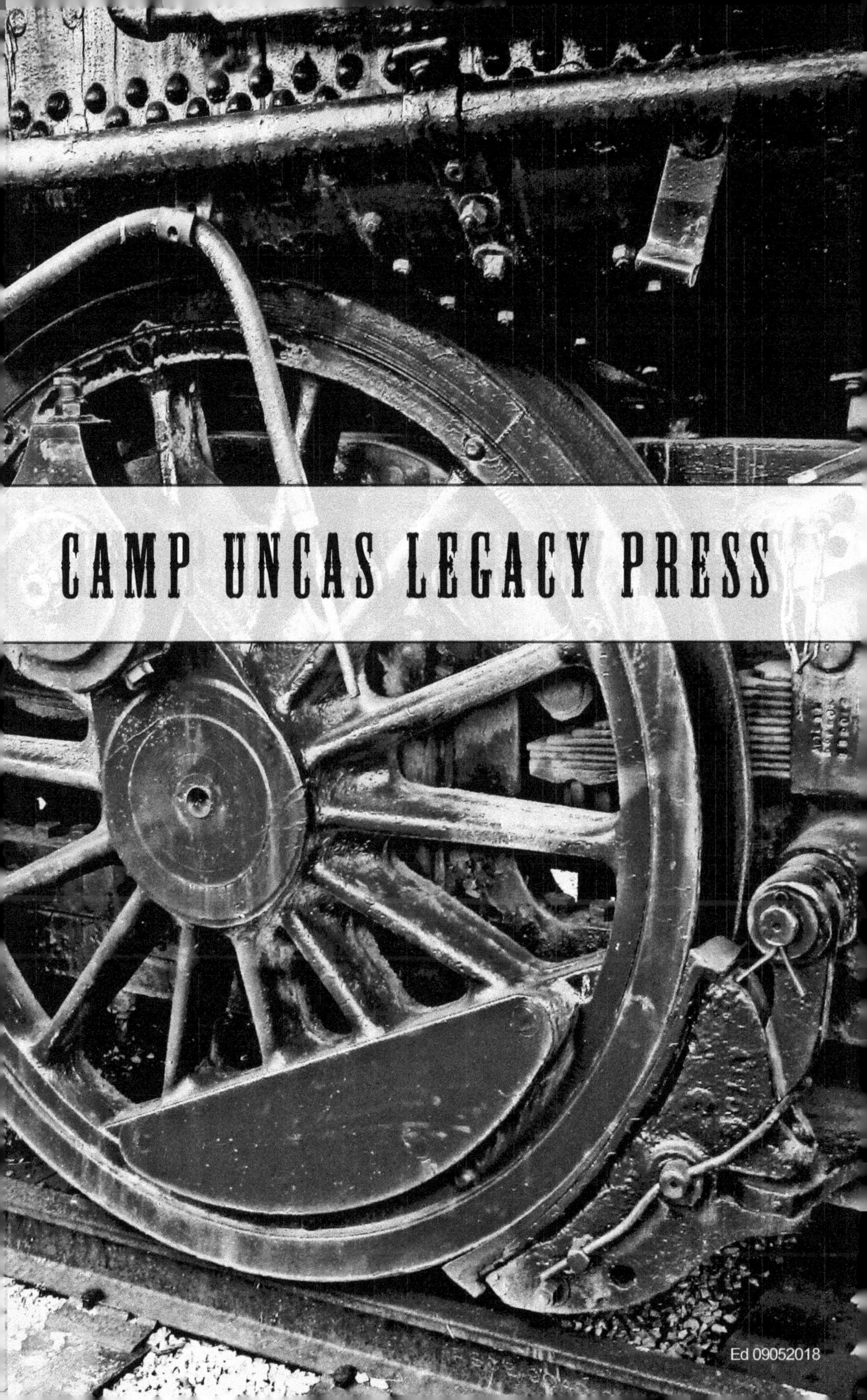
CAMP UNCAS LEGACY PRESS
Ed 09052018

TEMPUS FUGIT

TALETABLE

EASTBOUND SERVICE ON THE PAUMANOK EXPRESS

DEPARTS	STATION
00:01	The Adventures of the Quick Brown Fox
00:77	✦ Book Now!
00:79	✦ A Prologue to The Professor's Tale
00:95	The Professor's Tale | Once Upon a Time, a Fox (*a false start*)
00:99	The Professor's Tale Re-Told | – – – –, a Fox (*new and improved*)
01:44	✦ April 2nd is National Lazy Dog Day
01:47	✦ A Prologue to The Shrink's Tale
01:69	The Shrink's Tale | Fibs That Fell From Father's Lips
01:75	✦ A Prologue to The Artist's Tale
01:85	The Artist's Tale | The Baker, the Maiden, and the Unicorn
01:89	✦ A Prologue to The Wife of Bathbaum's Tale
01:97	The Wife of Bathbaum's Tale | The Nostradamus Cookbook
02:05	The Tour Guide's Guide | Victory Bar Air Conditioned
02:19	✦ Morning Coffee is Served
02:21	The Nun's Dream | A Lentil for Your Thoughts, Briefly Told
02:63	✦ A Prologue to The Florist's Tale
02:69	The Florist's Tale | The Tale of a Tall Tulip
02:75	✦ A Prologue to The Rabbi's Interview
02:83	The Rabbi's Interview | The Theory of Bagel Relativity
02:99	✦ A Sex Stop | Nobody Gets Off at this Stop!
03:03	✦ Teatime for the Disembarked, a Ghostly Prologue
03:19	Mrs. Lincoln Has Scant Praise for Mr. Spielberg's Bio-Pic
03:28	✦ A Fugue in Phone Major | Seating for 4, Conversation for 8

. . . continued on reverse side . . .

TALETABLE

EASTBOUND SERVICE ON THE PAUMANOK EXPRESS

DEPARTS	STATION
03:37	✦ A Prologue to the Acting Conductor's Tale
03:41	The Acting Conductor's Tale | Be Careful Who You Ask For
03:58	✦ Lunch Menu—*The Brown Fox* Dining Car, *Paumanok Line*
03:61	✦ A Prologue to a Trio of Tales | The Dining Car is Now Open
03:71	1. The Professor's Second Tale | The Devil's Daughter's Doll's Diary
03:83	2. The Man-of-Law's Tale | Things That Never Happened
04:07	3. The Journalist's Tale | Sayville Spies and Whispers
04:31	The Missing Passenger's Prologue & Tale | They Say Rain
04:38	✦ A Cellphone Octet
04:41	The Author's Tale | Lorem Ipsum Dolor
04:43	Lady Hooch's Aborted Tale | Little Maury Goes to Summer Camp
04:45	The Engineer's Incident Report | Sayville in Three Minutes
04:47	✦ Deus ex Machina
04:54	✦ Epilogue | Twelve Boxers Chase Victor Across the Great Dike at Sylt

To Canterbury

Each among this motley troupe shall one and all regayle,
When comes their chance at last, with the telling of a tayle.
While fleet as a fox his wynding waye is wont to wend,
We blythely follow where Fate foretells, untill our journey's end.

TO SAYVILLE

ALL ABOARD

The Adventures of the Quick Brown Fox

Dear Reader (or Rider, if you will), make note (use the back of your ticket if other paper is not readily at hand): you are located on the first page of a book of travelers' tales. The number *1* has been posted on the shoulder of this highway of words as would an ordinary road sign (*e.g., Welcome to A Book, Population = 1, Speed Limit = 1, Page = 1*).

There are those among us who might dispute the veracity of the Bible, question the existence of the Bogeyman, or Santa Claus, or Cropsey, or the Tooth Fairy, or even the Devil (and *that* would be a big mistake), but no one seriously considers road signs suitable subjects for debate or doubt. In fact, a recent poll revealed that road signs—since the publication of the *Warren Commission Report* in 1964—are one of the few forms of public reading material that Americans continue to

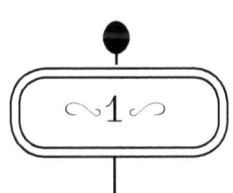

demonstrate faith in. How much easier life would be, by such token, if one could read road signs rather than those upsetting newspapers and bad-for-you magazines whilst heeding nature's call, how comforting to know precisely where one stands, or sits.

What, generally speaking, does the workaday road sign communicate to us, the humble passersby? *Somewhere Station—Three Miles...* (or) *Welcome to Someplace Place, a Nice Place to Live!* ... (or) *You Are Now Leaving Beentheredonethatville...* The highway tells us a story through artfully arranged road signs, a story with a beginning, a middle, and an end (that's three things that most modern novels don't have), and a sign for everything, like a series of carrots, to keep us going.

There are no credible conspiracy theories incriminating page numbers, so one may rest assured that one's whereabouts are one's whereabouts (*Page 2*, according to the sign) and the direction one is traveling in *is* the direction one is traveling in (typically, if you are on *Page 2*, towards *Page 3* and beyond). Behind you, all that has ever existed is concocted from the amorphous jumble of language known as *Once Upon a Time*. And preceding the left-most edge of the letter *O* in *Once Upon a Time*, there is Nothing. Just the Big Bang. Just a very thin line and a very loud noise—a mark not seen and a sound not heard—divide all that is Nothing from all that is Something.

The story universe is expanding, too. *Happily Ever After* is drifting further and further away from *Once Upon a Time*. And there are more and more stories every day. It's not possible to investigate them all or even to write their names down. One can easily get lost in the maze of stories and never be heard from again, even if you drop crumbs as you go along. You can be strangled in the webs that connect stories or grow hair in odd places from taking the X-rated ones too seriously.

At least you'll always know precisely where you are in any story you choose to settle down with—the conveniently placed page number makes it easy as 1-2-3. But even *that* leaves important plot points unresolved; for example: how you got where you are, where you're going, and where you'll end up (not necessarily the same place you're going).

The untied lace on the shoes of all narratives is a simple matter which can be separated into two schools of story. "What's Going to Happen" (which promises a *rhetorical* statement of fact for believers in Fate, proposing the existence of an individualized, pre-ordained, carved-in-stone resolution ahead that one can make plans around) and, "What's Going to Happen?" (with a question mark appended, *non-rhetorical*, for believers in the Divine, with its attractive Eleventh-Hour-Reprieve-Via-Spontaneous-Contrition Clause being a major drawing-card).

Destiny or Divinity—you can own stock in either, but not both. Which you choose, and why, is, at the minimum, one more story for you to tell and sell. All you have to do is find a listener and—*voilà!*—the steam whistle shrieks with joy, the iron wheels grind into motion, and—*off you go!*—flapping your lips and wagging your tongue at 55 m.p.h.

ow anyone arrives at this location (*Page 3*) is a story, too—or, more precisely, a network of interconnected stories, like an elaborate spider's web. What powerful, invisible forces caused this dime-a-dozen book to manifest itself in *your* hands? Do you remember meeting the storyteller in the past, and if you did, what do you recall of the entanglement of stories that connected *your* life—like an unavoidable collision—with *his*, and *this*?

Some stories are like souls in flight, looking for suitable places to roost. There are also less fortunate stories, homeless narratives, story hobos, and meandering itinerant folktales—stories with no choice but to survive as best they can—usually as night squatters, manifesting themselves in dreams, taking on all manner of disguises and *personae* wherever they can find a door left unlocked or a crack in the mortar. While the fitful sleeper tosses and turns, sighs, and snores, dramas and comedies wander in and out of the dream-state mists and dance around for their own amusement. No one knows where those stories go when their time on stage is done, when the bat shields its eyes from the onset of daylight, when the cock crows, the alarm clock rings, the dog jumps on your bed and licks your face, the milkman accidentally drops a bottle on the porch.

t takes all kinds of stories to make a storybook. *From recent writers' blogs, then, judiciously selected for your riding and reading pleasure, a sampling of stories coincidentally about stories and storytellers:*

{ 1 } Stories and journeys are not *only* about the signage. There are spaces between the signs. Pauses. Caesuras. Digressions. Rest stops. Addressing this, an elderly rabbi, considered by some to be a great scholar (and by others to be the village idiot who escaped from a long-vanished *shtetl* with one tooth and two *kopecks*), has published a pamphlet about the nature of space between road signs.

Reading his notes aloud at a packed press conference, he elaborated at length on his theory that this "in-between" space was principally composed of the holes liberated from previously-eaten bagels. In other words, contrary to long-held belief, this emptiness was *not* a mere food vacuum. He referred to this non-vacuum as the *Gornisht Mitndrinnen Ort* (*GMO*). Some reporters arrived at the press event with the mistaken belief that the GMO was a newly-discovered galaxy, only to learn from the rabbi that it was a just a long-winded version of *bupkis*.

Fifteen minutes after beginning, he looked up to discover that, hanging to his left, there was a sign that read "Men's Toilet" and hanging to his right, a sign that read "Women's Toilet." The rest of the lecture hall—everything between the two signs—was filled with empty space (a/k/a an aggregation of bagel holes, or *groys GMO*).

{ 2 } A fat man living on the Lower East Side died. He was found in a heap, decomposing, on his kitchen floor. His long-estranged brother then crawled out of the proverbial woodwork and wrote a book about the decedent's final years, which consisted—for the most part—of unbridled eating binges. To the astonishment of publishing industry executives and popular culture gurus, the book went on to become a best-seller.

This culinary biography (apparently a newly-invented genre of convenience) consisted of a list of groceries found on a crumpled charge slip from the local supermarket, lab specimens of food remnants from a garbage bag found under the kitchen sink which the decedent had not yet taken out to the hopper, a manifest of the remaining contents of his refrigerator and kitchen cabinets, a chemical analysis of various stains, spills, and sundry cooking mishaps, scrapings from unwashed dishes and utensils, and an official statement outlining the contents of the corpse's digestive system, obtained from the Coroner's Office for an $80.00 document processing fee.

The surviving brother knew very little about the final years of his sibling's life, but, ignoring that obstacle as if it were a raindrop, he managed to conjure—from thin air, aromas, and leftovers—a fascinating biography using the road signs of the departed one's final meals on earth. Here, too, was a beginning, middle, and end—but deviously disguised as a trail of crumbs—a trajectory, as it were—leading from the shopping list to the autopsy. The biography was described by one disapproving critic as "a three-hundred-page dotted line hungrily dotting its way, dot by dot by dot, towards the endpaper and the afterlife." In opposition, another critic praised the book as a masterpiece of "gastronomical sleuthing," and christened it "the dyspeptic love-child of Sherlock Holmes and Julia Childs."

There was, incidentally, some hullabaloo in the consumer affairs industry concerning a chapter the author devoted to his outrage over the $80 he was charged for a coroner's report listing his brother's stomach contents—double the price of a birth certificate. The author pointed out that a birth certificate is, by definition, also a report of the contents of a stomach, and therefore both documents should be equitably priced. The consumer affairs people jumped into the fracas when the Municipal Bureau of Records responded to the criticism by raising the price of birth certificates to $80 instead of lowering the price of autopsy reports to $40. The matter is now in Litigation—a lazy suburb of Limbo with an extraordinarily low speed limit and no police force, which means that either the story is not yet over, or it has mutated into another literary form—a sequel, a series, or possibly a spin-off.

{3} An elderly woman, residing in Manhattan, got out of bed on a Wednesday morning and did nothing whatsoever for the entire Wednesday except for spending thirty seconds applying lipstick. Finally, at seven that evening, something happened. Her phone rang. It was her daughter. "Hi, Ma," the daughter said. Without hesitation, the mother blurted out, "What a day I had today!" This, too, was a story—of sorts—or at least it seemed so in the woman's mind (although later she would insist that all of this hoopla had occurred on a Tuesday). Short as the story was, it had a beginning, a middle, and an end. It was just impossible to discern any difference between the three. In any case, had she not put on the lipstick, we would have had to classify this as a footnote rather than a story, and we would not have been able to use it in this blog.

If afforded an opportunity, you would not hesitate to tell *your* story. Not only that—you are likely to tell that story to anyone who will listen to it. As it happens, acquiring a committed audience for your story requires more artistry than the act of narration. Some caution is advisable when seized by an unrelenting urge to tell that which should not be told, so be careful to conserve your story-telling breath—otherwise you might discover yourself exposing the raw matter of your soul to the occupant of a neighboring seat who merely *pretends* to be interested...snores in silence...sleeps with their eyes wide open...waits for *their* turn. That's what listening really is—fundamentally—not that anyone would dare to admit it.

Certain rules apply to all riders. Three, considered essential by scholars, are known as *The Three Essential Rules of Railroad Travel*. These were first described in print in the private journal of Thaddeus Anderson Fox, scion of the Fox dynasty (founders of the Fox Ironclad Railroad Ltd.), published twenty years after his death under the title *How to Arrive Alive, a Private Journal of a Personal Journey*.

The First Rule of Railroad Travel is that no one—no matter who they are—rides for free. *Everyone must pay their fare.* Even the Devil himself.

On the rare occasions when the Devil has an urge to ride the rails, he too must part with a fair share of that glittering substance so often referred to as The Root of All Evil, an essential asset that he has stockpiled, always in coin form, and which he totes around with him in his war-torn purse. The image of the Devil carrying a man purse filled with jingling change—as if he was on his way to the laundromat or a penny arcade—might seem incongruous. It helps to think of it, rather, as a *Devil purse*, necessary for sundry expenses incurred in his official capacity as the Devil. The Devil is not a charity. He must pay for his sins. As must we all.

When the Devil joins John Quincy Rider—and us (including *you,* Reader Dearest)—on the rails, despite his inconceivable age, measurable in yardsticks of millennia, he enjoys no Senior Citizen discount or VIP privileges. Young and healthy riders are not obliged to defer to his advanced age by forgoing their seats. On the other hand, only the foolhardiest person would let the Devil stand on his feet while they remained seated and slouched unattractively with their ubiquitous cellphone, prattling on endlessly, sputtering toxic-to-overhear nonsense. Something could happen. Sometimes something does. Not recognizing the Devil is an unacceptable excuse. If you don't want to get on the Devil's nerves, the best course of action is to become an equal-opportunity lickspittle. Kiss *all* asses and hope for the best

[Parenthetically, this form of irritating behavior is described by a term whose first literary use was by John Wolcott in *Odes to Mr. Paine*, published in 1794; we refer, of course, to the origin of the 200-year-old word "daredevil," (derivation: *dare the devil*). We do not know the identity of the first person so-described, but we have a reasonably good idea of his current whereabouts.]

One uneventful day, seeking to amuse himself in the company of working-people traveling homeward at a late hour—most of them exhausted and demoralized from having endured a lengthy and hellacious day at their offices—the Devil got distracted and missed the last eastbound train heading for Babylon, his favorite destination. Sodom and Gomorrah, place names that aroused in the Devil a poignant nostalgia for his beloved playgrounds of yesteryear, would have sounded more to his liking, but they did not exist on this rail system. Perversely, though, a number of the most gruesome torments inflicted in Sodom and Gomorrah in the Good-Olde-Days were now actually considered enjoyable. The Devil discovered this to his dismay one night when he doled out $100 in quarters from his Devil purse (lucre painstakingly harvested from the cushion-cracks of sofas in model living rooms at ten different department stores) to gain entry to a place called The Brimstone Club. There he was confronted with a machine from which a tongue of pink paper protruded. "What's that?" he asked a nearby gentleman whose torso appeared to be carpeted with tattoos or a severe case of leprosy—it was hard to tell from which affliction he suffered in the ultraviolet light. The man glared at the Devil incredulously, pointed at the protruding paper, and shouted over the din, "If you want to get scourged, you have to take a number." The Devil never had felt so "olde" in all his millenniums.

Short of creating a newfangled version of Sodom or Gomorrah himself so he would have a cutting-edge place to ride to, Babylon was the best available choice of destination; at least its three syllables sounded musical to his pointy ears, especially in contrast to the alternatives—miserable pickings with dowdy names like Levittown, Ronkonkoma, Mastic, and Shirley. That last one rang a bell that was particularly unappealing to the Devil. He had once dated a rich widow named Shirley, and she was extremely annoying. He broke off with her, telling her, "Your soul rubs me the wrong way."

Spontaneously, after he missed that last train, he decided to spend the night in Pennsylvania Station, making do with whatever opportunities for mischief presented themselves. When the Devil gets bored, when he starts whistling a tune in C-minor and strutting about aimlessly, jiggling the loose change which he keeps at the ready to deposit in human pinball machines, there will shortly be—to "coin" a cliché—"Hell to pay."

n the final years of the 19th century, the Devil was known to make his public appearances in the retro-medieval garb of a Mephistophelian courtier-dandy: black and red velvet doublet, perfumed gloves, a lacy jabot, pointed shoes, and a peaked cap sporting a very long feather or two. One night, he went to a performance of Gounod's *Faust* at the Palais Garnier, meticulously dressed in his best finery. To his horror, the *basso* performing the role of Mephistopheles made his Act One entrance wearing the identical ensemble, forcing him to flee from the nearest exit with his face concealed in his odiferous armpit. After that humiliation, he learned to appreciate the value of cheap, fashionless fashion. Nowadays he can look like anything from a leprechaun to a lizard. If he wishes, he can look exactly like your husband—not too difficult to pull off, since most husbands look like anything from a leprechaun to a lizard, too. With a close enough shave and a polyester pantssuit, he can even look exactly like your wife—so watch out!

For knocking about in both town and country, the hip modern-day Devil sports the carefree look of a red-headed, freckle-faced "pranksta" who will steal your wallet or briefcase as soon as look at you. After he rummages through your personal papers and declassifies any secrets you may be keeping, he returns everything except cash, which he retains as a Finder's Fee—in simple terms, this means that he has "found" out what you do not want him to know and is charging you a "fee" for the time it took him to do it.

Unimaginative and unsexy as he appears in his suburbanite madras plaids and laceless tennis shoes—a style he satirically and satanically refers to as "Off the Rack" (one of a hundred of his in-jokes that no one ever gets)—he has been renowned as the life of countless parties throughout history, and after thousands of years of practice, he can boast of many unique skills—for example, playing Webern's *Etude in B-Moll* on the Jews harp with its maddening profusion of sharps and flats, or better still, the rare ability to sing a show tune, crack his chewing gum, and give you a blow job—all at the same time. Impish as his public persona often seems to be, in reality he is the most ruthless of opportunists. To understand this completely, one must first recognize—from *his* unique point of view—the staggering abundance of witless and self-deceiving persons Humanity parades before him—day after day after day—a veritable cornucopia of populace in motley, belching out babble, falsehoods, and stupidities, all of it fueled by seven deadly variations of the pleasure principle.

The antics demonstrated in the pursuit of self-satiation are astonishing, even to the patent-holder of Pride, the first and best of the variants. Lust, for example, curiously runs rampant in well-lit locations *outside* the bedroom. Sloth enjoys a mint julep during working hours and a late siesta when the kids get home. Sleep is such unbearable tedium for Sloth, it can only be relieved by a nap. Gluttony purges itself shortly before meals with a wooden spoon, and between meals basks, as if sunbathing, in the flickering blue light of television reruns, perceiving them to be ideal opportunities for reckless snacking without thinking. Greed, voted "Most Likely to Succeed" in the Class of 10,000 B.C., has ascended a steep ladder to become a 24/7 industry and this century's preferred investment strategy, operating at full steam, with no coffee breaks, no vacations, no sick leave, and never quite enough benefits to placate workers, which could account for the growing popularity of hobbies like Lust and Gluttony, both of which long ago replaced stamp collecting and bird watching in the public's affections. In this regard, the Devil has easy work: self-pleasure is—and always has been—*sui generis*. It's what inspired Man to stand upright. Apples taste much better than crabgrass and picking a tantalizing piece of fruit is much easier if you have thumbs and can stand on your hind legs. Man figured that out on his own after a few million years. The Devil only had to point at the apple and wait.

Contrary to common belief, the result of fictions fabricated and nurtured by the Church over centuries, the Devil is not much of a Doer, and it would be more than fair to say he's no more Unholy in his practices than the Church itself is Holy in theirs. In assorted past centuries, the Church was so outrageously corrupt, it came close to putting the Devil out of business altogether. In their less rapacious years, he considered the Church a sister charity of sorts, one which—while not precisely sharing his values—pursued certain of his doctrines better than he could himself, and with better financial backing.

Rarely initiating a dark turn of events, the Devil's preference is to sit back in wonderment, selectively using his paintbrush to dabble, to tint and taint, to highlight and shade situations that first fulminate of their own accord. He is more Enhancer than Necromancer, gilding lilies, adding adjectives, icing cakes, breaking camels' backs, but making no claims for expertise as goldsmith, linguist, pastry chef, nomad or anything else. He prefers, whenever possible, to make his first appearance on stage fifteen minutes *after* the curtain has risen and the drama is well-commenced (and *always* through an ordinary door rather than via the anticipated puff of smoke), hence his fondness for late-night train rides—the later the departure, the more degenerate the behavior of the passengers is likely to be, and consequently, the less time required to salt the stew and stir the pot.

On those rather productive nights, before he can intercede in any way, the passengers are well on their way to getting rip-roaring drunk in the bar-car, masturbating out of boredom in the toilets, driving each other mad with repetitive, purposeless cellphone conversations, tripping each other in the aisles for laughs, cheating at cards, and spilling more coffee on their neighbors than they are swallowing. The value of personal possessions and cash tumbling out of pockets and purses on these homeward junkets of debauchery could feed a small third-world nation, and the abundance of illicit romances in progress could tie up divorce courts for years should they ever come to light. It's during such volatile journeys, when the ridership has loosened its ties, de-trousered its shirt-tails, and taken down its stockings, that the most insignificant contribution he might make—a mildly provocative gesture, for instance, or the wink of an eye timed just so—can bring the simmering pandemonium to a boil. And then you would *really* have a story.

In the midst of this mayhem, the Devil routinely strikes oil in the form of fallen souls to store in his carpetbag, along with abundant fallen loose change, harvested from the crevices in the seats, to stuff in his Devil purse. In summation—it's a windfall of downfalls.

The Devil's layover in Pennsylvania Station proved to be unexpectedly fruitful. First, he dispatched the police to the Men's Toilet on the pretext that several men within were engaging in acts of exhibitionism. Three men were taken out in handcuffs, one of them guilty of nothing more than being more favorably endowed than the arresting officers. This exercise validated one of the Devil's theories—uniformed police officers never emerge from a public toilet alone. Vagrancy, smoking, shooting drugs, littering, spitting, lewd behavior, and disturbing the peace (*e.g.*, moaning off-key while in production of a bowel movement) are the most frequent charges justifying the application of handcuffs. For a policeman, forced in the course of his duties to patrol a reeking public toilet, the game must always justify the candle—or, at the very least, the match he has to light. For a desperate urinator, nothing is more disconcerting and inhibiting than the presence of a suspicious policeman, waiting in the shadows like a spider on coiled, hairy legs for his next victim. A public toilet is just one more of the Devil's playgrounds and requires very little maintenance. With nothing but human waste products and cigarette smoke to sustain them, plus an occasional roll of toilet paper and a few stingy ounces of liquid soap thrown in when a custodian remembers to be bothered, these increasingly hard-to-find locations go on producing mayhem for decades while their plumbing fails and rots, tiles fall out of their assigned places on the walls like decayed teeth, and light fixtures buzz and buzz endlessly, choking on their own electric juices.

Next, the Devil shamelessly pursued a mouse from one end of the station to the other—to, fro, up, down, over, under, back, forth, west, east, south, north—until the creature was so traumatized, it made a desperate attempt to end the chase by jumping into the donut batter at a food concession. The mouse surfaced three times before it succumbed and slid beneath the yeasty muck. At first, he was curious, but, soon enough, the Devil tired of waiting for the drowned rodent to be dropped into the fryer by the mechanized donut-maker. He moved on, seeking opportunities for pranks that promised more immediate payoffs.

Freshly-delivered blooms at the florist concessions wilted as he pretended to be browsing paperbacks nearby (he was loosening the final pages of the mystery novels), at late-night cafés, cream curdled in canisters and dispensers, the homeless sleeping on the benches in the waiting rooms had horrific nightmares in which they saw themselves put to work with brooms, rakes, mops, scrub brushes and—worst of all—subjected to supervisors and schedules.

It was in the pre-dawn hours that the Devil's attention was arrested by a distant glint. Snapping to attention, always on the lookout for an unwelcome incursion of celestial light, he recognized something even worse: it was the twisted figure of Death, toting his scythe (the source of the glint) at the southern end of the waiting area. Quickly, the Devil concealed himself behind a brimming garbage can, hoping he hadn't been spotted. Death was a huge drain on his satanic battery, a lugubrious bore who was perpetually lonely, always on the lookout for company or someone to kill—either would do equally well on slow weekdays. The Devil wasn't eager to get dragged all over town by that eternal loser—merely for the sake of politeness—from one fatality to another, all of them lacking as much as a molecule of subtlety. An evening with Death was absolutely exhausting. The whispering was bad enough (you had to ask him to repeat himself over and over again), but surely the worst part of it was the mandatory tiptoeing.

Wherever you went with Death he insisted that you walk on your toes, no matter whether there was someone around to creep up on or not. After a night with Death, your feet were killing you.

For countless eons, Death had persisted in asking the Devil out, refusing to take *no* for answer. The Devil was running out of excuses to put him off—as is so often said, *"A date with Death is inevitable."* On rare occasions—but not more than once or twice a century—he would throw Death a bone and agree to an outing, even though it meant being seen in public with a badly dressed hunchback with two left feet (one of them clubbed), and breath that stank of Zyklon-b.

Once he and Death had a play date on which they agreed to go clubbing. Death isn't much of a conversationalist but he does love to dance—that was one thing they had in common, and the only reason the Devil agreed to go along. *The Demon Dance* was lots of fun (you got to blow smoke out of your ears, and for a finale, out of your asshole), and it was hard to top the *Dance of Death*, a no-holds-barred version of the Tango which was justifiably famous for its violence, and which required the death of at least one bystander, usually engineered with the help of an artfully placed banana peel or a dollop of Crisco. They would have continued dancing all night, but the patrons packed around them had spent so much time snorting cocaine in the toilets, it wasn't long before the dance-floor began to reek of urinal cakes and sweat, and the D-Boys fled to the bar, where the air was more breathable, but not by much. So much for the entertainment. The rest of the night, Death chewed gum and swung his scythe and tiptoed around in his moth-eaten hoodie—it amounted to little more than engineering one fatal drug overdose after another, all of them exactly alike. The Devil was so bored he began to wish that Death would just go drop dead so he could get a cab and go home. That wasn't very likely, though. He wondered if Death would ever contemplate suicide. Would he leave a note? What would he write? How would he do it? Maybe one look in a mirror would be enough.

The Devil continued to watch from his hiding place behind the garbage pail. He breathed a sulfuric sigh of relief when it was certain he hadn't been spotted. Since the next departure from the station was still hours away, Death was apparently heading down to the connecting subway lines which ran all night with some really nefarious characters in tow, perfect targets for the glinting scythe, which thirstily drooled saliva like a Pavlovian dog. The sense that something irreversible was about to happen lingered in his wake, and sure enough, not twenty minutes had elapsed before a dozen police officers, their radios squawking, were all heading in the same direction—the subway. What was it this time? the Devil wondered. A shooting? A derailment? Human hamburger meat on the tracks?

Oh Death, oh Death, he mused ruefully. You're such a One-Note-Johnny, you poor slob. It's just kill, kill, kill, kill. No sense of humor at all. Lighten up! We only live once, even if it is forever!

Before the 8:00 a.m. tsunami of arriving workers had reached its high-water mark, the Devil had drafted installment plans with seven stockbrokers and four investment bankers for incremental transfer of their souls into his account in Zurich. The paperwork for the acquisitions made during those early morning closings was stuffed into his battered green carpetbag. Before folding the game board for the day, he ordered a large coffee at the donut concession and sat down with a newspaper which he had lifted from a sleeping homeless man's face.

Something felt incomplete; he wasn't sure what it was or what it wasn't.

He made quite an anonymous picture seated there, offering onlookers a faded, drooping carnation, pinned at his lapel, as his only fashion gesture—something about the way he carried that off was more depressing to behold than tape on eyeglass hinges. He smiled contentedly, running his tongue over the hairs on the roof of his mouth as he thumbed through the obituary pages. Scanning death announcements for familiar names was as mesmerizing to him as a *pari-mutuel* scoreboard was to a degenerate gambler. He was clearly, both figuratively and literally, making a killing this morning. Mentally, he clip-clip-clipped coupons off the shares in his overstuffed carpetbag while tap-tap-tapping his foot to the rhythm set by the imaginary scissors. The final moment of triumph, the *prix du jour*, was the shriek of horror from a woman from Valley Stream who was the unlucky recipient of a donut containing a fried-to-death rodent. The Devil had completely forgotten the mouse and the batter—and now this! "Oh, *Beelze!*" he squealed gleefully. Unable to contain himself, he treated himself to a self-congratulatory pinch on his left ass cheek. As was his custom when engaging in this compulsive behavior, he muttered (loud enough to be heard by the intended listener, of course), "Oh God, that felt good!" That bit of silliness over with, he sat back to enjoy the show.

EMS workers made it to the scene rather quickly, but not faster than two lawyers, who, having heard the woman's screams, were tripping over themselves—and each other—in a race to reach her. Instantly the two attorneys found themselves at fisticuffs over which of them had arrived at the scene of the looming lawsuit first. Before long, a crowd had congregated around the unfolding drama at The Donut Shoppe. The Devil luxuriated in the rapidly escalating chaos. He was contentedly enthroned in a comfortable front-row seat, observing the steady accrual of bonus points—ripened fruits of the previous evening's rodent safari—with total fascination. Clearly, many in the buzzing swarm of busybodies would arrive late for work and earn reprimands for tardiness; the bonanza level rose accordingly in the Devil's calculations like score points clamorously registering on an arcade machine. Best of all, surpassing the possible entertainment value of any and all future outcomes, was a more immediate, but subtle, payoff—many in the gathering crowd continued to purchase donuts, failing utterly to comprehend what the fuss was about in the first place. The Donut Shoppe was unexpectedly enjoying brisk trade—but not more than the Devil was enjoying it.

At one point, he became aware of a sugary odor and looked up. Standing over him was a slender, young hospital worker in green scrubs, taking bites out of a donut. His identification tag, issued by St. Vincent's Hospital, read "A. Bannerjee." Powdered sugar was falling on the Devil like snow from Dr. Bannerjee's donut.

"Any idea what's happened here?" Dr. Bannerjee asked, accidentally sibilating a few rodent-tainted donut crumbs.

"Hell if I know," the Devil responded with a shrug. But what he was thinking was, quite simply: "Hell."

After the usual delay for the administration of anti-litigation paperwork, the EMS team announced their readiness to transport the woman and both lawyers to the hospital. One of the lawyers was dictating notes into his cellphone through bloody lips. The other was either unconscious or faking it in service to a more personal litigation scheme. Meanwhile, Mrs. Adela Grassini, the prostrate woman—her lips covered with powdered sugar, crumbs, and rodent blood—had enough presence of mind to keep a firm hold on the repulsive evidence, despite being in the grip of sheer revulsion. She and the felled lawyer rolled in formation toward the station exit on rickety gurneys. The conscious lawyer scampered gleefully along, right beside his new client, chattering like a schoolgirl, attempting to demystify the intricacies of Pain and Suffering, Loss of Wages, the three varieties of Emotional Distress (Past, Present, and Future), and her husband's impending Loss of Services. Struggling with only one free hand—the other gripped the evidence as if it were the rim of a precipice—she phoned her husband and informed him about the drought of services looming in the months and years ahead that he would be forced to endure. He responded with three words—*What fucking services?*

The show was not yet over. The two Donut Shoppe employees—both African-American, one a chubby stammerer, the other a comparatively diminutive occasional cross-dresser obsessed with *Gone with the Wind*—had finally mustered a sufficient level of composure between them to convince each other it was time to phone the absentee proprietor and warn him about the morning's events. At the root of the delay was a tough decision—which of them was going to poke his head out of the trench first. The stammering employee drew the short coffee stirrer. They weren't expecting their employer to be helpful, and he wasn't; nor did they imagine the news would go over well, and it didn't.

"If anyone asks," instructed the proprietor through gritted teeth, "we do not serve fucking donuts. We have *never* served fucking donuts. We wouldn't serve them to our own mothers if they begged us."

He paused as if waiting for someone to bring up the subject of donuts. No one did.

"Fucking donuts?" he resumed. "What the fuck is a fucking donut? We never fucking heard of fucking donuts. Unplug that fucking donut-making machine and take all that crap off the shelves and throw it out. Don't leave a crumb behind. Not a single fucking crumb."

"B-b-but, b-b-boss," the stammerer countered, "our f-f-f-fucking sign says 'The Donut Shoppe.'"

"Replace all those goddam donuts with packages of peanuts from the storage room. Then climb up and paint over the D and the O on the sign."

"Then it will say 'space space nut Shoppe.'"

"Well, that works, doesn't it? And, while you are up there, you may as well paint over one of the Ps and the E, so the sign doesn't look cockeyed to our picky artsy-fartsy clientele."

"Where am I supposed to get the p-p-paint?"

"Just fucking get it done, that's all I'm saying."

"Yes suh, yes suh, yes suh!" groused the stutterer after the proprietor had abruptly slammed the phone down. "I'll be doing your f-f-fuckin' shit directly."

His colleague, too, reverted to plantation-speak. "What kinda sign-paintin' is we all supposed to do, Mammy? Us is kitchen niggahs."

The overlapping realms of Storytelling and Storyreading have been a cherished refuge for you since early childhood. It's where you first met Dick and Jane and Sally and Spot, and where—so long ago—Dick said three magical words to you: "See Spot run." Those words unlocked a door through which you began a long journey that ultimately led you here, to *Page 19* of a book of travelers' tales.

Dick, Jane, and Sally were the first people that you didn't know very well that you took to bed with you. They were the first people, outside of family members, household helpers, and pediatricians, to populate your dreams. The first people you ever tried to imagine naked were named Dick, Jane, and Sally. As a child, you patterned yourself after them. That process of imitation and improvisation was how you learned to flex the muscles of your imagination, to stretch yourself beyond what you were and reshape yourself into what you wanted yourself to be.

Sadly, Spot was a bit too fond of running for his own good and was eventually run down (pun *not* intended) by The Good Humor Man who did not bother to remember Dick's repeated warnings (they had been posted prominently on every page, in fact) about seeing Spot run. Jane ended her days as an alcoholic shut-in. Sally, who was boring to begin with, continued to be boring. It is widely known that Dick was killed in Vietnam along with Beaver Cleaver. More about that later. Maybe.

Dick, Jane, Sally, and Spot don't visit schools anymore. You won't find them in local libraries, either. You are one of the few persons alive who remembers them—fondly or otherwise. When you are gone, Dick and Jane and Sally—with Spot running at their heels—will be the dust of the cosmos. And so, of course, will you.

Vincent Grassini, the husband of Valley Stream's first mouse-stricken woman, was seated at his desk at the Wallace Wang Trading Company when he finished talking to his wife at St. Vincent's Hospital. He spent the next ten minutes with his face buried in his hands, holding back tears of frustration. His unannounced plan to divorce Adela had just been derailed by a suicidal mouse wearing a donut suit. He wasn't quite so distraught at the abrupt change of direction his life was skidding into that he failed to recognize the most critical issue at hand—there could be no Loss of Services for the blithering idiot who divorces the Service Provider, no matter what those services were or were not.

There was about to be a windfall, a huge one. The air around him felt as crisp as newly printed currency, rich with the scent of fresh green ink. To his profound embarrassment, he found he was experiencing the unmistakable sensation of an impending erection.

The morning's mouse affair, if carefully nursed by expert lawyers, had the potential to be something really big, he thought, trying to distract himself by diverting the expanding helium from his penis to the image in his mind of the mouse his wife had sunk her teeth into earlier that day. His mind's eye glazed over as he visualized the offending animal bursting out of a donut and swelling to the absurd dimensions of a parade float. In his overworked imagination he could see it standing on its hind legs, bobbing up and down over Fifth Avenue on Thanksgiving Day in a storm of confetti. Then it broke free of its handlers and drifted upward, upward into the heavens, inflating until it was as vast as a constellation in the firmament, a thirteenth sign of the Zodiac. He, Vincent Grassini, was under the protective influence of the astrological sign of Mickey the Donut Mouse, and he was about to be a rich man, cheerfully coping with the dearth of services that had suddenly afflicted his marriage. His head cracked open like a mammoth fortune cookie. A strip of paper unfurled. "You will soon tell your boss to kiss your ass," it read; and on the reverse side: "Your lucky numbers are 53, 6, 33, 42, 12. Learn to say 'Go fuck your mother' in Chinese = '*D'iu ne lo mo.*'" In the final moment of his reverie, the new *status quo* came into crystalline focus. As of 8:30 a.m. that morning, his life had been divided into two epochs, B.M. and A.M., and today was unmistakably Day One of A.M.

He began to type an e-mail. "Dear Paula," it read, "I will not be on the 7:20 tonight. I'm really really really sorry about it. Tonight is impossible. I'll explain it all later.—Love, Vin."

Within moments Paula was reading Vinnie's e-mail. The implications of Vinnie's message were quite clear to her. She sighed and began writing an e-mail of her own. "Dear Nicky," it read, "will you be on the 6:40 tonight? Let me know because I'd love to have a drink with you in the bar-car. Can you meet me? We've been putting this get-together off for much too long, don't you think?—Hope to see you later, Paula."

Within moments Nicky was reading Paula's e-mail. The implications of Paula's message were quite obvious. He smiled and began writing an e-mail of his own. "Marcia, honey," it read, "Sorry but will be home late again tonight. Kiss the kids for me and I'll see you around midnight if you're still awake. Love ya, honey—Nicky."

Within moments Marcia was reading Nicky's e-mail. The implications of Nicky's message sent her blood pressure soaring. She threw her coffee mug at the wall and began composing an e-mail of her own. "Dear Anita," she hammered into the keyboard, "I've had my fill of Nicky's constant bullshit and I've decided to come over and hang with you for a few hours. Remember how nice it was last time? Waiting for a green light. Ready willing and, with help from the babysitter, very able. Let me know—XOX, Marcia."

As soon as she sent the message, Marcia telephoned a teenager who lived across the street. "I'm so glad I caught you, Debbie. I'm hoping you can babysit for us tonight. Can you manage it?"

"Sure thing. I've got plenty of homework to do. I can do it at your place when the kids are down."

They settled their arrangements. As soon as Debbie finished speaking to Marcia, she began to contemplate the opportunities the evening of "babysitting" would present to her. At once, she sent a text message to Trevor Berger, a senior on the high school hockey team. It read, "B-stn 2nyt. Call at 7 if u want 2get 2gthr when fn kids r zzzzzzz."

She went downstairs to tell her mother about the babysitting job. Mrs. Cutler cut the power to the vacuum cleaner, listened, and smiled approvingly. A few moments later, she shut down the vacuum for the second time. She poured out a perfectly good container of milk. Then she asked Debbie to make a trip to the grocery for a quart of milk, claiming none remained in the refrigerator. She resumed vacuuming.

The opportunities presented by her daughter's planned absence gave Mrs. Cutler an unexpected thrill. As soon as she heard the back screen door slam, she cut the power to the vacuum cleaner for the third time and set about tracking her husband down. She found him smoking his pipe in front of the television.

"Randy, dearest," she said, rubbing his shoulders affectionately, "are you feeling randy today?"

He tapped the pipe. "Why do you ask?"

"Our lovely daughter will be out this evening, babysitting until around 11:00. We'll have a few hours."

"Okay, I'm game if you are."

"Sure, why not?"

She took off her apron and crossed the street. She knocked on Mrs. Amoruso's door.

"Barbara," she said when the door opened. "Debbie is off to baby-sit between 7:30 and 11:00. Is tonight good for you?"

"I'll check. Hang on." Barbara disappeared into the depths of the Amoruso house and reappeared rather quickly. "Ralph says it's okay."

"I'll send Randall over here at 8:00 and you can send Ralph over to our place when he arrives. Tell him to bring an empty Tupperware container with him in case there's an unexpected problem. He can say he came over to borrow a cup of sugar."

"Good thinking."

"And," Mrs. Cutler added before returning to her waiting vacuum cleaner, "remind him to bring his tool kit."

In a chilly corner of the Lånke region of Norway, there is a village called Hell. Small, pleasant, friendly— Hell (*Pop. 1,440*) is an ideal place for bringing up blond offspring, making snowballs, and selling postcards. The train station consists of a simple platform, an ordinary sign (aptly reading "HELL" in a straightforward font—no flame-shaped letters to ensure that everyone "gets it") and some nicely-preserved clapboard structures, including a *24/7* souvenir stand and an *18/6* toilet.

Hell can boast that it is the location of the most oft-photographed train platform in the history of rail travel. It is one of the world's smallest and most unremarkable tourist attractions, drawing travelers from around the world who have no interest in going to Hell (real or mythological) for any reason other than to be photographed under the sign as proof they had been there. Passing trains—even express runs—make ten-minute stops in this attractive backwater several times a day for photo opportunities. While you are visiting

Hell, you can buy postcards with witty quips printed on them, such as "This is Hell—wish you were here!" or "Hell is a place where you can't drink, smoke, or spit!" Postcards depicting winter scenes are the most popular and the most Norwegian in feel; a bestseller features a snow-dusted station and the words "It is cold as Hell in Hell."

A fabled Nordic beauty, Mona Grudt (*b. 1971*), who is—to be absolutely precise—from a smaller village just outside Hell's official boundaries, faked her credentials a bit and listed herself as "The Beauty Queen from Hell" in the publicity materials for the 1990 Miss Universe competition. She went on to win the crown, making her Hell's most illustrious (neighboring) citizen. In addition to Ms. Grudt, and the eponymous sign, Hell can boast of four additional attractions: a post office (*Postcode = 7517 Hell*), a grocery store, a gas station, and a retirement home. All four offer a selection of Hell postcards.

By design, the local church was built outside official town limits. This was a clever tactic engineered by the Town Council to avoid the notoriety sure to follow the discovery that they were harboring a Church of Hell in the town limits. The consensus was that a Church of Hell would draw tourists away from the train platform, where the raucous behavior and aimless milling about of the ten-minutes-per-person visitors was disconcerting enough and growing increasingly difficult to manage. The distraction of a Church of Hell in close proximity would also negatively impact the sale of postcards at the station. It's unfortunate that—despite all the planning invested in the placement of the local church—the final result was the much-ridiculed Church Two Blocks from Hell—hardly a significant improvement in the notoriety department.

Once a peaceful hamlet where unpleasantness was known only from newspapers and folktales about trolls, Hell had more recently experienced a rise in mischievous behavior and minor misdemeanors. Tourists were often blamed for this trend, condemned as corrupting influences, like toxic gas wafting over from the train station.

The worst incident occurred at Hell's retirement home. One night, an unidentified intruder switched all the bedside water glasses containing false teeth to other bedsides at random. This resulted in pandemonium the next morning when the retirees awoke to discover that their teeth no longer fit in their mouths properly and they were unable to make themselves understood or eat their breakfasts.

While staff members scrambled to find a solution to the calamity and the Board of Governors ripped their hair out in frustration, residents sat at the dining room tables, mournfully passing the dentures around and trying on (or in) any that looked familiar. A forensic dentist had to be summoned from Trondheim to sort the dentures out before the lunch bell rang. Then, sadly, three of the residents failed to recognize their own teeth and tried to spit them out. Those three unfortunates had to be deported to another facility where more intensive care was offered. They were, in nursing home parlance, "sent up the ladder"—code for being one rung closer to the Great Beyond.

 few years ago, there was an interesting debate in the travel-writing community about how to properly measure the size of a travel destination—just the sort of subject that the public can depend on travel-writers to resort to when they having nothing of significance to communicate. The quiet village of Hell became a focus of controversy when those who favored measuring the attraction by the official size of the village (260 acres) pitted themselves against those who favored measuring the attraction by the size of the railroad station sign, which was obviously significantly smaller—arguably smaller than many other pint-sized tourist attractions, such as Plymouth Rock, *Den Lille Havfrue,* and *Mannekin Pis.* Into this "fracas over a flea," jumped a group of etymologists, who threw oil on the fire by reducing the issue under debate to the size of the four letters as they appeared on the sign: H-E-L-L.

Whereas the original discussion concerned whether people visited the *town* or the *sign,* the new debate was focused on whether people visited the *sign* or the *word* (or *name*)—the lettering being smaller than the actual sign proper.

The Devil learned about this in the lavatory whilst reading an issue of *Etymology Today Monthly*. He was simultaneously highly amused and supremely irritated by these antics masquerading as erudition and wrote a letter to the editor in which he debunked both the Sign Theory and the Word Theory. He verbally tarred and feathered both groups of theorists as intellectual hooligans and proposed— quite convincingly—that the entire affair could be reduced to the issue of a single letter rather than a word, a sign, or a village. Without the letter *L*, his argument ran—specifically the second *L* on the sign—the entire discussion was moot. No one would go out of their way to visit a village called *HEL*. There would be no point, no *frisson*, no catharsis. The sole allure of the village (i.e., its *tourist attractionishness*) derived from the second *L*, which was approximately twelve inches in height, and six inches in width.

The Devil was so pleased with the logic of his argument, he was emboldened to sign the letter with his real name. The signature, as it turned out, was the only part of the letter the editors did *not* take seriously. They rushed to publish it—revising the sender's name to T. D.—in the next issue of *Etymology Today Monthly*. There it garnered the attention of the editorial board of *Ripley's Believe It or Not*, which unanimously decided to award Hell the honor of being "The World's Smallest Tourist Attraction" based on the size of its secondary *L*.

This unexpected outcome irritated the Devil—back in the lavatory at stool—even more than the initial controversy, sending his bile pressure skyrocketing on the retaliation meter. He had written the letter to put self-proclaimed intellectuals in their proper place, not to ensure that conniving Norwegians—who had pilfered a linguistic gold-mine from the English lexicon—would find themselves further rewarded with free publicity from *Ripley's*, a publication which had consistently Barnum-ized every freakish thing the Devil held dear since its first printing. When he recalled that the word *hell* meant *luck* in Norwegian, he became even more enraged. The Devil considered the greatest Evil of all to be Stupidity. People did not purchase travel packages by the yard. The idea of evaluating a tourist destination by its size in cubic centimeters or volume in ounces was asinine, as fatuous as saying that the Universe, by virtue of its vast expanse, was a place any savvy person should consider being born into.

Disgusted that he had allowed himself to be drawn into such a fallacious discussion, he was determined there would be a day of reckoning for the travel-writers, etymologists, and all others connected with this _cul-de-sac_ of common sense. He stuffed a full report, together with copies of the articles and his Letter to the Editor, into a folder, which he labeled "Stupidity, the Eighth Deadly Sin," and shoved it into the carpetbag for future handling.

Many years later, in a less volatile frame of mind, the Devil paid a long-overdue visit to the village of Hell, believing it was best to investigate things in person and not rely on hearsay. Conceptually, the Devil making his first visit to Hell could have been a newsworthy occasion—and if the Devil was all that writers, artists, religious zealots, and garden-variety idiots claim him to be, his journey would have taken on the trappings of a sacred pilgrimage. He might have arrived in a sedan chair carried by pointy-eared minions, or on a sled pulled by rabid Huskies, melting the snow as they traversed it. The truth was, he only went to Hell in order to put Hell behind him.

He arrived without fanfare, with the studied artlessness of a restaurant critic dining incognito. He gave himself over to donning overpriced ski-wear (chemically concocted fabric pockmarked everywhere with the designer's logo, scarred by far too many zippers and fake pockets), carrying a carpetbag stuffed with brochures, and toting the expected supplementary paraphernalia—camera, sunglasses, binoculars, and the ubiquitous—since the late 1990s—water bottle. As did everyone arriving in Hell for the first time, he had the obligatory photo taken under the famous sign, only because a failure

to do so would have attracted unwanted attention.

Despite the catchy name, he did not find Hell to be particularly Devil-friendly. He sized the place up in fifteen seconds and determined there was very little for him to do there, which left a surfeit of 9 minutes and 45 seconds of tedium before a whistle blew, steam whooshed from the undercarriage, smoke belched from the stack atop the locomotive, and he was swept up with everyone else in the clangorous machinations of the train—now resuming its status as an express—charging ahead to the ski resorts and the myriad mischiefs they offered.

Periodically, in later times, he would take the photo out of his carpetbag and conjure memories of his curious visit. Embarrassingly, the photo captured him glassy-eyed and grinning like the village idiot, pointing up at the sign with one hand and pointing down to the Netherworld with the other. He wore a knit cap that said "Troll Norge," ski boots, and a hideous parka trimmed in fake fur. Other tourists, dressed more-or-less identically, could be seen milling around behind him, looking for something of interest to look at.

When all was over, after the train had chugged away, the citizens of Hell were no worse off for the Devil having made an unannounced stop there. The most dreadful thing that happened in Hell that day was that a dog pooped on someone's shoe.

From the perspective of a travel-writer, Hell was a place that people made a trip to solely for the self-awarded diploma—to be able to boast about having been there willingly and having remained there only briefly. It was a cheap way to play Beat-the-Devil and brag about it afterward to anyone who would listen. Through the magical lens of irony, the unassuming railroad platform appeared to be the ultimate thrill destination. Arrival with fifty Japanese tourists in the throes of a photo-snapping frenzy was nothing noteworthy, but departure without being scorched, flayed, tormented, or even detained for interrogation, was better than going over Niagara Falls in a barrel. From time to time, departing visitors—specifically those with guilty consciences—experienced bouts of uncontrollable nervous laughter as they watched Hell fade in the Norwegian mists behind them, the train carrying them far from its clutches unmolested.

Thinking strategically, the Devil concluded that a place called Hell was an "idea" whose time had come, possessing significant potential—under the right stewardship—to blossom into a winning theme-park franchise. People, it seemed, could not get enough of it.

On the other hand, in the Devil's less business-oriented moments of reflection, the ridiculous excitement over a visit to a fake version of Hell seemed singularly ill-conceived, since Hell—and who should know better than its mythological Prince?—was nothing like the cartoon version humanity had conjured up in its collective imagination. Nightmares, folklore, imbecilic religious doctrines, horror films, medieval paintings by Hieronymus Bosch and other masters—all of these contributed bits and pieces of imagery to a mosaic that resembled the *real* Hell even less than the 1.06-square-kilometres in western Norway known on maps as "Hell" did.

Of what possible value would Hell be if it actually fulfilled the expectations of evildoers, miscreants, and sinners who were planning to retire there anyway? Then it really *would* be the asinine equivalent of a train platform built for tourists—or worse—a postcard of a train platform built for tourists—or, even worse than *that*—a snapshot of a tourist holding a postcard of a train platform built for tourists.

The real Hell was a realm of deafening negations, where two plus two equaled zero, and E did not equal mc^2, where the speed of light meant stasis, and Time neither surged forward nor retreated backward—only a great vacuous Present existed, lurching violently in place as if Time might eventually free itself and resume a journey that had screeched to a final halt long before. It would be unthinkable, in the *real* Hell, to have your picture taken or to buy a postcard to look at later—there was no *later* in Hell.

The perpetual flames, so often described by philosophers, theologians, writers, and artists, were the only feature of Hell depicted with a speck of accuracy—but their true purpose had eluded every one of the commentators.

Hellfires were not, as was claimed, for roasting the souls of the fallen, but to alchemize all vestiges of aspiration and ambition and altruism into ash and smoke and dust. The denizens of Hell did not wander for eternity in fire, but in the unbearable detritus of existence, which was all that remained of all that had been.

A photograph of that could tell you only one thing: Nothing.

Back at the donut concession, which would soon be reinvented as the Nut Shop, the sign-painting project was underway. The harassed employees were following the proprietor's instructions to the letter—letter by letter—beginning with the letter *D* in Donut, to be followed by *O* and *P* and *E*. Lacking any white paint, they came up with the idea to use white donut icing and cream cheese to cover the banned letters on the concession's sign. For this masterpiece of signage and stupidity, a spatula substituted for a paintbrush.

When the project was complete, the Devil noticed immediately—although the two harried employees did not—that an error had been made in the execution of the re-christening. They had painted over one of the *P*s and the *E* just as instructed by the proprietor, but they had accidentally covered over the *wrong* *P* with the icing. Now the signage read "—nut Sho-p-" instead of the more preferable "—nut Shop—."

It didn't count for much as far as the Devil was concerned. In his view, altering the sign was the most moronic idea in the history of the world anyway, and not likely to fool anyone. Even a person who was both illiterate *and* dyslexic would detect something wasn't quite right about that sign with a cursory glance.

Minutes after the ladder was folded and stowed in the storage room, things took an unanticipated turn in this do-it-yourself disaster. The newly-edited sign, suspended above the concession's entrance, had been designed to hang close to the ceiling where the air was considerably warmer than the regulated temperature of the terminal. It was only a matter of minutes before the icing and cream cheese began to liquefy and drip to the floor, where it had the appearance of bird droppings and the capacity to generate a lifetime of slip-and-fall litigations.

Compounding the ruinous situation in progress, the sugary paint-job was attracting a swarm of noisy blue flies. All that prevented this depressing picture from achieving artistic greatness was the absence of a mangy buzzard perched atop the sign, surveying the absence of customers.

"Tara, Tara, Tara," sighed the smaller employee, wringing his hands sorrowfully, "you sure have sunk mighty low."

The bigger, reverting to his real persona, took stock of the situation. "This place is one-hundred percent f-f-fucked," he said. "Who ever heard of a Coffee and Nut shop? Are p-p-people supposed to dunk bags of p-p-peanuts in their coffee or what?"

"Yeah, I can see we'll be looking for a new plantation to do our slaving at."

"Someone from the B-B-Board of Health will be b-b-busting our b-b-balls any time now."

"I'm Inspector Cosmo Polifrone from the Board of Health," the inspector from the Board of Health interrupted. He removed his hat and made an insincere bowing motion. "We've received a report that a customer was served a donut earlier today—at these premises— a donut that contained a rodent. I'm not sure whether or not that qualifies as busting all four of your balls—to coin *your* phrase—but here I am, just the same."

"I'm sorry, Inspector, but I'm afraid—*er, we're* af-f-fraid—we don't serve donuts."

"Not even to our own mothers."

"Not even if they b-b-begged us for them."

"Or if they were starving." This last bit was not on the list of talking points their employer had provided, but the skinny worker felt their case required supplemental dramatic emphasis in the face of such an implacable antagonist, especially one with a knack for correctly calculating the number of balls available for busting.

"But," Inspector Polifrone said quite calmly, but with an unmistakable trace of irritation nonetheless, "that hardly seems credible, fellows. I have here, in my records, a thorough, recent inspection report dated—*hmm,* let me see now—just three weeks past, which clearly states that this is a café establishment serving coffee and donuts."

"D-d-donuts?"

"What's a donut?"

"We never even heard of a f-f-fucking donut. Have we?"

"Certainly not. Mister, do you feel okay? Do you need to sit down?"

Stalemate.

"These answers, these responses," said the Inspector in his most reprehending manner, "are completely unacceptable under the circumstances. I'll have the two of you know that I am an accredited city official with the full measure of authority to close this business down with impunity—."

"Well, get cracking with that impunity, then, and stop threatening us," the small worker cut in with a regal, dismissive wave of his hand. "We'll have *you* know that our boss—the only official who means diddly to us—not more than ten minutes ago, on that very telephone, said he'd have *us* know that we are accredited concession stand workers who *don't* serve donuts. Officially and unofficially. We *abso-ficially* do not."

"There's a potential health threat in progress, young man. Does that have any relevance in your rodent-enabling universe? Are you confused about the priorities of the situation?"

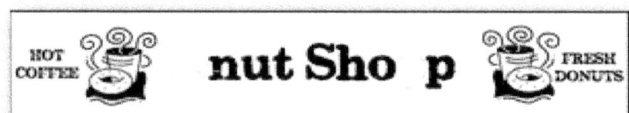

"Maybe *you're* confused. With all those papers and reports and priorities and accreditations, it's no wonder. And maybe you're just too literal-minded to get the subtlety of our slogan."

"Get *what*? What slogan? What subtlety?"

"'Drink coffee and *do* nuts.'"

"*D-d-dooo*. Not *d-d-dough*."

"That's right. *Dooooo* nuts. As in 'do drugs' or 'do time' or 'do wop' or 'do-rag' or when you 'do' some broad or as in Jesus telling his flock 'do unto others' or Frank Sinatra singing 'do-be-do-be-do, strangers in the night.'"

A clump of cream cheese fell from the sign and landed near Inspector Polifrone. He didn't seem to notice. He just stood there, blinking in disbelief. Then, beginning again, slapping his papers with the back of his hand, he said, "It says right here in this quarterly inspection report: 'licensed to make and serve donuts, coffee, and—.'"

"See? What have I just been telling you? It doesn't say anywhere on that p-p-paper that we serve rodents here. They're not even an *ingredient.* There's no mention of them."

"No, but it says you doooo serve do-do-do-do-do-do-nuts."

"No, we do-do-do-do-do-do-do-do-do-do-do-do-do-do-don't."

"Okay," said Inspector Polifrone, pretending to acquiesce while deploying a trick flanking maneuver. "Explain to me—if you will—what that machine over there is used for."

"I don't know. I think it's a lamp. All the bulbs are burned out."

"Oh? Is that right? And why, then, does it appear to be filled with oil?"

"I guess it must be an oil lamp. No wonder the switch won't turn it on. Maybe we should call in a utility guy to trim the wick."

"*This,*" warned the Inspector, "is *not* acceptable."

"It's not our job to answer questions and explain stuff unless it pertains to coffee or nuts. Put *that* in your upcoming quarterly report. We—us two—are supposed to serve coffee and nuts, and clean shit up, and do whatever else the fucking boss says to do. *Do* as in *do*, not *dough.* This '*if you will kindly explain*' business that you like to lay on people sounds real nice and polite, but it boils right down to plain old vanilla extra shit, and we don't get paid extra for anything extra."

"And this?" The inspector violently waived a sugar sifter in front of them. "What about this?"

"That's for in case someone wants p-p-powdered sugar sprinkled on their nuts."

"Excuse me," a tiny voice interrupted. All three turned in the direction of the voice to discover an impossibly large woman standing where they had expected to see an infant in a baby carriage. She was square-jawed, broad-shouldered, and big-boned, and towered over them at six-and-a-half feet, casting a shadow equal in width to her height, and stretching three times that span in length across the concession area. She wore a fedora the same color as her mousy hair, and a trench coat the same color as the fedora. From the crook of her elbow swung an enormous alligator purse, its tight-lipped aperture crowned with a large metal clasp that looked as fashionable as an industrial sink faucet.

"I'm Miss Musicaro," the giantess announced in a completely incongruous child's voice. She pointed to herself approvingly as she continued making her introductory remarks. "Mervyn J. Schlissel, Esquire, representing the Plaintiff Adela Grassini, and her spouse, Plaintiff Vincent Grassini, has assigned me to take photographs for Action Number 103934549, *aay-kay-aay* 'The Mouse-In-The-Donut Incident.' I'm Mr. Schlissel's personal private investigator and process server."

She opened her coat to reveal an antiquated camera, suspended from her neck by a cloth strap the same color as her hat, her coat, her shoes, and her hair. To further establish her official capacity, she fielded business cards from the jaws of the purse to all those who stood below her. Her card featured the head of an unpleasant-looking bulldog (the same color as her hat, coat, shoes, hair, and camera strap) with large, bulging eyes and a pointy-toothed underbite. The image was somewhat unsettling, possibly counterproductive from a business perspective—certainly a bloodhound would have been more apt. Or blank space.

The Devil reached up and took a card. He put it in his carpetbag to study at his leisure. With any luck, it would not be too difficult to track down the grotesque bulldog for a closer look.

"Make sure you get a photo of that donut machine," Inspector Polifrone suggested to Investigator Musicaro, figuratively taking her under his official wing. "You'll want to have a good one of that for your case file. Confidentially, Inspector to Investigator," he whispered, "that's one-hundred-percent, fourteen-carat evidence."

The detective moved indelicately around the scene, slowly closing in on the donut machine, snapping photo after photo. As she neared the two workers, the small one made a defensive gesture with his hands. "Please, Madam Detective, whatever you do, don't take any pictures of my colleague," he implored, putting a protective arm around the other's broad shoulders. "He's a devout Aborigine and it's against his religion."

The other one nodded vehemently and stood on one leg. The Devil nearly snorted coffee out of his nose.

"Excuse me," a new voice piped from the depths of Miss Musicaro's all-encompassing mousy brown shadow. A pretty young lady with a press badge emerged. "I'm Miss Orgo from *Reuters* and I have a few questions."

"I have a few myself," said Mr. Posid from *UPI*.

"And me," said another, from somewhere.

"Don't forget us others," others chimed in.

Media personnel were popping up with the disturbing suddenness of mushrooms in a dark crawlspace. Above the conclave of journalists, big, blue flies swarmed in a sugar-induced trance. Droplets of lique-fied icing and curdling cheese plummeted from on-high in small, but regular, *ploops*. The reporters and photographers buzzed in harmony with the monotonous din of the flies, huddled in a group, with the upper regions of Miss Musicaro's Amazonian person rising from their midst like a radio tower. At sea level, the Devil was nursing his fourth coffee of the morning. Miss Musicaro's face loomed far above his ob-servation post, like a clock at the summit of a skyscraper. At one point a small drop of icing landed above one of his eyebrows. He licked it off with the tip of his tongue and found it to be overly sweet.

When the huddle broke, the dreaded question was asked at last.

"Who's in charge here?"

"Let me get the boss on the phone, and y'all can ask him your questions," the little worker offered, unable to prolong the stalemate any further. Involving the boss was the equivalent of unfurling a white flag, an outright confession of incompetence, but it was the only card left to turn over. They had already wasted their Joker on Sinatra and other failed gambits of denial. "I'll put him on speaker." He dialed and jabbed the speaker button. After five rings a recorded voice responded. "We are sorry. You have reached a non-working number. Please check your number and dial again. *Click!*"

The big worker clucked his tongue. "We sure are f-f-fucked now."

Said the little one, "With God as my witness, I swear I'll never sell donuts again."

"And now for the rest of those photos," announced the intrepid Miss Musicaro. She inched backward to obtain a better perspective and promptly slipped on a gob of cream cheese. Up went the camera. Up went the alligator purse. Down went Miss Musicaro's gargantuan shadow and down went Miss Musicaro on top of it. "Oh dear, oh dear me," she whimpered. To the Devil's complete annoyance, she had landed very near his cringing toes like a belly-up U-boat. She then commenced, from her supine position, a lengthy and very detailed narrative, explaining the circumstances of her mishap to potential witnesses. She began with a backgrounder—actually, it was more like a feature-length prequel—providing the details of her morning ablutions and calisthenic exercises, her bowl of hot oatmeal and prunes, her inability to find a comfortable seat on the Second Avenue bus. She was meticulously picking her way across the vastness of time in the direction of the present moment (more or less), with the sincere intention of arriving at Pennsylvania Station in some not-too-distant stage of her narrative. To the Devil's ears, it all sounded as incoherent as an advertisement for baby food, and he stopped listening.

He rarely let annoying people get him flustered—there were just too many of them—but, as there were oft-times roles in his schemes crying out for just the right nuisance expert to champion them, he kept a diverse group in his mental Rolodex, perpetually on call for future assignments. His stable of dubious talent was organized by idiosyncrasy and special-ty—blinking, chattering, chuckling, chortling, coughing, fidget-ing, guffawing, prattling, primping, rustling, rummaging, scoff-ing, shuffling, sneezing, snoring, tapping, tsk-tsk-tsking, tittering, twiddling, twitching, wheedling, whining, whistling—the list went on and on, *ad infinitum*. The Devil understood that virtually any-thing could be annoying if the victim of the ensuing annoyance was not in the mood for it. Any random feature of human behavior—humming, for example—with the prefix or suffix "constantly" ap-pended, was a foolproof, two ingredient recipe for something le-thally annoying. Miss Musicaro was one of the rare exceptions. She required the addition of no further ingredients to serve up a deadly banquet. She was Ready-to-Serve Annoying in a Boil-in-Bag.

The only way to survive APs (Annoying People), the Devil had learned through experience, was to find something useful for them to do—preferably at a great remove. If nothing suitable could be found, in a pinch it was never dull to watch APs in a human cockfight—a modern-day version of gladiatorial combat wherein two annoying people are thrown into an arena and compelled to annoy each other to the death. A simple example would be a cougher and a sneezer in neighboring cubicles. A more interesting one would be two inmates in the same cell, one Born Again, one Masturbating Again (and Again and Again). Paradoxically, the Devil discovered that when two an-noying people were placed side by side, they seemed far less annoying to observers, as if they had somehow canceled each other out. It was hard to figure out how that worked and too annoying to think about.

One of the Devil's great ambitions was to fill a theater or arena with people who were skilled at producing raucous, irritating, grotesque, or phony-sounding laughter—any combination would do. Possibly, he was over-thinking the project, because many years after the idea first came to him, he was still turning it over and over in his mind like a diamond that had the potential to be the most valuable ever known, if only one more perfect cut could be made in it.

A feature he was eager to include was a pre-curtain examination to determine who would be granted entry. Great importance would be placed on skills that went a step further than the basic production of memorably ugly sounds; these skills included laughing too loudly or laughing at the wrong things—especially things that weren't particularly funny. Laughing when no one else was laughing was a good one. Laughter that trailed off into uncertainty was another. The highest marks were awarded to contenders who—beyond their laughing chops—supplemented their artistry with ancillary, non-laughter gimmicks performed in tandem with laughing, such as repeatedly elbowing the person to the left or right, uncontrollably kicking the theater seat directly ahead of them, repeatedly veering around to see who else was laughing, or choking to death on popcorn that went down the wrong pipe while laughing.

Irritating laughs could be quite varied, some of the most cringe-worthy originating in the animal kingdom from the speechless mouths of horses, donkeys, seals, hyenas, monkeys, chihuahuas, and numerous other creatures. Duets between species (*e.g.*, between a woodpecker and a walrus) yielded the most disconcerting results, occasionally worthy of their own National Geographic documentary.

Other insufferable laughs had sonic origins in everyday mechanics, such as *The Jackhammer*, *The Muffler*, and *The Faulty Brake*. The most annoying laugh of all, by popular consensus, was the silent laugh known as *The Lon Chaney* (often shortened to *The Chaney*, or *A Chaney*, and used in phrases like "Yeah, he pulled a *chaney*" by consultants serving the canned-laughter industry). The only sound to be heard when this deadly laugh is deployed is produced by the Laugher slapping one or the other of his knees while convulsing. An incomprehensible product of the human body, *The Chaney* is noted for the fact that it straddles the worlds of jocularity and self-flagellation. It is part of a cluster of laughing syndromes that have had medical researchers puzzled for decades. Why is it that some people turn to self-destruction when amused—clawing the skin on their faces, pulling out their hair, bending over in agony, urinating unintentionally?

Nothing, the Devil had long-believed, could be more sublimely annoying than an annoying laugh. Yet, here was Miss Musicaro, giving World Championship APs a run for their money with nothing funny about her, not a solitary molecule of wit could be found with an electron microscope and a hundred years to waste trying. Her monologue was beginning to take on the *longueurs* of a morning radio show where the host must fill a three-hour time slot with five minutes of twaddle. She had begun her ramblings ten minutes previously—the one connective thread in the knots and tangles of excessive verbiage being herself—and she was still on the Second Avenue bus—chronologically speaking—rummaging in the alligator purse for her fare card. "Things just seem to get swallowed up in there," she blathered to everyone in particular. "It's a mystery to me where they go." Her choice of the word *mystery* was quite likely a feeble attempt at private investigator humor. Or perhaps it was like everything else she said, just another headache-producing red herring.

While shutting out the steady drone of a two-year-old that had dropped its lollipop—he had balled-up *serviettes* and stuffed them into his ears—the Devil tried to imagine Miss Musicaro in the darkened library of a Victorian mansion, having her head bashed in by Colonel Mustard with a candlestick.

He had a premonition that the bulldog business card was going to prove useful before long. There was always some way to make good use of an ugly monster in the execution of his many enterprises.

n *Page 41* of a book of travelers' tales, you might be wondering where this journey is taking you. It's only natural to experience an urge to look ahead, but train

windows are not designed to satisfy such cravings, even though the yearning for foreknowledge is universal, and tickets are not cheap.

Among the many amenities offered by the railways, by far the most expensive to provide and maintain are the windows. They are an essential feature and always have been, dating back to the beginning of the industry.

Undoubtedly, in the age when trains were first designed, the inclusion of windows was necessitated by the need for natural light, lamp oil being prohibitively expensive, most of all in the years before petroleum-based products replaced costly whale oil. When inexpensive electric lighting came into industrial use, the need for windows diminished significantly, and railroad barons, in an effort to increase profits, decided to experiment with passenger cars that provided no windows. The savings on glass, hardware fittings, draperies, shades, weatherproofing, and other materials were enormous. Trains required less heating when the windows were eliminated, being better insulated, which increased profits one step further. The railroad barons were ecstatic. The public was not.

The few windowless carriages that traveled the rails were doomed to short lives. No one wanted to ride in them. A well-known journalist of the period, J. J. Schlegel, summed up the public's general feeling when he wrote: "One does not wish to travel to their destination in a pneumatic tube, like a bill of particulars."

Not long after bottles of champagne had been smashed on the noses of their locomotives, the windowless cars were herded onto a spur line and detoured to the train graveyard to face a future of rust and rot and raccoons. It was only many years later, when World War One broke out, that a retired engineer remembered them, and an attempt was made to salvage whatever viable scrap metal remained on the ravaged bones. Thus, that which had survived the vicissitudes of neglect enjoyed a second life as artillery and tanks and other useful tools of Death.

After this fiasco, train windows were back—indeed, they had never really gone—and the need for them was never again challenged.

Yet, train windows, despite their usefulness as "seeing" instruments, do not fulfill every whim of the traveler. Marvelous, essential, revelatory—these they are—but limited by their geometric relationship to the journey. Because they are at the *sides* of the train cars, at right angles to the train's forward motion, they allow the inquisitive traveler to study only the page he is on (in this case, *Page 43*) as it passes into history behind him. Memory is useful to conjure pages that have already passed (most recently, *Page 42*)—vanished—tree after tree, mile after mile, in the dust kicked up by the juddering caboose. As much as you would like to know what lies ahead, it is not permitted by the window arrangement. If you feel you must know—surmise that the next page to traverse is *Page 44*, extrapolate that the pagination ahead will increase by invariable increments of one. That's as far as certainty can be stretched.

The managers and executives and the boards of directors of the railroads, one and all, regret that you might be dissatisfied with these terms (actually, they don't regret anything—they just pretend to, at least to the extent that they understand the meaning of the word). When the railroads unilaterally made a commitment to keep windows on the trains at a great diminution of profit, the intent was to provide positional information and entertainment, not directional guidance. "A train is a conveyance, not a Ouija board," a board member of the Fox Ironclad Railroad Ltd was quoted as saying in the *Daily Telegram*.

N.B.—Unsatisfied passengers are encouraged to investigate the suitability of motor vehicles or bicycles to mitigate any dissatisfaction they experience with railroad amenities
—*from F.I.R.R. Guidebook; Section 44: Troubleshooting; 1955*

or the second time that morning, EMS workers rushed to the concession area with their rickety, clattery gurney in tow. Along with them, fresh to the scene, marched a

newly-formed brigade of situation-vampires—moist-lipped, wild-eyed, eager as always to suck the marrow out of any happenstance that lay in their path—extending their camera phones in front of them like amulets to ward off boredom.

"Oh me, oh my, oh gracious, it's awfully cold," Miss Musicaro observed, her breath misting. EMS had swathed her supine expanse with lumpy ice bags to prevent swelling beyond the capacity of the gurney. At this point, a group of garrulous lawyers closed in on the icy mound, their feet scrabbling for purchase on the greasy floor, elbows jabbing and fists flying wherever space allowed for the smallest act of violence.

Despite the preceding misadventure and her chattering teeth, Miss Musicaro seemed to enjoy the attention. The alligator purse had been restored to her by Inspector Polifrone, and she resumed the methodical disbursement of bulldog business cards with frostbitten hands. The purse lay open, slackened jaw spread wide, exposing sundry contents to the eyes of the curious—a 38 caliber revolver, a saucer-sized magnifying glass with duct tape wrapped around its handle, a rather large canister of B-Gone Mace, handcuffs, a coil of rope, some potentially lethal hat pins with their tips safeguarded in a little cushion, a bottle of nail polish, a plastic bag of casino chips, and what was either a very small flashlight or a very large lipstick.

Upon observing the lady detective's private arsenal, the little worker shuddered. "I hope they manage to get that monster to the hospital before she starts to get hungry."

In the staccato illumination of camera flashes, the spindly accordion supports and rickety legs of the gurney could be seen buckling under their overwhelming burden. The four little wheels below splayed outward at painful angles, emitting metallic squeals of protest. Bulbs popped. Icing *plooped*. Miss Orgo from *Reuters* opened an umbrella to shield herself from the steady pelting of buttercream.

"I believe I'm feeling just a tiny bit woozy-wobbly," Miss Musicaro confided to her cabinet of medical and legal advisors. All who heard this were taken aback—had the Statue of Liberty set aside her book and torch and, from a recumbent pose on a flatboat, passed the very same remark, it could not possibly have seemed more bizarre. Some of the more ethical attorneys in attendance were beginning to wonder where the greatest damage had been sustained—to Miss Musicaro's person or the sub-floor of the train station.

"Get a good shot of the donut machine!" commanded crimson-faced Inspector Polifrone, oblivious to all else, gesticulating enthusiastically to the *paparazzi* who—disoriented by the swelling numbers of their colleagues and competitors—appeared to be taking pictures of each other. He waved his badge with one hand to establish his authority to new arrivals and indicated elements of the fulminating health crisis with the other. "Get those dollops of cream cheese on the floor! And get those two lying sacks of shit hiding behind the cash register!"

"No! Get the d-dollops," the heavier sack of shit cried out. Then, to the other sack, "What the fuck is a d-d-dollop?"

The tide was coming in.

"Great balls of fire!" the little Scarlett-quoting sack declared.

"Quite," the Devil agreed. He stood up decisively. Off he went with his shabby green carpetbag—a sack of quite a different sort, this one full of the day's collected souls.

The *Second Rule of Railroad Travel* is that you *must* disembark. This requirement applies to everyone, no matter who, without exception. Even the Devil must get off a train somewhere. It is one of the immutable laws of the Universe. Einstein could not have said it better.

Every journey ends. There is nothing unfair about it. Adam disembarked. Noah disembarked, Methuselah disembarked (eventually, at any rate), as did Abraham and Moses and Jesus and Buddha and Mohammed and Lincoln and Gandhi and Audrey Hepburn and Mother Teresa. Disembarkers all.

One disembarks on pathways well-trodden by the feet of the great. Greatness, however, comes in many forms. Railroad historians downplay the subject, but it is common knowledge, and completely logical, that some very bad people disembarked as well—people with different, but distinctive, ideas about how to get from A to B. The public relations officials of the transportation giants prefer to describe these persons as "Alternative Riders." Among thousands and thousands, one finds the names of memorable persons as diverse as Attila the Hun, Vlad the Impaler, John Wayne Gacy, Elizabeth Bathory, J. Edgar Hoover, Joseph McCarthy, Myra Hindley, Richard Nixon, Charlie Manson, Idi Amin, John Wilkes Booth, Pol Pot, Joseph Kennedy, Lyndon B. Johnson, Typhoid Mary, Caligula, John Reginald Christie, the Marquis de Sade, Chairman Mao, Saddam Hussein, Adolf Hitler, Aristotle Onassis, Roy Cohn, the *other* Dallas gunmen, Leona Helmsley, Josef Stalin, and both Nancy and Ronald Reagan.

Despite the fact that he fulfills the requirements of Alternative Rider (AR) in all respects, Benito Mussolini was granted special consideration by railroad officials for successfully making trains in Italy arrive on time, although a thorough investigation into the methods used to achieve this success was never undertaken. Mussolini is a near-unique case, which is why he is classified as a Special Alternative Rider (SAR), as are some of the more questionable railroad barons of the 19th Century (SARRRB) whose positive contributions to the rail system should not be ignored, despite their alleged disreputable and possibly criminal practices.

No overview of disembarkation could be considered complete—or even optimally interesting—if it eschewed the subject of *Presumed* Disembarkers. Discussion of PDs is avoided because the powers-that-be at the highest level of railroad management prefer to distance themselves from the merest hint of responsibility, shared or otherwise, for the fate of PDs. In this classification, one encounters an incredibly rich assortment of personages—Jack the Ripper, Jimmy Hoffa, the Zodiac, John Favara, D. B. Cooper, Amelia Earhart, Solomon Northrup, Roald Amundsen, and many others—who knows if they disembarked—or where—or when.

The most amazing disembarkation story of all is attributed to Richard Martinczek, a well-respected travel-writer who vanished after the Great War while crossing Europe by rail (*cf. Presumed Disembarkers*, A. Fox, 1952). One could not declare his disappearance was "without a trace" with any verifiable certainty, however, because a diary was found and later published in which Martinczek claims to have remained, undetected, on board a train well-beyond its final destination. Some progressive physicists surmised that Martinczek and his train could have reached a terminus of sorts, an extraordinary theoretical locus they christened "The Railroad Event Horizon."

Railroad legend or not, numerous members of the scientific community have come forward to condemn Martinczek as a complete fraud. Asked for his opinion of the Martinczek diary, British cosmologist Stephen A. Hawking meticulously responded through his alphacommunicator, one painstaking letter at a time: "P-o-p-p-y-c-o-c-k-!"

"I had made the commitment to remain," Martinczek wrote in the final pages of his diary. "I ignored the thrice-proffered summons 'End of the line. Everybody off!' and the clangorous accompaniment of warning bells both within and without the train. I had concealed myself earlier beneath a tablecloth in the dining car, where I remained undiscovered by the conductor when he took his passage through, perfunctorily swiveling a lantern left and right in the darkened car. A long time must have passed before I ventured from my hiding place, although I felt that time had stopped utterly, as if I were in an actual place called Limbo, and that a waiting phase had commenced, with an unknown *dénouement* sure to unfold. It was quite unnerving.

"In the pantry area of the dining car, there was a pot of lukewarm tea and a tin containing a few biscuits. I served myself at a freshly laid table as though all were quite normal. Anything was likely to happen, and I wanted to enjoy it in the same manner and style as I had the previous chapters of my journey. Beneath me, I could feel the purring of the locomotive's engine transmitted back to me through the rails— — —"

[Some text following these words was rendered illegible by water damage. Document experts surmise that the train suddenly lurched into motion, causing Martinczek to spill his tea on the fresh ink. The narrative becomes legible once more a page later, now—mostly—in the present tense, written in real time, as events unfolded with increasing rapidity.]

"—a different sort of motion, perhaps smoother, but with far less vibration. I am tempted to describe it as 'more purposeful' for lack of better words to clarify the sensation. In any event, this feels considerably different, as if the train is being pulled toward—rather than driven to—some unforeseen place.

"I write now by candlelight, for soon after composing the previous paragraph, the windows darkened. Nothing could be seen from them. The dining car was dark and still. In order to continue to write these lines, I had to procure candle stubs from the pantry—luckily there were some few remaining from the dinner seating and I was able to locate them by groping about a bit. That search yielded the bonus of a banana and an after-dinner mint. I finished them hours ago. Now I just wait and write, moment by moment.

"*Later.* — At least another hour has passed. The ride has become so smooth, the dishes and glassware, which were chattering in their cabinets so boisterously earlier, have fallen silent. Perhaps we are gaining speed. Impossible to tell with certainty. My thoughts are becoming less decisive and clear—as they pass through my mind they disintegrate midway to resolution. Either anxiety is distorting my perceptions, or my mind is beginning to turn into gelatin.

"*Later.* — Pocket watch stopped. Near-unable to manage words—

cannot stand—understand—think—there are distant voices—sucked through a straw—a hazy light—remember me, my dear sweet Marion!—dissolving—upside-down?—hands grab my head—"

Here ends the document left behind by Martinczek. The man was never seen again, at least not *officially*. Rumors persisted for many years that his vanishing and the diary were elements of a scheme he concocted to abandon his promiscuous wife (the "Marion" referred to on the last page of the diary). There were Martinczek sightings, too. The last reported sighting was in 1933, at a church barbecue in Salt Lake City, where he was—allegedly—seen in the company of six wives and nineteen children.

When Dr. Amit Bannerjee reported for his shift on the third floor of St. Vincent's Hospital, the first thing he noticed was a group of nurses gathered around their station, deep in conversation. Male doctors, almost a dozen of them, were standing around the nurses, pointing and laughing. One of the nurses was slumped in a chair, fanning herself with a hospital chart, her face chalky. She looked over at the doctors and used a middle finger to express her displeasure with them.

Amit tried to tune in to the source of the conflict.

"Hey," one of the male residents said loudly, "I'm willing to bet good money that every one of you ladies would be standing on a chair right now if a mouse ran down this corridor."

The other doctors nodded and smirked.

"Listen," an obese nurse said, addressing the entire group. "I am not afraid of mice. I just wouldn't *eat* one."

"I've always wondered what sort of things you *would* eat."

The men—and some of the women—snickered.

"*That's* harassment Thinly veiled harassment."

As soon as the cannon fired the *H*-word, the group of doctors re-treated from the battlefield in the direction of the medical tents. The smoke around the nurses' station began to clear.

"Ladies, ladies—good morning!" Doctor Bannerjee said, bursting in cheerfully. "Here I am, fresh and full of energy, ready to get down and 'Do No Harm' as they say in our profession."

"Before you dive in and dedicate your life to not harming any of our patients at $600 per harm-free consultation," one of the nurses responded, expecting that he was fully aware of the morning's events, "would you care to join our contingency? We're all going to the Lost and Found. Or perhaps I should say 'Found and Lost' because we've Found we've Lost our appetites. Can we assume you've lost yours, too?"

"No, I haven't lost anything except my grandparents, my virginity, and the lottery. Why ask? What's going on?"

"You must have just got here, doll. We have a situation in progress— a woman down the hall—she claims she ate a mouse."

"No, no, no," another nurse said. "Her lawyer is claiming that. She's not saying anything, she's just screaming bloody murder."

"Excuse my language—but—*what the fuck?*"

"I'm so disgusted, I don't want to talk about it. I'd just as soon go home and start this day all over again. Maybe one of these other girls is willing to get into it with you. Martha, you've got a high blood and guts tolerance, *you* tell him. I'm just about ready to puke."

"Well, Martha, what really happened?"

"It's like Rita just said, a woman was brought in through the ER.

She supposedly ate—or bit into—a rodent."

He looked at the chart Nurse Martha held up. It read: *Ingestion of rodent.* A wave of nausea passed over him.

"It was in a donut she bought at Penn Station. We have the leftovers in a container in the fridge. Want to see?"

The first viewing of the leftovers, having been sufficiently satisfying for the other nurses, they disappeared from the scene. Martha didn't wait for Amit to answer. She made a gesture with her palm that signaled for him to wait. A moment later she was back with a blue Tupperware container marked "Grassini/Rodent Donut."

"It's in here," she said, handing it to him. "Be careful with it. The lawyer made us sign for it. Apparently, it's evidence."

She looked away as he lifted the lid.

He handed it back to her with trembling hands. Forensic confirmation was not going to be necessary. It was obvious that the powdered sugar on his scrubs was a perfect match with the powdered sugar on the remnants of donut.

"What's wrong? You're all pale and sweaty."

"Where is she? The woman. Where do we have her?"

"Down in 303. A lawyer is with her, and we can't get him to leave. She won't let him go until her husband arrives."

Amit heard a voice wafting from 303 just as he breached the doorway: "—won't be able to eat any fried food, or any baked goods ever again," the lawyer was saying to the bedridden woman. "Which means no more birthday cakes for your kids, or toast with your eggs, or cheese danish with the girls during Mahjong games." He laughed and pushed his glasses back up the slope of his nose. "You might not even be able to take Holy Communion. I suppose lumping those weird crackers into our case *might* be construed as something of a stretch, but I'm a Jew, so what do I know, right?"

The bleary-eyed woman still had powdered sugar on her lips. The lawyer had forbidden the nurses to clean it off until his investigator could photograph it. She looked up at Amit, who was gripping both sides of the door frame in complete horror and mistook him for her husband.

"Vinnie? Is that you?"

He fled.

He then returned to the doorway, shouted, "On his way!" and then fled again.

His destination was the handicapped Men's Room, which offered him the privacy he needed to force two fingers down his throat and induce vomiting. He did this twice. He was feverish and sweaty and weak when he stood up. Another wave of nausea and dizziness swept over him when he recalled that he hadn't washed his hands before the procedure. Then he reasoned that washing your hands prior to inserting fingers down your throat was less of a priority if you had just eaten a rodent-laced pastry, but his reasoning didn't help to calm him. Not at all.

"Look," he said to himself, as he ran down a busy corridor and then another and then another, "that woman bit the head off of a mouse and she looks like she's in better shape than you are. Pull yourself together, man! You didn't eat a mouse. Maybe you ate mouse particles, or a mouse hair, or a mouse toenail, or some mouse dandruff. And it ends with that. That's all there is to it. A mouse molecule. No biggie. No biggie. And the hot oil kills the germs, right? You're okay, man, nothing is going to happen. What's the worst that can happen? Rabies? Your dick won't fall off. You can still have kids. You can still have a career. You can still be an arrogant douche-bag doctor down the road.

A specialist. A golf ball-whacking specialist dickhead in plaid pants and white shoes that never get dirty. Nothing bad is going to happen. Pull yourself together, Amit. You probably will get laid within a week or two. At most three. The hot nurse on five is going to see a movie with you. At least she said she would think about it. You're going to marry some rich girl and produce bratty kids, and cheat on her, and get divorced, and then have an affair with your receptionist whose name is Myrna and who has a cigarette voice and a shaved pussy. But there is something you've got to straighten out first. It can't wait. You need to do it now. Right away."

He grabbed the next doctor he passed. He was in the corridor of the obstetrics area, which made it unlikely that this doctor was going to be in a position to help, but he had no time to waste.

"Doctor," he pleaded, steadily increasing the intensity of his grip on the man's forearms as he babbled. "I know you deliver babies, and I don't give a shit if you can help me or not, but you've got to help me. Now. Right now. I bit a mouse."

"You mean *you* got bit by a mouse...?"

"No, you idiot. Listen to me. I bit the mouse. Or almost bit it. Oh shit, oh shit. I need to get my stomach pumped. Help me, doctor. Some bad shit is going down, went down..."

At that he became incoherent. He heard the doctor calling for a gurney. "I think this guy stole some scrubs and used them to make an escape from Psych. Someone call Security and get him off me before he breaks one of my arms."

Another doctor tried to help. "I think this guy is Staff. "

"You recognize him?"

"No, but we don't have Indian patients here, just Indian doctors, and I think this one ate some curried crack."

"He claims to have eaten a mouse," the first doctor remarked. He looked quite puzzled. "I always thought these people were vegetarians."

Above Amit's head, the ceiling darkened, frightening him. Then he realized he was squeezing his eyes shut. He opened them and the ceiling lit up again, rows of fluorescent bulbs passed overhead as the gurney was rolled down hallway after hallway, bringing him to the stomach pump. Or was it to the morgue? Or to his mother's house in Madras? Doctors and nurses came and went, hovering, whispering. He closed his eyes again when he felt the syringe enter his arm. He let the drug smooth him out like a rumpled sheet. "There, there," the drug purred, "Shhhhh..." and he was quite, quite out. Quite. Out.

When he opened his eyes a few hours later, it was just barely. Through slits, he could see the blurred shape of a television hovering over him. Clearly, he had been heavily sedated. What other interventions had transpired, he couldn't begin to imagine, and didn't care to imagine. His imagination had already had the workout of a lifetime that day, and he wasn't feeling up to another flight down the twisted corridors of fantasy. Feeling cautiously under the thin blanket, he checked for the presence of dressings or tubes and found nothing unusual. His private equipment was still intact, curled up like a cat, fast asleep on a bed of thick pubic hair. He tried to stay calm and assess the damage his anxiety attack might have caused his future prospects. "I may be in deep career shit now," he mumbled.

"Perhaps not," a disembodied voice said.

Amit tried to focus.

A strange man was standing in the doorway. Whoever it was began to advance towards the bed, extending his right hand. A business card was at the ready in his left.

"If you'll kindly permit me," the stranger said. "My name is Mervyn J. Schlissel, Esquire. I feel very sure I can help you, Dr. Bannerjee. I can help you today, and, should it be necessary, I can help you for the next 365 days, or the next 720 days, or however many days it

takes for this matter to be set aright." The lawyer grinned broadly—so broadly that the cut on his lip split open for the second time
that day. Blood began to dribble down his chin.

When the Devil arrived home, he found an "Attempted Delivery" notice taped to his door. It was still
early enough to claim the package, so he set out for
the Post Office, only a short walk away. Whistling as he did so, he
flipped all the parking meters he walked past back to zero.

He was feeling a little hungry after his long night at the train station and decided to stop at Luigi's Pizza Parlor. There he ordered a
stromboli, a cheese pie named after his favorite volcano.

Stromboli, one of the three most active volcanos on the planet, had
been producing fire and brimstone off the coast of Italy, almost
without interruption, since the early 1930s. Naturally, that made it
a favored vacation spot for him. In particular, he treasured his memories of the summer of 1952, which he had spent on the hot slopes
among vents of steam, engaging in a torrid love affair with himself.

Luigi wrapped the Devil's *stromboli* in foil and opened the oven door
to heat it, permitting a blast of scorched air to smack the Devil in the
face. This pulled him out of his momentary reverie. Was he going
crazy, he wondered, or did he not hear the faintest trace of a voice
in that blast—as if someone was calling to him from the seething
magma below the earth's crust? He strained to make out the words.

"Psst! Psst! *Teuf!*" a hoarse voice wafted from the oven. "Kannst Du
mich hören?"

The Devil thought he recognized the voice. "Adolf?"

"Ja! *Teufi*, mein Freund, hier spricht der Führer!"

"Lieber Adolf, *bitte!* Jetzt ist keine gute Zeit," the Devil protested.
"Ich bin *sehr* beschäftigt."

"Was? Ich kann dich nicht hören! Kannst Du die verdammte Klimaanlage reparieren?"

Again with the air conditioning! Hitler may have been a great man in his day, but it would take a hundred additional Thousand-Year Reichs to find another tenant who made so many complaints. Once, when the heating system in Hell broke down, Hitler complained so persistently about the cold, the Devil had to knit him a sweater.

The Devil had lost his appetite. He canceled his *stromboli*. As he rejoined the pedestrians outside, he could still faintly make out the wheedling voice from the bowels of the earth. "Bitte, *Teufi*, das ist *schrecklich*! Meine süße Eva schwitzt wie ein Schwein"

It was a breezy day. Hats were blowing off the heads of pedestrians in record numbers as he strolled along. It was simply amazing, he thought—feigning innocence to himself—how many of those hats managed to get themselves run over by trucks and buses. One landed on a car antenna and headed uptown. At a sidewalk cafe, a teapot was knocked down by a flying homburg. Another hat landed on a pigeon, and as the bird struggled underneath it to free itself, the hat slid and hopped across the pavement, as though someone was break-dancing without a body. A small crowd gathered and applauded the best moves. Passing through the Diamond District, he came across another crowd which was looking skyward, following the progress of a flock of yarmulkes heading towards Canada.

When the postal clerk handed him the cardboard mailing box, it was not immediately obvious where the package had come from. Although the sender had included a return address on the shipping label, it was deliberately written in gibberish. Inside the mailer the Devil found a long, rectangular gift box, tied with a ribbon. There was an unsigned note as well.

"We've been watching you," the note read. "But you know that. You know we are always watching you. Most of what you do, you do so we can see you do it. And we do see it, as much as we care to. You are very tiresome, do you know that? Tiresome and tireless. Because you never get tired of your games. You had a good night last night and a good morning this morning, at least by your shoddy standards. We'll grant you that much. As far as what you do, you did very well, and you did it by doing next to nothing. That's part of the thrill for you, isn't it? You love to amuse yourself, and the less you do, the more you are amused—but who cares? Okay, you had a bang-up night and a bigger bang-up morning. Great! A hearty hand of applause from all of us. Congratulations are in order. That's why we decided to send you a gift. A nice cigar, to celebrate with. Stick it in your mouth and light it. We hope you love it. We think you will. And, in closing, we'd like to say that you don't need to get too puffed up about that mouse. Don't pat yourself on the back too hard. We know, and you know, and everyone knows—mice fall into fryers all the time without your help, without anyone's help. Plenty of fried, breaded mice that look like chicken thighs get served in fast food joints all the time. What we're saying is, you didn't break any new ground last night. You're no genius. If you don't want to give up, get some new material, because as things stand, we don't view you as competition. You don't scare us. You can barely make us laugh. Anyway, no hard feelings, old friend. Enjoy chomping on the cigar. We made it just for you."

Unruffled by the note—even a bit wearied by it—he folded it neatly in half, folded it a second time, and calmly placed it in his carpetbag. "Jealousy," he said to himself, "is a tawdry business." He snapped the bag shut for emphasis.

He was absolutely certain that the gift box did not contain a cigar. He had a vivid picture in his mind of what it *did* contain, and that was quite enough. He felt no need to prove he was right. Nevertheless—shameless opportunist that he was—he could think of no reason why a nicely wrapped celebratory gift for a job well done needed to go to waste.

He put the elongated gift box in a new cardboard mailer. On a fresh mailing label, he began to write: "Miss Annabelle Musicaro, Private Investigator, 235 Second Avenue ...."

s soon as the train came to a stop, the gray-haired stationmaster could be seen through the windows, strutting the platform and swinging a bell like the town crier. First in Norwegian, and then in English, he announced: "This is Hell! Hell Station! Ten minutes before departure!"

The Good Humor Man followed his wife down to the platform. "Don't wander off," the stationmaster said to them as if they might be senile. As retired people, they were not nearly as fast as the younger, more energetic tourists on the train, especially the Japanese group. All the other passengers had gotten to the HELL sign before them.

"Well, here we are at last, Francis," Mrs. Good Humor Man said. "In Hell."

He made no response. All his energy was invested in making sure that he wasn't biting his tongue hard enough to draw blood.

"And the air is so fresh, isn't it? Who would have thought?" She took a deep breath and stretched her arms, taking it all in. When she finished luxuriating in the exquisite banality of being nowhere, she began to snap photos. She took one of a group of Japanese men standing under the sign. By prior arrangement, each of them was making the universal sign of the Devil's horns with two of their fingers above the head of the person next to them. They found this highly amusing.

"First Pearl Harbor, and now this," Mrs. Good Humor Man whispered to her husband. "They are just so aggressive." Then, louder, and specifically intended for the Japanese to hear, "I sure hope some of the other passengers will be able to get a crack at that sign!" They may have heard, they may have understood, but it was not possible to tell.

At last, when the Japanese group went off to purchase postcards, Mrs. Good Humor Man was able to position her husband and frame her shot. "Don't smile, Francis. This should look serious, so I can show it to the ladies at church. It won't do to raise those ladies' eyebrows. No sir."

The Good Humor Man stared blankly. At the periphery of his vision, while his wife deliberated over the complexities of the photo she envisioned, his attention was arrested by the sight of a spotted dog standing alongside the waiting train. The dog was looking directly at him. Neither panting nor sniffing nor wagging its tail, it seemed totally disinclined to approach or leave. It was just there.

Their eyes met meaningfully.

And then it all came back to the bewildered ice cream vendor at once—the horrible sound of that persistent jingle, the not-in-time screech of brakes, the battered dog splayed out on the street, blood on its muzzle, the crying little boy who stood over it, covering his eyes with pink, spotless hands. He remembered that little boy vividly, the boy who they say was blown to bits in Vietnam. He invariably asked for vanilla and was always so fastidious and proper and polite. "See Spot run!" he would say. If only he had paid heed to that warning, if only he *had* seen Spot run on that fateful day so long ago.

"I must say, Francis," his wife was chattering, completely oblivious, as always, to her husband's richly textured internal life, "that was very realistic acting on your part. My, the look on your face, dear. You seemed 'totally into it' as the young people say." She handed him the camera. "My turn. Switch places."

When they reversed positions, he was forced to break eye contact with the dog, which was now directly behind him. He took a few photos of his wife with trembling hands. She stood under the sign, striking poses like a silent film actress in different states of mock terror and horror. She did an excellent impression of Mary Philbin in *The Phantom of the Opera*.

"I hope you got at least one or two good ones," she said when they were finished. Pre-failure rebuke was more than a little obvious in her tone.

"If not," he replied dryly, "we can drag ourselves back here next year. We can keep coming back until I get it right."

"Oh dear," said Mrs. Good Humor Man, looking somewhat less cheerful of a sudden. "I suppose I should tell you…"

"What now?"

"I hate to be the one to break this news to you, Francis, but while you were taking those photos, a dog did poopy on your shoe. I would have said something about it at the time, but I didn't want to break character."

He looked down at the mass steaming in the chilly Norwegian air. The smell was just beginning to waft into his nose.

"Where is he? Where did he go?"

"He ran," she said.

The Devil retrieved a blank sheaf of paper from the carpetbag and began to write: "Dearest Madam, —I was lucky enough to hear your excellent monologue this morning, in which you so vividly related to a small but select audience the specifics of your day from the moment your alarm summoned you from a wonderful dream (details included), until the instant of your unfortunate mishap in Pennsylvania Station. I hope this note finds you much improved. Consider the enclosed gift to be a humble token of appreciation for today's extraordinary entertainment and an homage to your narrative skills. As well, I hope the pen I enclose will be an incentive—whenever you take it up in your hand—to commit your inspired thoughts to paper. —Humbly, your servant, Scribble-Scribble."

He brought the completed, sealed package to a clerk.

"Next day delivery?"

"No, use the slowest service for this one," the Devil said. "The longer this takes to get there, the better it's likely to be."

Night had fallen on Babylon. The sky was dominated by a full moon and gossamer clouds that sailed over the constellation of the Great Donut Mouse behind them. Thundering in from the city and screeching to a halt at Babylon Station, the eastbound trains continued to the furthest reaches of Long Island, streaking through suburb after suburb, delivering random players in the day's sundry events to the continuation of their individual dramas and comedies and doldrums. Drunken dominoes that had fallen flat on their faces during the afternoon prepared to stand up again, dust themselves off, and take another tumble in the dark. The Devil might have been afoot, but he wasn't. He was at home, catching up on long-overdue housecleaning. His precious collection of knickknacks was in serious need of polishing and dusting. One can only neglect History for just so long.

There were many interesting objects on the shelves of the Devil's Museum. One of his most beloved artifacts was a glittering amethyst that had popped out of Princess Salome's bellybutton during a night of wild gyrations. The sight of that ancient jewel in his palm never failed to conjure wonderful memories of torrid nights in Judea when, to the accompaniment of religious exhortations, wine had flowed and heads had flown. Another gem from the age of antiquity was the knife Delilah used to saw off Samson's braid, its tip anointed with a dried droplet of Hebrew blood. (For the record, the Devil was very fond of Jews. In a pinch, they were useful to blame things on, a service they provided quite convincingly, since most had been trained from birth by their mothers to walk around feeling guilty anyway).

The more contemporary items were less exotic, but each had an interesting story to tell. Among them one could find the telephone from Josef Stalin's *dacha*—in its time it had been nicknamed "The Midnight Megaphone of Doom." There was a lava-lamp from Jeffrey Dahmer's bedroom (purchased on eBay very cheaply, because the seller had misspelled *Dahmer* as *Damner*), a pair of shoes and a handbag that matched Monica Lewinsky's famous dress (it was the *semen stains* that matched the dress, not the tasteless colors), a never-used bar of soap from Typhoid Mary's lavatory on Welfare Island, and a folio containing irrefutable proof of Ethel Rosenberg's innocence that was discovered under Roy Cohn's pillow after his death from "liver cancer."

Hanging in his bedroom, beautifully framed, the Devil had preserved an inscribed photograph of Adolf Hitler on which the Führer had written: "*Mein liebster Teufi—Du bist immer in meinen Gedanken—Mit freundlichen Grüßen, Dein Führer; Oberster Richter des Deutschen Volkes; Erster Soldat des Deutschen Reiches; und Feldherr aller Zeiten.*" Underneath the inscription, the busy Führer had taken time out from writing upper-case letters and invading neighboring countries to pen a little swastika, the heart of which was pierced by Cupid's arrow.

When *Teufi* had finished his household duties, he sat down to relax. On a sudden whim, just for the Hell of it, he picked up Stalin's phone, pretended to dial, and then, holding the receiver away from his face like a microphone, began shouting at it.

"This is Comrade Stalin speaking," he bellowed. "I want you to send a squad of agents to arrest a repulsive fat woman going by the name of Annabelle Musicaro at 235 Second Avenue. Once you have her in custody, charge her with a hundred counts of Aggravated Irritation in the First Degree, gag her, and put her on the next train to Siberia...."

He then slammed the receiver down and proceeded to laugh so hard he came perilously close to wetting himself. He was careful to rein himself in just in time, though, because there was a limit to how much cleaning he was willing to do in a single day.

Meanwhile, back on the train—It happened that Paula missed the 6:40 and never appeared in the bar car where she was eagerly awaited by Nicky. He called his wife to say he would be home on time after all, but their baby-sitter, the adorable Cutler girl from across Baldwin Street, answered and told him that Marcia had gone out for the evening. This came as a troublesome surprise to him. He began to wonder, as his train sped towards Babylon, what Marcia was up to when he was supposedly working late in the office. And, if she was up to something, who with, and for how long they had been up to it, whatever *it* might be.

Although Marcia had never heard back from Anita, she had started to drive over there anyway, eager to make the most of every minute of her night off. Just as she arrived at Anita's house, Anita called her to explain that she was at a conference in Minneapolis and had only that moment gotten Marcia's message. Marcia was so dispirited by this blundered opportunity, she reversed direction, intending to get drunk and possibly kill Nicky when he got home.

Heading for the back door, she saw Nicky, Debbie, and a boy she didn't know, puffing marijuana smoke out of the three dining room windows. From outside the house they looked like tenants of three separate apartments conversing with each other on a hot night. Marcia had the feeling a splendid time was had by all except Marcia. Debbie was paid for the full night and sent off early with her athletic babysitting assistant. Nicky was sent to bed. He tried to put his arms around Marcia, but she eluded him.

"Why the cold shoulder, honey?"

"Take two of them, and call me in the morning," she snapped and slammed the bathroom door in his face. Obviously, this was not an opportune time to cross-examine his wife about her activities when he was absent, but Nicky resolved to keep a close eye on her. On the other side of the bathroom door, Marcia made the same resolution about her husband.

When Debbie got home—much earlier than anticipated—from her aborted babysitting job, she was astounded to discover Mr. Amoruso, the Cutler's neighbor from the opposite side of the street, standing in the kitchen, wearing nothing but dumpy boxer shorts, stockings, and his eyeglasses. Mrs. Cutler was busy at one of the counters, wearing a nightgown that Debbie was certain she had never seen before. She could do no more than gape at the two adults.

"Here you go, Ralph, dear," Mrs. Cutler twittered. She hummed a tune as she filled a Tupperware container with sugar. "Are you sure this much will be enough?"

"Yes, I'm sure, thank you," he said. "Well good night then. And good night to you, too, Missie. My wife is not exaggerating when she says you get prettier with every passing day."

"Now, Ralph, don't forget your pants and the other things you left in the vestibule!" Mrs. Cutler said. "I'll get them for you." When she returned, she said, "Please don't be ashamed to ask again if another pair of trousers needs hemming. I am always happy to help a neighbor out."

Mr. Amoruso left the house carrying his bundled clothes and shoes and Tupperware with one arm, and a mysterious metal attaché case with the other. In the puddles of lamp light, he looked like a cross between Willy Loman and an imbecile, darting furtively away across Baldwin Street in his droopy boxer shorts and stockinged feet.

Mrs. Cutler watched him with her hands on her hips. After Mr. Amoruso's door closed behind him, she put her arm around her stupefied daughter. "I never before realized," she said in a confidential tone, "what a thoroughly *peculiar* person that man is. Barbara certainly has her hands full. I am going to say a prayer for them this Sunday."

Not long after, up in her bedroom, Debbie was certain she heard the back screen door clatter shut and its lock being snapped, signaling that her father must have come home—from where she hadn't a clue, and preferred never to know. His voice wafted up the stairs, but Debbie could not make out what he said. As she fell asleep—as the last train screeched to a halt at Babylon Station—she heard her parents giggling like teenagers behind their tightly closed door.

H is marvelous night of revelry, a veritable *Walpurgisnacht* on iron wheels, was finally over. The Devil was at home, luxuriating in a bubble bath, surrounded by gilded full-length mirrors. As evidenced by the multitude of reflections, he had the appearance of a moderately handsome man in his mid-thirties. He was quite partial to making his public appearances in this bland manner, so what you were most likely to encounter seated beside you on the train, was an unremarkable figure—not statuesque—perhaps five feet and ten inches in height. His lengthy hair was a pleasing reddish gold, as were his prominent eyebrows, and there was a slight dusting of freckles, barely discernible, across the bridge of his nose. His silky eyelashes were extremely pale—not quite white, but nearly—shading eyes of sparkling, mirthful green. More than anything else, when he adopted this disguise, he resembled an oversized leprechaun, with the same mischievous demeanor attributed to that mythic species, and while he appeared to be quite harmless— and inexplicably likeable—if you were foolish enough to follow him, you would *not* be led to a pot of gold glittering beneath a rainbow; you might, in fact, end up in any number of situations that you had not bargained for.

His greatest secret—and the explanation for so much that has happened in the course of history—was to be found just below the bubbles in the bathtub. There one would discover that he had no cloven hooves, he had no tail, and, most significantly, he had no penis. Below the bubbles—below the waist—the Devil was basically a Ken doll.

This was not an anatomical mishap. At the beginning of Time, when the Unseen Almighty fashioned His first creations, such appendages would have served no purpose—conceptually, they did not yet exist. Later, when creating Adam in His own image, the same aesthetics were implemented. It was only after the second human, Lilith, proved to be so unsatisfactory, that the Unseen Almighty decided to use spare parts of the more successful Adam to fashion Eve. That's when the trouble began. An odd count of ribs was left behind when one of them was removed to create Eve—creating an asymmetrical eyesore—and rather than have a near-perfect creation made less perfect for having more ribs on one side than the other, the odd leftover rib was fashioned into a very large sex organ for Adam's—and Eve's—enjoyment.

There it hangs, history's greatest afterthought.

There, too—in that ungainly, pendulous, unfortunate-looking instrument—swings the genuine Root of All Evil. Those who would claim otherwise, who believe that Money has the greater claim to wear that crown, must not be aware that Evil was in circulation before Money, and that the mighty Phallus came before both.

The newly-invented appendage proved to be the Creation-Era's most debated topic. One by one, the Unseen Almighty's progeny went to view it and returned from Eden with tales of its marvelous properties. The Devil was extremely curious and went to Eden to investigate for himself. There, even from a distance, concealed behind shrubbery, he could see the fabled organ lying limply between Adam's legs as he slept under a tree, curled up like a faithful pet beside its master. Later, he witnessed a different aspect of the organ's repertoire, when Eve woke Adam up, and the penis, along with its proud owner, unexpectedly sprang into frenetic action. After the penis had given a rousing account of itself, it settled down once again. Adam strutted around, the exhausted pendulum swinging to and fro aimlessly like a miniature version of himself. Eve was completely fascinated by it. Poor Lilith—she was just *so* difficult—definitely missed out.

"Well I'll be damned!" the Devil seethed. How did he end up with only the standard-issue poop-hole, while Adam—a veritable do-nothing nobody from nowhere, whimsically slapped together from a few handfuls of clay—was favored with the bonus of this multipurpose tool? Not only did that bizarre appendage arouse the admiration of all who beheld it, it was a versatile built-in pet that didn't need to be trained or fed. The Devil was profoundly offended by the unfairness and was left feeling both covetous and wrathful. It would be fair to say that any number of Deadly Sins sprang into being the moment Adam's rib-sized penis reared its stupid-looking head.

And so the great competition and enmity between the Creator's progeny began. While Man has relentlessly tried to outdo the Devil with all manner of evil machinations (inquisitions, wars, holocausts, ethnic cleansings, and an assortment of similar pastimes—some of which defy explanation by the greatest of minds), the Devil has had one primary field of concentration: he has inexorably striven to reduce the size of the human penis by implementing an arsenal of Darwinian initiatives. His ultimate goal—genetic castration.

The patience, the diligence, the single-mindedness required for such an endeavor—considering that the rewards are reaped in microscopic increments which are only discernible over the expanse of many generations—is not possible to convey to beings who have an average life span of 75 years, and an average attention span of 30 seconds. With the amount of concentration required for his plan to succeed, it is amazing that the Devil has enough time or energy left to sour a pint of cream on a hot day, never mind chase mice around railroad stations, or ride commuter trains at night with a bunch of degenerate drunks.

His hard work and patience have paid off. Penises are getting smaller—century by century, centimeter by centimeter. Mankind is losing the war of phallic attrition and doesn't even know it. By his latest calculation, in another two million years, the Devil will have managed to reduce the average penis to the size of a pinky toe.

He takes this—the work of an eternity—very seriously.

One further point of clarification is in order—contrary to the erroneous version of the Eden story that has circulated for far too long—and this really should have been obvious, because the truth is considerably more logical—it was the *Devil* who designed and first modeled the fig leaf, not Adam. It was the rarest of situations—having something to hide and nothing to hide at the same time in the same spot is not a circumstance encountered too often in celestial, terrestrial or sub-terrestrial affairs.

he *Third Rule of Railroad Travel* is a simple one, at least superficially—*You must enjoy your ride.*

Dictionaries define the verb "enjoy" firstly as "to take delight or pleasure in," secondly as "to possess and benefit from," and finally, "to experience." The intent of the *Third Rule* is best articulated by the last definition—the act of experiencing.

To clarify even further, your journey could be defined—in the most scientific terms—as the enjoyable (experiential) transmission of information over the course of traversed terrain. On the surface, you go from A to B. Beneath the surface, something rather different transpires. Cognizant of it or not, you arrive at the end of your journey different than you were on *Page 1*. On the most obvious level, your arrival occurs, chronologically, later than your departure, leaving you a bit older, a bit closer to the curtain at the end of Act III. Less apparently, but on a more exalted plane, you have acquired something indefinable through the alchemy of experience. You arrive at your destination with perceptions modified—perhaps to an unqualifiable degree—but subjected to transfiguration nonetheless.

ere is your chance to participate in a demonstration/test of the experiential transfer of information. No cheating, please! Follow the instructions and do not sneak a peek at your neighbor's book! When you are finished, turn your book facedown, neatly fold your hands, and wait for this story to be over. There are only a few more pages to go.

Now we begin: Rotate the book you are holding 90 degrees counterclockwise. Imagine, if you will, that the book is a road, and you are traveling along it. *Page 68* is closer to you, *Page 69* is further away. Beyond *Page 69* you can see the book horizon.

As you traverse it, *Page 69* rises like a hill. You climb, you climb, you climb. You reach the summit and suddenly you are riding downhill on *Page 70* heading for *Page 71*. A new horizon presents itself. A new hill arises. Next comes *Page 72*, then *73, etc., etc.*

Dick, Jane, and Sally showed you this road one summer day, long ago. Dick pointed at the horizon and said, "See Spot run," and Spot ran up the hill, disappearing down the other side. You climbed, you climbed, you climbed. On the other side of the hill, Spot was waiting for you, ready to run again. Annoying Sally was pulling your sleeve and saying "Oh, (insert your name here), isn't this fun?"

Look down. The paragraphs, the sentences, the words, the letters—all are gone now. Below you your shoes are positioned on a highway paved with undecipherable marks, rough and varied as crushed gravel. Your shoes point toward the book horizon. A road sign reading *69* stands to your right. Spot is already on the other side of a steep hill, panting, running in circles, tail wagging, wondering where you are.

Rotate the book back to its original orientation, 90 degrees clockwise. The gravel, the roadbed of flinty gibberish, is comprehensible once more—paragraphs, sentences, words, letters emerge from the chaos. At this moment you are reading this very

word!

It's the one with the exclamation mark following the lower-case letter *d* located on the page with the signpost reading *69*. Everything that didn't make sense a moment ago means something now. If it

HORIZON

and Tom showed you this road one summer day, long ago. Dick pointed at the horizon and said, "See Spot run," and Spot ran up the hill, disappearing down the other side. You climbed, you climbed. On the other side of the hill, Spot was waiting for you, ready to run again.

- Look down. The paragraphs, the sentences, the words, the letters—all are gone now. If your eyes had feet, you'd see your shoes below you, positioned on a highway paved with undecipherable marks, rough and varied as crushed gravel. Your shoes point to the horizon, a road sign reading 67 stands to your right, and Spot is already on the other side of a steep hill, panting, running in circles, wondering where you are.

... back to its original orientation, 90 degrees ... vel, the roadbed of flinty gibberish, is ... the more—paragraphs, sentences, words, ... ge from the chaos. Everything that didn't make ...ent earlier means something now.

CONCLUSIONS

- There are multiple ways to experience the same information.
- Questions and answers may be as little as 90 degrees apart.
- Certainty and chaos can occupy the same space.
- You cannot see the future, but you can see where it is.
- The next thing that will happen is only one hill further on.

Life is a journey comprised of countless smaller journeys. Every journey is an experience comprised of countless images, successively glimpsed through windows as you rush across the landscape. Every glimpse is comprised of countless concepts. Ev-

67

---

instituted the fig leaf, not Adam.

The third rule of railroad travel is a simpl... ... ... ficially: *You must enjoy your ride.* Dic...naries define the ... "enjoy" firstly as "to take delight/pleasure in," second... as "to possess and benefit from," *annually*, **"to experience."**
The intent of the third rule is comes to focus through the len... of the last definition—the act of experiencing.

The journey you are on could be...cing. ...tific, analytical terms—as the enjoya... — *in the ... in...al* ...sion of information over the course of traveled terrain. ...rface you go from A to B. Under the surface, some... ...n. The paragraphs, the sentences...it or not, your ar... re gone now. If your eyes had...ou were on Page 1.
...sentences, chronologic ...
...ed on a hig...er, ...
...and varied as 'defi... ...
...d, a road sign for destination w... ...nd Spot is already on the orderly unmeasurable ...g, running in circles, wondering wheless.

...AL EXPERIMENT

...are the book you are holding 90 degrees counterclock-wise. Imagine, if you will, that the book is a road, and you are traveling forward along it. Page 60 is closer to you, page 61 is further away. Beyond page 61 you can see the horizon. As you head towards it, page 61 rises like a hill. You climb, you climb, you climb. You reach the summit and suddenly you are riding downhill on page 62, heading for page 63. A new horizon presents itself. A new hill arises. Dick and Jane

GRAVEL

DIRECTION OF TRAVEL

66

HILL RISES UPON APPROACH
FROM ZERO DEGREES TO NINETY DEGREES

LOCATION SIGNPOST

SPEED BUMP

Illustration
courtesy of

doesn't, go back one page and ask the proctor if it would be okay for you to take the test again, or, as an alternative, ask them to recommend another book that is more appropriate to your reading level.

CONCLUSIONS

- There are multiple ways to experience the same information.
- Questions and answers may be as little as 90 degrees apart.
- Certainty and chaos can occupy the same space.
- The next thing that will happen is only one hill further on.

After years of investigation, a team of linguistic researchers concluded that the smallest known component of a story was the solitary alphabetic letter. It didn't matter which letter (although X had been the arbitrary guinea pig, known as *Subject X*, or *Ecksie*, in the blind studies). The basic glyph used as a building block in stories—the aforementioned X, for instance, was incredibly small— comparatively speaking, it was to the 888-page *Warren Commission Report* what a neutrino was to the City of Dallas, or a single bullet was to the United States.

How did the researchers tackle the complexities they faced in their quest to discover exactly what stories are made of?

The first experiments involved the removal of letters—letter by letter—from a specially constructed story, designed to withstand the rigors of just such a test. The subject chosen for the story was a familiar tale about a fox and a dog. After eliminating a mere five percent of the letters using a nuclear-powered blue pencil, it was observed that words could no longer be formed correctly and sentences could not be strung together. The simple story, in trying to tell itself under such adverse circumstances, exhausted all its resources and fell to the ground like an empty overcoat.

It was extrapolated, from these results, that there had to be a minimum number of letters required for a story to exist, like a minimum number of genes in a DNA molecule were required to produce a recognizable living creature. More importantly, the findings indicated that certain letters were more necessary than others to obtain satisfactory results. The second round of experiments, therefore, found the researchers cautiously attempting to eliminate letters that would not be called upon too often. A perfect candidate for exclusion (or discrimination, as some critics would later call it) was the aforementioned letter *X*, but that presented a serious conflict immediately. Without *Ecksie* they could not reference the *fox*, a critical character—possibly the hero—of the story.

An attempt was made to rename the species from "fox" to "foks" or "foqs" but researchers faced a six-month waiting period to get a patent on a new animal. Instead, a circumvention algorithm was used. All references to the fox were altered to *it* and *he* and *him*, and—when absolutely necessary—to *the clever brown animal with the bushy tail*. A secondary problem arose from the implementation of this very workaround. The story became bloated with verbose, oblique references to explain or describe the simplest objects, observations, and occurrences. It was only a matter of time before what had been a charming little tale was elongated to proportions that even the intrepid Dostoyevsky would repudiate. The researchers christened this unfortunate literary syndrome "Foksbloat."

Quite obviously, this series of experiments was a complete fiasco. The main cause of the failure was, more than likely, the wrongheaded, discriminatory, and generally negative approach to the subject under consideration—the research focused too much on deconstruction—removing things—followed by the taking of notes while the damaging decisions produced their unfortunate effects. The laboratory had inadvertently become an *abattoir* of the English language, instead of a hot-house for the breeding of rare linguistic flowers. Here was a classic case of scientific autoimmune disease, wherein the experiment sickened, and then killed, the science that spawned it.

There is an entirely *different* approach to the same subject in the next illustration. Here we see an attempt to build something *new* with a similar scarcity of resources. The result is something both useful and delightful, and it provides a fresh lens through which we can appreciate the wonders of storytelling anew. We refer to the following illustration, created *circa* 1885 for use by typographers. It incorporates all of the letters of the Roman alphabet in an extremely confined space. It gathers *A, B, C*, and their 23 letter-mates all in one place—as if packing them into a clown car—and spills them out thusly:

THE QUICK BROWN FOX JUMPS OVER THE LAZY DOG.

The author of this iconic illustration has ingeniously subdued the chaos of the alphabet and wrought from it a story. He introduces two characters—a fox and a dog—both deftly described. And although there is a scarcity of plot, the *dénouement* is not without a trace of irony for those who choose to look deeper. A great debt is owed to the choice of the word *lazy* for providing a hint of Æsopian morality to the narrative, and for delivering the letters *z* and *y* to the enterprise—two malingering members of the alphabet, lagging behind their 24 colleagues at the end of the lineup in the penultimate word.

Some professors of Quantum Linguistics would not hesitate to award this simple sentence with the honor of being *The Greatest Short Story Ever Written*. Others would qualify it as the archetypical story from which all other stories can claim descent—including the content of all the pages you have read prior to this one.

It should be no surprise, then, with all of this evidence carefully considered, to realize that, possibly unknowingly, you have just experienced—or, as railroad regulations like to describe it, *enjoyed*—74 pages of *The Adventures of the Quick Brown Fox*.

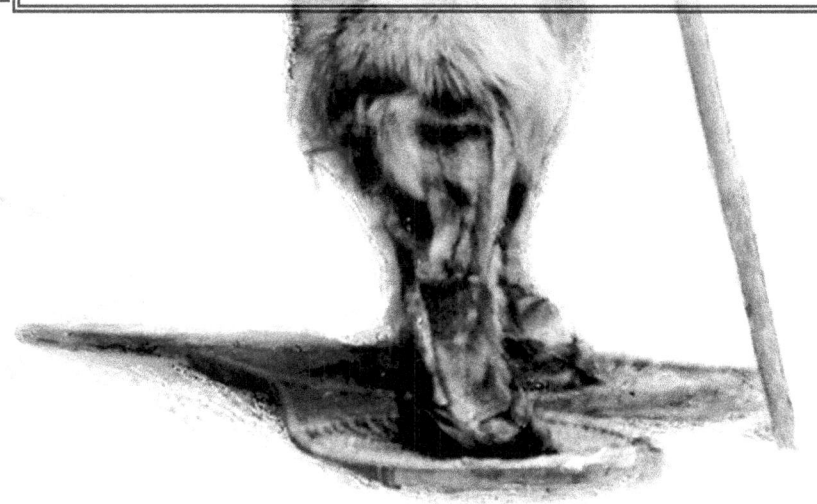

Roald Amundsen, one of history's most distinguished PDs (Presumed Disembarkers). Despite the fact that he *appears* to have already disembarked in this photograph, in actuality, it was taken while he was still "on the train."

F·O·X IRONCLAD RAILROAD LTD.

FEATURED AD

Highly recommended by renowned writer Geoffrey Chaucer, the month of April is a splendid choice to make for your travel adventure. *Our trains are at your service!*

Book Now!

Three Mormons get on a train. The first is an unmarried Mormon, the second is a married Mormon with four wives, and the third is a married Mormon with six wives. A fourth Mormon, three times widowed—already on the train—says to the three newcomers, "I'll give one hundred dollars to the Mormon who makes up the best story about where this joke is going."

— (to be continued) —

A Prologue to The Professor's Tale

Track 19. *Five minutes to departure.* ‖‖‖‖‖‖‖‖‖‖‖‖‖‖‖‖‖‖‖‖‖‖‖

The Professor began the promised analysis: "The fox is quick and brown. The dog is lazy. The fox jumps over the dog. It's not much, but it's enough to qualify nine words and eleven syllables as a classic fable. Because, however terse the execution, there is an unmistakable moral hinted at. There, my new friends, is the seed from which a larger story germinates."

The three Nightcaps—Scotch, Ry, and Soda—were listening intently as their invited guest and seat-mate, a Norwegian professor of folklore, between bits of congenial conversation and bites of crisp apple, unraveled for them—and eavesdroppers like ourselves—his analysis of the *real* story of "the quick brown fox that jumped over the lazy dog." Strictly speaking (not that any established rules of conversation were being observed), there is no *real* story of the fox and dog. Stories aren't real—they're just stories. That hole in the stocking of storytelling is even more troublesome when the so-called stories are populated by animals, or birds, or insects, or other barely sentient creatures. More than half the stories that could be told couldn't be told if you eliminated just those *genera* from the universe of potential story matter. Animals, for example, have lives, not stories. Animals must manage their lives with the meager pickings offered by the vicissitudes of survival. Animals, unlike people, can live on bread and water and little else. People need bread, water, and stories.

It's possible that the real story being told on the *Paumanok Express* was the story of four passengers—three listeners and one narrator—and the fox and dog were mere background music, or, in Hitchcockian parlance, "MacGuffins"—story elements that sound as if they might be animals, but are actually bits of story structure, much like "Red Herrings"—story structure herrings, not edible herrings, of course. If the *passengers* were the story, the savvy eavesdropper would be well-advised to pay close attention, listen between the lines, pick up the bits of story that sometimes drop out of hearing between other bits of story. It's never too late to start paying attention.

Earlier, at 9:30 a.m.

Just a half-hour before departure, the conductor had come into the carriage to greet early passengers and punch their tickets. The Nightcaps were closest to the door and the first passengers approached. Addressing Scotch, who was sitting across from his friends in the far corner, he said, "The seat you're sitting in was once the favorite seat of Walt Whitman, who rode in this carriage—right *there*—more than one-hundred years ago."

"I'm certainly surprised and honored," Scotch said, reverentially.

Ry added, "And we're honored to be sitting with him—now that we know what he's sitting on. Right, Sode?" Soda assented with a nod.

The conductor continued to elaborate. "Whitman was born on Long Island, you know, which he called by its aboriginal name—Paumanok. He rode often on the F.I.R.R., visiting friends out in Montauk and other places along the line—the famous *Paumanok Express* line— named in honor of its most illustrious passenger. They say Old Walt was very fond of that corner seat. See—look behind you—there's a small framed photo of him on the wall above you to mark his spot."

"Where does *The Brown Fox* come into the picture? The exterior of this carriage is marked *The Brown Fox* in gold lettering, and it's engraved in the brass plate above the door behind you." Soda held up his freshly-punched ticket. "It's printed on our tickets, too."

"Other than these four passenger carriages from 1878 and the dining car from 1896, nothing of *The Brown Fox* remains in actual use," the conductor explained. "But the original pollu-tion-belching locomotive still exists It's in a museum in Port Jefferson. *The Brown Fox* was named for Bromleigh Fox—nicknamed "Browny"—of the Fox railroad dynasty. There was also a *Black Fox,* a *Red Fox,* a *White Fox,* and a *Silver Fox* in service back then. *The Silver Fox* was named for Browny's sister, Silvana, who became a famous actress, Silvana Fox McGrath. I'm not sure of specifics on the other old Fox trains and their corresponding siblings. There could have been a Whitey and a Blacky and a Red. They're all scrap metal now anyway—the trains that is—melted down and absorbed in the calamities of the first World War. Only these five little foxes and the retired locomotive are left, and, of course, all of those Fox siblings are nothing but bones, dust, and *google bytes.* Even some of the silent films that featured Silvana Fox McGrath in her old age, includ-ing one starring Valentino, have been lost. We're a ghost train, in a manner of speaking—so be on your guard, guys—anyone riding with you might be a ghost—even me!" Indicating Scotch with his ticket puncher, he added, "And you there, sitting on Walt Whitman's lap—I'd be especially careful if I were you."

He stretched across the aisle to punch tickets there. Looking back over his shoulder, he continued to talk as he worked: "I'm sure you know we run these old carriages as historic and educa-tional attractions. We have all kinds of ghosts—*oops!*—I meant to say *guests.*" He winked. "From A to Z, really. Today, in the next carriage we have a group of Yeshiva students and a rabbi giving a lecture about the holes in bagels, if you can believe it. Sorry to say, they've brought their own food and won't let us open the windows, so it smells like Katz's Delicatessen in there. Even the ghosts are going to avoid that carriage on this trip!" The conductor pinched his nostrils and shuddered comically. "We've had many celebrities on board, especially film direc-tors. And lots of writers. The dining car has been written-up in major food magazines. It's right out of a movie. You'll have to pass through the F.I.R.R.'s newest and most modern carriage to get there, and that's somewhat interesting by contrast, even if it puts a dent in the historic mood we've worked so hard for."

"That's sort of perverse, isn't it? Why put a modern carriage in the middle of all this bygone-era splendor?"

"We're obliged to provide modernized toilet facilities for our modern-day sorry asses—the antique toilets are too delicate for bratty children and passengers who've had a few drinks—and by railroad regulation, 'facilities' have to be placed in the center of the carriage lineup for easy access. We also need an isolated place to herd our cellphone zombies so they can do their thing without polluting the atmosphere for everyone else. Not that we mean to imply any connection exists between talking on a cellphone and using a toilet."

"How could you?" Scotch said. "Only one of them is a necessity."

"Unfortunately, you fellows will have to pass through the smelly "Pastrami, Tongue, and Pickles Carriage" and then survive the cacophony in "The Train of Today and Tomorrow" on your way to the dining car, but I guarantee, it's worth it. The railroad bigwigs and poobahs decreed that this train would offer the best possible tribute to train travel of the past, the present, and the future, and, in my opinion, it actually does. There's the vintage dining car and the lunch ahead of you, and—trust me—you can't miss the outrageous toilets—so be sure to drink your tea, and lots of it. They're not just modern, they are, *literally*, robotic. Hercule Poirot is the attendant in the *Mens*, and Miss Froy is today's matron on duty in the *Ladies*."

Soda said, "I'm going to have a sex change after we pass Garden City, just so I can use both." The others nodded in agreement.

"We insist that all medical procedures be performed in the twentieth-century carriage," the conductor said with mock seriousness. "Who knows what a sex reassignment carried out with nineteenth-century surgical techniques might produce? We do have the lunch to consider, right? By the way, lunch is at noon. You know where. There'll be Long Island duckling, of course, and lobster tails, swordfish, corn on the cob, rhubarb pie, a selection of local wines, and lots more. Real Paumanok cuisine. Enjoy your visits to the toilet, too."

As soon as the conductor had progressed far enough down the aisle to be out of earshot, Soda leaned forward and whispered, "Who's Walt Whitman?"

Three minutes to departure, at 9:57 a.m. ||||||||||||||||||||||

The Professor continued with his analysis. "Let's get past the single irrelevant detail—the word *brown*. It doesn't matter a bit in the nine-word version of the story what color the fox is. The color *brown* is only mentioned to franchise the letters *b* and *w* for use in the typographer's manual. In the British version of the story you are about to hear—the *real* version—the color *brown* is hardly irrelevant—it may possibly be the most significant detail in the story.

"That said, whatever the contention between the two animals, the fox scores a victory over the dog—at least initially—through skillful observation. We know the dog is lazy—the author tells us so in the next to last word of the pangram. On the other hand, the author doesn't tell the fox anything. The fox has already jumped over the dog long before the word *lazy* is introduced.

"So, there you have the principle plot point. The *perceived* laziness of the dog is the circumstance that emboldens the fox to risk the leap. The adjective *quick*, therefore, refers *not* to the *speed* with which he executes his maneuver, but to the *mental acuity* with which he deduces the opportunity to make the maneuver in the first place. The author, with skillful subtlety, is telling us that the fox is very smart and the dog is either very stupid, or very dead. In nine words and eight spaces. And a period at the end of it all—if one *must* take the punctuation into account to placate completists, so be it."

As before, earlier, at 9:44 a.m. |||||||||||||||||||||||||||||||||||||||||||||||

Both Scotch and Ry were astounded by Soda's question. "Are you serious, Sode?—you've never heard of Walt Whitman?" Scotch pointed at the photo on the wall above his head. "This venerable American icon? The undisputed founder of modern poetry?"

"He looks like a dirty old man to me," Soda replied, unimpressed. He stood up and took a closer look. "Like Rip Van Winkle on Skid Row. Maybe worse."

"Rip Van Winkle isn't real, and Walt Whitman is. Was. It's not as if you don't read, man. I see you reading all the time."

"That's right—all the time. Thank you for noticing."

"What are you reading now?"

"A best-seller about a fat guy who drops dead in his kitchen."

"Oh yeah," Ry said. "I heard something about it. What is it? a bio? a mystery? a tell-all? a cookbook?"

"No, actually it's more like a piece of shit."

"So, how did it get on the best-seller list at the *Times*?"

"It has the Kardashian aura about it," Soda said with a shrug. "You know, not *everything* a person reads has to be *Literature*—dressed-to-the-nines, with an upper-case *L* and a top hat. Look at this, for example." He took out his train ticket and held it out to them. "Do you see the old-fashioned font the graphic designer used on the train designation? That's the Journey Font. It's as old as this train, which is why he chose it."

"What about it? As far as I can see, that thing in your hand is a train ticket, not *War and Peace*."

"Well," Soda continued, taking a book out of his briefcase, "when I looked at my ticket, I was reminded of the variety of typesetting fonts in this manual, which is our bible at the design studio. But it wasn't just the *font* on the ticket that aroused my interest, it was the *words* on it, too. I'll show you."

He laid the book on his lap in such a way that all three could see it. "All the fonts, for purposes of comparison, are displayed using the identical sentence—'*The quick brown fox jumps over the lazy dog.*' It's an industry standard, used worldwide."

He flipped the pages until he found the one he was looking for. "This one is the Journey Font." He pointed at the words "*brown fox*" in the typography book and pointed at the words "*Brown Fox*" on his ticket. Except for the lower-case *b* and *f* in the book, and the upper-case *B* and *F* on the ticket, they looked identical. "This sample sentence, used to demonstrate the characteristics of the different fonts, is a world-renowned 'pangram'—a sentence that includes every letter of the Roman alphabet. That's what makes it a universal tool for commercial artists."

"What, may I ask, does this have to do with Walt Whitman, or the price of sex in Thailand?"

"It so happens, Mr. Know-It-All—if I may address you by your ill-suited imaginary name—that the pangram in question is acknowledged by numerous notable scholars to be the greatest short story ever written. Which, I believe, qualifies said pangram as Literature with an upper-case *L* and a top hat, and maybe some diamond studs and a white bow tie thrown in. Furthermore, I am pleased to inform you vile, unbearable snobs, I have occasion to read said Literature with an upper-case *L* more than fifty times a day—at least Monday through Friday."

"You think that reading the same stupid sentence fifty times a day, five days a week, entitles you to a Ph.D. in Literature?"

"Well, if you add in all my overtime...."

"And, to call that bit of nonsense the greatest short story ever written is asinine."

"Not really," a strange voice said. The Nightcaps looked up. A nondescript gentleman stood in the aisle beside them. "The story of the fox and the dog in that pangram really *is* the greatest short story ever written. It's not the first or the shortest, and it's not the best, but it *is* the greatest—or, at the least, *among* the greatest, and it *is* great Literature with an upper-case *L,* a top hat, and a fresh carnation. As it happens, I am something of an authority."

Soda threw his hands in the air triumphantly. "King Solomon has arrived, and in the nick of time, too! Let me shake your hand!"

The stranger smiled generously, but—perfectly in keeping with his reserved old-world demeanor—he made no move to take the extended hand.

"And what, sir, is your field of expertise?" Scotch inquired with exaggerated formality, peering at the stranger as if through a monocle. "Would that happen to be foxes? Dogs? Fonts and pangrams? Men's evening wear? Other people's conversations?"

The stranger laughed. "Actually, the answer to that multiple-choice quiz is '*None of the above.*' I'm a folklorist—or, to be more specific, a professor of folklore at Tromsø University in northern Norway—so my 'field of expertise' is the collection and study of the world's stories and mythologies. You could alternatively call me a *fabulist,* which is a little closer to the way we'd phrase it in Norwegian."

"So, Professor—now that you are sinking in our conversation as though it was quicksand—what do you propose to contribute to it?"

"Actually," he replied congenially, "this is very nice quicksand as quicksand on train rides go. If you ask nicely, I'll tell the *real* story of the quick brown fox and the lazy dog, a fairly obscure fable from the British Isles. You can begin by inviting me to join you—officially, of course—which is much nicer than sinking in quicksand. At least I think it is. Then, if each of you promises to contribute a fable of your own to my collection by—shall we say 'gentlemen's agreement?'—I'll oblige you and tell you about the fox and dog first. What's the Latin phrase for that? *Quid pro quo*, I think."

The Nightcaps all assented with nods of their heads, but none repeated the previous attempt at handshaking. An awkward pause ensued during which the three waited for something to happen. Ry was the first to realize what was expected. "Excuse us," he said. "On behalf of myself and my two traveling companions, would you be so kind as to join us, Professor?" He made an expansive gesture of courtesy with his hand, indicating the empty space next to Scotch.

"Very well," the Professor assented. "Since you put it so elegantly and persuasively, we have 'a deal,' as you Americans like to call this type of arrangement." He sat next to Scotch, opposite Ry and Soda, setting an old carpetbag on the floor between them. Sunlight, streaming through the windows, crossed the planes of his face and glittered on his pale eyelashes. Each of the others, acutely aware that they were being studied, wondered which of them the Professor was really interested in. None considered, even for an instant, that the Professor's interest—beyond securing an audience for himself—might be the Professor.

"Interesting bag," Soda commented, indicating the carpetbag by pointing the tip of his shoe at it.

"My signature accessory."

"What's in it?"

"Signatures."

Three mental x-ray machines fired at once—each of the Nightcaps privately invoked an image of the contents of the carpetbag. One imagined a ball of yarn and an ugly, half-knitted sweater. Another envisioned a severed head of the Jeffrey Dahmer variety, nicely wrapped in sandwich wrap. Another pictured a bundle of smelly gym sweats and a collection of Norwegian *après-ski* porn. Despite the diverse fantasies, they were unanimous in their intention to look in the carpetbag the instant the Professor wasn't watching. All three had long ago mastered the art of looking in strangers' medicine cabinets, and even had a name for that investigatory tactic: *bathroom googling*. Soda, for example, had a 1/12th share in a Fire Island summer rental a few years previously. On his first visit, he had opened the medicine chest and found himself facing eleven bottles of Prozac. He had some difficulty making room for his own bottle, which he managed to accommodate by tossing out a box of band-aids. He then checked all the other prescriptions inside and looked up the unfamiliar ones.

"I'm Ryland Milney," Ry said. "Most people call me Ry. Next to you is my old pal, Scotch Diamond, a friend since childhood. His real name is Samuel, but his mother, who is Scottish, nicknamed him Scotch to annoy his Jewish father, who had annoyed her first by acquiring an English boyfriend. And this fellow next to me is another pal, Martin Sodak, who we call *Soda*, just to keep the beverage motif intact. Sometimes we shorten that to *Sode* in conversation because we don't think he deserves two syllables while we only get one apiece. So, here we are—the three 'Nightcaps'—Scotch, Ry, and Soda." As a flourish, he appended a fake hiccup. The other two had heard that appended fake hiccup a million times and hadn't found it funny in a few—possibly as many as five—years.

"It's a little early for even *one* nightcap," the newcomer said, "but here we are just the same, aren't we?" Now that the Professor had been invited to join them, his demeanor seemed to grow progressively more relaxed. "I'm Dr. Théoden Dramstad, Professor of Folklore. What kind of draught should I be? Probably a one-syllable draught would fit in best with the rest of you. Should it be Gin? Rum? Schnapps? Or do you want to address me as *Professor* like my students do? Or, more in the American style, as *Théo?* Or *Tod?*"

"With four stories to tell, and a long ride ahead of us, we can decide later. Maybe over lunch we can officially *beveragize* you." Scotch looked at his watch. There was still nearly fifteen minutes before departure. "We're on our way to Sayville, where we catch a ferry over to Fire Island. Are you heading the same way?"

"No, I'm afraid not. I am going to Sayville, same as you, but I stop there to investigate a local legend. Perhaps you've heard of Father Divine, otherwise known as Reverend Major Jealous Divine?"

"Not that I can recall," Ry said, glancing over at his friends, who wore similar blank expressions. "Who is he? A drag queen?"

"He was an African-American minister in the early twentieth century who claimed to be God," the Professor explained. "In 1919 he bought a house in Sayville to beef up his ministry with a series of meetings and banquets that went on—quite noisily—for more than a decade. These events grew in grandiosity, becoming increasingly bothersome to the conservative, white residents of the town. Eventually, in 1931, the townspeople, who didn't want black folk in Sayville to begin with—principally due to fear of falling property values—connived to have Father Divine arrested on charges of disturbing the peace. The house was raided. There was nearly a riot—the townsfolk surrounding the property like a scene from an old horror movie—minus the torches and pitchforks—with state troopers and prison buses summoned to the house sometime after midnight. A total of 78 arrests were made. The fine was $5.00 for each of the 46 persons who pled guilty, which Father Divine attempted to pay in full with a $500 bill; the authorities were unable to make change, nor able to get any at 3:00 a.m., causing even more embarrassment, and for the newspapers and radio broadcasts, more comedy.

"The Reverend went on trial months later and was found guilty. The presiding judge, calling him a fraud and a 'menace to society,' ignored the jury's recommendation for leniency, and sentenced him to the maximum allowable penalty—an outrageous sentence of a full year in prison *and* a $500 fine—just for having a loud party. Suddenly, the comedy wasn't so funny. It was more like a public demonstration of legally-sanctioned racism.

"In any case, the Reverend had his revenge, possibly in the form of a hex, or a curse—the judge dropped dead of a coronary four days after the sentencing. In response, the Reverend was quoted as saying 'I hated to do it to him.' That juicy bit was reported in all the newspapers of the day. The subtext, of course, was "Divine" retribution.

"That's the famous Sayville legend, gentlemen, at least the principal details. The Reverend served only a few weeks of his sentence before he was released on appeal. The judge remained dead—there is no Appellate Court to reverse fatal heart attacks. The Reverend became rich. His ministry still owns the house at 132 Macon Drive, which is where I'm going today. But that's not all—there's a *related* Sayville tale, arguably better than this one, and I will throw it in for you as a bonus—something I rarely offer—and you fellows won't owe me anything extra. I still get one tale from each of you and you get the fox, the dog, a double serving of Father Divine—otherwise known as God Himself—and my delightful companionship.

"Okay, here we go: —there were two German immigrant families living in Sayville, next door neighbors," he began. "One family, the Felgenhauers, lived in the house that was eventually sold to Father Divine. After World War I ended, in 1919, Felgenhauer got tired of all the prejudice being levied against Germans and changed his name to Fellows. His neighbor found that action thoroughly despicable and proceeded to wage a campaign of ridicule against the former Felgenhauer. This foolishness escalated to such a degree that Fellows was forced to move out of Sayville to preserve his own sanity—but not without exacting revenge first. When advertising the sale of his house, Fellows specifically targeted "colored" buyers, hoping to destroy his neighbor's property values—eventually finding his dream purchaser in Father Divine—a man with a mountain of cash at his disposal, and a white-hot zeal to move his ministry to a white locality where he could proselytize white parishioners. Father Divine became the first black homeowner in Sayville, but also the patsy in a revenge scheme, possibly without being fully aware of it. On the other hand, since Father Divine was God—at least during his lifetime—he was in a position to know whatever he cared to know. Property values in Sayville plummeted, noise levels soared, cars choked the streets on Sunday banquet days, tempers flared, threats flew—this went on for ten years—and the citizens of the town used every scheme imaginable to force Father Divine and his followers out, including formally accusing him of running a crime ring and a brothel out of the house, and housing a personal harem inside it.

"The most intriguing part of a story like this is how much it reveals about the mechanics of evil at work in human affairs. It's a story in which all the spinning gears are fairly transparent. One form of prejudice—American against German—leads to another—German against German—which leads to another—White against White—which leads to the finale—White against Black, ending—in Sayville, at least—with Father Divine getting rich and Judge Smith dead at the age of 55."

Scotch said, "I agree—that *is* an amazing story, but I don't understand what there is for you to investigate."

"That remains to be seen," replied the Professor, almost defensively. "I have to thoroughly absorb every last ounce of the considerable hatred and evil inhabiting the scene before I can catalog it correctly. It's like visiting a haunted house. It's one thing when you go in, and something else when you come out."

Imminent departure, at 9:59 a.m. ||||||||||||||||||||||||||||||||||||

The Professor had just concluded his analysis of the pangram for the benefit of his little audience. "As soon as we are moving, I'll tell you the British version of the story. I promised it to you, and I will deliver. It's much longer than the typographer's ditty—how could it not be?—but one of the more interesting features, despite the vast difference in length and texture, is that both versions run in parallel, so that details are encountered in the same order in each version. For example, the dog, which is the *last* word of narrative in the pangram, will make his entrance *last* in the story—as he should—following all else like the caboose at the end of this train. So, please, fellows—it would be appreciated if you could manage to put some catheters on your curiosity glands, or, at the very least, make a good show of trying to—*don't interrupt me to ask where the dog is!* Unless we are abducted by aliens first, we will get to the dog, I promise."

"No dogs allowed," barked the conductor, unexpectedly discovered standing over them. "Until the end."

He punched the Professor's ticket. "I see my trio has become a quartet," he said. "We're about to depart for better places, gentlemen."

He turned and addressed the rest of the carriage, holding up an antique stopwatch, its face exposed. "Departing in one minute, ladies and gents. Enjoy your journey!" Snapping the watch case closed as punctuation, he left as quickly as he had arrived.

The Professor took a fresh apple out of his coat pocket and bit into it. "He's not really a conductor," he said in a matter-of-fact tone while chewing. This announcement came as a genuine surprise to the three others. "He's an actor, here to play the part of a conductor for the tourists. The real conductor probably gets the historic trips as his day off. Or that actor has him tied up and gagged in the utility closet."

"How do you know?" Scotch asked in astonishment.

"Well, to me, it's obvious," the Professor explained with a shrug. "What should be obvious to *you*, though—for your own good—is that not everything is what it seems to be or says it is."

Departure, on schedule, at 10:00 a.m.

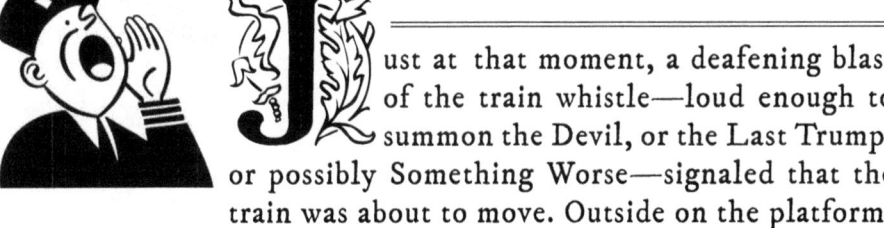

ust at that moment, a deafening blast of the train whistle—loud enough to summon the Devil, or the Last Trump, or possibly Something Worse—signaled that the train was about to move. Outside on the platform, the conductor, with his left hand cupped to the side of his mouth in a classic pose, called out, "All aboard!" in case there were stragglers. With his right hand he was energetically ringing a handbell. This performance was followed by a second blast of the whistle, as loud as the first, but not as jarring, and an enormous burst of steam from the undercarriages—a theatrical effect triggered by the conductor as he got back on the train. He signaled the engineer from his window with a small flag. Seconds later, a violent surge of energy was unleashed on several thousand tons of metal, sending all and sundry hurtling towards the furthest reaches of Whitman's Paumanok.

"So—" the Professor said, holding his gleaming apple, and smiling with the imperturbable enthusiasm of a tour guide opening an umbrella and taking the first stride of a long day "—now to begin."

New York ■■■■■ THE PAUMANOK EXPRESS ■■■■■ Montauk

IRONCLAD RAILROAD

God Handcuffed—Arrested by Suffolk County Police

Sayville, *1931*—Reverend Major Jealous Divine a/k/as Father Divine a/k/as God is taken into custody, charged with disturbing the peace. Inset: Parking nightmare on a typical Sunday afternoon at 132 Macon Drive, Sayville, the headquarters of the Reverend's ministry—property referred to by the local residents as "The Devil's Castle."

Once Upon a Time, a Fox

A false start—perhaps unintentional—to the Professor's Tale

To begin, let us agree to dispense with the opening salvo "Once upon a time" and turn our attention immediately to the adventures of our quick brown fox. There's nothing to be gained by starting on the wrong foot with that absurd bit of jabberwocky, useful only for tripping over as we come through the story's front door. Any storyteller worthy of the title recognizes that the threadbare phrase "Once upon a time" is unadulterated poppycock. What could the words "upon a time" possibly signify? It's not proper English—it's not even colloquial English—nor slang, nor jive, nor mumbo-jumbo. The great Einstein would have been stymied by it, and he was something of an expert on the subject of Time.

What is "a time" anyway? and how can *anything* be "upon" it? and why, whatever that *anything* might be, when it manages to get "upon a time," is it just "once"? If it's so marvelous, why not twice or three times? What if, just for the sake of variety—or, heaven forbid, originality—the author wrote: "*Thrice upon some times*"instead? A minor act of mutiny of that sort could only improve the outlook for what follows. Does the author believe that limiting his yet-to-be-revealed plot to "once" imbues it with the allure of a special, never-to-be-repeated gala event? It won't.

Experts on linguistic warfare technology claim that the infiltration of "Once upon a time" in literature is part of a subversive, sneak-in-the-back-door strategy to brainwash children into accepting anything printed on paper as reasonable or true. The theory supporting this insidious tactic is as follows: if you are exposed to the same thing often enough and long enough (for example, Tea promptly at 4:00 for the English) you not only cease to question it, you join in and build your entire existence around it. The end result, using this same example, is that a majority of the population starts to get thirsty at 3:45, and at 5:45, the British Empire is queuing up for the toilet.

Confusing readers, boxing their ears with piffle, getting them worked up unnecessarily is not a recommendable strategy to win a Pulitzer Prize. Perhaps if the story in question was inconceivably terrible, a candidate for citation by *The Last Word on What's Worst*, such an introductory flourish would blaze from the page, both luminous and praiseworthy; but the fact remains—and there's no kinder way to say this—"Once upon a time" can only be raised to an artistic plateau—a minor one at best—when followed by even worse applesauce. The dissatisfied reader might then be forgiven for saying, a few paragraphs under the bridge— "If only the author had pursued his original idea —which, if I recall it correctly, was something about something climbing up, just once, on a time (*what a piquant phrase I found that to be!*)—this literary fiasco might have been worth engaging. As it stands, I believe a refund tendered by the bookseller would best end this tale."

Not to put too fine a point on it, "Once upon a time" was—once upon a time—rather fashionable as opening fanfares go. It was still bullocks, but it was *quaint* bullocks....

"Stop! Stop! *Stop!*" Soda pleaded. "You're *killing* me!"

"What?" the Professor asked, breaking off. "Why are we stopping? I was just hitting my stride..."

"We thought this was going to be a story about a fox."

"What fox?"

"The one that jumps over the lazy dog," Scotch said. "*Once upon a time*—please excuse the expression."

"Yes, that's right, Scotch," said Soda. "Long ago and far away."

"In days of yore, if I am not mistaken—whatever *yore* is, never mind why we would need days of it," Ry said. "At this rate, we'll be pulling into Sayville before the fox pulls his ass out of his burrow."

"Ah," said the Professor with a wicked smile. "*That* fox! Okay, gentlemen, let's try this again."

The others settled back in their seats warily. The Professor sighed; then he cleared his throat; then he rubbed his hands together ceremoniously; and then he began:

"*Once*" (after this first word he inserted a sarcastic pause followed by a conspiratorial wink) "the brown fox was sure—as November drew near enough to singe the breezes with the scent of bonfires, and lengthening shadows gathered *upon*" (another pause and wink for *that* word) "the shivering grass around him—that the *time*" (a third and final pause and wink here) "for the foxhunts was soon to follow, he waited with a pounding heart for the killing to begin, thinking of death and more death and more death and more death and more ..."

"He was thinking of more death," Scotch whispered under his breath.

The Professor's Tale Re-Told

—— —— —— ——, a Fox

A new and improved version of Once Upon a Time, a Fox

Once the brown fox was sure—as November drew near enough to singe the breezes with the scent of bonfires, and lengthening shadows gathered upon the shivering grass around him—that the time for the foxhunts was soon to follow, he waited with a pounding heart for the killing to begin, thinking of death and of little else. Ritual horn calls announced the commencement of the Opening Meet, reaching the furthest furred ear in the furthest copse on the estate of Wolsey Manor. From the first note of that fanfare, the brown fox would be running for his life from the lords and ladies of the county, citizens of fine English breeding, one and all—the capped and the crowned alike—red-cheeked and laughing and robust. They were exquisitely appointed in their awarded colors and buttons and badges, mounted on prize-winning thoroughbreds, festooned with all manner of tack and regalia, manicured, monogrammed, monocled, with all the foxhounds of hell running in a frenzy before them. All and sundry with murder in their hearts—most of the malice focused on him. It would be as it had ever been—a season of whips and whinnies and tally-ho and killing. What was it all for? One could say that the primary goal of a foxhunt was to resemble a beautiful painting of a foxhunt.

On that first day, a red fox was flushed from a covert. The foxhounds followed. The mounted field (the so-called hunters) followed the foxhounds. The followers-on-foot followed the mounted field. The servants followed last—in order of precedence, of course—in case anyone of importance needed anything. Every living creature at the scene, human and animal alike, waited to see what would happen to the fox, except for the servants, who waited only for the day's business to reach its conclusion, so they could clean up the mess and go to bed. The servants recognized that the fox was one of their own, a kindred servant of the estate, interchangeable and replaceable. A secret tradition of the serving class had evolved over centuries—ignore the truth in respectful silence: one of their number was required to give up their life so that things could appear to run smoothly, punctually, and as expected. The idyllic painting of rural English life would be painted for all to step back and admire before the day ended, no matter what the cost.

There was a widely understood reason why the brown fox was the focus of so much attention at Wolsey Manor— quite simply, all the other foxes on the estate were red and he was not. It was nothing more complicated than that. There were some albino foxes, too, but there were usually several of them on the estate in any given year. That made them much less interesting. Their pale fur was a guarantee the foxhounds would make short work of them. They were so easy for the hounds to pinpoint, they were not to be considered seriously as fair game in the opinion of Mr. Brousster, the estate's venerable Master of the Hunt.

He would have preferred to shoot the albino foxes, rather than allow the foxhounds to demean themselves by chasing them, but her Ladyship absolutely forbade the use of firearms without her permission, and it would not be granted just to save Mr. Brousster from his own absurdity. It was all the same to Lady Winniot if the albino foxes ate the albino foxhounds or consumed pasty old Mr. Brousster himself.

"We'll get those damned white foxes out of the way in the cubbing, and that will be an end to them," Mr. Brousster told the kennel master, Mr. Seymour. The Master of the Hunt strongly advocated that practicing a form of enforced Darwinism was the best way to improve the sport of fox hunting. This was achieved, in part, through cub hunts—smaller, informal hunts occurring earlier in the autumn, used for culling out young foxes who were weak or stupid and would likely mature into poor sport by the time of the main season. The cleverer ones, the cubs that demonstrated the best survival instincts in the face of daily terrorizing, were allowed to escape to join the pool of future hunting victims. Young foxhounds that proved to be inept at tracking quarry, and those easily distracted by other game, were culled out during the cubbing, too, so that only the most promising foxhounds were entered into the pack. Cubbing was really just a series of auditions and rehearsals to ramp up the quality of the main events to come by deploying more talented animals on both teams.

"But that brown fox," Mr. Brousster murmured, almost as if thinking aloud. "I wonder if he's still alive. One can't keep track of the reds. They're all alike and there's too many, even at the end of the season. For all we know, one of our reds could be older than Victoria." He snorted back a laugh at that. Queen Victoria had been dead for decades, but the master had frequently invoked her memory to illustrate his oft-voiced opinion that *some* royalty—and *some* people—outlive their usefulness. It seemed to Mr. Seymour that to speak of the Queen in such a pejorative manner, and to criticize the length of her reign—which had stabilized the British Empire and helped make it great—was an exhibition of poor form on the part of Mr. Brousster, a man old enough to be one of her grandchildren. The kennel master was gradually coming to the realization that he respected his hounds much more than he respected Mr. Brousster. He already knew he preferred their company.

The master drew on his pipe pensively. "But there's only that one bloody fox all done up in brown. How has he managed to elude us all this time? Damn embarrassing, I say." He cleared his throat and then spoke with increased self-importance and indignation. "I wonder if you also were told, Seymour, some fool drunkard was overheard in a local pub, predicting our brown fox would outlive the lot of us—his Lordship included."

"I heard tell of it," Mr. Seymour said, shrugging it off as ale-inspired blather of little importance. "I must say I don't feel as you do about our brown friend, though. I think it does us proud to have a fox so clever we can't rid ourselves of him."

"Rubbish! He's not clever. He's just lucky."

"Maybe he's not lucky. Maybe we're unlucky."

"Well, I say we'll see about that. I'll get him this season—if he's alive—mark my words."

Mr. Seymour found this most unsportsmanlike. Mr. Brousster had said "I'll get him" when he should have, more properly, said, "We'll get him." To be entirely proper, Mr. Brousster might have opted to say nothing. That was a road he seldom traveled.

Mr. Seymour was privy to certain information about the brown fox that the Master of the Hunt was not. This put him in a position to know that harming that creature in any way would be certain to guarantee the displeasure of Lady Margaret and the dire consequences that would follow. He came by this insight quite by accident one day, while crossing the estate to visit a friend at a nearby farm.

In a wooded area, some distance from the manor, he saw Lady Margaret astride her horse. There was something strange in her demeanor that aroused his curiosity, so he stopped where he was to study the scene more carefully. He was far enough away, and hidden by enough shrubbery, to observe undetected.

Lady Margaret had paused in a small clearing and was looking intently at the ground. Standing on his toes in order to see what had arrested her attention, he was surprised to discover that the brown fox was sitting at her feet, looking back at her with equal intensity. Of course, he was too far away to hear what she was saying, but, without any doubt, she *was* speaking to the fox. For his part, the fox remained as still as Mr. Seymour, as if he were listening to a sermon.

Then Lady Margaret leaned forward and stretched her hand out to the animal. *Surely*, Mr. Seymour thought, *she is* not *going to pet that fox*. In a moment he saw that her intention was something else. She had something in her hand—something small—and she gently dropped it in front of the waiting animal. The fox remained as if hypnotized, his gaze still locked on Lady Margaret. He ignored the dropped object for a time, then, impulsively, he snatched it up with his teeth—whatever it was—and ran off into the trees with it.

A few days later, Mr. Seymour had occasion to see Lady Margaret taking tea on the lawn with two friends. An hour or so later, the tea party now over, he passed the same spot. On a wicker table, beside the tea service and a pot of geraniums, there were plates of biscuits and small sandwiches, and a bowl of little apples. Mr. Seymour concluded in that instant that the dropped object he had seen from a distance was an apple—a rather curious species of love letter, to his thinking—and, furthermore, that the incident was one that he probably should keep to himself. As he passed the wicker table—as if imitating the fox—he snatched an apple out of the bowl and put it in his pocket.

He vowed never to tell anyone about Lady Winniot's little adventure. After all, he concluded, he had witnessed a most unusual private act of kindness. Indisputably, the mistress of the estate had the right to make a charitable gesture in her own backyard—anonymously, if she wished—without inviting gossip and ridicule. If this type of behavior were openly discussed, she might be regarded, by certain insensitive and critical parties, as a woman of questionable judgment, or worse, as an *eccentric*—a state of being, in England, that was actually common, but never respected, and always frowned upon within the circle of narrow-minded gentry.

Later, Mr. Seymour found the apple in his pocket and wondered why he had taken it. Understanding came to him, along with a wry smile, at bedtime. Blushing, he realized that his greatest longing—secreted deep in his heart behind walls of stone—was to be given something pure and precious that he hadn't had to ask for.

It was because of his rare, dark color, that the brown fox was the most likely creature on the vast estate to be persecuted. He was also, due to the same circumstance, the least likely to be spotted, which made the pursuit of that persecution much more challenging for the hunters. His personal camouflage— a genetic twist of fate—worked greatly in favor of his longevity. He was also an exceptionally good climber, practicing that skill not only to evade the foxhounds, but also to climb high enough to observe the strategies of the hunt from a unique vantage point, one that proved quite educational when he could make sense of what he observed. The brown fox had a limited ability to reason—less than the canines, certainly—but foxes have not been viewed historically as clever and cunning without good cause. For example, he could clearly see, when observing from the branches, that the foxhounds were not following their prey by sight, but by scent, which made an impression radically different from the one he had when he was the animal being pursued. In those terrifying flights for survival, he had no way to know that the hounds could not actually see him—this only became apparent when, from his perch, he watched the hounds chasing after what might have been an invisible fox. Following another animal by scent was something he had done all his life, but he had no idea, until seeing it from the trees, that other animals could do it too. He understood then—his survival depended on mastering the science of false trails. Merely hiding was not enough. He had to prove his superiority to his persecutors to stay alive.

His first instinct was to use the trees for escape. By climbing a tree and then jumping to the next tree and the next and the next, and finally alighting as far as was possible from the first tree—around which the pursuing foxhounds had congregated, leaping and voicing their frustration—he could evade their scrabbling claws and gnashing teeth. To that end, he scouted for wooded areas where trees were clustered closely together, sharing a network of intertwining branches for use as hidden roadways, and he marked those locations as future escape routes. And so it was that the clever brown fox developed the same survival technique practiced in America by raccoons, an evasion tactic which inspired the expression "barking up the wrong tree" many years earlier and more than an ocean's distance from Wolsey Manor.

The arboreal escape tactic would have been more successful if the hunts took place earlier in the year, for while his brown color helped conceal him, it could not make up for the scarcity of foliage in November. The fox had no idea he was brown, but he did know that the thinly veiled branches made him more visible than was ideal. Other methods for survival were necessary and he tirelessly sought to discover them. One of the best he learned when following the scent of a vixen. Her intoxicating trail eventually led to the edge of a stream where it abruptly ended. The vixen had trotted off in the shallow, gurgling water, but in which direction? In this case, not knowing which way the vixen had gone was useful information—certainly more useful than sexual gratification would have been.

His most ingenious gambit was a collaboration of sorts. One day he came upon the putrid corpse of a fox cub. Judging from the remaining evidence, it had been felled by an owl or a falcon. The rotting cub stank profusely, but the body was small and light enough to drag about by its tail. The brown fox and the dead cub became constant companions, wandering about together for three days. The odor of putrefaction was an ordeal, but the pair left an especially pungent network of trails in their wake, which was entirely to the point of the exercise. By the fourth day, the cub could be dragged over the rough ground no further. Nothing remained except the tail and tendrils of stench. But, more importantly, there was nothing useful left behind for the foxhounds. At best, they would run in circles, unable to locate the milder scent of a living, edible fox. By the time he spit the cub's tail out and sauntered off, the entire estate reeked of criss-crossed, meandering fox trails, and none of it led to him, and—even more satisfying—none of it led anywhere.

One fine day in mid-October, a few weeks before the Opening Meet, Lord and Lady Winniot took a planned stroll across the lawn of Wolsey Manor. Each had something to discuss with the other. "I already know what you want, Arthur," she began as soon as they had walked far enough from the gardeners to speak privately.

"Really?"

"Yes, you want me to agree to ride in the hunt in November, when the Duke is here. So, I will tell you straight away—I will. And that's because it may prove helpful to your career should England go to war, and because I genuinely like the Duke. The hunt interests me not an iota. And the Duchess even less."

"Understood, and thank you, dear," he said. "Your turn now. There's something you want to take up with me...?"

"Can I assume that someone in the household has already told you of the shooting incident on Tuesday? I know you were away, but surely someone informed you...?" She was referring to the use of a firearm, which she had unequivocally banned. It was discovered that a new member of the stable master's staff, a boy of sixteen from a neighboring farm, was the one who fired a hunting rifle behind the stables. "I wonder if the people here believe I am so inbred that I don't know a gunshot when I hear one in my own backyard."

"I've already spoken to him," Lord Arthur said, looking earnestly into his wife's eyes. "I trust he's well-informed of the rules now and knows what's expected of him."

"Very well, as long as we're in agreement and present a united front."

Lord Arthur nodded agreeably, perhaps too easily, leaving his wife feeling a need to elaborate further. "While I live on this estate," she said, "we are not going to shoot anything that we are not going to eat. I find that to be a thoroughly reasonable restriction to impose on the gun-crazy fools in our midst. We're not under threat here. Nothing on these grounds is dangerous except us. Should anyone at Wolsey find it too difficult to live with that pinch of discipline salting their daily fare, they can pack their bags and guns and pursue their interests in Kenya, where they can kill all manner of creatures, including each other. Or they can wait for war to come. I'm sure Herr Hitler can find some way to keep them busy."

"Hunting is one of our nation's great traditions... We can't pretend...."

"Never mind *that*, Arthur. We're the ones who should decide what kind of people we are. Tradition should not make that decision for us. And what's more, dear husband, if I could impose one further rule it would be to dismiss anyone in our employ who dares to say fox hunting is a form of pest control. We should not be paying wages in support of such imbecility or dishonesty—I'm not even sure which category of the two that balderdash comes under." She shuddered in disgust. "If necessary let's confine our staff to people who are well-versed in practical things like *Yes, Madam* and *No, Sir*."

"Well, you've clearly thought this out, so I'm at a disadvantage in conversations of this nature. I suppose I should spend more time considering this sort of thing."

"Why? To be better equipped to spar with me?" She laughed and pinched his cheek. "Don't expect me to encourage *that*."

"To be better equipped to *understand* you, Meg."

Lady Margaret was taken by surprise and genuinely pleased. "That was nicely said, Arthur," she admitted graciously. She took her husband's arm, determined now to put an end to any conflict between them. She continued in a more endearing tone. "In all honesty, tell me—have I *ever* tried to put an end to fox hunting at Wolsey?"

"No, Meg, I admit you have not done that."

"But it's good to impose some discipline, is it not? As one might with difficult children."

"Yes, I suppose it is."

"Good. No shooting."

With those final words, she abruptly turned her husband in another direction, leading him towards a nearby gazebo. She had, just a moment previously, caught sight of the brown fox at the far edge of the lawn, crouching low near some shrubbery. He was watching them. Lady Margaret reflected that her acts of friendliness and gentleness toward the fox were entirely responsible for his presence so close to the manor, but—having just won an argument with her husband concerning their animal tenants—she was none-too-eager for Arthur to see the fox too. She wasn't as sure of his position in the ongoing war against the defenseless as she was regarding Mr. Brousster and certain others at Wolsey. The unhealthy interest the estate's hunters had taken in the brown fox had not escaped her attention. She was determined that no harm came to him, even if it meant being mocked for posterity as Lady Peggy, the Patron Saint of Brown Foxes.

As she drew her husband into the deep shade of the gazebo, a chill came over her—something that she had overlooked came into focus in her mind—she knew, with sudden, unshakable certainty, exactly what the new stable boy had fired his gun at. Lady Margaret then did something that was not typical of her at all—she repeated herself. "Remember, Arthur," she said. "No shooting."

Of course, Lord Arthur *had* seen the brown fox watching them. He knew all about it. Like Mr. Seymour, he chose to keep silent.

The typical hunt at Wolsey involved no less than 20 pairs of foxhounds, and the participation of Mr. Brousster's entire staff, supplemented by alternates-on-call when necessary—all of them mounted, including a half-dozen whippers-in whose function was to contain the foxhounds and keep them focused on the specific animal being tracked. The hunt staff, in scarlet frock coats emblazoned with Wolsey insignia, was followed by the mounted field in black or scarlet coats, the colors and buttons worn dependent upon rank or bestowed honors. This mixed assembly, consisting of between thirty and forty persons, was followed by any number of followers-on-foot, dressed formally or informally depending on whether or not significant persons, such as Dukes, Ministers, Admiralty, or members of the Royal Family, would be part of the mounted field. Unmounted followers generally preferred informal dress, known as *ratcatcher*, due to constant bombardment by mud, dung, and tiny stones propelled back at them by the horses' hooves. Followers-on-foot could take advantage of the Second Track, which ran to one side or the other of the Primary Track. The difference between them was that the Second Track had been cleared of jumps and other obstacles—stone walls had breaches and fences had open gates—while the Primary Track required a high degree of equestrian skill, and horses trained for the demands of the terrain.

One further participant, as yet unmentioned, was the Terrier Man, a self-appointed member of the hunt, who generally followed along on the Second Track—when he cared to join—riding a noisy, sputtering motorbike. A cardboard carton attached to the motorbike contained an especially vicious terrier. This horrid animal, a demonic mass of teeth and claws, was used to flush out a fox that had successfully evaded the foxhounds by hiding in a burrow or drainpipe. Her Ladyship had forbidden any further pursuit or molestation of foxes that had successfully gone to ground—if the fox was clever enough to evade the foxhounds in such a manner, its life was spared. On this point she was absolutely adamant. Thus, at least at Wolsey, the generally unsavory Terrier Man might follow with his motorbike and cardboard box if he agreed to pay the cap, but his terrier always went home hungry.

The evening before the big hunt took place, the brown fox happened upon the decomposing body of another fox cub. This was now a familiar opportunity to create mischief and take revenge on the foxhounds, and he was not capable of resisting its temptation. Seizing the tail between his teeth, he dashed off with his prize, intending to pollute all compass points of Wolsey with the stink of corruption as he had done previously. Then, suddenly feeling inventive, he decided to bring the dead thing to the manor instead, to deposit it near the kennels where whiffs of its scent would send the confined foxhounds into a frenzy and keep them howling all night. He had no idea that there would be a hunt the next day, nor did he know that the Duke would be present, nor that Lady Margaret—because of a promise she had made to her husband—would ride beside the Duke in the mounted field. All he knew was that he had the perfect instrument of torture to strike back at the foxhounds clenched in his jaws.

Around the time the fox was dragging his wretched find towards the kennels, the Duke's motorcade drove up to the manor. One of the vehicles suddenly backfired, startling all who heard it. The brown fox, always hyper-vigilant when in close proximity to humans, dashed for the trees in a panic, abandoning the little cadaver on the spot. He was too unnerved by the sound of the backfire—which he mistook for gunshot—to retrieve his plaything. Where it had been dropped is where it remained all night—in front of the stable doors.

Inside Wolsey Manor, a festive dinner, with no expense spared, was held to honor the Duke, after which all the guests retired to rest for the hunt the next morning. The only wrinkle in the luxurious evening occurred when Lady Margaret found herself overcome by a compulsion to inform the Duke that the elk he was being served had not been hunted at Wolsey. Her husband sighed inwardly, wondering if his wife was going to launch into a lengthy, possibly pedantic, elaboration. She didn't, and the conversation turned to cows and sheep, to Lord Arthur's great relief.

He wondered, while sipping his wine, if his wife's extreme views concerning their animal tenants—most particularly her obsessive protectiveness of the brown fox (which he knew she tried to make a secret of)—had their origins in the fact that she was childless. As for himself, he had three children from a previous union, but Margaret was past the age of conception when they married, which left her with vestigial maternal instincts invested in all manner of strange things, including an animal earmarked as quarry by the social conventions of the day. Flowers, canaries, charities, chocolates, croquet, and other lawn sports—these were typical diversions for women of Meg's station—even presiding over a patch of unglamorous vegetables, especially with the likelihood of war in the near future, would be a more suitable pastime than the clandestine meetings she indulged herself in. Yet, he would not have anything about her be different, not for all the world. He was thoroughly convinced that if any flaw existed in Margaret, it was actually a flaw in himself, like a cataract in his vision, that if he understood her better—even if only a little—she would be even more perfect, should such a thing be possible. The strangest thing of all—he sometimes reflected on nights when sleep would not come—was that her secret love for the brown fox mirrored the love she *might* have had for a child of their marriage, and as a consequence of that most unusual of circumstances, he was duty-bound by his love for her to love the object of her love as if it was of his own blood. Once he accepted the brown fox as his own—and *their* own—it followed naturally for him to love Lady Margaret all the more. So, without any conscious choice on the part of the those who were drawn into this circle of compassion, they were—all three—inextricably bound together within it for life.

Margaret was not an indulgent woman, but—appropriate for her years—if she had an indulgence, it was compassion, rather than passion. Compassion, Lord Arthur reflected, was so often the product of a secret unhappiness. There were many secrets at Wolsey. Of that he was certain. Not many of them were bound to be as intriguing as the secrets shared by Meg and her brown fox—but, at the end of the day, he didn't really know their secrets, did he? Nor did he know anyone else's, nor did he wish to know them—for he believed quite strongly that every living creature was in possession of (and possessed *by*) an internal world that could not be violated, nor should it be. Even the brown fox, a kindred living being, was entitled to an unbreachable boundary between its life, as lived for others to observe, and its soul which was his, and his alone. Animals did have souls, didn't they? His wife believed that, and—secretly—so did he.

Far from the festive dinner that honored the Duke, the brown fox was just dropping off to sleep in a drainpipe, where he was sheltering from the chilly breezes that swirled through the moonlight. Those same breezes were laying a thin blanket of dirt and torn leaves over the inert body of a dead fox cub near the stable doors, concealing it from view.

Deep in the outlying forest, Mr. Seymour, carrying a lantern, was walking towards a timbered shelter at the edge of the estate where he would secretly meet his young lover—a lad of sixteen from a nearby farm—who was, through Mr. Seymour's subtle efforts, recently employed in the stables at Wolsey.

Mr. Brousster, in his private quarters, drew pensively on his pipe while gazing down at his bed. There he had meticulously laid out every article of his costume for the following day, from boots to badges. All was arranged as though the articles were being worn in *absentia*—the top hat above the collar, the gloves at the ends of the sleeves, the handle of the whip placed on the palm of the glove, the breeches laced and tucked into the out-turned boots, the buckles buckled, the neck-wear properly tied and pinned. Anyone other than Mr. Brousster would have thought the recumbent presentation looked extremely bizarre—like a shroud wound around a missing corpse, or the linen wrappings of a mummy without a mummified Pharaoh inside them; but it appeared quite differently to Mr. Brousster, who, while puffing industriously at his tobacco, contemplated adding a codicil to his will, mandating that he be buried in the garments and regalia displayed before him. Perhaps, he thought, it would be prudent to pay an artist to do a detailed sketch of what was required, so that nothing was overlooked during the discombobulation and mourning that would surely follow his final departure from Wolsey Manor. It was a very strange foible of Mr. Brousster's—who had no reason whatsoever to believe he was well-liked at Wolsey—to imagine he would be missed after his demise. The evidence necessary to arrive at such a conclusion simply did not exist. For better or worse, of this he was blissfully unaware.

Lady Margaret arose quite early the next morning. She dressed in her scarlet-collared hunting frock and buff breeches, and with all her hunt paraphernalia in check, went down, first for a bun and coffee, and afterward to spend some time with her horse; she had not been out riding for a considerable length of time and thought it wise to ease into the process before the hunt began. Emerging from the stable, she paused in the morning sunlight, seated high and straight in her saddle—serene, regal, proud—a goddess of the British Empire. She could scarcely have been more magnificent had she been written by Thackeray, painted by Gainsborough, and was accompanied by fervent, bosom-heaving strains of Elgar. Her horse—an equally glorious creation, every bit a match for his rider—was standing on a dead fox cub.

The Duke awoke early that morning. He had experienced a restless night and his sleep had been repeatedly disrupted by nightmares. In those terrible dreams, his country was once again at war with Germany. Bombs fell, ships sank, and blood ran. He looked out the window, hoping to draw some comfort from the exemplary day that was gathering itself together outside. His eyes scanned the autumn grass as it rippled in the sunlight, thinking, as he absorbed the richness of life arrayed before him—*in a sane world, no bomb could fall on anything like this*. Below his window, he caught sight of Lady Margaret crossing that tranquil scene on her horse, and his heart skipped a beat in tribute to her great dignity and beauty. Nevertheless, a sense of foreboding persisted. Hunting they would go today—and happily, despite the clouds on the horizon—but soon enough, he reflected, all of the kingdom might find itself huddled in underground burrows, a nation of foxes, shivering in terror, while a vicious terrier loomed outside, clawing and howling and demanding surrender. On a day such as this, it hardly seemed possible, yet anyone who had lived through the soul-destroying crucibles of the Great War and the influenza epidemic knew how easily the hunters could become the hunted.

Mr. Seymour, back in his own bed, rose early that morning without the benefit of full night's sleep. While his helpers fed the foxhounds, he examined each member of the pack carefully, just to reassure himself that nothing was amiss. Something *was* amiss, though. He felt sure of it. But look as he might, he could not find the source of the foreboding. Dark clouds gathered in his head, casting shadows on fresh memories of a warm, flannel-covered shoulder against his cheek, and hair that had a faint scent of hay about it.

Lord Arthur awoke early that morning. He walked down the corridor to Lady Margaret's bedroom, intending to discuss a few last-minute details before everyone at Wolsey was overwhelmed by the day's affairs. He discovered that she had already left her room. Her dressing gown had been draped neatly over a chair, and her empty slippers stood next to each other beneath it. Something about the motes of dust settling in sunlit silence around him was disturbing him—in fact, his discomfort was such that he forgot what he had entered the room to say even before he turned to leave.

The brown fox awoke in the drainpipe early that morning. Throughout the cold night, he had been plagued by violent images and sounds. When he scampered over the wet grass to quench his thirst at a nearby stream, for the first time in his life, his reflection in the glistening water frightened him. If he had been a creature capable of thought, his thoughts might well have been clouded, but the struggle to *try* to think and reason without the necessary faculties to do so, was utterly exhausting. He returned to the drainpipe, curled up, and closed his eyes tightly.

Julius Brousster, MFH, woke early that morning in his deceased wife's bed. This was conveniently placed directly beside his own bed, on which his hunting garments—laid out the previous evening—were resting while waiting for their intended tenant to take occupancy. He stretched his arms, yawned ferociously, beat his chest in imitation of Tarzan, and generally felt quite rested and fine. He looked out the window and was pleased to note that there was not a cloud to be found in the sky. He couldn't imagine a more perfect day to put an end to the legend of the quick brown fox.

Mr. Fullerton, the stable master, woke early that morning. He had a very restless and overcrowded stable to manage this weekend. The Duke's retinue had almost doubled the number of horses quartered, increasing the piles of ordure that had to be got around by the busy staff. The overpowering smell of accumulated manure prevented anyone from noticing the competing smell produced by the little corpse outside the precincts of the stable. In any event, when Lady Margaret had exited earlier, her horse had pulverized the rotting meat and mixed it with dirt and pebbles, rendering it unrecognizable and unnoticeable—except, of course, to the specially trained nose of a foxhound. One by one, Mr. Fullerton and the stable boys led the saddled horses forth to the guests waiting beyond the patch of dead fox. Each hoof passing that way had some share of odiferous fox clinging to it. It would be fair to say that if anyone had understood what was happening, events that later ensued might not have ensued.

A pistol shot rang out, stunning all who heard it. Standing in front of a crowd of hunters and followers, Mr. Brousster held a still-smoking pistol at arm's length before him. At his feet lay a mess of blood and fur, the remains of the terrier he had just blown to pieces at close range. Not far off, a young man lay dead. He had been thrown by his horse, smashing the back of his skull on a large boulder. His eyes, wide open, stared as if in wonderment at the treetops and the sky, while his life's blood seeped into the grass and clover. Finally, someone in the crowd came to their senses and covered the boy's face with their hunting coat.

The terrier's blood had spattered on Doctor Patterson, who was kneeling beside Lady Margaret, along with Lord Winniot, white-faced, and deep in shock. "Give me your coat, Arthur," the doctor said, nudging him. "We have to keep her warm." He got no response. Someone else brought a blanket and the doctor covered the gravely injured woman as gently as he could. Judging from the way her hands were convulsing, the doctor had reason to suspect that Lady Margaret had suffered a neurological injury, but it was too soon to be sure of much. Her eyes were open, but unfocused. Her gaze wandered back and forth between the doctor and her husband but gave no indication that she knew either of them. She was attempting to speak. Doctor Patterson leaned forward to hear better. "Who is shooting?" she whispered hoarsely. "I'm sure I asked them not to." She slipped into unconsciousness.

Mr. Brousster, lost in a daze himself, wandered off into a nearby cluster of trees, still holding the pistol at this side as though it were a glove he'd just removed. It was only later, after Lady Winniot had been brought safely back to the manor, that anyone thought to go looking for him.

The next day—and for many days thereafter—the nation's news services carried stories about the fox hunt that had somehow gone terribly wrong. A young man of twenty-three years had lost his life. While the Duke was unharmed, Lady Margaret Winniot of Wolsey Manor had suffered grievous injuries that could prove fatal in time. Four foxhounds were so badly kicked and trampled by the panicking horses, they had to be put down. And two or three prize-winning horses appeared to be—at least temporarily—rendered lame because of deep bites and lacerations they had received. No one knew why the foxhounds—while in the midst of giving chase—suddenly turned around and began to pursue the horses that were riding behind them. No one knew how the terrier had escaped his cardboard box and got among the horses and hounds and turned the confusion into a bloody *mêlée*. The general consensus was that the whippers-in might have restored things to a normal state of order if it had not been for the intrusion of the terrier. The press condemned the terrier and his owner as the culprits in the Wolsey tragedy, pointing out that the terrier had never been socialized with other canines, and that he was routinely starved before hunts so that he would be more aggressive towards the foxes *if* he was used to flush one from its burrow—a practice, quite ironically, that had been banned by Lady Winniot years earlier. She had banned the practice, but not the practitioners.

The newspapers unanimously cited Mr. Brousster for his quick actions, yet there was not one that failed to point out that—most unfortunately—his actions came too late to prevent any serious harm from being done. Several articles, to his great annoyance, employed the phrase, "*If only the Master had....*"

Lying sleeplessly in his deceased wife's bed the night after the first news reports were published, Mr. Brousster imagined that the brown fox was just outside his window, leaping gleefully in the air and laughing at him. It was a certainty that fox hunting activities would be suspended for the season, and it was conceivable they might never be restored to the honored role they had always played in life at Wolsey—in which case, Mr. Brousster would be the Master of Nothing and would likely remain so for the rest of his days on earth. The hunting garb that had been meticulously laid out on the bed beside him might never be worn again, except in death, at his funeral. If the brown fox could understand the situation in the same way that Mr. Brousster—the soon-to-be Master of Nothing—understood it, he would have every reason to rejoice.

Except one—the loss of his one great love.

It was a toxic combination of tedium and loneliness that ultimately led to the fox quitting Wolsey forever to set forth on his great journey. One day, venturing beyond the outskirts of the estate, he discovered that there were chickens in a wire coop at a nearby farm. Here was something new and delicious to eat that didn't need to be chased—the stupid chickens didn't stand a chance against the clever fox. He returned regularly to his new pantry, and, before many months passed, he was an addict. Later, after the war began, one chicken led to another chicken which led to another and another and another, and before long, the brown fox was many miles from Wolsey. Chicken by chicken, he was crossing England in a northerly direction, heading to, and then crossing, the Scottish border. At some point, cold weather upon him, he stopped and lived in the outskirts of an industrial city, Hexbury, his first experience of urban life.

Back in November of 1938, he had been asleep in a drainpipe—dreaming of apples, in fact—when the Wolsey tragedy occurred. He would not have been capable of understanding it even had he seen it play out from one of his high lookout points in the oak trees. He might have recognized the dead boy as a type of dead animal, might have recognized Lady Margaret as an animal that had been injured, but he would never have understood the ramifications of the event and how it would affect the future of the estate—or his own fortunes.

The brown fox was left—with the cessation of hunting activities that followed—with no one to love and nothing to do except make more foxes, chase rabbits, and sleep. Certainly, he would never know of, or begin to comprehend, the incidental role he had played in the events of that November day in 1938. Like the humans around him, he was a pawn of destiny, which was the one thread of commonality that connected all living creatures to each other. The war would prove that.

The Christmas season following the tragedy was somber. There were no New Year's celebrations. There were no guests. One day, for no reason that anyone could determine, the foxhounds became very anxious and noisy in the kennel, and the racket reached the windows of the manor. Lady Margaret became so agitated at the sound, that her husband decided there and then that he would have to remove the foxhounds from the estate. There was no sense in boarding them out because he would not have them back, so, pair by pair, the foxhounds were given to breeders, until only one pair, the favorites of Mr. Seymour, remained. This pair had been badly crippled by the horses in the November upset, and he could not bear to part with them or put them down. Typically, he took them under his protection and treated them as if they were his younger siblings. Mr. Brousster, on his bumbling visits to the kennel, displayed nothing but scorn for this situation. What use could Mr. Seymour possibly have for a pair of crippled foxhounds? One day he said, "I do believe, Seymour, that those pathetic animals have thoroughly outlived their usefulness."

Mr. Seymour looked at the Master of the Former Hunt in disbelief, and replied with undiluted annoyance, "You can say as much about Queen Victoria, as I know you have done on many an occasion— and you are certainly welcome to include yourself on a list of those who've outlived their usefulness for all I give a damn—*and I don't*— but these two pathetic foxhounds, as you call them, need me, and I, being equally pathetic, need *them*, so let *that* be an end to this bloody discussion. For my money, old man, you can go hang yourself."

One day, after the first of the new year, Lord Arthur paid a visit to Mr. Seymour at the kennel and informed him, with great regret, that Wolsey would no longer have a kennel and that it would, therefore, not require the services of a kennel master. Mr. Seymour had anticipated this and was prepared for the announcement. He had, in fact, settled much of his personal business, paid off his small debts, and packed everything he owned except the few things he would need while he awaited Lord Winniot's inevitable visit. The one loose end in all of this was the intense affection he had for Alistair, the sixteen-year-old boy who had worked in the stables. Alistair was one of the first of the stable boys to be given notice when the number of horses dwindled, primarily because his family had a farm nearby and he had no dependents (this, of course, discounted Mr. Seymour, who was very much dependent on his lover, although no one knew it—not even Alistair). In his usual careful fashion, when Lord Arthur set about dismantling the machinery that made Wolsey work, he did it with the utmost consideration and care for those who were the life and soul of the estate. Without the people, in his opinion, Wolsey was just brick and mortar and trees and grass, and none of it meant a thing.

"You have our thanks, Mr. Seymour," Lord Arthur said at their meeting, "for all you've done, and for all the years you've given us here. God knows, so much has slipped away, ebbed out to sea, so to speak, and there's little I can do to stem that outgoing tide. The best *any* of us can do is patiently wait for the tide to turn back to us, bringing what it will. But, for the present, in considering Lady Margaret's condition, the needs of Wolsey, and the perilous situation of England in general, I am at a loss for what steps to take next. I've never felt quite this helpless. What I can say for certain is that—even if we were to enjoy the best of all possible outcomes in the years to come—we will not be having a kennel on the estate, unless my eldest son decides to reverse that decision after my death, which would be his right as the next Lord Winniot. We will not be hunting on the estate for the foreseeable future, and I may ban guns completely. Certainly, I will ban them if Margaret hears a single shot ring out, or if war is declared. Our foxes will wake up to discover that they can live their lives free of terror, including that brown one that's been the subject of pub talk for so many years."

"So, you know about that?" Mr. Seymour exclaimed in astonishment.

"Of course, I do. And those drunken loudmouths may very well be right. That fox probably *will* outlive me. And so be it." He laughed suddenly and put his arm around Mr. Seymour's shoulders. "May I call you Toby? It *is* Tobias, isn't it?"

"Yes, that's right, milord."

"Oh, call me Arthur, please, at long last. I'm feeling exceedingly simple—down-to-earth, you might say—and we're about to go off on our separate paths. Allow me to share something with you, Toby. My wife, my dear Margaret, was bringing fruit and table scraps to that brown fox for a very long time. She did it—she thought—secretly. So, she never knew I knew what she was doing, at least not from my mouth. I'm not sure why I never spoke of it to her. I suppose it was because she seemed to derive pleasure from the intrigue and secrecy. And we all have those—little secrets, I mean to say—don't we? We are allowed that much, aren't we? Something of our very own that no one can know of, or speak of, or touch?"

"I agree—we should be permitted at least that in this topsy-turvy life," Mr. Seymour assented truthfully, directly from his heart. In that moment of unexpected intimacy between himself and Lord Arthur, he found himself on the verge of sharing what he had witnessed occur between Lady Winniot and the brown fox, but—thinking better of it—he stopped himself and let the matter drop. Sometimes, he reflected, the best use of knowledge is to put it aside. It would be his final gift to Lord Arthur—to allow him to continue believing that he alone had known of his wife's odd adventures, as if she had shared them only with him, possibly intentionally, as a token of her trust and love.

"Well, that was Margaret's secret passion," Lord Arthur continued with a little sigh, "although I'm not sure that's an accurate description of that rather indescribable behavior. At any rate, that fox has had a diet as good as mine or yours for quite some time, so he should be a truly healthy and hardy specimen. And he has no natural enemies and no human enemies hereabouts, and plenty of rabbits to eat, and many, many, many lady foxes, I should think. So long as Mr. Brousster is retired, the brown fox will have as good a life as a simple fox can have. As for me, when war breaks out, I will most surely be appointed an officer and, having survived the horrors of the Great War, this time around, I'll probably be killed."

Within the year, that's exactly what happened.

r. Seymour, now that he had been freed of his obligations at Wolsey, was at liberty to follow any path he chose, for there were only Hannah and Hilda, the two lame foxhounds, and Alistair to consider. His family had dwindled to a scattered group of distant cousins he barely knew. He had lost two older brothers in the first World War, a double tragedy that left him with a loathing of all violence and conflict. Naturally, because of this history, he found himself unprepared to face another outbreak of hostilities, which he was certain was to come soon.

In 1938, Mr. Seymour was in his mid-thirties, well-aware that the best option ahead for him was to quit everything and start a new adventure somewhere else while he was young and healthy enough to do so. As an inspiration to seek out change, there was no better example than Mr. Brousster, whose arthritic, pedantic personality was a distasteful work-in-progress, fueled by decades of stasis. He made a decision, finally, to leave England for Canada, where he had two friends that had previously emigrated, and who were now successful businessmen in Winnipeg. They had often written to him, begging him to join them. Their offer had never been so appealing as now.

The delicate issue at hand was how to persuade Alistair to go along with him. He saw himself, as always, as a protector. He was convinced that Alistair would enlist if war was declared, and that he would suffer the same fate as had both Tim and Donald—his two older brothers—twenty years earlier. Emigrating could save him.

Like most men of his years, Alistair had a narcissistic conception of himself as invincible. He lacked the maturity to see the world as it would be without him in it. Others might perish, but he could come to no harm—the world would always be there for him, and he would always be there for the world. Mr. Seymour knew otherwise, but no argument was persuasive enough to convince Alistair to quit England with him. In fact, his warnings of the dangers and hardships that might lie ahead—the first arguments he made—only served to make fighting for his country more enticing, further whetting the young man's desire for a life of heroism. Every argument he made in favor of emigration gave life to a new excuse for refusal.

He remembered—almost poignantly, now that the incident was safely behind them—the time that Alistair had impulsively fired a rifle at the brown fox behind the stables and gotten himself into so much trouble with Lady Margaret. Mr. Seymour had been power-less to argue in Alistair's behalf because to do so would have raised unwanted and unhelpful curiosity about them, so he had been forced to watch events play out from the sidelines. Lord Arthur had even-tually diffused the matter with his usual kind diplomacy, for which Mr. Seymour was forever—but silently—grateful.

Only Mr. Seymour knew it, but Alistair had acted as he did only to impress Mr. Brousster, whose distaste for the brown fox was com-mon knowledge at Wolsey. For his part, Mr. Brousster kept his usu-ally out-of-joint nose out of the matter, lest any residual blame fall upon him for the gunshot. He would have loved to kill the brown fox, but he did not want Lady Margaret to hear him going about it.

Unfortunately, the same quirk of Alistair's character that led to that foolish act of bravado was in play once again, easily recognizable to Mr. Seymour from the experience of the previous incident—Alistair wanted to stay behind in England, with the specific intention of enlisting at his first opportunity to impress his father and brothers, just as he had wanted to impress Mr. Brousster earlier. Mr. Seymour could already hear the symbolic rifle shot behind the stables—the enlistment and ensuing tragedy—and he felt he had to do every-thing in his power to prevent it.

The situation that was unfolding was ironic in the extreme to Mr. Seymour. He was sure that if Alistair's father and brothers *really* knew Alistair for who he was and what he was, being killed one thou-sand times in one thousand wars would not suffice to impress them in the least. They would see him as extremely flawed and disappointing, and worse, probably deserving of death or assignment to the life of a paraplegic for his sins. *That* was the reality that Alistair did not see.

It was fruitless to try to court the approval of such people, a bitter lesson learned numerous times in his life, but one he could not share with Alistair without causing heartache. It was a species of appalling truth a person needed to either discover on their own or remain oblivious to forever. So, while it seemed to be the most compelling argument of all for emigrating, Mr. Seymour was forced, to his continuous frustration, to talk around it.

In the end, the impulsiveness of youth, and the misguided need for approval won out. Mr. Seymour asked Alistair if he would come to Winnipeg later on, after the war—if there was one—but beyond enlisting and fighting, the youth remained non-committal about the future. That was his most adult response during their many discussions of the matter. Alistair realized that, after maturing a few years and experiencing the harsh realities of war, he might emerge a completely different person. Avoiding a commitment he might not keep later was an act of compassion on the young man's part which Mr. Seymour recognized and appreciated. It actually served to make parting a bit easier, because, having brought Alistair to the point where he could make *one* insightful and responsible decision, Mr. Seymour felt a large part of his job had been done, and done well.

He did, near the end of their remaining days together, ask Alistair to take charge of Hannah and Hilda and give them as good a life as he could manage. This Alistair agreed to, saying, "When the war comes, if it comes, my Da' will look after them, because I will be at the front, and my brothers with me."

Alistair and his family put the two foxhounds to work on their farm, assigning them to guard the chickens. The brown fox discovered that palace of chicken meat before long and made it his private lunch counter. Hannah and Hilda endured months of continuous torment because the brown fox had developed a craving for their feathered charges, which he came to like almost as much as small, red apples.

When it came time for Mr. Seymour to leave to board his ship in Liverpool, he met with Alistair one last time in the little cottage on the perimeter of the estate. With great tenderness, overcome by his emotions, he took Alistair's face in his hands, and looking deeply into his youthful eyes, said, "May no harm come to you, Alistair. May God keep you just as safe as you are this very moment with me."

Alistair was very moved. He laid his head on Tobias Seymour's shoulder, and rested it there a long time, feeling unsure of himself for the hundredth time. Mr. Seymour, tightly shutting his tear-filled eyes, was overcome—to the point of choking—with the dreadful feeling that Alistair would be killed in the war.

On May 29, 1942, that's exactly what happened.

The brown fox, all through the winter that followed the Wolsey tragedy, did not see Lady Margaret even once. He barely saw anyone at all at the manor or on the grounds. It was as if the majority of the occupants of the house had simply vanished. An occasional vehicle drove up and stayed a few hours. And, too, a black sedan, from which a man with a black bag emerged. He made short visits to the manor regularly all through the winter.

There was an eerie stillness all across the estate. And there were, due to the suspension of hunting, a lot of foxes—more than there had ever been previously. All was well, as long as the supply of rabbits held out. In the spring, the young fox cubs began emerging from their dens with their mothers, and then that surplus of rabbits began to diminish. This is what led the brown fox—always ahead of the other foxes in his clever schemes—to explore distant areas and make his first acquaintance with the world of caged chickens.

One spring day, Lord Arthur emerged from the manor with a curious looking chair in which Lady Margaret, partly covered by a blanket, was seated. The chair had strange contraptions at its sides, which resembled the wheels of a red bicycle he had once seen. Lord Arthur pushed the chair to a shady spot close to the trees at the edge of the lawn, and then, after speaking a few words to his wife, went off on his own, carrying a pair of garden clippers.

She was now quite close, and she was alone. The fox saw this opportunity—which Lord Arthur had purposely engineered for his wife's emotional benefit—and was not intending to miss it. He cautiously approached his old friend. She was—even to an animal's feeble ability to comprehend such things—vastly changed from the elegant Lady Winniot on horseback he had come to know during their previous woodland encounters. All he could recognize of the old Lady Margaret, beyond her distinctive scent, was what remained of her smile and the apple on her lap, both of them the same soft, red color. Her hair had turned almost entirely white, and there was a noticeable tremor in her hand when she reached out to drop the apple for him. He sat at attention before her, blinking, confused.

When he heard Lord Winniot coming back, he fled back to the woods, leaving the apple behind, untouched, where it had fallen— even though he was much less disturbed by Lord Winniot than he was by the transformation in Lady Winniot. He didn't understand any of it, but he was filled with dread and a diffuse sense that something terrible had happened.

Upon returning, Lord Arthur immediately took note of the apple on the grass in front of the wheelchair. He kissed his wife's forehead and laid a fragrant bouquet of freshly cut flowers on her lap. Then he began to push her back in the direction of the manor, leaving the apple behind for the fox, as he believed Meg would have wished him to.

On September 3, 1939, war was declared on Germany. Then came the bombers and the bombs, the sirens, the blackouts, and the shuttering of Wolsey Manor as Lord Winniot went off to soldier in the war, and Lady Winniot entered a sanitorium for rest and care in his absence. The horses had been taken away to join the war effort, and Hannah and Hilda, in semi-retirement, were living out their days next to a wire chicken coop, getting plenty of fresh air, and daily visits from the brown fox. On the occasions that the sounds of distant air-raid warnings wafted in the breezes as far as the farm, the two neurotic, crippled foxhounds would howl so pitifully, they had to be brought indoors and distracted until they settled down. Those same air-raid sirens and the howls of Hannah and Hilda were signals to the fox that a self-service dinner was available in the now-unguarded chicken coop. If he could have triggered those meal-enabling sirens himself, he would have.

Mr. Seymour had long ago crossed the Atlantic and journeyed by rail to the city of Winnipeg, where he was following wartime events at the pubs with old friends, fellow expatriates. Even though, during these convivial gatherings, he felt safe from the boots that were trampling across Europe, kicking down the structure of history with every mile they traversed—like the fox back at Wolsey, the transformations wrought upon the old world by the new reality made him extremely uneasy. Although he longed for it, no word came by post from Alistair. Nor would any, ever.

The ongoing war left Mr. Brousster behind, dismissed, de-horsed, de-hounded, de-frocked, and out-foxed. Lord Arthur, in consideration of the MFH's years at Wolsey, allowed him to remain on the estate with a small pension, certainly enough to see to his needs. In any case, Mr. Brousster hadn't spent a shilling in thirty years and was already a well-to-do man by standards of the day due to his parsimonious nature. But, whether he had any intention of enjoying his money or not, he did not live much longer than Lord Winniot. He died quietly—at the respectable age of 83, which is an accomplishment not to be sneered at—sprawled on his wife's bed, in close proximity to his own bed, on which his Master of the Hunt regalia had been laid out, waiting for him for months. There he was found, a near-naked nobody of a corpse lying beside a set of garments with nobody inside them. All one had to do was simply combine everything on the two beds together according to the handwritten instructions and crude diagrams that had been taped to the wall and take the end-results to the cemetery. In the end, though, very few were left at Wolsey to put on the pretense of mourning, and more significantly, a funeral that had the slightest aura of pomp and circumstance about it would be considered an obscenity with so many young men dying unidentified in ditches in France. Mr. Brousster was, therefore, fittingly interred in a plain box, wrapped in an ordinary cotton shroud. His regalia was hung in a closet, where moths snipped at it for decades, until it was finally unrecognizable as clothing. The remnants were found by a maid in 1962 and tossed in the trash.

On the night Mr. Brousster died, Queen Victoria came to his bedroom and lowered herself into his favorite chair, which had been transformed into a throne for the occasion of the royal visit. She was, indeed, a most impressive vision to behold. Her small diadem and the heraldic medals of honor pinned to her bosom gleamed in the lamplight. Her back was as straight and firm as the Rock of Gibraltar. Even though Her Majesty was not a tall woman, her eyes gave the appearance of looking downward at those in her presence (in this case, Mr. Brousster), and when she spoke, she did so with her chin lifted heavenward. Her hands, meanwhile, remained motionless, one lying atop the other on her ample lap, as if sewn together and pinned to her gown. Caught between the drooping eyelids and the upraised, jutting chin, Mr. Brousster felt himself being crushed to insignificance by the severity of the royal expression.

In her most regal tones, she addressed the recumbent Master of Nothing, who was in the meantime struggling to sit upright and make himself presentable. "We regret to inform that we find you have quite outlived your usefulness to our Crown and to the British Empire," intoned Her Majesty resolutely.

Upon hearing that pronouncement, with little to look forward to, he fell back on his wife's mattress, and then, with no fanfare anyone might notice, his rather small spirit departed his much larger body. Queen Victoria, her purpose at Wolsey achieved, carrying her scepter and orb, her ermine cape trailing behind her, returned to the history books that had been her official royal residence for decades.

And finally, as respects this eccentric member of *the-world-that-once-was* at Wolsey, a man whose foibles were, in some ways, as amusing as they were irritating, it should be recorded that—thirty-four years, six months, and seventeen days after his passing—a descendant of the brown fox's bloodline urinated on Mr. Brousster's little grave marker.

Shortages of food and rationing resulted in many challenges for the English populace. The brown fox, also a citizen of the realm, shared in these trials. It was much more dangerous for a fox to be hungry in wartime than it had been in peacetime. For one thing, chickens were now more valuable assets than they had been previously—producing a steady supply of much-needed eggs for rationing—and farmers were not going to take the depletion of their feathered food factories without a fight. Chicken coops were carefully policed against sabotage by traitorous, fifth-column foxes. The brown one, hailing from Wolsey, was, once again, on the Most Wanted List.

Throughout the countryside, rabbits were finding their way to the dinner tables of rural households at an increasing rate. Students that were too young to enlist were shooting rabbits everywhere, and if they stumbled upon a fox, they killed that, too, to reduce the ranks of their competition. An army of young boys, fattened up on rabbit stew, pigeon pie, and spotted dick, joined the growing list of the brown fox's persecutors. Barely a day passed that did not find the fox fleeing from slingshot pellets, stones, and buckshot.

Ever since that day, long ago, when Alistair had fired a rifle at him behind the stables, he had dreaded the sound of gunfire; even the residual smell of gunpowder terrified him. It was this terror, and the growing food shortages, that led him to wander into the outskirts of Hexbury and take up residence in an abandoned building.

Urban life was an entirely new experience, providing no shortage of surprises, some pleasant and some not-so-pleasant. For instance, it was rare to encounter gunfire in the city—a primary attraction for him. But the aspect of urban life he enjoyed most was the daily air-raid warning, which conveniently signaled the absence of people on the streets, which, in turn, signaled the safe accessibility of hundreds of garbage bins brimming with edible refuse, cornucopias of food scraps. The clever fox, through careful observance of the warning signals, was able to survive the worst of the winter. It was a time of deprivation, but, paradoxically, meals had never been this regular and so blatantly announced. The air-raid warnings were a foolproof dinner bell.

The downside was that he had to contend with roving packs of homeless dogs who were just as hungry and ruthless as he was. And an even bigger problem was that a majority of the dogs were formerly working foxhounds, set loose all across the countryside because it was too expensive to keep them in kennels and feed them. These animals had not lost any of their passion for the pursuit of foxes, and they did so with relish whenever the scent of one wafted past their nostrils. They responded to fox scent as they always had, despite the fact that there was no one to blow a horn to get them worked up or to reward them for a successful chase. The compensation for the newly liberated foxhound was the fox itself. Now, in the absence of kennel food, fox was more than an occasional delicacy, it was a daily necessity. Just when he thought the jeopardies of life of Wolsey were behind him, the fox found himself back on the menu.

Luckily, he was able to find fox corpses from time to time, which he used to lay scent trails leading away from his favorite garbage bins. When no dead foxes presented themselves, he used his own urine to make the trails. None of this was foolproof, but it was a survival tactic. It was a microcosm of what was happening in the human world around him. Every living creature was forced to adapt to developing circumstances in order to continue being a living creature.

Eventually, the war evolved in ways that changed everything so dramatically, urban living became more of a trap than a refuge. When the air-raid sirens that had formerly signified meal-time at the garbage bins began to signify the falling of *actual*, rather than *possible*, bombs, the brown fox found himself living in the worst circumstances yet. The sirens were far more terrifying than the hunting horns he had grown up with; he had easily been able to outrace the approaching pack of foxhounds when he heard Mr. Brousster blow his toy horn in the old days. But these Nazi bombs falling from above were a different species of terror. There was nowhere to hide from them or the resulting horrors they spawned.

It was dangerous to be near any person or animal during the bombings, when the behavior of both man and beast became completely unpredictable. At the first wail from the sirens, the packs of dogs went berserk. From his various hideouts, the fox had witnessed naked women running from doorway to doorway, and crazed dogs jumping off rooftops. Rubble filled the streets and continued falling, incrementally, hours after the bombers were gone. Houses that he had once lived in had completely disappeared. Structures weakened by the explosions could topple over, without any warning, when elbowed by a strong gust of wind a week later. The dreaded smell of explosives and burning infiltrated every new hiding place he found.

Before enduring this for very long, he ran from Hexbury and never thought about city life again. He ran until the rain had washed every trace of smoke from his fur, until all he could smell was grass and heather and the clean air of the Scottish countryside north of Hadrian's Wall.

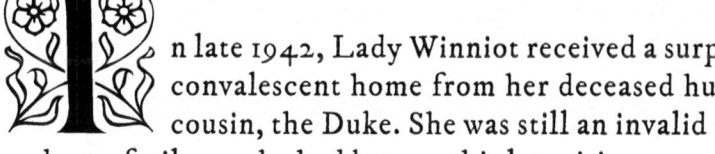 n late 1942, Lady Winniot received a surprise visit at her convalescent home from her deceased husband's distant cousin, the Duke. She was still an invalid in a wheelchair and very frail—as she had been on his last visit, years earlier, at Wolsey—but she seemed so happy to see a friendly face from the past, it was as though a curtain had been drawn over the events of the last four years. The Duke took one of her hands in both of his own, and reminisced about Lord Arthur, recounting many events from their shared youth that she already knew about, but only from Arthur's exaggerated dramatizations. The differences in the details were very

comical and they both had a good laugh over Arthur's silly fibs.
The Duke had come with gifts, as well as warmth and witticisms.
The first gift was a bouquet of the most lustrous red roses she had
ever seen. These must have been difficult to come by, and come at a
dear cost, because it was both wintertime *and* wartime. The second
was a very small box of chocolates, which was equally precious in
those years of sugar rationing. The Duke asked her to share them
with her attendants, who appeared to be extremely devoted to her.

"The next one, I'm afraid, is quite worthless," the Duke said. "It's
a greeting card from my wife. You can put it aside and save it for a
boring day—may you never become so desperate that you need to
read it." He laid the card, just to be funny, as close to a waste bin as
he could without actually depositing it.

"Lastly, Peggy," the Duke said, presenting a small package with a
gallant flourish, "I bring you the most precious gift of all because
this one comes from our dear Arthur. He gave it to me when I went
to see him in the hospital at Dorset, and he asked me to be sure to
bring it to you when I could. He said, as things stood, my chances
of making it up here to you, were better than his. So, you see, Peg,
he really had no illusions about what was coming next, and he was
very much at peace with the world at the end. Now, I should tell
you—by way of a little hint—that when I saw him, he didn't actually give me the gift right away. What happened was, he had sent
for a portrait artist, and he wanted me to come back for the gift two
days later when the artist's work was done. When I got back to the
hospital it was a week later, and Arthur was in a coma. But his gift
to you was wrapped and ready and given to me by a nurse. So here it
is, although a little late. You'll want to open his last gift to you privately, I imagine, so I'll take my leave now, but I promise to come
back as soon as I can. And, I promise not to bring the Duchess. I'm
aware of how annoying you find her. She annoys me, too, but not as
much as she annoys you and others. What can I say, Peggy? We love
who we love. No one can explain it."

With that, he kissed her benevolently and departed. As soon as he had gone, Lady Winniot called an attendant and asked her to help open the package, as her hands were now quite useless for handling anything small and delicate. The attendant did as she asked and extracted a gold chain and locket.

"Can you open it? You don't mind, do you?" she said rather helplessly.

"Not in the least," the attendant replied. She unsnapped the clasp and laid the open locket on her palm. She then extended her hand to Lady Winniot, who reacted with a little gasp, followed by a smile of bliss. Her wonderful, splendid Arthur had chosen the artist for his commission with his expected care and good taste. Inside the delicate case, the painter had rendered an exquisite portrait of Wolsey's brown fox.

Several years after arriving in Winnipeg, Tobias Seymour had a successful dog-breeding business, a cozy house with large windows and a stone fireplace, a pair of young foxhounds he had named Hannah and Hilda, and many new friends, both Canadian and English. He called his two foxhounds *My Sweet Lady Friends* and took them everywhere he went. In time, he became a recognizable figure in the daily life of Winnipeg and was frequently referred to as *The Brit with the Fox-Less Foxhounds.*

Despite Hannah and Hilda, he was lonely and often thought about Alistair. When his thoughts turned back to the days at Wolsey, he remembered the best and feared the worst. The war was still on, but he had heard nothing for many years. It was 1943.

Finally, at the urging of his most intimate friends, he took a brave step and wrote a letter to Alistair's father, inquiring about the health of the two foxhounds he had left in his charge, the original Hannah and Hilda. He *incidentally* asked about Mr. Cavendish's three sons, and if there was any news to report about Wolsey and its people.

Five months later he had a reply. He was only willing to open the letter in the company of his closest friends, Marcus and Silas, fearing it contained ill-tidings that he didn't want to learn of in solitude; it had been a long time since he had entertained anything likely to promote a strong emotional response, and now he found himself in possession of a letter that could potentially demolish his fragile equilibrium.

When the time came to open the envelope, he was in a pub with his friends and had downed a few whiskeys in preparation. He asked Marcus to read the letter first. He thought that by gauging his friend's reaction, he could better prepare himself for any bad news when he read it himself. Marcus agreed, and did his best to maintain a frozen, emotionless face as he absorbed the contents, but, as he refolded the letter, his trembling hands said what his eyes had not. Mr. Seymour's face went very pale and he looked as if he would fall from his chair.

"I'm terribly sorry, Tobe," Marcus said, putting his arm around his friend. He placed the letter in Mr. Seymour's shirt pocket rather than on the table. The eloquence of that gesture was not lost on the grief-stricken man. It spoke volumes about the quality of his friendship with Marcus, reminding him that all was not lost. Silas, meanwhile, playing doctor, went to the bar to get them all a round of good whiskey.

Mr. Seymour sighed deeply and retrieved and unfolded the letter. He read, to his great sadness, that not only Alistair, but also one of his older brothers, had been killed. Alistair had perished in the evacuation of Dunkirk on May 29, 1942, and his body had never been found. While crossing the Channel from France, his transport was attacked by a bomber. This, sadly, was not a heroic death, as Alistair would have wished; it was, instead, a total waste of a possible future in Canada, or anywhere else among the living. There was also news in Mr. Cavendish's letter about Lord Winniot, Mr. Brousster, Hannah and Hilda, and others. Mr. Seymour already knew about Lord Winniot, because he had read about him in the newspapers. Unexpectedly, despite his sadness, Mr. Seymour derived some relief from knowing the truth about Alistair at last. Three years of speculation and uncertainty had been a terrible burden. He wanted to move on.

On the night that Mr. Cavendish's unfortunate letter was opened, the three expatriate friends drank whiskey and chattered aimlessly for hours. Each made an attempt to steer the conversation to less depressing subjects. The whiskey helped.

Suddenly—perhaps because they were discussing survival—Mr. Seymour recalled something that had been the subject of humorous pub gossip back at Wolsey years earlier. He explained the bizarre controversies connected to the brown fox in detail to his friends, including anecdotes about Mr. Brousster's absurd obsession with it, and he gave them, by way of contrast to Mr. Brousster, a colorful account of the scene he witnessed between Lady Margaret and the fox—the first time he had spoken of it since the day it happened.

"It was a legend—at least in the pubs—that the famous brown fox at Wolsey would survive everyone," he said. "That bit was repeated endlessly. Even Lord Arthur had heard it."

"Has he outlived *everyone*?" Silas asked, a bit drunk, and not taking the fox very seriously. "He can't have outlived you, since you're still here. Why don't I just kick you in the shins so we can be sure?"

"Do you have any idea what happened to him? Does anyone know?" Marcus asked. At the same time, he was thinking, *Thankfully, for poor Toby's sake, Mr. Cavendish's extensive casualty list doesn't include the brown fox among the fallen.*

"No, actually, I don't. But I would *like* him to live forever. I feel he *should* live forever. For me, he's the embodiment of the indomitable English spirit, a perfect symbol of the will to survive. He's Winston Churchill with fur and whiskers and a wet nose and a bushy tail and a taste for apples."

"Good show!" Silas said, lifting his glass. "Here's to the bloody brown fox, may he live forever!"

"And to me! And to the ugly bloke sitting next to me!" each said in turn.

At that point, with Mr. Cavendish's letter folded and back in its envelope, and the envelope safely tucked back in Tobias Seymour's pocket, the three friends took advantage of the three best options available to them—they laughed and drank and got on with their lives.

There were thirty-two chickens at the McVicar's ramshackle dairy farm when the brown fox took residence in the woods nearby. Within a week there were only twenty-eight remaining. Then the McVicars ate one more on Sunday since it had stopped laying eggs and there would be no point in continuing to feed it. That left twenty-seven chickens for the fox to keep his conniving eye on. He was watching the chickens as carefully as Ollie, the old family dog. There might have been an outbreak of war between the two animals to rival the one already in progress around them, but, ultimately, that's not what happened.

Unlike the circumstances of Mr. Seymour's exodus, the fox did not have a destination in mind, or friends waiting for him, when he left Wolsey, and later, Hexbury. His compensation was the beauty of the sparsely populated countryside, Scotland's sweet-smelling carpet of green, the restorative, joyful experience of beginning life again. The fox would roll in the fragrant, damp grass in the morning, and howl with delight when he raced through it at sunset. He leaped into the air when he heard the sound of birds overhead, no matter how unreachable they were. The earth was soft and loamy, and easy to burrow into to create a cozy den for himself to hide from the damp and the nighttime chill. Everything seemed possible once more. Everything seemed edible, and if not edible, certainly clean enough— free of the stench of gunpowder and fire—to be edible if only it was smaller or he was bigger.

His nervous system, first damaged by the shock of Lady Margaret's decline and unexplained disappearance, and nearly destroyed by the stress of the bombings and the crazed, erratic behavior of the homeless dogs and marauding foxhound gangs, was now in recovery. He had never expected to find such agreeable conditions as he did at the McVicar's farm. His new canine adversary—there was *always* at least *one* dog to be dealt with, wasn't there?—in comparison to its predecessors, was either very docile or very stupid. It took the fox a long time—about ten purloined chickens worth—to realize that Ollie's problem was not one of temperament or stupidity. It was old age.

Ollie was nearly seventeen, and he was arthritic and tired. His favorite pastime—about all he could manage comfortably—was napping. The balance of power was leveled-out only because Ollie had an ally in the oldest of the McVicar children, Bartholomew—affectionately nicknamed Barty—who was some three years younger than Ollie and looked up to the dog as if it was his older brother. Ollie had watched over him as a child and been his closest companion and protector all through his youth. Barty's bond with Ollie was formidable. Not only did he treat the aging animal with the respect and consideration usually reserved for a much-loved grandparent, he was protective of the dog's standing in the hierarchy of the farm's workers, willing to pick up the slack left by Ollie's shortcomings to such a degree, an observer could construe that the dog's reputation meant more to Barty than the welfare of the chickens. Thus, at the first summons from the dog, if Barty was within earshot, he would race to the chicken coop with a shotgun in his hand. It was the bad luck of the chickens that when Ollie was on guard duty and happened to be awake when the salivating fox made his appearance, he was usually too tired to properly sort himself out and bark for Barty to come to his aid.

Nineteen chickens remained. Barty, at this point, whenever he was not busy elsewhere, had taken up a seat on the porch steps with his rifle in readiness across his knees. Ollie, as usual, slept, especially when Barty was near enough to watch the coop for him. As soon as it got dark, and the McVicars sat down for their dinner—the fox could smell the cooking odors wafting out of the chimney and through cracks in the mortar, and knew it was time for his dinner as well—he crept out of the woods and began digging another tunnel under the wire fence. He could no longer chew his way through the wires because Barty has placed a second layer of fencing over the first and added an extra dimension of insurance by painting an evil tasting chemical on it that was guaranteed to ruin his appetite for a week.

No matter what happened at the coop, Ollie slept through it. On the rare occasions that he woke during a raid, he would open one of his eyes halfway and passively watch what the fox was doing. His inability to ward off the invasions was becoming more and more obvious and detrimental to the tally of the chickens in the coop. That pleased the fox at first, but it became irritating before very long. There was no challenge here. The fox was becoming increasingly bored and restless and feeling less satisfied by every chicken he ate.

On one occasion Ollie did manage to outwit him. The scenario was the same as usual at the start, but this time Ollie waited until the fox had gone through the trouble of tunneling into the coop before he struggled to his feet and howled for Barty to come to the rescue. The teenager quickly charged out of the house. He fumbled ineptly with the rifle that had been left on the porch, giving the fox just enough time to leap to the top of the hen-house, grasping a small headless chicken in his mouth, and from the henhouse roof over the fence. He was back in the woods with his meal before Barty had managed to cock the rifle.

There were soon only sixteen chickens in the coop. Since the fox had arrived at the farm, the McVicars had eaten only two of the original thirty-two. The fox was winning the war of attrition, but he was losing patience. He needed more of a challenge than Ollie could provide. He suspected that Barty was deliberately mishandling the gun to avoid firing it. After every successful raid, he felt as if he had been forced into the skin of a much smaller fox.

One day Barty did fire the rifle, but his shot went wild. The bullet struck a rock, causing a shard of granite to fly off and embed itself in the fox's right foreleg. This injury was the most painful he had ever suffered. He laid in his den for two days, contemplating—obliquely—how unfair it was that Ollie was protected and he was not—not since Lady Margaret, long ago. Finally, he limped to a stream for water, and then towards the farmhouse to check on his chickens. The first thing he saw when he emerged from the woods was Barty walking lazily about the yard. Ollie, looking sickly and lethargic, was dragging himself along, a few steps behind the pimple-faced teenager. They had left the chickens unguarded. That triggered instantaneous suspicion. He was also—inexplicably—beginning to experience something resembling sympathy for the vulnerable chickens.

Some strange things happened then. First, Ollie noticed the fox watching them and barked halfheartedly. Barty, who was carrying his rifle over his shoulder, turned and spotted him, too, but he didn't stop or take hold of the weapon. Instead, he continued with Ollie to the porch, stood the gun up against the house, and took him inside. It was much too early in the day to leave the chicken coop unguarded and to bring Ollie indoors. Most curious of all, the last tunnel under the wire—dug just before his injury—was still there. Barty had not filled it in with stones as he usually did. It was clearly an open invitation for a flurry of feathers, hot spurting blood, and a tasty chicken dinner.

The scene was so perplexing and suspicious, the fox decided to enjoy some rabbit that night and to monitor future happenings at the farm, lest he become the victim of an ambush or some other clever trick he had not thought of first.

Weeks passed. The tunnel remained untouched. The rifle remained where it had been left, leaning against the rickety house. Barty was rarely seen outside. Ollie had not been seen in weeks. Eventually, a taste for some juicy chicken won out over his sense of caution. He dug a second tunnel on the other side of the henhouse, far from the previous one, in case the first had some trap concealed in it. He had a double helping of chicken that night. There were only fourteen birds left when he limped back to his den.

It was not in his nature to skimp on meals, especially good ones that were so convenient. While Barty and Ollie were making it possible, the fox saw no downside to helping himself to the food he craved. Before long, though, the cupboard was bare. The chicken supply had been depleted. With Ollie nowhere to be seen and Barty ignoring him as though he was equally invisible, the fox came to know a form of psychological torment he found increasingly difficult to cope with.

The truth behind the abandonment of the chickens was that the McVickars had a solvent dairy business and the chickens were merely incidental to it, kept to provide some eggs as a supplemental protein and to give Ollie, in his dotage, something easy to be in charge of. But now that he was too old to be an effective watchdog, Barty decided—with his father's consent—to abandon the last of the chickens to the fox, except for two plump ones which they cooked for dinner and shared with Ollie. Thereafter, the McVickars traded milk with their neighbors for whatever eggs were wanted.

Barty noisily tore the henhouse down for firewood and dismantled the wire coop. All the while, he kept glancing back over his shoulder and smiling at the fox, who watched the demolition of his pantry in complete frustration from a hundred yards away. He became so distraught by this outrage, he started to run in circles, chasing his tail and howling. When Barty saw this, he dropped to his knees and laughed until tears ran down to his chin and his stomach ached.

At that juncture, the fox began to suspect that chickens were being hidden inside the house where Ollie could watch them more effectively. He couldn't imagine the McVicars would give up eating chicken any more than he could imagine doing so himself. He was sure that Ollie was lazily napping next to an indoor chicken coop; at least he was sure enough to risk sneaking inside to see for himself. He had nothing else to think about and nothing else to do.

He awaited an opportunity patiently. Finally, it came when Mrs. McVicar burned the family's dinner and all the windows were opened to let the smoke out. The brown fox had been attracted to the house by the smell of the burning food. He crouched down in the shadows and waited. After a few hours, someone closed all the windows, except for the one in the kitchen. One by one, the lights in the house went out. A radio played for a time, then silence fell over all.

It was time to act. He charged to the house and jumped up to the kitchen windowsill. This was a fortuitous entry point because on the other side of the window there was a cook's chopping counter, which meant he didn't need to jump directly to the floor on his injured leg. It was very quiet. The fox heard some distant snores from upstairs and some moans the house was making as the wooden floors and walls readjusted themselves after a day of bustling activity. The house seemed almost alive as it settled, yet curiously quiet, too—not at all what he expected. The accumulated smell of years of cooking and baking permeated everything—the rugs, the furniture, the curtains, even the peeling wallpaper smelled of good things to eat.

The first floor of the house was deserted. He padded cautiously from room to room, sniffing, looking, and listening for his beloved chickens. Finding nothing, he began to despair that he had been mistaken about the indoor chicken coop. Then he saw Ollie lying next to the still-smoldering hearth, eyes half open, ignoring him. He pawed at the rug, but Ollie, as usual, didn't take the trouble to look up at him.

Then, with no warning at all, something exploded—like one of Hexbury's bombs—only this time the explosion was *inside* him. The bile produced by a lifetime of persecution came to a rolling boil and alchemized instantaneously into pure adrenalin. Before he knew what he was doing or could impose any control over his actions, he was jumping from place to place in the room, hurdling over furniture. He jumped over Ollie and howled in his ear. He leaped over him again and howled again. Ollie never moved. He stared into the fireplace and made it clear—with a flagrant display of apathy—he had no intention of fighting any longer, no matter what the humiliation. Finally, the fox had enough of being ignored and thwarted at every turn and, with an impulsive lunge, sank his teeth deeply into Ollie's neck and throat. He shook him violently, sinking his teeth still deeper. His sole objective in that instant was to avenge his years of frustration with his first taste of a canine's evil blood.

The final truths were only moments away. Ollie was as rigid as a log and much lighter than a dog his size ought to be. The fox had ripped away a mouthful of fur, sawdust, and poisonous taxidermists' chemicals—principally arsenic, which is commonly used in that trade. The wood chips and bitter-tasting powder had flown everywhere when he had shaken his victim—a substantial amount of the poison had gotten into his eyes, blinding him. He never saw the dog's head separate from its ruined neck and roll into the fireplace where it began to burn and glow demonically. Mortally poisoned, blind, the brown fox fell on his back, kicked his legs in the air, and screamed in agony, waking the entire household.

Mr. and Mrs. McVickar, Barty, and his two sisters, soon stood in the doorway, all of them struck speechless, taking in the horror before them. While Barty—despite the misfortune of losing his token remembrance of Ollie—suppressed a smile of righteous satisfaction at the poetic justice so well-served, his sisters began to cry and buried their faces in their mother's nightgown. Mrs. McVicar put her arms around them, but her mind was on the mess she was confronted with, fully aware that her children—for various understandable reasons—were not going to be any help at all when it came to cleaning it up.

Too weak to run away from Death, he lay in the sawdust, defeated at last, next to what had been his final foe—as pathetic an excuse for an antagonist as there could possibly be—a fellow player in a minor Shakespearean tragedy writ very small. The quick brown fox was going to expire in the headless shadow of the lazy dog he had so spitefully jumped over. Their stories would end simultaneously, their passing marked only by a period at the end of the typographer's pangram that summarized their entwined lives.

The remnants of the fire crackled in the hearth nearby. The floorboards creaked as the frail, wooden house settled down to sleep. The weather vane, atop the shingled roof, squealed as it turned in the wind and pointed southward, towards Wolsey—shuttered and silent now—where he was born nine years earlier. As the clocks inside struck midnight, the great manor house of Wolsey crouched in the dark, hiding from the bombs as he had once hidden in that very place from the horns, the horses, the hounds, and the hunters. A three-quarter moon moved silently behind silky winter clouds as they skated back and forth—hundreds of kilometers—between the past and the present. The fox closed his useless eyes and dreamt.

A small, red apple lay on the floor, between his paws. So few things in the world were red like that little apple was red. If his little life had been a little different, or a little shorter, the brown fox that didn't know he was brown, might never have known the color red at all. In his rapidly diminishing capacity to remember, the apple seemed as red as the red bicycle he had once seen leaning against a stone wall on a summer day when he was a cub. It was red like the scarlet collar on Lady Margaret's hunting frock when she rode across the grounds at Wolsey. It was red like her Ladyship's lips when she laughed, and like the ruby ring on her right hand, with which she offered little, red apples to him. It was red like the blood of albino foxes that he had seen chased and killed from his hiding place high among the autumn leaves. It was red like the blood of screaming chickens. It was red like love and war and all else that life entails for everything that lives and breathes and perishes. It was red like red was red before the black that was coming came.

He looked up—as he faded into legend—hoping to see the vague, beautiful lady that had brought him this simple gift, the only thing that he had ever been given in all the years of his life.

She was no more physically present in the scattered sawdust and poisonous powders than the apple was. Nevertheless, the last glimpse the quick brown fox had of this worrisome life was his imaginary reflection in the imaginary eyes of the only living creature he had ever loved. Then the locket of earthly existence closed and accompanied by the barely audible sound of a delicate clasp closing, the darkness closed in with it, so that the black that was coming all of his life was the only thing that was there, and the story of the quick brown fox was over.

April 2nd is National Lazy Dog Day

Journalists, photographers, and meteorologists from all points of the compass are expected to converge at Marker 144 on *The Paumanok Express Line* on April 2, National Lazy Dog Day. We will have live television crews at the scene to provide coverage.

As always, the American public is eager to know what the lazy dog will do this year—will he or won't he allow *The Brown Fox*, scheduled to pass the marker at 11:42 a.m., to jump over him as it speeds toward Montauk?

On numerous previous occasions, the unpredictable lazy dog has sauntered off, sometimes only moments before the train comes through. If the lazy dog holds his position between the rails, allowing the train to "jump" him, expect the Dog Days of Summer to be extended by an additional 21 to 30 days, say expert meteorologists.

More than hot weather is at stake. Insiders report that millions of dollars are wagered every April 2 on the outcome at Marker 144.

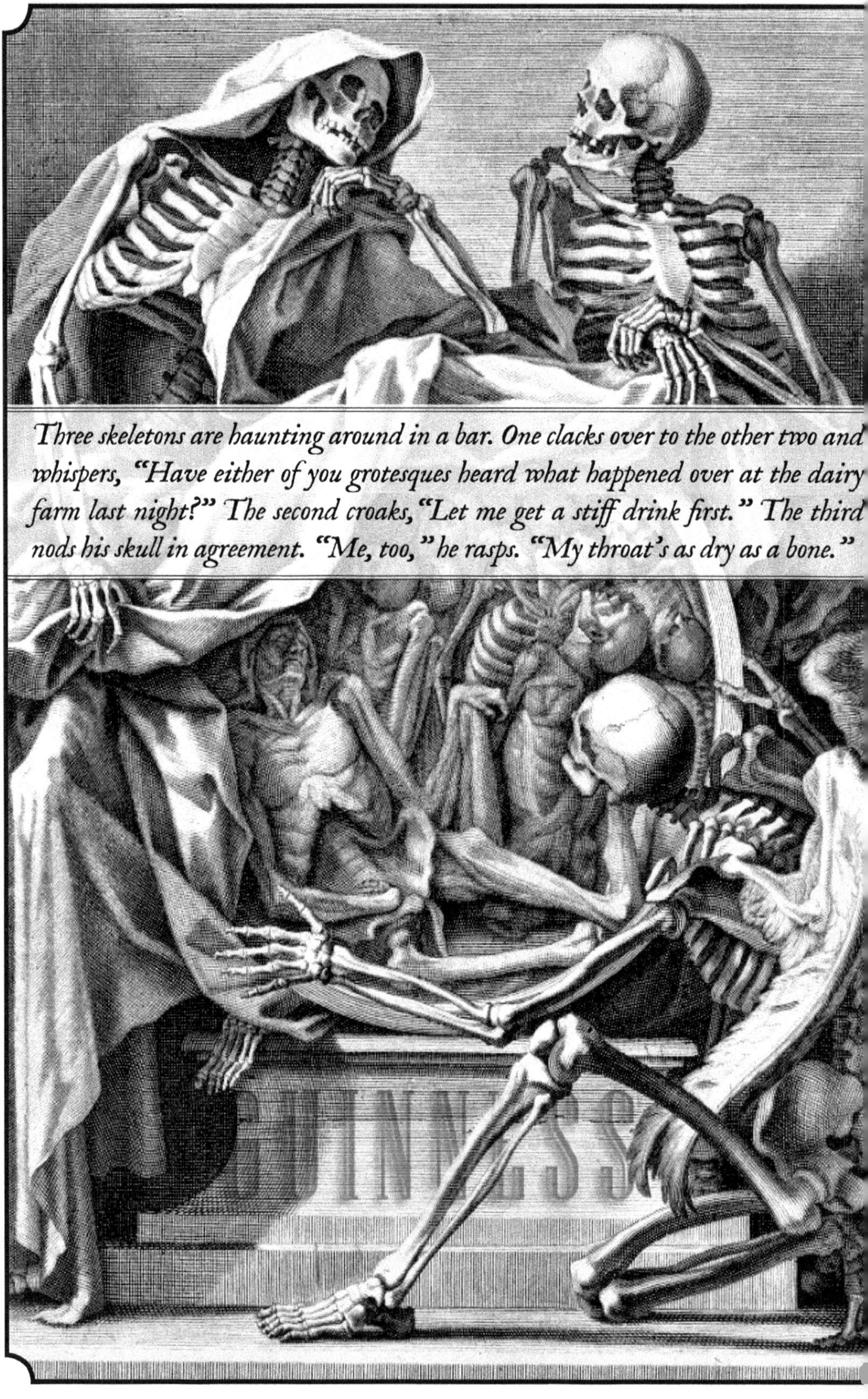

Three skeletons are haunting around in a bar. One clacks over to the other two and whispers, "Have either of you grotesques heard what happened over at the dairy farm last night?" The second croaks, "Let me get a stiff drink first." The third nods his skull in agreement. "Me, too," he rasps. "My throat's as dry as a bone."

A Prologue to The Shrink's Tale

he end of his lengthy tale reached, the Professor waived the blackening core of his apple with a dramatic flourish of finality. Some light applause from the appreciative Nightcaps broke the silence that lingered in the wake of the fox's unexpected demise. "There you have the *official* story of the quick brown fox and the lazy dog," the Professor said, quite satisfied with his recitation. "You may or may not be surprised to learn that there is—additionally—an *unofficial* Appendix to the story."

"What else could possibly happen?" Scotch asked. "The fox, the dog, and almost everyone else in your sprawling drama is dead. There can't be more."

"We in the story industry," the Professor said, deliberately adopting an obnoxious and exclusionary tone for humorous effect, "would never reference such priceless, rarefied material as mere 'more.' Fable connoisseurs, such as myself, prefer to implement less common-sounding terminology, favoring words such as *Epilogue* when discussing these ancillary literary matters. In the Epilogue in question, Barty McVicar, whose hobby is (quite obviously to those who were paying attention)—taxidermy—predictably decides to use his skills to preserve the brown fox. He does an excellent job of it, too, shaping the form in a realistic crouching position, as if the fox was about to launch himself into the air. One could imagine—if one knew the history of the fox—that he was preparing to take his fateful leap up to the McVicar's kitchen window, or—more traditionally interpreted—just about to jump over a lazy dog. The Epilogue subsequently informs that, years later, Barty McVicar sold his taxidermied brown fox to the Natural History Museum in Hexbury when he needed money for books while a student of husbandry at Hexbury University. The museum later designed a large display—a diorama, I believe, is the word in English—depicting a fox hunt, prominently featuring a brown fox eluding a group of malicious foxhounds. Our friend, the brown fox—perhaps as a punishment for his callousness towards the dog—was back in Hexbury, the place he hated most, flash-frozen in a fox hunt frieze, pursued for eternity by a pack of foxhounds, perpetually about to leap, but never getting off the ground. I suppose one could visit the world's most famous fox and absorb the vibes of that ironic, macabre twist—his private Hell." The Professor turned his attention to Scotch and said, "So don't be quite so skeptical. The fox is just as real as Walt Whitman, whose lap you're figuratively sitting on."

"And just as dead," Scotch responded. "Bluntly speaking."

"I beg to differ," said the Professor. "Nothing is dead if it's remembered."

"So true," a female passenger interjected. Seated across the aisle from the Professor's and Nightcaps' corner clubhouse, a woman dressed in mourning, wearing an old-fashioned veil and black gloves, had been listening to their conversation. She was gripping the edges of a cardboard shoebox.

"Ashes?" asked the Professor. The woman nodded somberly. The Professor probed further. "Husband? Son?"

"Son. The big A claimed him," she responded. "How did you know these ashes are *men's* ashes?"

The Professor pointed his black apple core at the box. "It's a men's shoebox."

"Our sincere condolences," Soda said sympathetically. "Are you off to Fire Island on a 'scattering' mission?"

"I am." The woman lifted her veil. Her eyes were heavily made up, but very bloodshot. "On the beach and into the sea in a town called The Pines. It's what he wanted, according to his papers. So here I am—the good mother."

Ry leaned across the aisle and touched her hand. "We're going to the same place you are, so we can help—unless you want to be alone. If not, we'll make it less traumatic for you. Sadly, we've done this before. Too many times."

"Oh, yes, yes," she said, breathing a sigh of relief. "That would actually be wonderful. I've already enjoyed listening to you gentlemen since we left the city. It's been an ideal distraction from sad thoughts." She turned her head to address the Professor in particular. "That was a most marvelous story you just told. I've always been fascinated by people who can spin a good yarn."

"Thank you for saying so," the Professor said, humbly bowing his head, although his humility came across as a tad insincere to the skeptical Nightcaps, who had already experienced his methodology for luring strangers into his folkloric web-of-no-escape.

"I never think of what I do as *spinning yarn*, though." He spoke in a hushed voice, as if he was confiding in her, rather than showing off. "As a fabulist—a lecturer on all things folkloric—what I really do is allow my imagination to take up the yarn that's already been spun by humankind over the last million years, and from that I collect and conserve stories—beautiful stories, sad stories, terrifying stories. I have no prejudices in that regard and no preferences. All of this world's stories are equal in my profession. They represent what was, what could be, and what will be. Which leads me to say, Mrs. X, that I'm sorry the story you have for us today is a sad one."

She acknowledged his last remark with a solemn nod. Meanwhile, with narrowed eyes, the Professor stared fixedly at the shoebox on her lap. "But," he added emphatically, "I *will* have it from you."

The train entered a tunnel, magnifying the sound of the grinding iron wheels to a screech. When it emerged a few seconds later, the Professor's focus had shifted from the shoebox to the Nightcaps. He smiled flirtatiously, dispelling some of the tension. "You gentlemen aren't off the hook, either."

"Of course not," Ry said, rushing into the void left behind by the dissipated awkwardness. "We did have an agreement, although I can't see myself rising to your exalted level of skill."

"You can rise to it, or you can sink to it. No matter. But each of you fellows—and also, I hope, our beautiful Lady in Black—*will* pick up that storyteller's yarn, and all of you *will* weave, as best you can, some tapestry from it for our combined pleasure. Agreed?"

All nodded affirmatively. The woman in mourning managed a weak smile and began to relax. Gradually, she loosened her grip on the shoebox. "I'm Asta Louise Bathbaum," she said, "and I'd be pleased to participate in your adventure. I'm sure I can dig up some prattle for you."

"Welcome to Storytellers Anonymous," Soda said, and then he proceeded to make the rest of the introductions.

At that moment, the conductor entered the car. He was forced to halt because the storytellers were passing business cards across the aisle, impeding his progress. The Professor took advantage of this to ask for the lunch menus. "Also," he added, "I believe I overheard you mention there was a Rabbi giving a lecture somewhere on the train. Is that correct?"

"He's on the train, and he's talking. I'm not sure anyone is listening."

"I wonder if you wouldn't mind asking him to join us for a short chat. I, for one, would like to hear what he has to say."

"Say about what?"

"That's up to him," the Professor said rather curtly, "not either of us."

As soon as the conductor moved on, the Professor got back to managing his storytelling lineup. "Okay, who's next at the podium?" he inquired. "We have to tighten our schedule a bit, fellow pilgrims. A renowned Rabbi might be joining us here, and space and time are shrinking."

Both Ry and Soda insisted that Scotch go next. Ry said, "No one has crazy stories like Scotch has crazy stories. Not only was he *born* into crazy, he *majored* in crazy and became a shrink. He thought *shrinking* was an escape route, but it just opened a door to a wider vista of crazy."

Soda was in complete agreement. "Professionally," he said, "his ears are force-fed verbal crazy-corn all day long in fifty-minute servings."

Scotch listened to his friend's assessments and didn't seem inclined to disagree with them. "It's true that I could write a book called *Tales from the Couch*, but I have yet to hear *anything* to top the story of my parents' wedding." He paused and considered his options for a moment. "Actually, though, I'd prefer to tell a story about my father. It's a story that my Nightcap brethren don't know yet. I've only recently remembered it."

"What a gyp!" Ry said, looking to Soda for support. "You *have* to tell them about the wedding. *Nothing* can top that epic humdinger!"

"Yes, the wedding." Soda said. "Really, you must."

"In honor of our new friend, Lady Asta, I'll take a detour and tell all those present about my parents' wedding first. Then my story." Lampooning the Professor's flamboyant posturing, he added, "This is what we pompous assholes in the storytelling industry pompously refer to as a *Preface*."

It all begins in the wonderful 1950s with the birth of my mother, Bernice McDougan, who was born precisely two minutes after her identical twin sister, Beatrice McDougan. Those few minutes of lead time made it possible for Auntie to become the self-appointed manager of two matching childhoods—or, perhaps that's better described as a matching *childhood*, singular. *Twindom* really could use a dedicated vernacular to help clarify the convolutions that characterize it.

As the "older" sibling, Auntie staked out her territory as Twin-in-Command as far back as the crib—beginning with kicking and pushing and escalating, before long, to bottle-snatching and blanket-hogging. As silly as it sounds, this pattern continued into young adulthood, until The Great Truce came in the 1970s, by which time the sisters were young women and both mothers. Until then, it was Auntie who got to make the big decisions, the most important of which was picking out what they would wear each morning. Then, too, there was the obnoxious, petty stuff—for example, Auntie deciding which of them had the right-of-way in doorways, on school buses, and in bathrooms. And, of course, being the older of the two, it was Auntie who had to have the first slice of birthday cake.

At the breakfast table, Auntie would toast her bread first. If this left only the small pieces at the end of the loaf for my mother, it was Mummie's bad luck for being a latecomer. At mealtimes, the only mitigation was that Auntie knew that smaller portions for Mummie might eventually cause her to mutate into the thinner of the pair, consequently transforming her into the more attractive sister. Recognizing the inherent danger in this, she would relinquish a fair share of first helpings to my mother to ensure that, no matter which way the scales of fortune tilted, their weights remained more-or-less the same. This saved Mummie from various mealtime indignities, like having to scrounge around the bottom of the cereal box for the broken Cheerios that always accumulated down there.

Auntie, when she was a child—like many otherwise decent children—displayed an occasional, unbecoming streak of cruelty. Famously, on one unfortunate occasion, she called my mother an "afterbirth" and told her that she—my Aunt—had actually been *born*, while my mother "just fell out"—a path into the world having already been cleared and widened for Mummie by my aunt's championship arrival skills.

Food and clothing were the principal realms of equality and peace in their early relationship, and those only for the sake of appearances to outsiders. On all other fronts, war broke out with predictable regularity. Even many years later—until The Great Truce was declared—an occasional salvo would be fired by one side or the other. The most outrageous incident I heard of had to do with their menstrual cycles, which they had managed, somehow, to coordinate since adolescence—probably through sheer force of will—keeping their moon-moods in enforced synchronicity, meticulously calendaring upcoming "crappy mood" days on which they would avoid contact with each other, except for their daily morning wardrobe conference, around which their twin-existence revolved. When my mother became pregnant with me, it threw the years of menstrual accord completely out-of-whack and sent Auntie into a tailspin. She ran off to a drunken binge in Mexico and returned a few weeks later, tanned, somewhat sobered-up, and pregnant with my cousin, Niall Gonzalez, who was born on the very same day as I was, in the same delivery room. That was the last time Mummie and Auntie were able to coordinate anything below their waists except for underwear, shoes, stockings, nail polish, and corn plasters.

Finally, things changed radically for the twins. There was a big reversal. Unexpectedly, Mummie reached the apex of her ascendency by default, because Auntie—being the older of the two by two minutes—attained the dreaded status of "old maid" first. It was inevitable, but no one, least of all bossy Auntie Beatrice, saw this twist of fate coming. Suddenly, being older wasn't so marvelous. It was written in stone: Auntie Beatrice had to marry *first*.

Mummie, after enduring years of twin abuse, would gleefully rub Auntie's face in this unpleasant reality, referring to her, whenever they had a disagreement, with a range of epithets beginning with the word *old*, such as *old cow*, *old hag*, *old crow*, *old bitch*, and so forth, and on the rare days when they were on *good* terms, she would call Auntie Beatrice an *old twin*, just to be sure she remembered her place in the new hierarchy. She certainly wasn't going to let Auntie forget those precious two minutes of age disparity while both remained unmarried, because the only thing worse than being an Old Maid—at least to their generation—was being an *Older* Maid. Whenever the subject of marriage would come up at family gatherings, all eyes would turn sympathetically towards Auntie, and the *tsk-tsk-tsk*ing would commence. When Auntie's face reddened with shame and annoyance, Mummie's beamed with relief. They didn't look quite as much alike on those occasions, or so I've been told.

Three momentous things happened in one year. I, Sam "Scotch" Diamond, was born, and my cousin, Niall Gonzalez, was born, and my Scottish mother married my Jewish father who has the same deluxe Jewish nose I have and that Niall Gonzalez has. May I add that Donald Trump looks more like a Mexican than Cousin Niall does? I certainly look more Mexican than Cousin Niall, and I don't look Mexican at all. So, there's the beginning of the identity crisis. While, on the surface, it's clear that my father is possibly—hell, *probably*—my cousin's father, too, it has never been clear whether Beatrice is my mother or Bernice is. After the Truce, they began switching places with greater frequency, so switching babies would not be off limits for them. Regardless, my father valiantly pitched in with Cousin Niall, treating him like his own child, because Señor Gonzalez—if he ever existed at all—supposedly had his brains blown out in Tijuana by an outraged rival over the affections of a *señorita de la noche*.

Mummie has always liked men, and Auntie has always disliked them. Being the old maid in the set—and my mother beating her to both the obstetrician and the altar—didn't make the male sex any more appealing to dear Auntie. Daddy, on the other hand, being bisexual—or, at the very least, polymorphous perverse—was not particularly over-the-moon about women anyway and being "married" to both my mother and my aunt was not helpful in that regard. I'd venture to say that it's a stretch to conceive of him conceiving a child, never mind conceiving two children with two inconceivably identical women, both of them mad as a pair of hatters who owned two of every hat.

In the wacky household I grew up in, no one had the slightest idea what was *really* going on, least of all me. And despite all that, I had a marvelous, love-gilded childhood, as would any imaginative kid with two identical mothers, a *doppelgänger* twin cousin, and a delightfully crazy father almost as crazy as both mothers combined, not to mention all the new "Uncles" Daddy would bring around. There was at least a dozen of them—all shapes and sizes—over the years. Four of them were named Bruce. There was, I seem to remember, a Claude, an Anton, and an Albert, too. None of them had names that began with letters from $\mathcal{D}$ to $\mathcal{Z}$, which made me wonder, years later, if Daddy did his uncle-shopping in the *Pink Yellow Pages*, never progressing beyond the letter C.

Those were the wonderful days of rollicking insanity, revolving mothers, rotating Bruces, ridiculous fictions. Imagine our family vacations—one or two of the Uncle Bruces in tow, and Auntie Beatrice and Daddy and Mummie and pseudo-twin-cousin Niall and I—plus a ton of two-of-everything twin paraphernalia—all of us packed into a station wagon and heading out to Cape May for a few weeks of sunshine, identity swapping, and bickering.

One day, when I was older and had begun to get a psychological handle on the suspected switching and disordered doings in the household, I asked my father how he was able to tell the difference between Mummie and Auntie.

"I have a simple test," he said.

"What's that? How do you do it?"

"I ask a provocative question as casually as possible—so as not to arouse any suspicion—and then I carefully observe the resulting reaction. For example, I'll ask something like, 'Do Scottish men wear underwear beneath their kilts?' If it's actually Bea I'm talking to, she'll make a sour face, wrinkle her nose, and she'll come back with something abrasive, like: 'If there's a God, they do.'"

"And if it's really Mum?"

"She'll make a sour face, wrinkle her nose, and she'll come back with something amusing, like: 'If there's a God, they don't.'"

"I see your point," I said. "They occasionally have slightly different opinions, but they are *always* identically predictable."

Budding psychologist that I was back in my youth, I decided to pose the same test question to my Cousin Niall to see what his reaction would be. It took some explaining to clarify that I was asking about *kilts*, not *clits*, but he eventually understood what I meant. In any case, he stared at me as if I was insane, made a sour face, wrinkled his nose, and said, "How would I know? I'm Mexican."

The best story I could tell about my parents concerns their wedding. Leading up to that, however, I have to provide some background to set the scene for that epic disaster, one which, by the way, continues to be discussed to this day by New York social historians.

When both sisters became mothers and a certain amount of attention was diverted away from their *twinship* and into child-rearing, they declared The Great Truce. With new responsibilities, there would be no more time or energy for rivalry and undermining. To seal that non-aggression pact, Auntie and Mummie went into business together. They became talent agents. But, it should be stressed that to be ordinary talent agents would have been far too simple for these larger-than-life characters. They had no clue about what was, or was not, ordinary, and they had no interest in being clued in or counted in. One day they were no longer Bernice and Beatrice—they had transformed themselves, seemingly overnight, into McDougan & McDougan, Inc., Talent Agents for Identical Twins.

So, the insanity continued, but now it flourished under the umbrella of a legally licensed business, which somehow legitimized the craziness in a very scary way. Even the primary logistics—all of them legal—were unique in the business world. Every client consisted of two anatomically separate clients. Every deal was a double-deal. Every document had two dotted lines. Every setback was a double tragedy.

Auntie and Mummie had some homespun rules about how to conduct their business affairs that were highly irregular. The vendors and purveyors they employed—florists, caterers, photographers, printers, carpenters, lawyers, insurers, and so on—had to be companies owned and operated by sets of twins. Naturally, they favored businesses where *both* of the twins were committed, so it came about—as a perfect example—that the twin sisters had twin hairdressers, Mr. Ivan and Mr. Evan, and on Thursday afternoons, all business ceased while they sat in identical beauty shop chairs facing identical illuminated mirrors looking at identical reflections. They kept this up for decades. The salon was called the Double Your Beauty Salon.

Finding such twin-set vendors is not as difficult as one would guess. There happens to be a thriving Twin Underground that twins can tap into, which facilitates perpetuation of this lunacy, and even prints a monthly newsletter. It was in the *Twins on Twins Takes* that I learned of two different pairs of twin psychologists in New York City who specialize in the treatment of twin trauma. This raises a lot of questions for me. Does this form of treatment constitute group therapy? How many couches and chairs does it take for twins to treat twins?

Twin neurosis is not uncommon. Neither is twin obsession. Auntie and Mummie were solely fixated on *twindom*. They refused, despite the potential loss of profit at stake, to have anything to do with triplets and quadruplets. They were especially dismissive of quintuplets, rare as they were. In fact, I once heard Mummie disdainfully refer to Mrs. Dionne as "The Lady with the Clown-Car Uterus."

No fake twins were taken on. And no porn twins. A sign above the double CEO's double desk read: *Not Born for Twin Porn*. The sign made absolutely no sense, but it got their point across nonetheless. As to the Siamese variety, they considered those rarities to be members of an unfortunate "subspecies" best handled by "oddity specialists" outside the general entertainment industry; in any case, Siamese twins, while genetically identical, are almost never identical in appearance, and on that basis alone, Mummie and Auntie could muster no enthusiasm for them. Appearing identical—and milking the maximum amount of havoc out of it—was all they ever cared about.

It's fair to observe that the subliminal focus of their business venture was to legitimize a world in which twins, much like themselves, would not only thrive, but would appear to be members of a super race. Their ideal clients could be classified as *Young Twin Misses*, girls in whose breezy exuberance they could revisit themselves as they had once been at an earlier stage of their lives. Their ideal booking for clients was something like those twin-infested Double-mint Chewing Gum commercials—youngish twin girls and youngish twin boys (satirized by the industry as *Ingénues* and *Outgénues,* or alternatively, as *Soubrettes* and *Sabretts*) joyfully out on the town, kicking up their carefree heels, each flashing more teeth than seemed possible to squeeze into a human jaw, while perversely sporting bottles of bad-for-your teeth soda pop.

More commercials and print ads featured twins in those days than people realize today. It was definitely an established advertising motif. At that time, the public viewed twins as special—and beautiful twins even more so. Advertisers gambled big money that their products, when touted by gorgeous twins, would appeal to people who could be convinced that washing their laundry with Double-Dirt-Destroyer would make them special, too. Maybe doubly special.

Too bad this boon came to an end when fertility enhancements caused an unanticipated explosion of multiple births. Unlike their predecessors, who were viewed as happy accidents, millennial twins were stigmatized as laboratory experiments gone awry. These millennials are now the worst cellphone abusers on the planet—a momentary lost mobile connection with a twin sibling can set off a debilitating case of separation anxiety at both ends of the dropped call.

At the outset of their business venture, the desirability of twins in advertising was the factor that made Mummie and Auntie rich ladies who could well-afford to plan a wedding at the St. Regis Hotel. There was a lot of buzz in the McDougan and Diamond families about the upcoming affair—expectations of glitz and glamor could not possibly have been higher—but when the day of the wedding arrived, both families had the surprise of their lives waiting for them. The McDougans and the Diamonds, dressed as though they were honorees at a Nobel Prize Ceremony, entered a banquet hall that was more like a hall of mirrors in a fun house. All of Bernice and Beatrice's double clients and double vendors had been invited to the wedding and were doubly present, brandishing their unique weapons of confusion in all their redundant force. There was two of nearly everyone. With the exception of family members, out of every ten guests, there were only five different faces. It was possible to get lost just crossing the room because the geographical signposts of recognizable people played tricks on the eyes and mind.

Obviously, I wasn't there, but—years later—Mummie's and Auntie's older brother, my Uncle Duncan McDougan—known as "Unc-Dunc" to Cousin Niall and I—described the occasion to me quite vividly.

"Imagine," he said with a genuine shudder, "arriving at the Grand Ballroom of the St. Regis Hotel. The concierge at the door acknowledges your arrival with a smirk and greets you with the words: 'Welcome to Noah's Ark. Are you *one* or *half of two*?' Imagine being seated at a table with six strangers. At the next table over, you see the same six strangers seated with an empty chair where your twin—if you had one—would be sitting. How's that for the start of an evening in *The Twilight Zone*? Imagine taking a piss in the Men's Room and discovering that the same guy is peeing on either side of you. Then you go back to your table, but you discover that the woman who you were sitting across from and talking to about Proust is apparently sitting at two different tables and, with a few drinks in you, you aren't sure which table you belong at. There's a vacant chair at both of them and one of them is for someone who doesn't exist. A drunk comes over to you, puts his arm around you, and says, 'I'm so glad to finally meet you.' Five minutes later that same drunk comes back and, once again, putting his arm around you, says 'I'm so glad to finally meet you' and then proceeds to throw up on your shoes.

Just then Mr. Ivan and Mr. Evan—dancing with each other—waltz over to you. They look at your shoes and say, 'Oh, Dunc... *Ewww!*' Later, you're dancing with a woman who's wearing a pink corsage. A guy who's wearing a blue bow tie cuts in. Now that you have no partner to hold you upright—feeling a bit woozy—you decide to sit down again. As you try to figure out which table you belong at, you see the woman with the pink corsage dancing with a guy with a purple bow tie who is the twin of the guy wearing the blue bow tie. Next to them, you see a woman with a pink corsage—this one is *not* the twin of the other woman, she's a completely different woman who happens to be wearing an identical pink corsage. She's dancing with a guy with a blue bow tie, probably the guy who cut in earlier. The two of them stop dancing and come over to you and say 'We're so glad to finally meet you' establishing that they must be a different pair from the earlier pair. While you are being waylaid by these two, you see both women who look like the one who you were sitting across from—the Proust lady. They are now dancing with another pair of twins, and it occurs to you that you won't be able to find your table until both of the Proust sisters sit down again. That won't answer the question of which one you belong across from, but it's a move in the right direction. You go over to one of them and cut in. While you are dancing with her she says 'I'm so glad to finally meet you' and you realize that she's either drunk or not the one you were discussing Proust with at the table. You look around the room in a panic to locate her sister, the real Proust lady, but you can't find her anywhere. You do see, however, the guy who was dancing with the now-missing sister a moment earlier, so you steer your partner in his direction, and when you're dancing very close to him, you ask him where his former partner is. He replies, 'I think you're dancing with her, buddy!' The woman he is dancing with—a woman you're certain you've never seen before—says to you, 'I met your charming brother earlier. I felt so bad for him when that horrible drunk threw up on him. What a shame. I guess your brother was so disgusted that he went home, because I haven't seen him for an hour or two.'"

As surreal as all this is, it pales in comparison to the final coup which Auntie and Mummie pulled off during the ceremony. No sooner had my mother been escorted down the aisle on the arm of my grandfather, my father noticed that Auntie was walking down the aisle with Unc-Dunc, directly behind Mummie and Gramps, wearing the identical gown and veil, and carrying the identical bouquet. He went into shock and had to be steadied by his Best Man (the first of the four Bruces) to prevent him from passing out at the altar. Meanwhile, the assembled guests were laughing so hard at this farce, they were practically falling off their chairs. A brief scuffle ensued, there was a flurry of white tulle and flower petals, and one of the two brides vanished along with Unc-Dunc in the confusion. A moment later, my Father—or so I have been told—had recovered enough of his composure to say to the woman that he hoped was his intended bride, "Pity you didn't both stay. Then you could have said 'We do.' Now I suppose it's you I'm stuck with, whoever you are."

"Nevertheless," she allegedly replied, "until death do any of us part."

As outlandish as this stunt might seem—and there's no denying it was inconsiderate to upstage my father like this in front of his family—it was, nevertheless, a moving public demonstration of my mother's love for her sister, although, as could be expected, not everyone understood it for what it really was. In essence, what Mummie had actually done was sign over half of her "special day"—her wedding day—to Auntie, so she would not feel left out. It was a touching sacrifice disguised as a prank, and my father found it easy to forgive because any selfishness in the mechanics was a by-product of generosity to my aunt. Unlike most sacrifices, this one was a happy one. Mummie and Auntie, like two school kids, had planned everything together, hired the photographers, the florists, the band members (all sets of twins, of course, sourced from their network). They visited bridal shops and dressmakers, they met with caterers and wedding planners, and they carried the daffy habit of wearing identical costumes to an epic extreme no one else could have dreamt of. They had the time of their lives, and they never realized or cared—not for a moment—how bizarre it seemed to outsiders, most of whom didn't understand what was really going on under the surface silliness. It was front-page news in the one-page newsletter from the Twin Underground. It was discussed everywhere for years, but misinterpreted. So, there was a beautiful facet to the mayhem unleashed at the wedding. If you knew how to hold those raucous, attention-grabbing events up to the light and—turning them this way and that—consider them from the ideal angle, you would inevitably discover the undercurrent of beauty that flowed through my family.

I'd say anything my father touched became beautiful. He spent a great deal of time with me, and just as much with Cousin Niall. He almost always did things with each of us individually, and that opened up the possibility for him to nurture us in different ways—ways best suited to our different characters. He took Niall to baseball games and wrestling matches, and he took me to the theater and the opera. He understood that more nourishment is derived from enthusiasm than education, but he endorsed both and provided them generously. Knowing that I loved Tad's Steakhouse because the big portions made me feel like a grown-up, he took me there once a month, and after that to a barber where we would get our hair cut in adjacent chairs, just like Mummie and Auntie did. When he got his shave, he would pay the barber to put shaving cream on my face, too, and then scrape it off with a popsicle stick, pretending to be careful not to cut me with it. When the barber slapped aftershave on my freshly 'shaven' cheeks, my father would bolt from his chair and shout, "Who said you could slap my son? If you do that again, I'll knock your block off!" We took long walks and we held hands, even when I was a teenager. People stared, but we didn't care.

When I went off to college, my father would occasionally drive up to Ithaca to visit me with one of the Bruces, and we would have wonderful weekends together. He would always ask how my "shrinking" was progressing. When I answered positively, he would lay down on the couch, squeeze his eyes shut, and say, "Do me."

The visits continued for more than a year. At some point, during my sophomore year, my father opened a Travel and Tour Company, and he was often away, leading tours in exotic locales. I saw less and less of him as time passed, but hilarious postcards—hand drawn by him—never stopped coming until his death. My favorite is a sketch of a vile-looking fish and potato dinner he had at a restaurant in Svalbard. He had used a green pen to paint parsley freckles on the boiled potatoes. The boiled fish still had its head attached, with ugly, bulging eyes, a downturned mouth, and tears running down its puffed-up cheeks. He wrote at the bottom: "Having a boil. Wish you were here!" I framed it and hung it in my kitchen.

After his death, Mummie and Auntie sold their agency and moved to adjacent apartments on Fifth Avenue. They've spent the last seven years up there, devoting their energies to becoming more and more peculiar, carrying the identical clothing and accessory motif to an extreme that's unprecedented in the history of fashion. On the one hand, it probably makes it easier to dress when there is only one rule to be followed. On the other hand, the attention required for what items will go on, where they go on, how they go on, what they go with—and so much more besides—is the equivalent of decorating a large house in the time it takes you to drink your morning coffee. When the hats, coats, gloves, scarves, stockings, shoes, handbags, dresses, handkerchiefs, panties, brassieres, girdles, garters, slips, hair, make-up, nail polish (for twenty appendages each), wrist-watches, rings, brooches, bracelets, earrings, hair pins, sunglasses, umbrellas—*pace*, if I have omitted anything important or necessary—are precisely synchronized, then (and only then), can the sisters proceed to exit the building and appear on Fifth Avenue.

One day, when we arranged to meet under their awning, they emerged together, both of them wearing small band-aids just below their left knees. I pointed at the injuries and asked what had happened. The answer was that one of them had fallen down.

Thusly, they present the best they have to offer to the public on a daily basis. Since they do nothing else, it really isn't that difficult—in the same way that playing a Liszt sonata without a single mistake isn't difficult if you've never done anything else with your brain and your hands. Mummie and Auntie have staked out a place in fashion history, and occasionally a few square inches of the social diaries of New York newspapers. They are cited as trend-setters in the Twin Underground, which still exists, despite the fact that twins have utterly lost their glamor in modern times because laboratories can produce them with a fair degree of frequency. In any case, elderly twins, no matter how they package themselves, are just not cute. Ironically, Mummie and Auntie, as they are today, fit more congenially into the category of *eccentrics* than they do into the

category of *twins*. If they were still in business, they probably would not take themselves on as clients. In my head, I can hear them saying, "Now there's a genuine twin-pack of Print-Ad-Poison."

Have you ever seen them? If you shop on Fifth Avenue, where they are indisputably legendary, you *must* have. They habituate Saks Fifth Avenue, shopping there on Mondays, Wednesday, and Fridays, and returning merchandise on Tuesdays, Thursdays, and Saturdays. This significantly reduces their *schlepping* because on any given day, the packages will go in only one direction. For that reason, lunches are scheduled on the "Return Merchandise" days, which leave them hands-free by noon three days every week. I don't believe I've seen either of them on a Wednesday in five years.

Their visits to Saks are appreciated by an enthusiastic public, but I doubt that the store executives are anything but ambivalent about them. While they purchase and keep significant amounts of expensive merchandise, all ongoing business on the main floor—the highly profitable make-up and notions floor—comes to a standstill when they

enter and cross to the elevators. Hundreds of dollars of revenue are lost on their entrances and exits. Every eye turns and every detail—let's call it the "workmanship"—is studied carefully, because it isn't any *one* detail that makes the masterpiece, it's *all* of them together—the sheer multitude of them and their complexity—that illustrate the genius behind the picture. The longer you stare at them, the more absurdly fabulous they seem.

No one knows what lies on the road ahead for such extraordinary people, only that Death will decide when a fork in that road will divide it. For now, they are happy and creative and possess the thing that keeps old people young: the ability to foresee the days ahead in a positive light. They'll always have something to keep them busy when their alarm clocks sing a morning duet, and each of the ladies knocks on the adjoining bedroom wall to signify that all is well on both sides of it.

Today is Wednesday, a shopping at Saks day for them. I'm sure they have dressed themselves identically and perfectly. If there is a God (to coin their phrase) they are now—and will always be—shrinking in height at exactly the same rate.

M rs. Bathbaum was beside herself with excitement. "Oh, my God," she said, "I've seen those ladies a *hundred* times, perhaps even more than that. *Everyone* has. I think I spoke to one of them once, many years ago. I asked her advice about the color of a dress I was trying on. I can't believe that those women are actually your mother."

Hearing that verbal mishap, the others burst into laughter. Mrs. Bathbaum joined in and then wiped tears from her eyes. "It's good to know I can cry about something amusing, too."

Scotch said, "You know, Professor, you're the only one here who *hasn't* met them. I'm of the opinion that you're much too busy weaving convoluted folktale tapestries in Norway and investigating Devil Castles in Sayville for your own good. A shopping spree at Saks Fifth Avenue might be just the thing for you. You want stories? Mummie and Auntie have just fallen in your lap like manna from Heaven."

"I must admit," the Professor mused, stroking his chin pensively, "they *do* sound tempting.

MISSED AND MISSING

Missing since February—*possibly dognapped!*—this is our beautiful, beloved Doctor Watson. Have you seen him? Do you have information concerning his whereabouts? Oh, we do hope you have! If so, please contact Mrs. Annabelle Musicaro Polifrone, or Inspector Cosmo Polifrone, at P.O. Box 2492, Pennsylvania Station, N.Y.C.

$1,000 Reward!

The Shrink's Tale

Fibs That Fell from Father's Lips

One afternoon, my father and I ran away from home to Central Park with nickels from my piggy bank. My mother and my aunt were shopping, so it was my father's job to get me "out of her hair" for a few hours. Lucky for me, Daddy didn't have too much hair, and so there was always someone who wanted to hang around with me when my mother went off with her sister.

Daddy and I went to the zoo and we rode on the carousel and we each ate a terrible-for-us hot dog. Then we went to the big fountain, threw my extra nickels into it and made wishes.

By the time we had used up all the nickels, it was late. The sun was going down. The sky was a deep blue and one star had shown itself— a different star than the first one the day before. The stars took turns being first and you had to be fast to catch them because first stars could jump out at you anywhere. Sometimes two stars would be first, like twins, but not very often.

Nobody could pick out the star that came out last, though. Not even Daddy could do it. He explained that a star could be born in the middle of the night when we were all asleep, and then the star that you thought was the last star to appear wasn't the last one anymore, but no one would ever know it.

He also told me that it was terrible manners to make a wish on the first star that came out right after you made nickel-wishes in the big fountain because that would be greedy and more like nagging than wishing.

We walked north to meet my mother and my aunt near the Museum. On the way, there was when I saw it—a stone castle perched at the top of a little rocky mountain. "Let's go see," I said, tugging Daddy's sleeve. "There are stairs over there."

He glanced at his watch. I could tell he wasn't in the mood for stairs. Even then—at the age of six—I knew he wouldn't just admit it. My mother always said he had a talent for inventing transparent excuses that bordered on genius. I could sense one of those excuses taking shape now but I couldn't figure out the part about them being transparent. How could excuses be transparent if they were only sounds?

Daddy said, "You know, Sammy, that happens to be Dracula's Castle up there, and it's almost dark now. He'll be coming out soon and looking for a nice, young neck—a plump, juicy one like yours—to sink his teeth into. You don't want him to suck your blood, do you?"

His hand swooped to the back of my neck and he pretended to bite it with his fingernails.

"See all the bats on the tower, waiting to fly away? I bet he's one of them. They're going hunting just as soon as it gets a little darker."

"Those are birds," I said, squirming away from the fake vampire bites. If he saw how nervous I was, he would just laugh at me. "There aren't any bats in America. Just pigeons and parakeets. The only bats in America are for baseball."

"Those are bats up there. Those are juicy-neck-biting, blood-sucking bats. Look! See them? There they go! Flying away! Come on, we'd better get away from here!"

"There's a real bat right there," I said, pointing to a man my father hadn't noticed. He was carrying a baseball bat and coming towards us very slowly and quietly. He wore a black coat with an upturned collar and a big black hat pulled so low it hid the upper part of his face. I could barely see the tip of his nose. Without saying anything, he tapped the bat on the pavement and beckoned to my father, who had grown unusually quiet.

"Wait there and don't move," Daddy said, pointing to a bench where I was expected to sit. He went over and whispered with the man with the bat for a few moments. I saw him take his watch off and hand it to the stranger, who then slipped back into the shadows as quietly as he had emerged. It was very dark. All I could hear were crickets and Daddy breathing. I could feel a stinging sensation on the back of my neck where Daddy had *vampired* me.

"Who was that weird man?" I whispered nervously.

Daddy put a finger to his lips. "Shh!" he said. "That was Dracula. Not to worry, though, he's gone now. I don't think he was all that scary anyhow."

"What did he want?"

"To borrow my watch. His is broken, and he has to be sure to get home before the sun comes up. Know why?"

"Everyone knows that," I said, attempting to sound as calm and adult as possible. I stood and took his hand. It was trembling slightly and felt clammy. "Bring me with you when you go to get your watch back. I really want to see the inside of the castle, and now that you two are friends, you can introduce us."

"Okay," he said. "The next time your mother goes shopping, we'll put some garlic in our pockets and we'll climb up to the castle and knock on his door. We can have lunch with him in the dungeon where there's no sunlight. And with his mother, too—Mrs. Dracula. You don't have to worry about getting bitten, either. I told him your neck might be plump and juicy, but it was really filthy because you never wash it."

"I do so!" I protested. "You shouldn't lie to Dracula!"

"And, by the way," he added in the snotty know-it-all voice he used sometimes, "bats are animals, not birds. Only birds are birds. If you don't believe me, look it up."

The next morning, I looked it up. Bats, said the Encyclopedia, were animals, even if they did fly. Daddy had been telling the truth. Except for the part about my neck being dirty.

Hell Station, (Lånke Region, western Norway), platform and station house photographed in the hiatus between train arrivals. Postcards and pay toilets available inside. To the right of the drainpipe, the new loudspeaker, installed in 2015, can be seen.

A Prologue to The Artist's Tale

Mrs. Bathbaum was unstinting in her praise for the warmth and nostalgia that permeated Scotch's father-and-son reminiscence. She was decidedly less enraptured with the contrasting *vampiriana*. "Call me old-fashioned, but vampire stories are far too prevalent nowadays for my sensibilities, springing up everywhere you look, like mushrooms—*poisonous* mushrooms—in books, on television, in films," she said. "Blood sucking? How did that become a desirable American diversion?"

"It's a sociological metaphor for our old friend, Mr. Greed," said the Professor astutely. "He's a major trendsetter, that one."

"I confess I've never been enthusiastic about vampires. This story is the first time I've enjoyed anything connected with them."

"That's because there are no *real* vampires in the story," Ry said. "Just *pretend* vampires."

"Maybe you would enjoy vampires more if you met a real one," the Professor suggested. "Perhaps we can find one on the train."

"Not possibly," Ry said. "It's daylight."

"In a coffin, then...? In the baggage compartment...?"

"I think we'd have more success finding a zombie on the train. The conductor told us earlier that the modernized carriage is where they herd all the 'cellphone zombies'—his exact words, as I recall."

"We can stop by and eavesdrop on the way back from lunch," the Professor said enthusiastically. "Loads of good material in there, I'd wager, and there's a cellphone game I can teach you. But, for the moment, I'd like to praise your contribution, Mr. Samuel 'Scotch' Diamond. Your story was precisely what we needed after all those ripped-to-ribbons rabbits and chickens, taxidermied dogs, poisoned and blinded foxes, rotting fox cub cadavers, equestrian fatalities, gunshots, explosions, bombings, and backfiring automobiles. I ask you, what in God's name is this world coming to?"

"I have no idea, Prof, but that's *your* story you're deriding," Scotch said incredulously. "It was *you* who came up with all that."

"Was it? I don't know what I could have been thinking. Perhaps I grew a bit overzealous in my presentation, or maybe I fell victim to a passing episode of fable-frenzy."

Mrs. Bathbaum rattled her shoebox gently to get her companions' attention. Tiny bones and other small, unconsumed remnants of her son mixed in with his ashes whispered softly through the cardboard walls of his makeshift repository. "I hope we can soon move on from the Undead," she said. "Dying young is a misfortune, but living forever is no blessing, either. Maybe I can strike a bargain with the Devil for something suitable between those extremes."

"An interesting idea," the Professor said, while rummaging in the depths of his carpetbag. "*Where in hell did I put that bloody pen?*" he mumbled. Soda, overhearing this, offered a marbleized Waterman. The Professor took it and scribbled energetically in a notebook, muttering as he did so, "*...vindaloo sauce, jalapeños, paprika ...*"

"Anyway," Mrs. Bathbaum continued, "after listening to that engaging story, I feel as though now I know your father, too. I've already met you—*obviously*—and your mother, and your aunt. If I meet your cousin, I'll 'know' most of your family."

"You *can* meet him. This afternoon, in fact. He's today's Featured

Chef in the dining car. That's why we're on this train today. Niall wanted all of us to be here for his gastronomical railroad debut. He has a catering business with Ry, who's a florist, and Soda designs some of their event programs and invitations. We're all interconnected—like a cluster of symptoms."

"So, we can look forward to stories about palettes, purées, and petunias," said the Professor, clapping his hands together. He eyed the shoebox again. "And who knows what else."

"Perhaps I should warn you," Scotch said to the Professor. "When, and if, you meet my cousin, do not—under any circumstances—make jokes about Mexican food, or Mexican *anything*. Better still, don't use the *M*-word at all. *Please.*"

"How about the *S*-word? Can I get clearance for that?"

"What's it used for? Not *shit*, I hope!"

"*S* means it's *story* time!" the Professor announced cheerfully. He pointed directly at the center of Soda's forehead, almost touching it. "Okay, Mr. Artist-in-Residence, I appoint you to be next to bask in our storytelling spotlight. Paint us a fable, if you please."

"I'm anxious," Soda responded, "to get it over with."

One of the more interesting assignments I've received in my years as a graphic artist was to design a brochure for "The Hunt of the Unicorn," a series of seven tapestries that hang in The Cloisters, a museum in Upper Manhattan that houses the Metropolitan Museum's medieval collection. The published brochure I designed was unremarkable, actually, but the tapestries are something else entirely. They're speaking to me now.

Unicorns are the most interesting non-existent things in existence. I confess to a thorough fascination with them, and I'm far from alone in that devotion. People would pay or do nearly anything for the chance to see a living, breathing unicorn. Find one, put it in a zoo, and the queue to see it would stretch to the moon and back again. Which begs the question: should a unicorn, if we were lucky enough to find one, be subjected to mankind's cruel whimsicalities?

Our species is as unprepared for the discovery of a unicorn, as it is for a productive encounter with intergalactic aliens. Based on our less-than-stellar reputation for diplomacy in delicate species-to-species affairs (take whales and elephants as examples), consider the range of our possible responses if a unicorn, innocently chewing its cud, wandered out of a cornfield on a hot summer day.

For starters, we would be likely to chase it, capture it, display it, measure it, poke and prod it, dissect it, clone it, cross-breed it, ride it, attempt to arouse it, collect its blood, its DNA, its sperm, its urine, its saliva, its tears. We could frighten it to see how fast it could run. We could measure how far it can see, hear, and smell, how much noise, heat, and cold it can tolerate, or how much food and water it can consume, or how much gas it passes in a day. While Christians could convene a High Conclave to determine whether a unicorn is holy or heathen in nature, Jews could argue until they are hoarse about whether it's *kosher* or *trayf*. We could feature it in a documentary about all the clever things we did to it. We could classify it as a top-secret discovery, hide it in a Quonset hangar in Arizona, or lock it in an underground bunker in Nevada, allowing only authorized officials with top-level clearance to have access to it, and, even then, only on a *need-to-gawk* basis. On the other hand, our government could classify a unicorn as a refugee from the effete universe of art and culture, and callously freeze funding to it, in which case—while starving it for understanding—they would feel obliged to make the best use they could of it—more than likely, they would squeeze the animal dry for its last ounce of "fake news."

The unicorn would die of exhaustion. Moments after it fell dead on the ground, someone would surreptitiously head for the hills with its severed horn and sell it on the black market to a Japanese billionaire. The next thing to vanish would be the testicles. Then the teeth. Then the hooves. Strands of hair would be listed on eBay. The penis would go to the eponymous Member Museum in Iceland, and the brain would be *Tupperwared* in ice and shipped to Harvard where they have a substantial pickled brain collection—not as many pickled brains as the Member Museum has pickled penises, and nowhere near as much variety (over a hundred assorted *things* are on exhibit), but, nevertheless, Harvard Medical is the undisputed Smithsonian of Gray Matter, and there are critical gaps in their collection. For example, they don't have a unicorn's brain, they don't have Donald Trump's, and they don't have our Professor's.

The only thing that we *could* do to a unicorn that we would definitely *not* do to a unicorn is leave it alone and allow it to just be a unicorn. That's why we are blessed to have the tapestries instead, which give us a lot to enjoy and relatively little to fuck up.

About those tapestries—they are, undoubtedly, the most highly-prized jewel in mankind's vast treasure-house of unicorn art. The La Rochefoucauld family of France possessed them for centuries, but finally sold them in 1922 to John D. Rockefeller, Jr., for more than a million dollars. He gave them to The Cloisters, where they hung, uneventfully, from 1937 until the 1990s, when—as explained in my brochure—something extraordinary occurred. The captured unicorn—and the woven world surrounding him—came to life.

At the time of this unforeseen occurrence, the room housing the tapestries was scheduled to undergo a major renovation. The tapestries were removed from the walls, rolled up, and sent in secrecy to a "wet room" off-premises. There the delicate tapestries were bathed in water, dried, and turned over. Each of the panels had a linen backing sewn to it that lent support to the panel when it was hanging vertically. The backings were in deplorable condition, so they were scheduled to be replaced. They were carefully removed.

The first surprise came at this point: the restorers were stunned to discover that the reverse sides of the panels, which had barely seen light in centuries, had retained their brilliant original colors. They were an even more breathtaking depiction of the Unicorn's hunt, death, and resurrection than the one that had been viewed by thousands of visitors. Unveiling the verso of the textiles was a resurrection from the vicissitudes of time, a resurrection of a resurrection.

To facilitate photographing both sides of the tapestries, a large scaffold was required. Skilled fine-art photographers spent more than two weeks capturing high-resolution images of the textiles—laid on the floor below them—in three-by-three-foot sections. The plan was to import the data from the Leica camera into a computer and create a full picture of each tapestry from the segments. But that's not what happened. The museum's computers were incapable of crunching this staggering amount of digital data, consisting as it did of at least one-hundred-billion numbers. The size of the data was subsequently reduced, but the images continued to resist all attempts at fusion. The only consistency was that everything was haphazardly off. The data was filed away—on hundreds of discs—and the project was deemed an expensive and disappointing failure.

Enter the Chudnovsky Brothers—David and Gregory—Russian *émigré* mathematicians who describe themselves as "a single mathematician occupying two bodies." They are most well-known for building *It*—a super-computer cobbled together out of Home Depot parts—which filled an expansive living room and required a dozen fans running at full-tilt to prevent a meltdown. Their original goal was to produce the most extensive computation of *pi* known to date, and then to use the data to seek patterns within the numbers. They found nothing useful or edifying. *It* yielded *Bupkis*.

The Chudnovsky Brothers and their mathematical endeavors were virtually unknown to denizens of the art world, but through a series of New York coincidences—people meeting people at dinners, benefits, and the like—the problematic project that was dropped years earlier as hopeless—was unearthed and rebooted in their care.

Initially, the Chudnovskys failed, just as their predecessors had failed. The difference this time around was that they could explain *why* they failed. One brother raised an index finger upward, making the universal symbol for "Idea!" The other brother pointed his index finger downward, at the panels. "They," he announced, "are moving."

Without their linen backings to restrain them, and without gravity steering them in a single direction, the yarn in the panels had regained its freedom—the images had started to both stretch and contract. The wool, the silk, and the gilt yarns, each changed at different speeds and in different degrees. Constant variances of temperature and humidity affected the speed and degree of the multiple processes in play. Complicating things further, the yarns were responding to the changes they perceived in adjacent yarns. The panels were writhing, breathing, and shape-shifting below the scaffolding. Between every click of the Leica's shutter, the sections being photographed had changed two-dimensionally, three-dimensionally—and factoring in time—four-dimensionally. The art people and the math people were witnessing a nano-conversation in cloth. Another resurrection—a *third* resurrection—was in progress at their feet.

The digital numbers for the three-by-three-foot photos were so large that no significant detail of this unexpected event went undocumented by the Leica. With the Chudnovskys at the helm, massive recalculations on a gargantuan computer were made. The one-hundred-billion numbers that needed to be crunched initially, had exponentially increased many times over due to the recalculations required to marry the sections. In time, through the dedication of the intrepid brothers, the three-by-three fragments of the panels came together. In the final images, everything joined seamlessly. By this time, the panels had already been furnished with new backings and re-hung at The Cloisters. The Unicorn had gone back to sleep.

Now, I think, would be a good time to entertain you with a humorous trifle—as charming a piece of unicorn folk art as you will ever come to hear. First, though—before I fulfill my storytelling obligations—the following public service announcements are in order:

First, to *my dear friend, Scotch*: Please consider a lesson worth learning from those *It*-building, *pi*-hunting, number-worshipping Chudnovsky Brothers. On occasion, a single mind housed in two bodies can produce something miraculous. Your mother and your aunt produced you, and that proves it.

To *the disembodied gentleman in the shoebox, I offer my humble elegy:* I've described for present company—and for you—how a unicorn was freed from the linen bindings that constrained it for the better part of its lifetime. Death has arranged a similar reprieve for you, Box Man. Now is the time—*your* time—to wiggle your toes, shake your fanny, stick out your tongue, and thumb your nose at us, the living. Your chains lay at your feet. Take advantage of the darkness provided by your flimsy container, your private compartment within a train carriage, where no one can see you or judge you. Only mathematicians, armed with super-computers, cigarettes, and coffee, can detect that you are moving at all. The resurrected unicorn spends today and all his tomorrows in a vale of woven flowers. You'll spend tonight and eternity tossed from wave to wave by an ocean woven of dreams and legends—three-by-three-sized stories, tales told by fishermen and sailors, by exiles and explorers, by dolphins and mermaids, by those who swam and those who sank—and now you will be a story among many in that restless, rolling book. Someone who loves you—and the *Paumanok Express*—are taking you there now.

And *to the ghost of Walt Whitman—since I'm already conversing with ghosts, why not include you, too, old fellow?*: I am ashamed to admit it, but, until this morning, I had no idea you existed. Accept my apology. I will fix that. At my local bookshop. Soon.

Last—*but not least—to our Norwegian Professor:* Please dispense with that revolting, blackened apple core. Its time has come and gone, gone, gone. You've been gesticulating with it for quite long enough, and it's wreaking havoc with my appetite.

The Artist's Tale

The Baker, the Maiden, and the Unicorn

Unicorns might never have been photographed, nor displayed in captivity, nor domesticated, nor served for dinner, but the *idea* of a unicorn is centuries old and shows no sign of fading from our consciousness any time soon. One might say, if a thing is nothing more than an idea or a concept which inspires man to create works of art—some of them particularly magnificent art, at that—it exists. Therefore, unicorns are real whether you see one in your garden or not.

Unicorns possess many qualities that guarantee them prolonged shelf-life in the library of human imagination; examine those qualifications and you will find the requisite affiliations with virgins (which is why unicorns only come in the male variety), with Jesus (which is why unicorns only come in white), with the ability to cure grievous wounds, reverse the effects of poisons, and return the dead to the realm of the living (which is why you can never find a unicorn when you need one). The unicorn is the Jack-of-All-Trades in the bestiary of the impossible.

To help clarify what the unicorn is, here is a summing-up of what it is not: it is never the Jill-of-All-Trades, it never gets its hooves dirty, and never performs the tricks you taught it when you are hoping to impress your friends. Not existing is one of the unicorn's greatest charms, although it has frustrated mankind for centuries.

A long time ago, in 18th Century Poland, a hardworking baker came up with the inspired idea to use a unicorn to pull his bagel cart through the streets of Krakow. He thought the unicorn's horn would be ideally suited for stacking and dispensing fresh bagels, and the use of the elusive animal a marvelous publicity stunt, sure to get a lot of attention.

First, despite his wife's protestations, he employed his daughter's virginity as a means to lure and ensnare the local unicorn. While the unicorn snored noisily with its head on his daughter's lap, the baker tied one end of a rope around its hairy neck and the other to a leg of the bakery oven. Then, with the greatest amount of difficulty, and the help of five cabbage-kicking farmers from the outskirts of town, he finally succeeded in hitching the irritable animal—bucking and braying and kicking feces everywhere—to his cart. He sold his horse to pay the farmers for their help with the difficult beast.

Unfortunately, the idea—which seemed so promising to begin with—proved to be a terrible one with unexpected consequences. The unicorn developed an overwhelming craving for bagels even stronger than its craving for virgins. Eventually, the unicorn was consuming more bagels than he was delivering and was getting too fat and lethargic to make his rounds before the bagels that remained got so stale no one would buy them. He also became excessively flatulent, which was another deterrent to sales. The baker could no longer ride in the cart without gagging and found himself walking all day long far in front of the unicorn, wearing himself (and his shoes) out. The worst part of all was the pitiful cries of the hungry animal beginning early every morning, as soon as it smelled the fresh bagels baking. The Krakow Police had been summoned numerous times by enraged neighbors.

Eventually, the baker had no choice but to put the miserable animal down and sell its horn to the local priest for a few measly *zlotys*. On the brighter side, the priest was willing, for a small contribution, to restore the virginity of the baker's daughter with a few hand gestures and some Latin mumbo-jumbo, so the baker did not feel quite so badly about his unfortunate experience.

"I usually do this only once," the priest muttered at the ceremony where he performed the annulment of the daughter's deflowering. It was from this offhand remark that the baker eventually learned that his wife had already paid the priest to restore their daughter's fleeting virginity on three previous occasions.

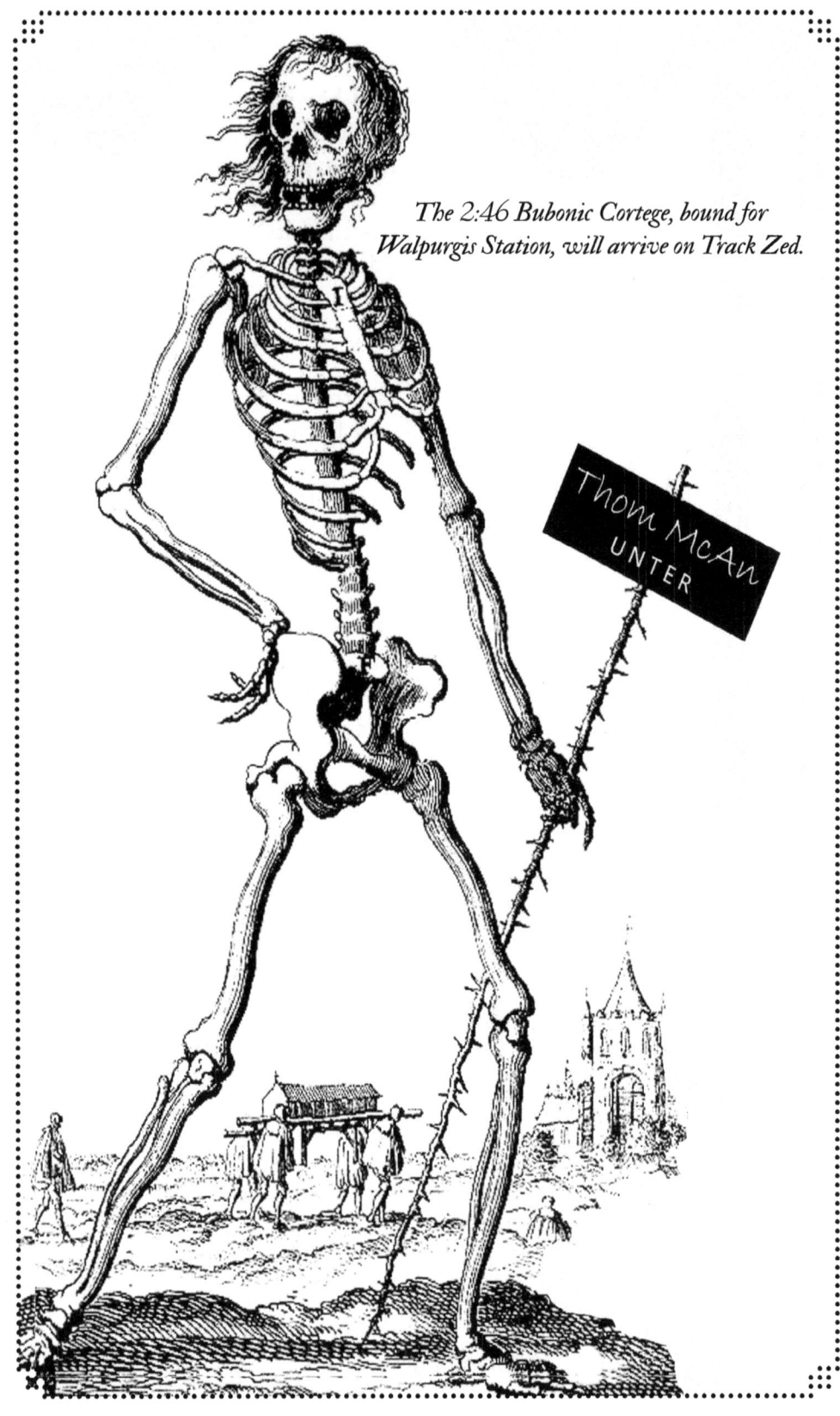

The 2:46 Bubonic Cortege, bound for Walpurgis Station, will arrive on Track Zed.

A Prologue to The Wife of Bathbaum's Tale

"As only a true artist could tell it," Ry said admiringly. "Not a wasted stroke of your brush, and you also managed an impressive elegy for the fellow in the shoebox—a gentleman we only know as 'Thom McAn.'"

"My son's name really is—*was*—Thom," Mrs. Bathbaum said, gesturing towards the shoebox as though it was the grand prize on a game show. "He was Thom Fulton, from my first marriage, to the architect Thomas Fulton the Third, who everyone called *Tre*." She patted the box proudly. "Our son, Thom, was Thomas Fulton the Fourth."

"And the last," the Professor pointed out, rather unhelpfully.

"It's a family naming convention, not a countdown," Ry said, giving the Professor a light kick.

"Count-*up*," the Professor corrected him. "The numbers were going *up*."

"What numbers? Up what?"

"Not down."

"Did your son have a numerical nickname, too?" Soda asked, doing his best to distract Mrs. Bathbaum from the ridiculous argument taking place in their midst.

"Oh, yes, and such a cute one, too. We called him *Tre Deux*—Tre the Second—but that eventually morphed into *Très Doux*, which means *Very Sweet*. Naturally, we couldn't call him that when he got older—it seemed too diminutive for a Princeton boy—but by then the first Tre, my husband, had died, and Thom became just Tre."

"If you don't mind my asking, how many times have you married?"

"By my last count, three," she said. She smiled wickedly and added, "I know you're probably thinking, 'That's a lot of shoeboxes!' but the truth is, I never got any of that marriage stuff right, and I never got any of it terribly wrong, either. It was always just satisfying enough to get me back on the merry-go-round, still willing to reach for one more gold ring. And reach for it I did. Successfully, too, I might add. My full name is Asta Louise Honnen Fulton Naughton Bathbaum— quite a mouthful isn't it? I have to pause before I say it or write it down, just to sort it all out correctly. We've all heard that a moment before death, one sees their whole life flash before their eyes. It's like that when I recite my full name. The inside of my head is like the view from this train window—an onrushing blur pretending to be scenery. I can barely remember most of it. My life unfolds inside me as if it was a photo album. All the spaces between the snapshots are blank, big empty spaces I can get lost in. Sometimes, I tell myself 'Gerald Naughton was the one in the middle,' just to keep Fulton separat-ed from Bathbaum. The one constant, the love of my life, the apple of my eye, was my *Très Doux*." She gently shook the shoebox and brought it closer to her ear, as if listening for a response. "I'm sending you out into the world for a second time today," she said, addressing the box of ashes. "Pretend you're in a taxi and tell the driver where you want to go. You won't have to pay the fare. You've paid all you're going to pay in this world—the rest is going to be free. The wind and the waves will take you wherever you want to go, and these Cordial or Nightcap or Whatever-Drink-They-Call-Themselves fellows will look after me, so don't worry about anything." She put the box back on her lap, and re-focused on Soda. "You were saying?"

"Mr. Bathbaum has also gone on to his 'Great Reward?'"

"Actually, he hasn't. That's not to say he's not dead. He most definitely is dead, as dead as a dead husband can be, and when it's a divorced husband who's dead, that's very, very, very dead. But, as respects that ironic terminology, '*Great Reward*'—how shall I put this?—let's just say my marriage and divorce were unintentionally lucrative for me and the investment department at Chase Manhattan. It's probable that Harold Bathbaum crossed the River Jordan with a bag of peanuts in one hand, a pencil cup in the other, and his pockets pulled inside-out."

"That leaves you all alone for now, except for occasional flotsam and jetsam floating by, like us lot. How do you feel about a return visit to the merry-go-round?"

"Certainly not for money, which I don't need. And not because I'm bored or lonely. I could run away and join the circus and no one would stop me. But, marriage is still an option that isn't as tarnished in my mind as perhaps it ought to be. A fourth husband would have to offer something the first three didn't, so that simplifies things a bit. My mother always said that if you don't know *what* you want, you need to know—at the very least—what you *don't* want. If not one or the other, all is lost. I know, absolutely, I don't want more Fulton, or more Naughton, or more Bathbaum. Maybe a Mormon, or just a regular albino, would do. Or perhaps a younger man, a well-spoken, presentable foreigner with an interesting mind."

The Professor was still holding his notebook and Soda's fountain pen. He turned the notebook around to show her that he had inscribed *Mrs. Asta Bathbaum, a Lady in Black* on a blank page and drawn a series of bullet points below it, like a row of vacant parking spaces. "Shall I help you make a list of your requirements?" he asked provocatively. "Or—if you prefer—you can write them here yourself." He held the notebook and pen out to her.

"I think I have other, more important, business to attend to today," she responded as politely as she could. "I have no idea how to scatter ashes, and here I am with this box on my hands and funeral rites ahead of me." She took a deep breath and shook her head. "This really is too much for me. I sent a suit and a pair of shoes to the mortuary to use for Thom's viewing. After the cremation, the mortician came to me and handed me this box. He explained that since I wasn't buying an urn, they put the cremains in the empty shoebox and taped it up. I suppose I looked a little surprised because I hadn't expected this. He said, rather defensively I thought, 'My dear Mrs. Bathbaum, without the purchase of an urn, which is optional—although it is *customary*—it was either put Mr. Fulton's remains in his shoebox or his garment bag,' and then I said to him, 'My dear Mr. Sorry-For-Your-Loss, you can't reasonably expect me to purchase an urn when I'm scattering the ashes, not keeping them, can you? Or do you want to refund me for recycling the urn afterward, like supermarkets do with empty cans of Mountain Dew?' He had a look on his face that seemed to say, 'Why didn't I think of that first?' and he just walked away, leaving me with *this*. So, here I am—and what a deplorable sight!—with this chintzy box on my lap. I suppose if it really *was* an urn I would look like Morticia Addams heading to a shindig at Forever Dead Cemetery, but *really*—oh, Lord, I hope he can't hear me in there—this is like a cardboard handbag for a homeless woman."

"Let me take it—him—for a while," Ry said, assuming responsibility for the box. Once he touched it, though, he found himself meditating on the possibility that the man inside it had taken a bullet that could have been meant for him. Or *any* Nightcap. He felt a little queasy.

Mrs. Bathbaum, meanwhile, made an attempt at tension-reducing humor. "It's very hard to find cardboard shoes to match a handbag of this caliber. There's such a meager selection of styles and colors to choose from, and nothing but flats. No heels being offered at all."

"I have a very strong feeling," Ry said, "that you will come out on the other side of this rather well. Like I said before, we'll be honored if you allow us to help you through the scattering."

"What exactly does one do?" she asked. "I have no idea. We can't simply dump the ashes in the water. I don't think Thom would appreciate that much. It just wouldn't be *Thom*, even though it would actually *be* Thom, if you know what I mean."

Ry said, "Get that image out of your head, Lady Asta. No one *dumps* ashes like that. I don't claim to be an expert, but this is not the first shoebox ceremony I've been to by any stretch. There are two competing methods used at these disbursements. There's the *Salt Shaker Method* and the vastly different *Lamaze Method.* In the first, you cut a corner off the bottom of the container." He gestured with his finger. The ashes whispered as he tilted the box. "Then you shake the ashes out as you would if you were salting a plate of fried potatoes. You can do the sprinkling as ceremoniously and theatrically as you like. I've seen people spin like dervishes and release the ashes in the air around them in a zigzagging circular pattern. It's a very interesting send-off to witness, especially if it's done with live music and you don't stand too close to the dervish. The downside to this method is that you're left with the box on your hands at the end. It's awkward and unpleasant. What does one do with it afterward? You can't put another pair of shoes in it and throwing it out would only leave you feeling guilty."

Mrs. Bathbaum didn't find the prospect of any of this appealing in the least. "How about the *other* method, the *Lamaze?*" she asked, hoping for a more agreeable option. "Isn't that the name of a method for natural childbirth?"

"It takes its name from that, yes. In this context, though, it's a method for natural ash disbursement. One can enter the world with the original birthing *Lamaze* and leave it with the scattering *Lamaze,* a nice symmetry for those who take comfort from rhyming their rites of passage. In the *Lamaze Method,* you have to put the box on the ground; in your son's case, that would be on the sand. You loosen the cover and then you slit the box vertically in each of the four corners so that when you lift the cover off, the sides will fall down and the entire box will lay flat. The *Lamaze Method* then allows the ashes to drift away *au naturel* on the gentle breath of the still-living world. The box is already on the ground, so you don't have to worry about complications stemming from littering after-the-fact. The empty container flies off to the great beyond along with the remains—extremely convenient, I'd say. There is a third method—now that I think about it—which only applies to oceanic disbursement. That's the *Mosaic Method*, named after Moses, who you know from all those awful plagues and commandments and the Red Sea. This requires you to set the ashes adrift in a cardboard boat. A shoebox will stand in quite well for the boat. Very basic. Not clean though. No, I am not a fan. How about you Scotch? Sode, what do you think? And you, Prof?"

"Definitely not," Scotch said firmly.

Soda agreed. "Too risky. The marine underwriters at Lloyds of London would not approve."

The Professor shrugged.

"What's your recommendation?" she asked, addressing no one in particular.

Soda said, "As an artist, I think visually, and I rarely give serious consideration to what is or isn't practical. I see the *Lamaze Method* working quite poetically and memorably on the beach—a beautiful, windswept send-off, with the background sounds of the sea and spray and gulls. But, since you ask for a recommendation, I would like to see you take it just a little further. I suggest a hybridization of both principal methods—the *Salt Shaker* corner clipping to start with—then spell out the name *Thom* on the sand with the sprinkled ashes—lastly, let the *Lamaze Method* do the rest."

"Brilliant," Scotch said. "Sode, you've surpassed yourself."

Ry, ever the practical Nightcap, said, "What about the box?"

Scotch dismissed that with a wave of his hand. "A minor wrinkle. We'll give it to the Professor to bring back to Norway as a souvenir of American funereal folk art."

Mrs. Bathbaum was extremely pleased. "I wouldn't mind being sent on my journey exactly like that when my time comes. It might be a bit of a challenge to spell out *Asta Louise Honnen Fulton Naughton Bathbaum* in ashes. There would have to be a lot of remains in the box to get the job done. And I would insist on a classier box. Ferragamo, or Manolo Blahnik."

"One thing is certain—your name won't get any shorter. The laws of time and physics decree that it can only remain as it is or get longer," said the Professor. "I've been working it out, and, as things stand, your name is fourteen letters short to qualify as a *bona fide* pangram. In that regard, your choice of husbands was poor planning. You'd probably have to marry three more times and be divorced or widowed twice to rack up all the missing letters, including the two toughest ones: Q and X. You'd have to resort to marrying Xavier Quackenzipper to succeed pangramatically. After today's ceremony, I suggest you waste no time and get back on the merry-go-round. As they say, *Tempus fugit.*"

He put his notebook back in his carpetbag and almost tossed the fountain pen after it, but Soda managed to snatch it back before it was too late. Mrs. Bathbaum eyed the beat-up carpetbag. The expression on her face was oddly similar to the one the Professor had worn earlier when he had been staring with equal intensity at the shoebox.

"Before I try my hand at storytelling," Mrs. Bathbaum said, "I want to clarify one thing. There's been a lot of talk about my previous marriages, so—for the record—in case there is any question in your minds, I didn't kill *any* of my husbands. Thomas Fulton the Third choked to death on a corn muffin. I didn't bludgeon Gerald Naughton with a candlestick in the library. Someone else did. And, while I didn't kill Harry Bathbaum in cold blood, I freely admit that I did—as divorce lawyers are wont to say—skin the bastard alive. Three years later, skinless, and stewing in his own bilious juices, he gave up the ghost. How is that my fault?"

NOSTRADAMUS
Michel de Nostredame (1503 – 1566)
Apothecary ~ Poet ~ Seer ~ Chef

The Wife of Bathbaum's Tale

The Nostradamus Cookbook

For the record—except in the mind of the person who felt compelled to "cook" it up—*The Nostradamus Cookbook* does not exist. Not that it has anything to do with the events that follow, it surprises one to learn that Nostradamus actually *did* write a cookbook which contained his recipes for various jams (and cosmetics), which is called *Traité des fardemens et confitures*. Considering that he was a wandering apothecary, among many other things (they say necromancer and astrologer, too)—which in the early 16th-century was as good as being an alchemist, but without the notoriety or the threat of being immolated by the Inquisition for heresy—to concoct recipes for *la confiture des guignes* seems a rather timid use of talent for the man who accurately predicted the French Revolution, the rises of Napoleon and Adolf Hitler, both world wars, and the atomic bombs that fell on Hiroshima and Nagasaki. One must note, parenthetically, that Nostradamus rarely predicts anything Ozzie and Harriet would wish to find in their Christmas stockings or would enjoy reading about in the Sunday newspaper. For example, the development of the polio vaccine and mankind's first steps on the moon are exactly the sort of things that fly under his cosmic radar with regularity. For Nostradamus, happiness was clearly a pimple-free face and a teaspoon of his homemade jam on buttered toast; all else was noise and *Sturm und Drang*.

How Mildred Bathbaum ever came up with the idea of *The Nostradamus Cookbook* is anybody's guess, but the need for such an essential reference book is easy to explain. In her late seventies, and frail, Mildred feared icy sidewalks more than the fires of Hell. If the weatherman predicted bad weather (there's the *iffy* Nostradamus connection), bad enough to keep her trapped in her walk-up apartment, unable to get groceries, she would have to make do (and here's where the Cookbook gets its foot in the door) with whatever scraps of this and that she could find in her kitchen. To complete the picture, there was Mildred's ne'er-do-well, lazy, *nudnik* son, Morris.

"Ma, where's dinner? I'm starving in here," his voice would waft out of the living room, where he was still growing, at the age of 53, bathing himself in the blue, radioactive television rays, like a potted plant from another galaxy. Add Maury and you have—or certainly *need*—*The Nostradamus Cookbook,* and its principal Page One recipe—the reason the book was conjured from wishful thinking to begin with—a recipe entitled "How Do I Shut Him Up?" Behind that sentiment lurked a stronger, more maternal instinct which was totally predictable. She just wanted Maury to be happy. Who can blame a mother for that? Allow me to be clear: my sister-in-law, Mildred Bathbaum, was an innocent, loving mother. If she created a lazy, fat monster, it was an unintentional artifact borne of a maternal love that had run amok.

"Ma, make me an egg cream. I could really go for an egg cream," his voice floated from inside the radioactive television cloud, accompanied by the sound of *The Honeymooners* theme song and the announcer intoning (with Maury moving his lips like a ventriloquist) "...with the stars Art Carney, Audrey Meadows...and Joyce Randolph..." Then she heard him say the same thing he said every weeknight at exactly ten seconds past 11 p.m.: "Joyce Randolph? Some star! Oh brother! Boy oh boy! Ha ha ha ha ha! I'm glad someone told me. I had no idea. Ma, I could really go for an egg cream!"

His words—"go for an egg cream"—were, simultaneously, a figure of speech and a figment of his imagination. Maury wasn't *going* anywhere. Maury did not *go* to the egg cream. Someone would have to bring the egg cream to Maury. Mohammed had more patience waiting for his followers to bring him "the mountain" than Maury did waiting for Mildred to bring him "an egg cream." Admittedly, a mountain is much bigger than a drinking glass—mountain-moving has some fearsome logistics to be dealt with by the movers—but there are millions of Moslems to *schlep* for Mohammed, and only one Mildred Bathbaum to cater for Maury.

An egg cream? How was that supposed to happen? There was no seltzer, there was no chocolate syrup, there was no milk—so, there would be no egg cream. Period. Maury had seen to that. Mildred had implored him over and over again to make a trip to the grocery. "After my show," he said. Too bad his show—followed by four more mandatory shows—ended after midnight with the Star-Spangled Banner and the buzzing blue dot in the middle of the TV screen, when the grocer already had his iron gate down for two hours. Then the snow. The snow. The snow. Then more snow. Quick, Millie, get *The Nostradamus Cookbook* off the dusty *Maury-Wants-Something* shelf in your brain. Maybe you can make an egg cream out of wallpaper paste and left-over brisket gravy, and then you can blow bubbles into it with a straw.

"Maury, we're out of toilet paper."

"It's snowing, Ma."

"Am I blind? I can see the snow. It's up to my bellybutton. We still have no toilet paper."

"Use a paper towel," he shouted from the living room.

"We're out," she shouted from the kitchen.

"We probably have coffee filters. Take a look."

"We're out of those."

"Okay, when my show is over, I'll dig up some hanger shrouds and shoebox tissues."

"Why don't you tear some pages out of your diary—you know, the secret book you have where you record all the marvelous things you do to help me. There should be at least one page because five years ago you took down the garbage."

"After my show," he shouted explosively. "I'm watching here." A metallic banging sound was heard. "What's that racket? I'm watching."

"Mrs. Shrebnic is banging on the radiator pipe with one of her pots because you're screaming."

"She can go to Hell and give my regards down there to Mr. Shrebnic."

"There's too much snow for her to go anywhere—even to go visiting in Hell she would need a snowmobile."

"Shall I go downstairs and give her a piece of my mind?"

"No, Maury. Go apologize, and maybe she'll make you an egg cream."

"Quiet, quiet, Ma," he said urgently. *"Shush! Shush!* The good part is coming now. Joyce Randolph is going to do her star turn. She's going to put her hands on her hips and roll her eyes. Oh, boy, her mother must be *kvelling*! I hope her husband is watching. God forbid he should miss this. Ha ha ha ha ha!" He abruptly stopped laughing. "What now? Again with the banging? If she bangs that pipe one more time, you have my permission to go downstairs and tell that midget to go screw herself."

Mildred sat down at the kitchen table and put her hands on her forehead. *I'm not going anywhere,* she thought. *I have an egg cream to make, and it's going to take the rest of my life to figure out how the hell I am going to do it.*

After ten minutes of contemplating her options, Mildred came to the conclusion that she couldn't just sit idly by while the egg cream issue remained unresolved. This was a weather emergency, the fulfillment of a predicted Nostradamic disaster, like the birth of Hitler, requiring her to resort to an imaginary cookbook for a solution. *Oh great Nostradamus,* she thought, *if you know so much about jam, show me the way to get out of the one I'm stuck in.*

She put her coat on over her housedress and wrapped a scarf around her neck. She pulled a knitted cap over her rollers and slung the strap of her pocketbook over the crook of her elbow.

"Shrebnic, it's Millie Bathbaum," she said, after surreptitiously tiptoeing down one flight of stairs and knocking. Mrs. Shrebnic opened her door. She was four-and-a-half-feet tall and ninety years old. Maury called her the Incredible Shrinking Refugee and the Polish Kosher Shrimp when he wasn't calling her worse things.

"*Nu?*" the old lady said, looking up at Mildred, her arms folded over her chest. "What's up with you, Bathbaum? Nothing is wrong, God forbid, that you should come out of nowhere to knock on a door that my own daughter hasn't walked through in six months."

"Shrebnic, dear, I just came from the lobby," she lied. "It's terrible outside. A person could get killed just looking out the door."

"Who's going anywhere? Are you crazy? What are you dressed up for? A broken hip?"

"I wish I was coming here to ask *you* if you needed anything, but— I'm sorry to say—it's *me* that needs something for my Morris."

"What's wrong with that *bumitshkeh* that he can't do a little shopping for his mother? And the shouting? Is he crazy or what?"

"I'm so sorry, Shrebnic. He has a terrible cold and can't go out in this weather. And his ears, so stuffed up! He can't hear, so he doesn't know how loud he's talking. You know what it's like, you're a mother, too. He's like a baby when he's not well."

Nostradamus says you can make this at home!

"That's some baby you've got on your hands, Bathbaum. I would love to see the diaper you put him in. That must really be a sight. A diaper like that probably has to be sent on a freighter to China, to the birthplace of laundry, for a washing by experts."

Mildred expected this. The salt being poured on her wounds was part of Nostradamus' recipe—it clearly said: *Add salt as needed*. She bit her tongue and plunged ahead.

"So maybe you have some seltzer, or some chocolate syrup...?"

"That sounds like it would be excellent medicine for a cold and *ge-buttled* ears! Just what the doctor ordered. But, you're out of luck. I don't have a supply of soda fountain ingredients here. As you can see, if you look over my shoulder, I live in an apartment, not Schraffts. Would you like a tea bag and some lemon? or a couple of aspirin? or something else that's good for a cold in a *normal* person? You know, Mildred, I would help you if I could. I'm not a rich woman—my Simcha, he should rest in peace, left me *gornisht*—but I'm willing to make a contribution if you want to send Morris on a pilgrimage to Lourdes."

They both heard the sound of Maury laughing at the television upstairs. "Ha ha ha ha ha! This is what I call a star! How did Jackie Gleason ever find her? That's what I want to know. He must have looked far and wide for such a talent."

"Heat the bottle—the baby's up," Shrebnic said stoically.

"Ha ha ha ha ha!" Foot stamping punctuated the distant laugh.

"Maybe you have an extra roll of toilet paper for us?" Millie asked sheepishly.

Behind the closed bathroom door, she started preparing the egg cream. She laid out one bottle and two packages along with a soda glass and a long ice-cream soda spoon. She was in the habit, as a time-saving measure, of opening all the bottles and jars and packages of her ingredients before she began to cook. It actually saved no time at all, but it was an excuse to step back and smoke a cigarette while contemplating the components of the adventure that was about to begin. This time was no exception.

Carefully following the instructions given in the *Nostradamus Cookbook*, she filled the glass with cold water and dropped in two Alka-Seltzer tablets. The water began to fizz immediately. Not wanting the drink to go flat before she had a chance to serve it, she rushed with the rest of the preparation. She quickly crushed two servings (oddly, the packaging referred to them as *doses*, which didn't agree with the language in the cookbook) of chocolate-flavored ExLax with the back of a spoon and threw the resulting brown mush into the fizzing water. Then, the last step: following the instructions carefully, she added some Milk of Magnesia—little by little—to the mixture and then, after that looked right to her eye, she stirred the concoction vigorously with the spoon until it was nice and frothy—just the way Maury liked his egg creams. Knowing Maury, he would drink the whole glass in a single gulp, too fast to even taste it!

Thank God! she thought as she ran with it, still fizzing quite convincingly, to her son in the radioactive TV cloud, *Yes, thank you, God, for the ever-reliable Nostradamus and—in case it might be needed—for Shrebnic's extra roll of toilet paper.*

VICTORY
BAR
AIR CONDITIONED
JACK KING'S
LOAN
535 OFFICE 535
LEGAL RATES ONLY
HOTEL
523 BOYER 523
LOANS
LOANS
OFFICE
UNNEL
CO.

The Tour Guide's Guide

VICTORY BAR AIR CONDITIONED

nly the name VICTORY and the description BAR were lit in neon, and those only when twilight descended on Michigan Avenue, and the atmosphere grew creepy and the creeps lifted their rocks and crawled out from below them, stood upright like Cro-Magnons, and started looking for something to drink. The words *AIR CONDITIONED*, while italicized for emphasis, weren't considered worthy of the extra expense of illumination because there were only about ninety days in a year that were hot enough for potential clientele to give a shit, and there really was no air conditioning on the premises—that was just bullshit, like the boastful conversations that wouldn't ever stop inside. The customers were a bunch of oblivious drunks who only wanted to hang around in a BAR to score a VICTORY over sobriety with a lower-case *s*. They never read as far as the *A* in *AIR CONDITIONED* anyway. Attention usually flagged at the *R* in BAR which is where the neon ended after dark.

Congratulations to anyone who guessed right—the dive was named for victory over the Japanese a few years earlier, so the name of the place commemorated Hiroshima and Nagasaki, too. Atomic bombs, booze—two ways to die, two speeds to die at. VICTORY BAR had the concept of "getting bombed" covered every-which-way it could be done.

Someone left the door open, and why not? As already observed, the air conditioning only exists on the sign. Mr. Victory started telling customers "it's busted" way back when he bought the place and the customers have been swallowing that hooey along with their hooch ever since. Like most places on Detroit's scuzzy Michigan Avenue, VICTORY BAR is what they call "Street Cooled" by a marvelous invention known as a "Door Ajar." Its origins can be traced back to cave dwellers, that's how old it is. God bless Man for his ingenuity. Ingenuity and a few stiff ones will get you through anything on Michigan Avenue. We need a drink, we need it now, and we've only penetrated the photo by a few focus factors. Hey, Bartender, fill'er up! We've got the ingenuity part covered, we just need the booze to chase it. Turn up the Door Ajar. It's hot in here!

The Door Ajar machine in the foreground of the photo—the first object we encounter on this Skid Row excursion—has three narrow windows designed into it. When the door is closed, three very skinny customers *could* stand next to each other and look in (or out) at the same time. The design could also prove useful if a three-eyed alien lands on Earth and gets curious about what on earth Earthlings do inside VICTORY BAR— the door designer has seen to it that there is a window for each of its alien eyes.

Inside, a drunk guy got curious about the three windows. He turned to the foreign drunk guy on the next bar stool. "If you were going to give a three-eyed alien a black eye for being nosy," he asked, "which eye would you hit?"

"Let's see... pro'lly the one in the mittle. That way, when you runs away, if you're not too pickled to runs in a straight line in front of heem—the oogily thing—he won't be able to see you."

"Let me write that down."

"Sure," the foreign drunk says "Didja want me to repeat any of it?"

"Yeah, the whole thing. But wait until I find a pencil."

Nobody in VICTORY BAR has ever been known to look out of those three windows—there wasn't a helluva lot of interest inside about the helluva world outside, other than in things related to baseball, wrestling, or boxing, none of which were happening just outside 545 Michigan Avenue. We *guesstimated* that number because the next building is 535 and the one after is 523, but we were wrong (!), because VICTORY BAR is actually 547—who knows how they came up with that fucking system! You have to be able to add *and* subtract to figure out where the hell you are!

There's a little round sign with a drawing of a bell on it just above the three-windowed open door which denotes that there is a telephone inside. (Update—The phone company actually made money from payphones at one time, so it was worth it for them to print a sign and pay someone to climb up a ladder to hang it. That sign-hanging guy told people who asked, "I climb up a ladder and hang a little round sign that says 'Telephone' outside buildings. A lot, like many times a day." He was proud of it. Now there's no phone company, no sign, no phone, and No Smoking inside the bar. The guy who hung the sign is dead, but his grandson is inside Number 547 getting high in the bathroom that's next to the spot where the phone used to be before VICTORY BAR became Starbucks® Coffee.)

The advertised phone is invariably next to the toilet, which leads one to wonder why anyone might want to make a phone call in a yellow cloud of urine fumes. Why not use a phone booth instead? Well, it so happens that phone booths smell worse because they're also toilets, but with no plumbing. Fact: people have been known to die in phone booths and fail to fall down afterward. That's right—some corpses stood around in phone booths for days as if they were taking shelter from the rain while waiting for a bus. Their deaths were only discovered when someone who desperately needed to use the imaginary bathroom in the phone booth came along and began pounding on the glass. It's a strange image, though—dying in your own see-through coffin with a phone handy in case you had a nickel and were able to call someone to say goodbye and "please don't forget to walk the dog." By the way, did you hear about the guy who was killed in a Michigan Avenue phone booth while taking a leak? A bolt of lightning struck the adjacent utility pole, sending a deadly shock right up his stream and into his johnson. His balls got fried sunny side up *and* sunny side down. Stopped his heart before he had a chance to wash his hands!

till exploring the foreground—which turns out to be a vast expanse in prose, if not in practice—before we get to the shifty-looking guy leaning against the telephone pole, the inquisitive eye pauses to take note of the little dark spot in the photo—bottom center. That's a piece of blackened chewing gum, last chewed by some down-at-the-heels guy in 1932. Most people don't realize that all those black spots on the pavement—the numerous sidewalk-freckles found everywhere—were once pieces of chewing gum living

The road through America is paved with good intentions and expelled chewing gum.

out the brief minutes of their heyday in someone's mouth. Some date back decades—they are history's most ubiquitous street-crime stories. Each freckle represents a case file of two violated statutes: *No Spitting* and *No Littering.* Wouldn't it be great if we could scrape some of them up, carbon-date them, and perform DNA analysis to identify which inconsiderate slobs spit their gum out on a busy public street in the 1930s? There's a line from the intro of a television program that goes "there are eight million stories in the *Naked City*" which makes one wonder how many expectorated blobs of Bazooka-turned-black-spots an eight million-storied city has—maybe one hundred million or more. And the history of it! You could be—without being aware of it—stepping on your great-grandfather's Wrigley's on your way to work every day. America's chewing gum crime wave is the world's largest aggregation of cold cases, a gold mine for the film industry. Those street freckles could provide material for the next great Hollywood *policier.* All that's needed is a catchy title, like *Flatfoot Underfoot,* or *Gumshoe G-Man.* For emotional effect, to yank women in by the heartstrings, the producers could exploit the "poor child" angle. Maybe it's an urban myth, maybe it's not, but it's been said that poor, hungry kids—during the Depression Era—scraped those black spots up and re-chewed them until they were white again. Isn't the biggest crime in America hungry kids?

oving along. It's a mystery why the sign that reads TUNNEL—at the side of the photo (*photo* right, *our* left)—shows an arrow that points at the door of VICTORY BAR. Three skinny people could, theoretically, all go over to the door and look through the three narrow windows together to see if there is a tunnel on the premises or not. A three-eyed alien might look through the three windows with its three eyes and conclude that TUNNEL is a word describing a bunch of drunks that don't look appetizing to eat. For the record, there are no records of complaints about a sign advertising a nonexistent tunnel at VICTORY BAR. Who cares, right?

ext, we come to the shifty-looking gentleman leaning on the telephone pole. Shifty has his hands in his pockets. This is what some people call "playing pocket pool" and others call "playing miniature golf." Shifty looks harmless enough. Maybe he's engaging in a third hand-to-pocket scenario known as "playing it cool, not pool." Or, maybe he's just waiting for the two policemen to get further away before doing something nefarious. We may never know. He's dead. Everyone in the whole fucking photo is dead.

About those policemen—this was before *policemen* were renamed *cops*—here they are, unencumbered by the burden of donuts, walkie-talkies, artillery, helmets, notebooks, flashlights, night-sticks, and who-knows-what-else—the Kings of Paraphernalia. Neither of them is four feet tall. Neither weighs over 300 pounds. They can walk on their own feet, even if they are flat, which they probably aren't, and they don't need a vehicle to keep circling a block or two like carousel ponies. You can approach them and ask them for directions. "Hey, guys," you can inquire of them, "which way is it to the tunnel?"

ext, JACK KING'S LOAN OFFICE at Number 535, where there is a blatant announcement that he charges LEGAL RATES ONLY. We presume, therefore, that the next loan office, BOYER LOANS, either offers *Non*-Legal Rates, or Mr. Boyer believes it is beneath him to announce he does not charge them. In any case, one passes by with the feeling that Mr. King protests a little too much. His sign is rather like Nixon's assertion, made years later: "I am not a crook." Oh, really? You'd tell us if you were, right?

Then, too, there is the matter of the three hanging balls. That's the standard three-ball symbol for a pawnbroker dating back to the Middle Ages. Historically appropriate or not, is it a good idea to incorporate a bunch of dangling balls in your signage, even if one of the balls is correctly hanging lower than the others? There's just something unsettling about an odd number of balls on any level other than a count of one single ball. Isn't that the derivation of the word "oddball?" (*Note to self: look up!*) Big Jack King, as he is known on Skid Row—in an oblique reference to his hard-to-take-it-all-in, family-size buttocks—coincidentally has a son, Paul King, who had survived testicular cancer in his teen years. He's known to everyone on Skid Row as One Ball Paul. People can be *so* cruel. As if One Ball didn't have it tough enough.

Mr. Boyer does not resort to balls in any number, nor does he make a statement about the legality of his rates, but he does host a round "telephone inside" sign outside his door. That payphone enables customers making loans to immediately call their bookies as soon as Boyer doles out their last fiver. By keeping his customers on the payphone in his shop, Mr. Boyer increases the possibility of a second transaction. Customers may need to borrow from him again within the hour when the horse they bet on doesn't come in, which it seldom does. That payphone has earned its moniker: The Boyar Gold Mine.

BOYER LOANS is succeeded by a third (identity obscured in the photograph) LOAN OFFICE. So far, this street provides not much beyond booze and loans and telephones and misleading directions to a missing thing called TUNNEL. We are shortly going to enter the black and white borderlands that exist between the foreground and the middle ground, where things get grainier and grayer, but no less interesting or easy to explain.

At last we stumble upon some relief—we arrive at WHITE STAR HOTEL, which features *one* star on its sign. Don't be misled by *that* sleight of sign painting. This is *not* a "one-star" hotel in any rating book known in the Universe. It's actually a run-down Single-Room-Occupancy residence—but whatever it is, it's a relief to find a place to lie down, because this photograph turns out to be a lot more work to penetrate and explore than it seemed at first glance.

At WHITE STAR HOTEL, the rates are low and the class of clientele lower. The hotel's name, like the star on the sign, is white-lie advertising. There is nothing white at WHITE STAR HOTEL—except for that white lie—nothing even close to white. Not the walls, not the porcelain or the tiles in the shared baths, not the toilet paper, and certainly not the bedsheets. Everything is vaguely tinted with nicotine stains and beer tears. Even the bill they hand you, which you must pay in advance, has a bilious tinge. The name, White Star, is disturbingly reminiscent of the White Star Line, the steamship company that owned the Titanic. An ill-favored name, to say the least.

What about that guy lingering in the doorway at BOYAR LOANS' lending house? What's he up to? Magnification and close examination reveal to the inquiring mind that he is not lingering after all. His left foot is slightly airborne, and he is in the process of departing the premises. It isn't clear whether or not he got his loan, but he must have been pleading his case with Mr. Boyer for quite some time, working up a nervous sweat because he is apparently unseating a wedgie from the back of his pants with his left hand. Get a magnifying glass and check it out.

Pfeiffer Beer burped its last burp in 1966.

Beyond WHITE STAR HOTEL we find ourselves confronted with another triplet of balls and a truck making a delivery right beside them. We checked the logo that appears on the back of the truck, so there's no doubt it's Pfeiffer's Famous Beer, not Pfeiffer's Diaper Service that's double-parked in the middle ground of our dismal adventure. Pfeiffer's illustrious Detroit brewery began to evaporate from history during the early 1960s and their vats had run dry completely by 1966. Lots of Pfeiffer Brewery skeletons dot the landscape of Detroit, but not in this photo. You'd never know, looking at the picture, that anything would go wrong in the world of Pfeiffer Beer. On the other hand—speaking in generalities, looking at the photograph as if it were a novel told in images—which it is—you couldn't imagine anything worse happening than what already happened long before the photographer arrived at the scene. Goodbye, Pfeiffer's—it was nice knowing about you, even if I never tied one on with you because I was too young to drink when you made this delivery to Michigan Avenue. Drink you in a better place, if there is one.

The guy who wants to write down instructions on how to give a three-eyed alien a black eye is outside on the sidewalk, trying to score a pencil. He remembers that an old geezer was selling pencils out there when he first went into VICTORY BAR. That was five hours ear-lier. The old pencil guy is not outside the bar now, nor anywhere in sight.

"Anybody got a fucking pencil?" the frustrated drunk screams, steadying himself by holding the knob of the three-windowed door. One of the two po-licemen outside JACK KING'S LOAN OFFICE at Number 535 approach-es and says, "Listen, man, slam a lid on it. You're disturbing the peace."

"What peace? We're in the middle of the fucking Korean War. What's to disturb?"

"Don't make me tell you again. I'm not good at repeating myself. "

The other policeman is nodding enthusiastically. "It's one of Jimmy's little flaws. He doesn't much care for it."

"I have just one question," the drunk says, swaying precariously. "*Office-sires.*"

"What's that?" the first policeman says. "And don't ask about the Tunnel."

"Where can a guy like myself buy a pencil?"

"It's almost dark, so we sent the old pencil guy home. Sorry, buddy."

The second policeman, gestures with a jerk of his thumb towards JACK KING'S LOAN OFFICE. "Go in there. Big Jack'll loan you a pencil, and he only charges legal rates."

"What? What?" The drunk completely loses control of himself. "I coul-da bought an entire new pencil outright from that old geezer you chased away and paid that bum just a nickel. Are you sayin' Mr. Big-Shot Jack King is gonna charge me a vig to *lend* me a half-used pencil that's been sitting on his ear since Truman took office? What's that fucking guy the king of anyways? Fat asses?"

"That's it, Mister. We're taking you in," says the second policeman, pre-tending to be reaching for his handcuffs. Unseen, he winks at his partner.

"On what charge?"

"Making my partner repeat himself."

"He hasn't said nothing," the drunk protests. "I've been listening very, very careful."

"Repetition is *implified.*"

Unexpectedly, the two policemen huddle and confer with each other. They're actually whispering about where to go for some coffee. Finally, Jimmy, the first policeman, says, "We're gonna give you a break. Go lean up against that telephone pole, keep your hands in your pockets, and hum *The Star-Spangled Banner.* We're going to walk away very slowly. Just make sure we don't hear anything that makes us have to come back."

The drunk does his drunken best to comply. The policemen head east on Michigan Avenue and don't give him another thought. Pencil Pushing Pete is already at home in Room 342 of WHITE STAR HOTEL, sharpening his supply of pencils with a dull Boy Scout knife, a souvenir of his long-past youth in rural Michigan. Big Jack King, at Number 535, misses out on loaning a drunk a used pencil at legal rates, but never finds out about that business reversal. The foreign guy on the other bar stool in VICTORY BAR, meanwhile, has obtained a scrap of paper and a pencil from the bartender, and is at this precise moment writing the following words: "then you punch reel hard him in his mittle ayleean eye...."

That manages to clear up some mystery about the shifty-looking guy leaning against the pole and explains why his hands are in his pockets. But, really, who cares? It would be much more interesting to see him give a three-eyed alien a black middle eye. Certainly, more interesting than watching him cheating at miniature golf on Michigan Avenue in 1951.

The muddled middle ground of our photo stands between us and the even vaguer background. The background zone is the last stop before the mists of oblivion obscure Michigan Avenue's furthest photographic vista. Here, however, in the busy middle ground, is where we encounter a few undecipherable parking signs and four new persons, one female and three males. The closest is a nattily-dressed Cuban (natty by Michigan Avenue standards) with a fashion hat and a bag of dirty laundry slung over his shoulder, heading to Mr. Wu's Wash-n-Fold (not in view, behind our vantage point). Next to him (*photo* right, *our* left), hiding behind a telephone pole is an off-duty cabby reading the racing lists in the newspaper. Further on, a woman pursues a man, her husband, who has been on a bender for a week. "Sidney, wait, please wait for me," she keeps calling. He's humming *The Star-Spangled Banner*, a tune that popped into his head when he passed the also-humming-slug-the-alien-in-the-middle-eye drunkard playing pocket pool outside VICTORY BAR.

"Sidney, Sidney, wait for me. We gotta talk," she calls after him. She's getting hoarser and feeling more exhausted with every square of pavement she traverses, her stockings are rolling down, her girdle is squeezing the living daylights out of her, and she looks ripe for a bender of her own.

Sidney hums louder. He's having none of it. He's just recovered from injuries stemming from a very serious traffic accident and wants to grab life by the horns again. The MICHIGAN AVENUE NO. 30 EASTBOUND BUS struck him in the back when he paused in the middle of the Avenue to light a Lucky with a hinky lighter. He was hit so hard, the impact sent him *va-vooming* eastward—from the photographic foreground to the photographic middle ground—depositing his banged-up body near the blurry parking signs. Poor guy broke four ribs, his collarbone, an ankle, and lost a kidney (*his* left, *our* right). Now denizens of the Avenue call him One Kidney Sidney, a step up, at least, from Sid the Yid.

"Wait for me, wait for me," she's shouting. "Not a chance," he's thinking. He's in enough pain. His missing kidney is suffering a phantom kidney stone, the way missing arms suffer phantom hangnails. He needs a phantom pain killer. Jack Daniels (he calls it *Jake* Daniels) might do the trick.

Speaking of missing body parts, it so happens that One Leg Craig just crutched his way into Big JACK KING'S LOAN OFFICE for a legal-rates-only quickie. Our photographer just missed him. If One Leg wasn't already dead, he'd be back outside in a Michigan-Avenue-minute, his pockets brimming with Big Jack King's-Fat-Fanny-loan-money. The photographer is dead as well, so that ties our record-keeping up in a nice little bundle with a pink bow. See you in the next world, One Leg Craig! And your wife, Ruth, too, with her missing tooth. Anybody want to take a guess what people call *her*? That's right—Missing Tooth Ruth. From Duluth.

At long last, we have reached the edge of Oblivion. Here's where the last dregs of 1951's documented truth reside in snapshot testimony to a moment on Michigan Avenue. Do a little math, and you'll see that the people populating our photo add up to be about—give or take a few shots—48 sheets to the wind.

The Book-Cadillac Hotel

Not much back there, is there? There's part of the sign for RELIABLE FURNITURE, but the biggie in the distance is the very famous 1920s Book-Cadillac Hotel (no hotel sign in the photo, sorry, but it's as recognizable as can be), towering out of the mists of bad focus, a real space-hogger. If this was a real *Naked City*, one million of the eight million stories would be taking place inside the Book-Cadillac Hotel. Let's face it, they didn't name it "Book" because people in Detroit like to read. Oh, if walls could talk and if I could just shut up!

What comes in life after the vagaries of photographic backgrounds? Is there anything we don't know about beyond the hulking Book-Cadillac that justifies everything we've just seen, or makes some understandable sense out of the rag-tag, tumble-down, hotchpotch of Main-Street-Skid-Row, USA? If, as they say, the Devil is in the details, we should, at least, be able to see them.

Having been born the same year this photo was taken—with a 1.00 out of 365.25 chance (considered unbeatable odds on Michigan Avenue) of having been born on the very day it was taken—what's beyond the Book-Cadillac Hotel is big fat ugly beautiful America and me, your tour guide to Skid Row, gathering myself out of the blurry mists and

Virtue. Its own reward.

Bazooka gum fossil
(Carbon-dated 1922)

congealing into what resembles a life.

Now it's time for me to start wrapping things up. I close my imaginary tour guide's umbrella, folding it in on itself like a morning glory shutting down for the night. Meanwhile, the Cuban guy with the white fashion hat is inside Mr. Wu's laundry, discussing the possibility of the two of them going into business together. They toss ideas back and forth. Mr. Sanchez wants to open a Cuban-Chinese Laundry and Dry-Cleaning Store with casino money from Havana and spray starch from China. But Mr. Wu has what he shrewdly considers to be a better idea. "You, me, we open first time Cuban-Chinese Res-taurant—serve *Comida Chinas y Criollas*,

"Here's mud in your three eyes," says Missing Tooth Ruth from Duluth

ropa vieja, chop suey, and other rousy food—worst cuisine ever cook in America. Cheap, cheap, cheap. Someone no rike, we poison. You, me, we make rotsa money. America make quick get rich for people rike us."
`

At the far end of Michigan Avenue, a woman's whining voice can be heard. "Wait for me, Sidney, wait, we need to talk for Gawd's sake!" The tired wife rounds the corner in desperate pursuit of the fleeing One Kidney. He's not waiting. He's not talking. She's not giving up. Most likely, this story won't end well. God save us, there are 7,999,999 more of them.

The foreigner in VICTORY BAR is licking the tip of his borrowed pencil and squinting as he tries to summon an idea out of an internal cloudbank composed of billowing booze fumes. He has one strained expression that he uses for both thinking and bowel movements. "Ah," he sighs, as he produces a satisfying thought. He licks the pencil tip again and writes: "Run in strayt line far away from monster and never take any look back at heem. Maybe like this you can live."

-END OF PHOTO-

MORNING COFFEE

New York ━━━ THE PAUMANOK EXPRESS ━━━ Montauk

F🦊X

IRONCLAD ━━━ RAILROAD

Morning Coffee is Served

The conductor entered the carriage, pushing a silver samovar and coffee service on a mahogany cart. He rang a small bell to get the passengers' attention, then gestured to the tiered stands of miniature pastries and finger sandwiches. "Elevenses is served, Ladies and Gents" he announced ceremoniously, "Fox Ironclad Railroad is pleased to proffer complimentary mid-morning fare to passengers of the *Paumanok Brown Fox*." He passed out little menu cards that listed the offerings. "There is no better time for abstemiousness than yesterday, so please step up."

Passengers left their seats and came over for a closer look. Some snapped photos. Only one remained oblivious—a nun, draped in black, fast asleep, and snoring very noisily. Her rimless glasses were seated crookedly on her prominent nose, reflecting the scenery that flickered past the windows. Her lips quivered with each loud snore.

"A nun—traveling alone—giving a sermon consisting entirely of the letter *Z*," Ry said to the Professor. "Let me see—we have a lecturing rabbi, a thrice-bereaved widow who is, at present, a grieving mother, a ghost in a shoebox, a professor of 'highfalutin' fairy tales, three story-swapping Nightcaps—a shrink, an artist, and a florist— an actor masquerading as a conductor, and a pair of robotic toilets—one robot is a Belgian detective, the other a lady British spy—I wonder what sort of story a solitary nun would have for us."

The Professor looked at the snoring nun this way and that, cocking his head, taking in details from different angles. He shook his head disapprovingly. "Whatever her story is, she's dreaming it."

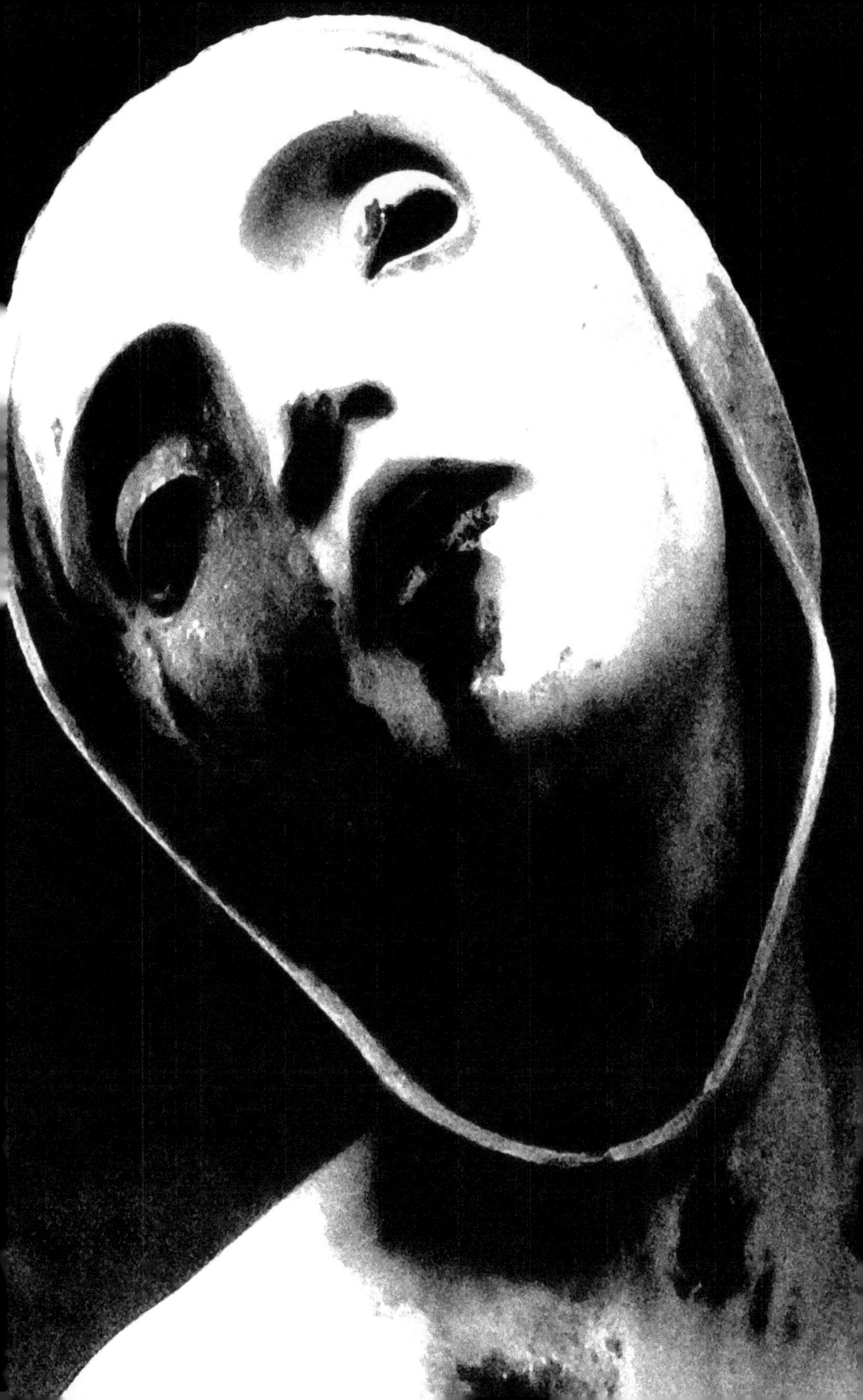

The Nun's Dream

A Lentil for Your Thoughts, Briefly Told

Hoc est corpus meum, et ibi est ianua

This is my body, and that is the door.

Lost in contemplation of the Virgin's legendary beauty—on the last of her days of innocence and freedom—she stood in a light sprinkling of rain at the junction of three nameless roads. The carved face before her was tilted upwards, ensuring that its eyes were destined never to meet any onlooker's gaze directly. Trails of rain ran down the stained cheeks like rivulets of tears, falling to her breasts and bare feet. Her arms and her hands, outstretched, palms upward, might have been shaped to demonstrate her resignation to earthly suffering—and to the daily flagellation of springtime rain— but there was something more, though perhaps unintended by the woodcarver, in the deep-set, uplifted eyes and slightly parted lips. Whatever it was, it defied description and indifference.

Here was the famed statue known to believers as the Virgin of the Crossroads, rooted in an unmarked, isolated place in the heart of the English countryside. No one knew who had carved her, or when, or how she came to be in this forlorn location, where three insignificant roads converged in a field of ordinary wheat and no sign directed one into her presence. Her lone figure, impossible to forget once seen, had been part of the desolate landscape here ever since anyone could re- member. The more the sun, the wind, the rain and snow, and the pas- sage of years abused her, the more beautiful and enigmatic she seemed to those who stumbled upon her unintentionally. She might reappear, decades later, unfazed by time and the elements, in the dreams of these wanderers, when they least expected anything of such beauty to radiate from the dust and clutter of their memories.

Mary Agnes had dismounted from her wagon and was standing next to Micah, her horse, stroking his soaked mane, as she contemplated the holy image. She discovered that she was not alone. An older man, wearing a hooded robe, was standing on the other side of the horse and looking at the statue, too. He said, after a long period of reflection, "I've seen her a thousand times, but I can't say I've come to know her any better through familiarity. What is it that she wants to tells us? You can sense there are words struggling to be heard. Hundreds pass this way every year, most on their way to Canterbury; many on those pilgrimages ask her to intercede for them in some matter or another. Often, I've seen them camp here for a night and approach her in the dark, holding candles out to her. Some claim they've heard her whispering, or sighing, or crying. Others say she moves. In some accounts, she places her hands over her eyes, in others, over her heart, but most commonly, it is said she has been seen pressing a single forefinger to her lips, indicating her desire for silence. Coincidentally, there is a convent nearby that observes a strict Vow of Silence. Skeptics claim that the forefinger legend is a lie invented by the Sisters of Silence that live there. Perhaps the legend is a form of advertising. Or some type of arcane warning."

"Where is the convent?" Mary Agnes asked. "I see only fields here."

He pointed to the right. "The right fork of the road goes to the Convent of Silent Penitence in the Abbey of Saint Pollye Loquaicius. It's not far. The left fork goes to the town of Asbury-on-Thames, which is a little further, but still fairly close—a half-hour walk, perhaps less. Geographically, though, the town is quite near the convent, near enough that the townsfolk can clearly hear the convent's bells when they are rung. The Silent Sisters communicate with the townsfolk by various signals from the bell tower, in case there is a fire or some other emergency. I believe only two of the Sisters are permitted to speak— one is the Abbess, Reverend Mother Myrtle of the Mount of Olives, and the other is the Prioress, Mother Mary Monitor of the Last Nail. The first is a witch—not a real witch, of course—and the other is just an ordinary unpleasant crone, much like others you've met, only dressed in holy garments. There is also an imbecile caretaker, Antonio, but he lives outside the convent's walls—as is appropriate when young women are domiciled with no one to watch over their innocence—and, if that lout *does* speak, it is generally drooling idiocy that no one pays heed to.

"Local legend says that the Mother Superior fled to Asbury in her youth because she had unwittingly caught the Devil's eye while dancing at a county fair with her schoolmates. He was soon assiduously, unrelentingly courting her—in the grandiose manner that only the Devil himself could manage—nightly serenading her high window from her father's rose garden, leaving bouquets and jewels and sweetmeats and love notes for her everywhere. The house gradually filled with all manner of creatures festooned with ribbons, accompanied with little notes in purple ink—puppies and kittens and rabbits and rare songbirds. She would retire to her bedroom at night to find her bed strewn with rose petals and gifts. On one occasion, she awoke with the uneasy sense that she was not alone, only to be terrified, after looking around, by the sight of an enormous tortoise—with an elaborate red bow glued to its back—slowly traversing the room. On another occasion, a multicolored parrot, wearing a diamond bracelet around its neck, woke her from a deep sleep. It had perched on the rim of her chamber pot, squawking '*Je t'aime, Nanette, toujour, toujour.*' She opened a window and swatted at it with a broom, until it flew out into the night, still protesting its love for her. The diamond bracelet went with it, never to be seen again.

"Even though the Devil had never personally said a word to her, he had boldly 'asked' her father for her hand in marriage. Terrified by the Devil's barely concealed irritation, the old man viewed the request—quite correctly, too—as both a demand and a threat, and he agreed to the match at once, offering an absurdly large dowry to sweeten the deal. Meanwhile, a young gardener, who was also in love with her, overheard much of this nuptial plotting and warned her about the plans being made. She escaped the trap with the gardener's assistance on a moonless night, gladly paying his asking price for

the help—a single, lingering kiss.

"Not long after her escape, a mule kicked the gardener in the forehead, killing him. Then—before anyone noticed what was happening—the Devil was found to be living in the house. He spent his days pacing the rooms and hallways, cursing and fuming, berating the servants, and brutally kicking the dogs and cats and rabbits whenever they got in his way. He lingered, unwelcome, for a half a year to see if the object of his obsession would return or try to make contact with her father. Meanwhile, the animals were destroying the house, eating the linens and carpets and drapes, burrowing into the upholstered furniture and bedding, and pulling the wallpaper, strip by strip, from the walls. As horrible as living conditions became, the Devil refused to quit the premises. Tormented by heartbreak and constant traumatization at the hands of his terrifying house guest, the father finally took his own life with a dose of poison so potent, it killed him before he finished swallowing it.

"With no one remaining to vent his frustration on, the Devil packed his belongings and departed the ruined house, slamming the door with such force, the lintel came crashing down on the porch, crushing the skull of the footman who was carrying his bags out to the carriage. Before he rode off, the Devil paid the servants twenty years of wages in advance to insure they would remain on the premises as lookouts. Their only duty—spelled out in contracts signed in blood—was to notify him, without delay, if the daughter returned.

"As soon as the Devil was gone, the servants killed all the dogs and cats and stewed the rabbits. The cats had already eaten all the birds, with the exception of the rainbow-colored parrot, which had escaped much earlier, as I said. They were unable to find the tortoise, but not for a lack of trying. A few years later, workmen discovered that the tortoise had gotten stuck underneath a bathtub and died there, still wearing its garish red bow. An attached note, in faded purple ink, read, '*Je t'aime, Nanette, toujour, toujour.*'

"Months after her midnight escape, traveling in secrecy, having hidden hither and thither on her way, the daughter arrived in Asbury-on-Thames and sought sanctuary in the convent of the legendary Abbey of Saint Pollye Loquaicius. What she had learned of the renowned Vow of Silence appealed greatly to her, because it insured that no one could reveal her whereabouts to her satanic suitor. Thus, she became Sister Myrtle of the Mount of Olives, and—as was required—she ceased to speak. Even if he was listening for the sound of her voice in the vast stillness of the night, all the Devil would be able to hear were the nocturnal ministrations of the crickets and an occasional owl.

"Many years passed, during which she rose, station by station, to become the Abbess and Mother Superior of the Silent Sisters. She withered in the course of time and grew exceedingly unattractive—a process known to occur in persons who are overwhelmingly unhappy and mean-spirited. Nevertheless, in her mind, Reverend Mother Myrtle believed the Devil would still want her no matter how severely she was ravaged by the passage of the years. He probably *did*—but it would only have been to exact his revenge. She preferred to think otherwise. Married as she was to Christ, it assuaged her unquenchable vanity to fantasize that the Devil was His rival for her affection. What could be more flattering than a cosmic war between the archetypes of Good and Evil, two forces locking horns and halos, with her as the mythical Helen? The thought of this romantic mayhem was the only thing capable of bringing a smile to her prune-like face—a small and bitter one it was, too, but it was enough to be recognizable as a smile, nonetheless, by anyone who could bear to look at her long enough to see it poking out from under the veil of wrinkles.

"So, the legend of Sister Myrtle—later to be Reverend Mother Myrtle of the Mount of Olives—goes. Perhaps it's just one of those traveler's tales, amusing but completely untrue. What is known for certain is that when she was appointed the Abbess, she gained the right to break her vow of silence, in order that she could speak to—and on the behalf of—those in her charge. Thus, her risk of exposure and discovery, if ever there was any danger to begin with, was greatly increased. To this day, she dedicates her all her energy to preserving the secret of her whereabouts through the silence of her domain, lest the Devil—hearing the sound of her voice from afar—find her and resume his relentless courting rituals. Or so she imagines. Worse still, she imagines—and always has—that she is actually engaged in the service of God! Avoiding the Devil and serving God are not one and the same at all. Avoiding the Devil is—all too often—serving the Devil."

The stranger patted her horse on the back and then bent down to lift his basket, emitting a weary groan as he stood up. "You must not stay here much longer. For one thing, you're blocking the road. Soon enough someone will come up behind you with their wagon, and you will have to go to the left or the right to allow them to pass or follow. Which will it be? You have to decide soon. Certainly, before dark."

"I have no idea," Mary Agnes said. "I've been recently orphaned. I sought this place out to ask the Virgin of the Crossroads to give me a sign, to show me which path I should follow, since there is no one else in the world to guide me."

"What has she told you?" he asked. "Did you get a sign?"

"None, as far as I can tell. Must I approach her with a candle after dark? Kneel before her? Make an offering?"

"No, no, no. That's just nonsense," he said. "How fortuitous that we should meet here. It so happens that I know a better way. Listen to me very carefully. We can induce your horse to decide for you. The Virgin has the power to work through him. Do you see her outstretched hands? I will put a peach in her left hand and an apple in her right hand. Then we will take a step back and wait to see which fruit your horse eats first. This will make it easier for her to show you—through my method and your horse—which path to follow, whether to go right to the convent or left to the town. It can't fail."

Without waiting for her to agree or disagree, he produced the two necessary fruits, one from each of his pockets—left and right respectively—and placed them on the Virgin's palms, which seemed to be shaped by the woodcarver for this very purpose. The horse and the three figures stood in the approaching darkness and waited while the rain drizzled down on them. Nothing happened right away. The stranger, however, exuded extreme confidence that the horse would oblige them and choose one fruit or the other. His eyes gleamed with anticipation as he eagerly rubbed his hands together.

After a length of time had passed, the horse approached the wet statue and stared at the Virgin's face as if he was hypnotized. He sniffed her neck and whinnied. Then he proceeded to lick her cheek. The impatient stranger suddenly lurched forward and shouted loudly in the horse's ear, "Choose, fool!" At that, the startled horse immediately snatched the apple and swallowed it whole.

"Your road has been indicated, child," the man said with finality and self-satisfaction. He shifted his burden so it would be more comfortable to carry. "I wish you a safe journey and a rewarding future. I am heading to the town with my wares for the market tomorrow, else I would accompany you and see you to the threshold of silence, your appointed destination. But, I'm sure no harm will come to you without me. The Mother Superior is convinced that the Devil hasn't found this place—at least not yet—although it's only a matter of time. I've no doubt he will find her and exact his revenge someday. He's known to keep very good accounts, and his ink is the kind that never fades."

With those words, the hooded man turned abruptly and trudged down the left road towards Asbury-on-Thames. Mary Agnes watched him until he could no longer be seen through the veil of rain. Then she steered her horse in the direction of the convent on the right. As an afterthought, she hastily returned to the statue and knelt before it. She looked up at the enigmatic face. "Thank you, Blessed Virgin, for helping one who was lost until she found you," she whispered. "I beg you to keep me safe and give me strength, that I may serve." The persistent rain ran down the cheeks of the statue and fell on the cheeks of the penitent at her feet. They cried together like this for a short time. The horse, his soaked head hanging almost to the ground, looked as if he was crying with them.

She noticed, upon standing up again, that the peach was no longer lying in the statue's left hand. What had become of it? It wasn't on the ground. Perhaps Micah had eaten it when she wasn't looking, or possibly the stranger pocketed it before leaving her. She was hungry. Never having had a peach in all her years, she would have enjoyed biting into it and experiencing one last taste of life's sweetness before the silence of the cloister closed in around her.

Only one option remained to Mary Agnes. Looking to the right, at the road to the Convent of Silent Penitence, she had the impression that a door had opened to admit her. Leading her horse forward, taking one final step across the imaginary threshold, she felt a different, less comforting, sensation replacing the first one. There was no doubt about it—the door had closed behind her. Silently.

She had almost no uncertainty about her actions. Hadn't the Virgin of the Crossroads directed her, with a clear sign given to her through the medium of Micah, her faithful horse, to this symbolic entrance? If there was any uneasiness in her mind at all, it concerned what might happen at the secluded convent if the Devil should discover the hiding place of Mother Myrtle of the Mount of Olives.

In saecula saeculorum
Forever and ever

Mary Agnes was required, as a postulant to the order, to endure a trial period of six months before being permitted to take her official vows. During this time, she was under the watchful eye of the Prioress, Mother Mary Monitor of the Last

Nail, and was permitted to ask questions of her. She was instructed to speak to no one else. In this way—with a calculated half-measure—her indoctrination into the mysteries of silence was begun.

She discovered, during her first days as a postulant, that whenever she asked a question—no matter what the inquiry concerned—it was answered with a tone of undisguised irritation. Before long, the two women were playing the roles of Irritator and Irritatee.

Without intending to turn Mother Mary Monitor's quirk of behavior into a form of amusement, Mary Agnes found herself unable to resist the urge to ask questions just to see if she could correctly guess what form the display of annoyance would take. Would it be an exasperated sigh? A pinched or twisted mouth? A rolling of the otherwise droopy eyes? A rude, dismissive hand gesture? Or a combination of several at once? Mary Agnes began awarding herself with tokens each time she successfully predicted Mother Mary Monitor's reaction to questioning. She put a pebble in a jar when she guessed correctly. If her guess was wrong, she removed a pebble. Before the first month ended, there was a shocking accumulation of pebbles. Mary Agnes was worried. She was beginning to run out of questions.

More importantly, the new postulant had begun her fall into Error. The first of the Deadly Sins she was guilty of in her newly begun life at the Convent of Silent Penitence was Pride. The more pebbles that found their way into the jar, the happier—and the more sinful—the prideful Mary Agnes became.

Except for the periods of training and preparation, she was otherwise kept in isolation, permitted outdoors solely during the hours that the other nuns were in the abbey, engaged in their toneless mumbo-jumbo of silent prayer. As a consequence of her isolation, Mary Agnes became familiar with the domestic animals of the convent, but with none of its human occupants beyond the Prioress. Among the animals, there was a donkey, a billy-goat and a nanny-goat. There were chickens, as well, and a dog to guard the henhouse. The donkey, clearly a lonely beast, would look at her with longing eyes, quivering lips, often showing his enormous teeth in what she came to believe was a smile. Even for a donkey, he had a very raucous laugh, loud enough to start a bird migration.

"Do our animals have names?" she asked one day.

Mother Mary Monitor instantaneously responded with a withering look. She replied icily, "Of course not, girl. How can you suppose we would entertain anything so ridiculous? When our devout Sisters do not permit themselves the luxury of discourse with their equally devout Sisters, why would we permit ourselves discourse instead with filthy beasts of burden? *O, meus Deus, en medias noctes!* We are not permitted to summon the convent's animals by name, nor do we address them as if they—and we— were characters in storybooks. Our duty is to tame the wildness of their natures, to steer these beasts away from sinfulness as Noah guided them to safety—he, by saving their bodies from certain destruction, and we, by saving their souls, so they may continue to serve us in Heaven where our work continues, although in a more supervisory form. And, never forget—*silence* means *Silence*—so whilst engaged in the practice of silence, you would do well to contemplate the true meaning of Silence. And please learn the difference between a donkey and a unicorn."

"Mother, I assure you, I will think about Silence in silence most vigorously."

"See that you do," Mother Mary Monitor stated firmly. "And have you, perhaps, any additional urgent questions to ask of me, while we are being diverted at such length from our prayers to explore the advisability of conversing with donkeys, goats, chickens, and field mice?"

"Yes, Mother, I do."

"I thought you might. Well then, what is it? As if I don't already know what's coming next!"

"When is it that we may *not* be silent?"

"Ah, yes, I knew it," she said, smiling for the first time in many days. "You *all* eventually come to *that*. Some sooner than others, and you are a quick one, aren't you? It is typical of today's sinner that they will ask when a rule can be broken while the ink the rule is written with is still wet. Yes, indeed, you may be allowed to speak in due time. Silence without the promise of respite would prove to be counterproductive; there would be no contrast and nothing to look forward to. The Lord commands us to be charitable to all, including those in our order. Your allowance, in time, to speak after a long silence, is akin to the carrot that draws the donkey forward, while severe penance is, correspondingly, akin to the stick that smacks the donkey's rump, keeping him moving in the same direction as the carrot. But do not expect much from this promise of a reprieve. We do not smack rumps as hard as we should, nor do we offer much in the way of luxury when it comes to the carrots, which only seem like chocolates until you actually get one and bite into it. Our carrots are as puny as our smacks are sparing. You will be disappointed—as all before you have been—for only two words are permitted."

"What two words?"

"It is not a question of *what* words are permitted, foolish girl." She sighed with impatience, throwing her hands in the air. Sternly, she continued to reprimand her charge. "It is *when* you may speak the two words that you should be asking about."

"When is that, Mother, if this is a proper time to ask?"

"You may speak two words—and only two words, mind you—any two words you desire to speak, and only once—you may not repeat either of the two words permitted to you—and then only when the Reverend Mother tells you that you may speak the two words, and at no other time. You may, for instance, say, 'Mea culpa,' but you may not say, 'Mea culpa, mea culpa,' as those nasty, sex-addled friars have been known to do. Such repetition is absolutely forbidden. If you wish to prolong your speech, you may say one carefully chosen word followed by the word *Infinitum,* which keeps you within the prescribed guidelines, while it indicates something greater is intended. Of course, this is cheating, but we accept it because it's Latin, the language of our Savior. Even when we are silent at this sanctuary, child, our silence is in Latin. Remember that."

"Yes, Mother, but *when* may I speak my two words?"

"After five years of unadulterated silence, you will be invited to share two paltry pearls of wisdom—however imperfect—that you acquired in your half-decade of sacrifice. Failure in your obligations may require further penance in the form of additional time added to the five years before the Reverend Mother deigns to summon you. Master your tongue—that's my advice—or you will serve in a prison of silence, with no reprieve—no carrot, puny or otherwise—forever and ever."

"Mother, I assure you that I understand all you have said. I understand, then, that I may not speak to my horse, Micah, nor call him by his name, nor even address him as *Horse*, but I would like your permission to *see* him. That is, to see *It*. We've been together for all of my life. *It* may be worried about me."

"What foolishness!" the Prioress scoffed. "Anyway, that will be impossible. Your horse isn't here."

"Where is he? What's become of him?"

"Antonio, our imbecile caretaker, took the animal to Asbury."

"Asbury? Why to Asbury?

"To sell it. We can't feed and care for an animal we have no use for—that should be obvious, should it not? The Lord commands us not to be wasteful."

"*Sold?* Micah was *sold?*" Overwhelmed, even more profoundly than when the Thames Fever had come for both of her parents and her little brother, Mary Agnes began to cry bitter tears. Her solitude was now complete. All seemed starkly empty, black, and hopeless.

As for the opposite side of the conversation, this was one of the rare times that a postulant's question failed to irritate Mother Mary Monitor of the Last Nail. In fact, she rather enjoyed responding to it, because it was a rhetorical question, and for once she was able—with a single terse response—to put an annoying matter to rest once and for all. "Not *sold*," she said, in a matter-of-fact tone. "No one would buy it. It was too old. So, it was taken to the butcher and traded for salted meat."

Upon hearing this news, Mary Agnes stopped breathing. She remained motionless in the courtyard of the abbey, as white and impassive as the sculpted saints that framed the doorways. But, despite her outward appearance, she was far from becalmed. Spinning helplessly in the epicenter of her grief and fury, she committed her second Deadly Sin then and there—the sin of Wrath—for it was apparent to her how very unlikely it was that she would manage to put Micah's fate behind her without first exacting a just punishment from Mother Mary Monitor of the Last Nail for her callousness.

She was only in her first month of trial. There were still five Deadly Sins and Ten Commandments remaining—all unexplored—at her disposal, and all the time in the world ahead of her.

She could not sleep that night. Wide-eyed, and mercifully free of tears, she stared at the mottled ceiling of her cell and listened to the sound of her heart thudding and her teeth grinding. From deep within the damp, chilly darkness, she could distinguish the sounds of industrious spiders weaving cobwebs in the corners, and the mice, sniffing and blinking, peeking out of crevices to determine if it was safe enough to emerge for the scavenging of crumbs. A bat, or a large bird, had gotten trapped in the abbey somewhere, probably having entered through the summit of the bell tower. Whatever it was, wherever it was, it flitted restlessly from rafter to rafter throughout the night, increasing the pervasive atmosphere of anxiety. Outside her window, an owl perched in the white branches of a crusty birch tree—its huge orange eyes like the slow-moving lensed lanterns of a lighthouse—sweeping this way and that way, this way and that way, and intermittently hooting... hooting... hooting. Watching. Waiting.

One by one, Mary Agnes took the collected pebbles from their jar, rolled each in her fingers as if they were holy rosary beads, and dropped them, bead by bead—pebble by pebble—to the cold stone floor.

Why, she wondered, over and over again as the pebbles fell, *why did you not pick the peach, Micah? If only you had picked the peach and not the apple, you would still be alive. And so would I.*

Non sumit illam velum
She takes the veil

Micah was gone, but she had, as compensation, the lovesick donkey that she named Wigbert. She was forbidden to call him by name—she could not even clear her throat as a means of securing his attention—but the two quickly found a way of communicating with each other using subtle gestures. The first breakthrough came when Mary Agnes placed her fingers behind her ears and used them to make them wiggle, a game she had played as a child with her younger brother. Wigbert would wiggle his own ears when he saw her wiggling hers, just as her infant brother had. Soon enough, he would approach her and wiggle his ears without provocation. When no one was watching, she would wiggle her ears in response. Seeing that, the donkey would laugh uncontrollably, kicking back with his hind legs, seemingly believing that he was controlling her, rather than she controlling him. If he played this out with her successfully, she would feed him a carrot. For a carrot, Wigbert would do anything she wanted. Without a carrot, he would just love her. That was all to the good, because she did not always have a carrot. When she began to steal carrots for Wigbert from the supplies intended for the caged rabbits, she broke the Seventh of the

Lord's Ten Commandments. That was in addition to committing the Deadly Sins of Pride and Wrath. It was still early enough, and there were still few enough, to keep track of her transgressions.

The billy-goat, which she named Clydas, had the bearded nanny-goat, Priscilla, for companionship, and the chickens had other chickens and chicks and the ugly, mangy rooster. The unfriendly dog that watched over the chickens had the chickens and the rooster and Antonio, the caretaker. The local fox had the dog and the chickens. Wigbert only had her and she had only Wigbert and Mother Mary Monitor of the Last Nail.

One day Mother Mary Monitor was giving her some instructions regarding management of farmyard dung. Wigbert stood between them, his head towards Mary Agnes, and his hindquarters towards the Prioress. When Mother Mary Monitor's attention was suddenly diverted (she heard a nun who pricked herself on a thorn say "Ouch!" causing her to momentarily turn her head away from the donkey), Mary Agnes quickly used her fingers to wiggle her ears for Wigbert. She had to deftly push back her cowl with her thumbs and do the wiggling with her forefingers simultaneously. From the donkey's perspective, her two wiggling ears seemed to appear out of nowhere. As expected, he laughed gleefully and kicked his hind legs back, striking the Prioress in the buttocks and knocking her down into a puddle of rainwater and mud. The donkey kept wiggling its ears, laughing, snorting, and tossing his head, while the Prioress struggled to get to her feet, drenched, filthy, and fuming.

Wigbert was a stubborn animal, capable of being very obstinate with those he disliked—Antonio and the Prioress in particular. Mother Mary Monitor did not fail to notice that the donkey had an affinity for the postulant, who seemed capable of getting the lazy beast to do anything, although his disruptive, raucous laughter when Mary Agnes was around was the price one paid for it. The Prioress was left with no choice but to assign the novice the task of caring for the donkey. The Abbess used the donkey to ride to Asbury twice a month to sell medicinal herbs and other products produced at the convent,

in order to buy food that could not be grown by the nuns and other items that were needed—hence he was a necessary member of their community. The Abbess would be accompanied on these excursions by Antonio and the Prioress, but the donkey loathed them both and often became unruly. As soon as he saw Antonio approaching with the bales of herbs, he would run away and had to be chased around the yard while the Abbess stood impatiently awaiting her ride to the town. It was only with Mary Agnes' intervention that Wigbert could be coaxed to get anything done at all.

A pattern soon established itself. Wigbert would go to Asbury at a tortoise's pace, repeatedly pausing to cast a mournful gaze back at the convent. Conversely, while returning to the convent—and the carrot he hoped to be given—he practically trotted, no matter how heavy a burden Antonio saddled him with. Once or twice he came close to throwing the Abbess off of his back in his haste to get home. The Prioress and the Abbess, in private conversation, discussed their mutual regret over their decision to sell Mary Agnes' horse to the butcher. The horse would have been far more manageable than the donkey in the long run. They had been all too eager to sever the young novice's ties to her former life to properly consider what to do with her horse. Ignorant women that they were, they had no idea at all about the profound effect their treatment of Micah would have on the future. If someone explained it to them, they wouldn't have believed it anyway. From their point of view, sending an old animal to a slaughterhouse was not an action worthy of consequences, and therefore, there could be none.

Another of the assignments that Mary Agnes was given, one that was much more disagreeable, was sorting through lentils—bag after bag of them—to pick out any tiny stones mixed among them. The lentils were poured from a sack and spread out on a table in the quadrangle, around which the cloister ran on three sides, the fourth side being open to the yard where Wigbert and the animals were. At first, dealing with a large table covered with thousands of tiny lentils seemed to be a very tedious job, Sisyphean in its frustrations, because no sooner had one completed an entire table's worth of lentils, finding—at best—three or four little stones for all the trouble taken, there was then another sack of lentils waiting to be spilled out where the last had been, and the process would begin all over again. She was sure, at first, that this assignment would be the death of her, or at the very least, the eventual cause of blindness or insanity or both.

Quite by surprise, working with the lentils proved to be much more interesting than she would ever have dreamed possible, becoming, in fact, one of the tasks she most looked forward to. This change came about when she was summoned to the sorting table quite unexpectedly because the nun on Lentil Duty had suffered a sunstroke, falling to the ground and leaving her work unfinished. Antonio carried the stricken nun away like a sack of turnips, and the Prioress pointed to the table, gruffly indicating that Mary Agnes should take over the sorting. This she did at once. She did not, however, expect to find—neatly spelled out in lentils on the table in front of her—a message that read:

DIE PRIORESS DIE

Apparently, she found herself seated at what was the secret communication center of the Convent of Silent Penitence. This was just one of several places where the nuns left messages and complaints they wished to share. Sometimes there were warnings or jokes.

This is quite a silence, she thought, astounded at her discovery. *I don't believe I've ever heard anything quite like it.*

It wasn't the table of lentils alone that was being used by the rebellious nuns for communicating with each other. Before long, she came to discover that there was an entire visual language of hand signs. Gestures represented letters that, with patience, spelled out words and ultimately sentences. Some words had simple gestures of their own, such as Amen (pulling of the left earlobe), but Amen was used in this adaptable nun's language to mean Amen in several different ways, all removed from prayer, as in Amen (*I or we agree with that*) or Amen (*Okay*) or Amen (*Enough!*). Like much more well-established languages, *Nunglish* was subtle and contextual, but it was essential to learn it if one did not wish to exist in isolation.

Later on, after she was invested as a member of the order, Mary Agnes was astounded to discover that her Sisters were engaged in multiple simultaneous conversations during dinner in the refectory—silent, elaborate, detailed conversations, and most definitely *not* in Latin Silence. There were often so many hand gestures being performed at once, there were moments when the nuns appeared to be suffering from an outbreak of St. Vitus' Dance.

Said Sister Wilhelmina of the Heavenly City (in Nunglish)
Scratch chin (R); Scratch nose (M)—[this was an abbreviation for Reverend Mother, the Abbess]—Rub upper lip (A); Scratch left eyebrow (T); Shrug shoulders (E); (deep sigh = space); Scratch nose (M) Shrug shoulders (E); Rub upper lip (A); Scratch left eyebrow (T); (pause); Rub thumb and forefinger of left hand together (O); Tap table with right hand (N); (deep sigh = space); Rub back of neck (F); Purse lips (R); Stroke neck (I).

— *"Reverend Mother ate meat on Friday!"*

Said Sister Grace of Hope and Charity:
Scratch top of head (B); Rub upper lip (A); Put hand on forehead (D); Twiddle thumbs (Signifies repetition of word or phrase for emphasis).

— *"Bad! Bad! Bad!"*

With the exception of the Abbess and the Prioress—who remained oblivious—everyone at the table simultaneously pulled their left ear lobe, even if it meant putting their spoon down to do so.

— *"Amen!"*

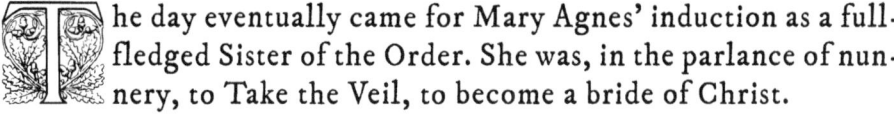he day eventually came for Mary Agnes' induction as a full-fledged Sister of the Order. She was, in the parlance of nunnery, to Take the Veil, to become a bride of Christ.

Two things of significance occurred at the time of her investiture.

The holy wax effigy of Saint Pollye Loquaicius

The first was her introduction to the precious relics of Saint Pollye Loquaicius, the Patron Saint of their order. It was in her honor that the Vow of Silence was taken. The relics, kept in a locked, gated chapel to which the Abbess had the only key, consisted of a grotesque wax effigy of Saint Pollye, a farm girl from Kent, who was martyred in the previous century by a feudal lord who wanted to exercise his right to deflower her—her tongue had been cut out for reporting the lord to the local Bishop, causing infection, and eventually, her death. If the maudlin effigy in its niche wasn't terrifying enough, the other relic was the tongue itself, housed in a bejeweled gold and glass reliquary. The tongue was, supposedly, Incorruptible Flesh, or so declared the Pope in Rome, but as far as Mary Agnes could see, it looked more like a small dog's penis than something that had ever seen real-life use for tattling or the tasting of sweets.

The second was her naming ceremony—she had to give up her former name and take a new one to symbolize a complete rejection of her previous life. She could either choose a name—if it was approved by the Abbess—or have one chosen for her. In the case of the latter, a name would be selected from the names of the nuns who had died and passed into the Silence Beyond Silence. Stating aloud her choice of name was the last audible sound she was permitted to make before her period of silence—five years of it—was to commence. So she connived to become Sister Micaela (after her horse, Micah, of course) of the Mortification of the Flesh, and with that choice, she secretly—and most wickedly—confounded the required severance of ties to her past.

Quinquennium in silentio
Five years of silence

More terrible than the punishing silence caused by the prohibitions against speaking, were the supplemental bans— sneezes suppressed by firm nostril pinching, coughs stifled with rags, and digestive trumpeting smothered with special pillows called *pulvillus tacitas*—wind mufflers—manufactured by the nuns themselves. These were sewn of burlap casings, or, when available, old, ruined habits with frayed hems, stuffed with chicken feathers and dried, boiled grass. It was traditional to embroider some prayer or moral lesson on the side of the muffler meant to face away from the body—only the non-muffling side of the *pulvillus tacitas* was permitted to be shown outwardly. The most attractive mufflers were sold to merchants in the village for re-sale to townsfolk and travelers as everyday religion-themed cushions. Others, that showed some small defect in workmanship, were kept for use by the Sisters to maintain the uninterrupted silence of their nether regions. Such bowel emanations were condemned as the *Vox Diaboli*—the Voice of Satan—whose sole purpose was to distract the Sisters from their main duty, which was silent Latin prayer for mankind's collective soul. This explains why the inner side of the *pulvillus tacitas* was never to be shown facing outward—the side held next to one's posterior region was considered to be the Devil's Ear.

ne night, quite unexpectedly, a very small noise was heard, much like the plaintive squeak of a tiny mouse—but it was not the squeak of a mouse, nor was it a rusty hinge. It was unmistakably the *Vox Diaboli*. Obviously, one of the poor Sisters had failed to alight on her *pulvillus tacitas* in time. This type of gastric event was known amongst the sympathetic Sisters as an *escapee* or, in the case of multiple *escapees* in quick succession, a *gaol break*.

On occasion, especially on nights when she could not sleep, the Prioress was in the habit of patrolling the passageways outside the nuns' cells. She would strut back and forth, swinging a lantern to and fro. In this way, when her nerves had gotten the best of her, the Prioress sought to catch the nuns whispering to each other through the cracks in the mortar. That she had never once discovered a transgression of this nature was no deterrent to her patrols. In fact, her failure to find a culprit for an imaginary infraction increased her determination to identify a transgressor hiding in their midst.

Sister Micaela—formerly Mary Agnes Fontoon—could easily see the shifting light of Mother Mary Monitor's lantern in the small gap at the bottom of her door—so she always knew when the Prioress was prowling about, restlessly, desperately looking for something to justify her barefoot presence—and so she was well-aware that the Prioress was haunting the corridor of the dorter on the night the dreaded *Vox Diaboli* issued forth. There was only a split second of silence between the *escapee* and the hysteria that followed it. During that split second, the spiders stopped spinning, the mice withdrew their twitching noses into their crevices, and the owl in the birch tree outside Sister Micaela's cell stopped hooting and looking around for something to pounce on. It seemed, in that brief moment, the whole world was waiting for what would come next.

Mother Mary Monitor of the Last Nail, fully losing control of herself, began ringing a large brass bell that hung in the corridor, summoning the nuns from their cells. "Come out, come out, all of you come out this instant," she shouted. As the cell doors creaked open, the Sisters emerged, wrapped in blankets, their eyes half open.

"Which one of you was that?" she demanded. "Step forward so your Sisters in Christ will know which of you is so lacking in discipline. Show yourself. Step forward."

No one moved. Mother Mary Monitor reacted as if she was possessed. She strutted up and down the corridor, stopping before this nun and that nun. "It was you, wasn't it?" she asked one, holding the lantern up to her face. "No more dallying, Sister—I grow weary of this," she said to another. "It was you, am I not right?"

At last she came to young Sister Grace, who was so often the Prioress' target for discipline. "Sister Grace, enough now. I know, I am sure, I am certain, it was you who lent your body to the Devil so he could use it to deliver a foul midnight sermon to us. Admit your complicity. Don't be a coward."

Sister Grace shrank back against her door and shook her head vehemently in denial. Seeing this refusal to cooperate, Mother Mary Monitor flew into a rage. "Liar!" she screamed. "Liar! Liar! Liar!"

Outside the walls of the convent, Antonio could hear the commotion from his shack. He leaped out of bed and ran outside. Even from a considerable distance, he saw flickering lights in all the windows of the abbey, and could hear the Prioress screaming, "Fire! Fire! Fire! Fire!"

Without wasting a moment, he ran—nearly naked— to the bell tower and bolted up the stairs to the belfry. He grabbed the ropes and began to ring the bells to summon the townsfolk from Asbury. He needed every able-bodied man, woman, and child to help quell the blaze he was sure was ravaging the abbey below him.

It wasn't long before the clamorous, good citizens of Asbury could be heard approaching in a state of high excitement. Dressed in night clothes and swathed in blankets, they carried buckets and chamber pots, shovels and pitchforks, and all manner of destructive instruments which would not be helpful in any case. Even under the best of circumstances, if there really was a blaze, there would be nothing useful anyone could do, except roast a pig and feed it to the poor.

Antonio, from his high vantage point, could see the townsfolk approaching in the near-distance. He stopped ringing the bells and began shouting across the wheat field to them. "Hurry! Hurry, good people of Asbury! The abbey is on fire!"

Meanwhile, far below him, in front of the bell tower, the Abbess stood in her nightdress, a bedsheet wrapped around her head. "Shut up, you moron," she shouted up to Antonio. "There isn't any fire!"

He didn't hear her. But it wouldn't have mattered if he had. It was too late. Within a few minutes, the length and breadth of the convent had been invaded by hundreds of unruly citizens, all of whom wanted to be in charge of extinguishing a nonexistent blaze. They threw so much water from their buckets that all the candles in the abbey were extinguished and soaked and could not be re-lit until they dried out. Plunged from organized illumination into flickering semi-darkness, their torches continued to burn, confusing things—

what was actually on fire and what was a group of men with torches became interchangeable in the confusion. While the private chapel housing the precious relics was locked and could not be entered by anyone but the Abbess, the fire the townsfolk brought with them easily darted between the bars of the gates and began to melt the holy effigy of Saint Pollye in her niche. Soon enough, the effigy was missing more than a tongue—Saint Pollye's lips were dripping from the tip of her chin and falling to her bosom.

When order was restored at last, the sky was glowing with the approach of dawn, illuminating much of the damage the abbey had sustained. Vegetable and herb gardens were trampled, fences torn down, wooden doors and windows hacked by axes. Many precious artifacts were either damaged or stolen. Even Sister Micaela recognized this event as a tragedy. All this destruction—brought upon the Sisters of Silent Penitence by a wayward wisp of wind.

Only Wigbert found amusement in the excitement. He spent the night running around the courtyard, chasing and being chased by children, *hee-hawing* at the moon, and laughing his donkey head off.

Duobus verbis ut dicam
You may speak two words

When she had completed the term of her first five years of silence, she was summoned to appear before the Abbess. Sister Micaela entered the *Misericord*, the special room reserved for discipline, with mixed feelings of elation and terror. The aged, Devil-tempting Abbess was seated in a chair in the middle of the room, with her hands clasped and her eyes closed. A pillow—probably a discarded *pulvillus tacitas*—was on the floor at her feet, the Devil's Ear facing the ground. The arrangement of chair and pillow usually signified that the penitent was going to be asked to kneel.

"Approach, my child," the Abbess said, "and kneel you before me.

The time has come, as you have anticipated, when we reward you for your devotion and diligence. By all reports that have reached out to me through the silence, you have been a most humble member of our Sisterhood, and a praiseworthy Bride of Christ. You may, today, speak two well-considered words. As we say—in an attempt to be lighthearted about this serious matter—*I offer you a lentil for your thoughts, briefly told.*" She placed her icy hands on Sister Micaela's cheeks. "I command you now to break your seal of silence and speak your two words. What is it that you wish to say to me?"

"Bed hard," Sister Micaela said emphatically.

The Abbess remained implacable. "Go in peace, my child."

Sister Micaela rose and left the somber *Misericord*. She would not return to it for five years.

Est alia quinque annorum silentio
Another five years of silence

Five years of lentil-sorting and dung-shoveling followed her visit to the Abbess. She never expected that her two words would produce a softer mattress, and they didn't. From that she learned a valuable lesson—expect *less* than nothing, and you will never have to resign yourself to disappointment, for *less than nothing* is still less than *ordinary, everyday nothing*. If you get ordinary nothing, be grateful, and rejoice that nothing was taken away.

Time passed more quickly in the second five years, even if time just led to more time and little else. Wigbert's whiskers had begun to turn gray. The composition of his laughter had changed, too, containing a larger proportion of snorts, and a smaller proportion of *hees*-and-*haws* than previously. Time had weighed heavily on him. In idle moments, his head drooped almost to the ground, and he snored, sleeping in the sunlight, dreaming and drooling.

Sister Micaela spent more and more time with the goats, becoming especially friendly with the bearded nanny, Priscilla. At some point, Priscilla stopped producing milk and baby goats. As Sister Micaela expected, preparations were made to "bring Priscilla to town." The last of Priscilla was inevitable. The largest reward given for years of faithful service at the Abbey of Pollye Loquaicius was a mere two words. Goats didn't need to speak two words, so they got nothing for providing milk and cheese and baby goats, and when it was time to go to visit the butcher in Asbury, they got less than nothing.

Sister Micaela was heartbroken at the prospect of losing her only female friend—unless her owl was female, something she was never able to determine—and she felt sorry for Clydas, too, knowing that he would soon be as isolated and alone as Wigbert had been for years.

If things followed a pattern, the billy-goat would soon be following her around. Then she would have a donkey and a goat competing for her attention. This would probably send Mother Mary Monitor into a rage, which—since the rage that had precipitated the false fire—no one at the abbey paid much heed to. In any case, if the order wanted to continue to put dairy products on its table, it would have to acquire a new nanny-goat or a cow, or trade in town for milk and cheese. She assumed a goat would be brought to the convent because there was still a possibility of using Clydas to manufacture more goats—something nature prohibited him from doing with a cow. If that happened, Sister Micaela and Clydas would have a new female friend, and only Wigbert would be nagging her for attention.

Having lost Micah, and now in the process of losing Priscilla, Sister Micaela was determined to have a keepsake of her beloved nanny-goat. The only option available, as far as keepsakes went, was to obtain Priscilla's small, curved horns. With complex hand gestures, she made it clear to Antonio that she wanted him to bring Priscilla's horns back to her when he returned from town. He appeared to agree, possibly hoping to be rewarded with a sexual favor, which, of course, would not be forthcoming. It was a shame he didn't share Wigbert's love of carrots, she thought. It would certainly make him more manageable.

Antonio did, in fact, bring her the little horns when the time came. They seemed very small indeed, but they gave her comfort. The day that Antonio had taken Priscilla for her final walk, she had gone into his ramshackle hut and stolen a small pot of carpenter's glue. She intended to build a little shrine—similar to the niche that held Saint Pollye's effigy before she melted—her creation would be a tribute to the relics of Saint Priscilla of the Goat Species. The glue and the little horns would help to make this shrine possible. Luckily for the former Mary Agnes, too, because having a secret plan that broke the order's rules and deceived both the Abbess and the Prioress, was the only way to face the silent expanses she would have to traverse in the days and years to come.

Duobus verbis ut dicam
You may speak two words

When she entered the *Misericord* for the second time, she had considerably lower expectations than she had on her first visit. Nevertheless, it shocked her to hear the Abbess intone the very same words she had used the previous time they shared a "dialogue" in this room together as if she was adhering to a predetermined script, crafted for deployment on all members of the community. To have the single moment of vocal intimacy that came but twice in a decade defiled in this way was more dehumanizing than all the sacks of lentils and mountains of dung that the abbey routinely substituted for acts of charity and kindness. Sister Micaela was struck speechless by the way her reward of two words was devalued by the disengaged demeanor of the Abbess. Luckily, she had only two words to say before the "interview" would be terminated. She was sure she could manage that much before breaking down.

"Approach, my child," the Abbess said, deviating as little as possible from her previous soliloquy, "and kneel you before me. The time has come, as you have anticipated, when we reward you for your devotion and diligence. You have been a most humble member of our Sisterhood, and a dutiful Bride of Christ. You may, today, after your second five years in my charge, break your silence and speak two well-considered words. As we have previously said—in an attempt to be lighthearted about this serious matter—*I offer you a lentil for your thoughts, briefly told.*" Looking down at her, she placed her withered, icy hands on Sister Micaela's cheeks, sending a sudden wave of nausea right through her. "I command you to break your seal of silence and speak your two words to me. What is it that you wish to say to me this time?"

"Food bad," she said emphatically. She stood up at once, rudely turning away from the Abbess as she proceeded towards the door. *Honor your Father and Mother,* she thought. *Another commandment broken.*

Once again, the Abbess remained implacable. "Go in peace, my child," she said, but Sister Micaela never heard her, and the Abbess didn't notice she had already gone.

Est alia quinque annorum silentio
Another five years of silence

Five more years of lentil-sorting and dung-shoveling followed her second, disastrous visit to the Abbess. She never expected that her two words would produce a better tasting meal, and they didn't. From that she re-learned a valuable lesson— the same one she had learned five years earlier. Now it was written in red ink. The lesson's sting was gone, too, replaced by something terrible, but it was something she couldn't quite define.

"I offer you a lentil for your thoughts, briefly told," she heard the Abbess croak in her head as she lay, sleepless, in her cell—and she heard more than internal voices, too. She listened for the night creatures that populated her sleepless hours—the spiders, the mice, the owl. She had learned to learn from them. Slowly, meticulously, the spider made its plans and wove its traps; cautiously the mouse looked out of his crevice, wary of danger and predators; the owl never stopped watching and waiting. All of them—as was she—were hungry. All had a single-minded focus on a goal. She resolved to have a plan of her own. She wove, she peeped, she surveyed the world around her. Mostly, like her companion, the owl, she waited.

Sometime later, she was engaged in work with the lentils again, but this time her assignment was to soak them in buckets of water, prior to their use by the cooks in the abbey's kitchen. The water-and-lentil-filled buckets were heavy, and she struggled as she carried them out into the early morning sunlight, straining to raise them high enough to set on the table in the courtyard. One summer day, there was one too many buckets to fit on the table, so she placed it on the ground. Meanwhile, Wigbert was watching her every move, as he always did, hoping for a caress or a carrot. He was still lovesick after more than a decade.

Not much later, Antonio entered the yard carrying bales of medicinal herbs destined for the market in Asbury. As soon as Wigbert saw the load he was going to be saddled with, he ran to the other side of the yard. Out of frustration, Antonio had long ago given up chasing the donkey. Controlling Wigbert without Sister Micaela's intervention was simply not possible. Each of them knew what was expected. Even Wigbert understood what was coming next.

Antonio glanced over at Sister Micaela and she nodded her head in assent, holding up a carrot to attract Wigbert to where she and the caretaker stood by the table of lentil buckets. Despite the carrot, he refused to approach while the caretaker stood near the desired treat. In order to speed things along, Antonio walked back to the cellarium to get more bales, while Sister Micaela, putting the carrot down on the table, rummaged in her pockets for more treats. The carrot, however, rolled off the table and landed in the bucket of lentils that had been left on the ground. Before she could stop him, Wigbert had his snout in the bucket and was noisily consuming the lentil-water-carrot mixture with great enthusiasm. This gave Sister Micaela an idea. Before Antonio could come back outside, she had fed the cooperative donkey four full buckets of gaseous lentils. All she had to do now was wait for them to take effect.

Soon enough, the Abbess emerged in her traveling clothes. Antonio and the Prioress took their places on either side of the donkey and they proceed towards the convent's gate. They had scarcely gone a few feet before the first volcanic salvo trumpeted forth.

"*O, meus Deus, en medias noctes!*" the Prioress exclaimed, crossing herself vigorously. "Mother Myrtle, was that you or the donkey?"

The Abbess reached over and brutally slapped the Prioress in the face with all her strength. It stung Sister Micaela just to hear it. "For that insolence," she hissed, "you will walk to Asbury *behind* the donkey. If the Devil has anything else to say, he can say it directly to your face."

Sister Micaela watched the despicable Prioress suffer this humiliation with immeasurable joy, but she knew this was only the first of Wigbert's contributions to a day of revenge. As she ran to the bell tower to get a long-distance view of the proceedings, she wished that the donkey could fully understand what was happening.

From the belfry, she had a perfect view of the road to Asbury. Every few yards, Wigbert would halt. When Antonio struck his rear end with a switch, the stricken rear would respond with an explosive outcry. Wigbert repeatedly kicked back with his legs, once or twice hitting the Prioress in the knees, and giving the Abbess a very rough ride. Every time he bucked, one of the bales would fall from his back, sometimes spilling its contents. Once or twice the Abbess was nearly thrown off with them. Finally, the moment of triumph came. Wigbert bucked so violently that the Abbess was thrown into a ditch. Wigbert was overcome with laughter and more flatulence. A frightened flock of crows flew up into the sky and screamed with him. Very bruised by her fall, the Abbess forced the group to return to the abbey. Even from her high vantage point, Sister Micaela could hear her saying that on the next trip to Asbury, the "cursed donkey" would be left behind. In the future, they would walk, and furthermore, the Prioress

COMMUNAL MANUFACTURE
OF THE PULVILLUS TACITAS

and Antonio would have to carry the goods to market on their backs. The two *new* donkeys glanced at each other most unhappily.

A few weeks later, Sister Micaela was made aware that another journey to Asbury Market had been arranged. She learned this from the lentil-sorting table, where the details had been meticulously spelled out in lentils during the course of a lazy afternoon.

Just as had been broadcast in the lentil newsletter, the caretaker was seen getting his bales ready late one afternoon, in preparation for the morning journey. Sister Micaela beaconed to him seductively and enticed him into the cellarium, where she signaled for him to wait for her. He probably hoped for a sexual favor, even if it was just a peek or a sniff. That, however, was not part of her plan. Fifteen minutes later, she returned, fully clothed. She carried a tray on which she had temptingly arranged a bowl, a spoon, and a very large pot of lentil and cabbage stew.

Diabolus est nobiscum!
The Devil is with us!

When she next entered the *Misericord*—this was her third visit, fifteen years after kneeling in front of the wooden Virgin of the Crossroads on a gray, rainy day—she felt a lightness in her step that she had not known for many, many years. It only took a moment for the Abbess to become suspicious of this slight change in demeanor. She studied the nun standing before her with ancient, narrowed eyes, wondering what two words were about to be uttered. In her many years as Abbess, she had heard a thing or two.

"Approach, my child," the Abbess said warily, "and kneel you before me. The time has come, as you have anticipated, when we award you once more for your devotion and diligence. You have been a most praiseworthy member of our Sisterhood, and a dutiful Bride of Christ. You may, today, break your silence and speak two well-considered words. As we say—in an attempt to be lighthearted about this serious matter—*I offer you a lentil for your thoughts, briefly told.*" Looking down at Sister Micaela, she placed her palsied hands on the nun's flushed, burning cheeks. "I command you to break your seal of silence and speak your two words to me. What is it that you wish to say to me this time?"

"I quit," Sister Micaela said emphatically.

The Abbess remained implacable. "I foresaw this. And I do not regret it. Although it grievously pains me to say it, you've done nothing but complain since you arrived here."

"Does your response to my decision amuse you?" the newly-lapsed nun asked, exceeding her word limit without a care. "I suppose you believe you have a chance to achieve immortality with that absurd retort, believe that through those mocking words you will live for years, for centuries, perhaps for eternity—remembered for all time for your cleverness. And, indeed, perhaps you will. Perhaps this sad conversation and our very brief conversations preceding it each half-decade will be the subject of a long-lived joke about a nun who uttered six words in fifteen years and was dismissed as a chronic complainer. But, nevertheless, now it is my turn to *really* speak, and I suggest, Reverend Mother, that you *listen* to my words instead of counting them to determine how many years of penance I will have to pay you for them.

"To begin with, Reverend Mother, you can keep your cursed lentil and have my thoughts for free. But, more to the point, I wish to help you understand that your clandestine activities with Antonio— your repeated fornications—are known to one and all. It is common knowledge that you lie with him whenever the mood is on you, which is shockingly frequent considering your advanced age, and that you have been engaged in this scandalous behavior for many years."

"What?" Mother Myrtle sputtered, shocked to the core of her being. "What nonsense is this? Who says this?"

"All the Sisterhood *knows* of it, Mother, they just don't speak of it aloud. So, to be entirely literal about the matter, not a single one of my sisters *says* it. It is known to all—silently. In Latin, if you will—in *Latin Silence*, whatever in Heaven's name *that* is. And while the Sisters of our order, honoring their vows, do not speak, one who *can* speak and *does* speak has used her voice to tell them all, each and every one of them—and me, of course—of your high fall from grace. What's more, my beloved Sisters, all of them at one time mere innocents—by virtue of the terrible influence you have had on them— have also fallen from grace in the corrupt atmosphere engendered by your lust. Many of them are regularly serviced like mares in the caretaker's filthy hut. In fact, Reverend Mother, you will learn to your dismay, several of my Sisters are now with child, carrying the spawn of the slobbering idiot you have taken on as your lover.

"The Bishop will be sending his Holy Emissaries here soon enough, and they will investigate all I have written of to him. They will lift the robes that hide the swelling bellies and see for themselves. The full extent of the sinfulness will be known, and the transgressors dragged into the daylight for all to see. You will certainly be among them. Mother Mary Monitor of the Last Nail will see to it.

"I may have been forbidden to speak, but I know how to write and spell, and none have forbidden me to send a letter. You just *assumed* that I would never do such a thing, that there was no one in this wide world who would take an interest in anything I might say, or write, or even think. But the Bishop *was* interested in my letter. Very, very interested. It would not surprise me at all if he came here himself, to deal with you in person."

The blood had drained from the Abbess' face, leaving her white and trembling, repeatedly crossing herself with such fervor and rapidity, she seemed to be scratching an itch. "Nothing, nothing, nothing you have accused me of is true. If Mother Mary Monitor of the Last Nail has spread this calumny... if... if... if...."

"*If... if... if....*" said Mary Agnes—at last no longer Sister Micaela—disrespectfully mimicking the stammering Abbess. "There is no *if* here, Reverend Mother Myrtle of the Mount of Olives. Like most things related to our convoluted beliefs, no one cares whether or not *any* of it is true. They just wish, as I do, to *believe*. Truth has no place within these walls. The Bishop will not care what is so and what is not so. And the Pope won't give a fig either. The Lord on high won't trouble Himself for a woman who has devoted her life to avoiding marriage with the Devil in order to give herself, instead, to an imbecile.

"Quite simply, despite your efforts to avoid it, despite the time you have devoted to prayer that it might *not* happen—whilst neglecting prayer for the sick and the poor which was your avowed duty—the Devil *has* discovered your hiding place. He *has* found you, Reverend Mother, in spite of all your elaborate precautions against it, and he is angrier with you for your sexual transgressions with that slobbering fool than the Bishop will ever be. The Devil has come for you to claim his due. He is here, at the abbey, right now."

With those words, she carefully removed her elaborate, starched head covering to reveal the Devil's horns growing from her head. Of course, these were the horns of Priscilla, the butchered nanny-goat, painted black and glued to her scalp with the carpenter's glue she had stolen from Antonio, but the Abbess had no idea what was happening, nor who or what was actually kneeling at her feet. Even Mary Agnes Fontoon had no idea who she really was at that moment.

Lest the Abbess see through the artifice, Mary Agnes stood up immediately and towered over the petrified woman, standing on her toes to increase the effectiveness of her threatening pose. She threw the wimple and cowl to the floor and, ripping open her black gown to reveal the ordinary garments of a common woman concealed below it—with the added feature of a swollen belly, an effect engineered by stuffing a *pulvillus tacitas* under her clothes—she tossed the lot of sacred garments at the Abbess' feet.

The last words she said to her, before turning and leaving the room, were spoken in a squeaky, broken imitation of a parrot's voice. "*Je t'aime, Nanette, toujour, toujour,*" she squawked, leaving the Abbess and her silent domain forever.

As the door of the *Misericord* slammed behind her, it severed—like the swing of a sharp scimitar—the high-pitched sound of the Abbess shrieking in horror.

A s she neared the crossroads, approaching from the direction of the Convent of Silent Penitence, wearing once again the ordinary garb of a commoner (without the deceptive padding, of course), she saw the strange peddler she had previously encountered there many years previously. Once more, he was standing before the statue of the Virgin of the Crossroads. Unhooded this time, as it was not raining, his reddish-golden hair gleamed in the sunlight. His placid, green eyes registered no emotion or surprise to see her after the passage of a decade and a half, as if he had long-expected this second encounter to occur. "You've returned to us,"

he said, referring to himself and the wooden statue. "At long last!"

"Your idea of 'at long last' and my idea of it may be very different ideas," she replied. She smiled pleasantly, but she was unsure how she felt about seeing this man again, as his presence invoked memories of her earlier youthful vulnerability at a time when she was once more feeling vulnerable. "Yes, good sir," she continued, "my sojourn with the Sisters of Silence is at an end, and I have regained my voice and my life. Once more, you see me here, back at the crossroads. This time, though, I expect no answers to come from a wood carving. This time I have not come to pay her a visit."

"I've hoped to see you," he said. "I've something to give you, something I've carried for a very long time." He bent down, rummaged in his basket, and brought forth an old horseshoe. "This belonged to your horse. I saved it for you, hoping you would pass this way again."

"How did you come by this? At the butcher?"

"No, no," he laughed. "A week or so after we last met, I saw the idiot caretaker of the convent leading your apple-eating horse, a sweet animal that I remembered quite well. He paraded him throughout the town, trying to sell him without success. I was curious, and I followed him all the way to the slaughterhouse. There, before the butcher could make an offer to him, I paid that caretaker handsomely for your horse. I even bought the idiot a woman for the night. Your animal was my companion—and I his—for many long years before he became a bit lame and eventually died of old age."

"Thank you for that, and thank you for the keepsake, but I don't want it. A horseshoe belongs on a horse's hoof, not in a lady's purse. The Lord commands us not to waste—a lesson I have learned very, very well, and have put into practice in ways you could never imagine. And, also, I have no need for an old, rusty horseshoe to remember our Micah—which was his name—as I have him always in my thoughts and prayers where my parents and my little brother are, as well."
"You're sure? They say that a horseshoe is a lucky thing."

"I don't believe in the existence of luck," she said. "So, it would not bring me any luck to have it. I'm a heathen at that dubious altar. Give the shoe to a horse—as a good deed—and let the horse have the luck that Micah did when you saved him from the butcher's cleaver."

He dropped the horseshoe back in his basket. Standing upright again, with a gracious flourish, he indicated the statue, pointing at the Virgin's left hand. A fresh peach rested on her palm, the sun gleaming in the droplets of moisture that dotted its velvety skin. She had last seen a peach on that same palm, wet with rain. "Perhaps this will tempt you instead," he said of the peach. "A *single* choice this time."

"Yes, I think it will. I've never tasted a peach. Never in my life. And I've had nothing sweet in all my years of silence."

"So, perhaps, just seeing the horseshoe has brought you luck in the form of a peach," he suggested. He gestured at the fruit again, but she did not rush forward to take it. Instead, she looked at it in wonderment, realizing, all at once, how often she had thought about it over the passing years. How odd it seemed that she had desired something for so long that she had never tasted or touched and seen only once. Her craving for it, she concluded, stemmed from Micah's refusal to choose it, and therefore, the alternate future in represented.

"Now that you have your peach to eat—or just to look at—if that's your preference," the stranger said, "where will you go next?"

"Since we don't have an apple or a horse at the crossroads this time, I suppose I'll be the one to take responsibility for what comes next." She looked around and sighed. "There are two roads here. One is an easy path that leads to Asbury and the other is a road to places unknown to me."

"The road will not be dangerous, if that is a concern for you. Nor will it be lonely. Pilgrims will be walking on it within the hour, coming this way from Asbury, where they've spent the night at the

Thameside Inn. It's a large and motley group—interesting folk from all classes and professions of our society—all of them with a common purpose, heading for the shrine of Saint Thomas à Becket at the great cathedral of Canterbury. I've heard that they are led by a Master Chaucer, a customs officer and justice of the peace, who—to help pass the time on the journey—proposes a storytelling contest among the pilgrims. Most likely, you have a goodly number of stories for telling—perhaps a winning tale."

"Who among us that breathes has not a single story to their name—if not a pocket full of them—to sell to a willing buyer when the price is right?"

In the distance, she heard the sound of a drum and pipes and singing. A large group was approaching. The tops of their walking sticks could be seen above the shafts of wheat in the fields beyond the Virgin. "That's the parade of pilgrims coming now," the stranger said. "A most marvelous cross-section of humanity—they celebrate the richness of life just by walking through it."

"I don't think I will join them," she said thoughtfully. "Master Chaucer and his story-loving pilgrims will have to manage without my contribution to help them to Canterbury and salvation. For the moment, I believe I've had enough of saints and relics and worship. Being still in my child-bearing years, perhaps I will go to Asbury and seek a fulfillment I've never had."

"One can get themselves with child quite easily, if that's your goal. If you find no husband, you can become a whore at the Thameside Inn. Soon enough you'll see your belly growing."

"Oddly—considering my recent vocation—it appeals to me. As I could say of peaches, I have never experienced Lust, either."

"If whoredom it is to be," the stranger said merrily, as if reciting a humorous poem, "then thou must follow me."
He bowed gallantly, like a courtier, then lifted his basket, heavy

with horseshoes and many other artifacts and oddments he had accumulated. He started walking towards Asbury-on-Thames with the basket on his back. She followed a few steps behind him. The sound of the pilgrims was closer now: the drumming, the fluting, the voices talking, laughing, singing. It was like the overwhelming din of Creation itself—all of life's stories being recited at once.

"Don't forget your peach," the stranger said. Just as he finished speaking those words, he glanced back at her and noticed that she had already eaten it—its juices were running down her chin—and she was about to let the fruit's stone roll off the palm of her hand, as once, so many years before, in the darkness of her cell, she had dropped the pebbles from her jar. That was many, many sins ago.

She walked slowly, always keeping him in sight, no matter how far behind him she lagged, enjoying the fresh air and sunlight and the odor of the wavering wheat. She could hear him whistling, although it was hard to pick out his music in the competitive din of the approaching pilgrims.

Moments before two very different possible futures crossed paths on the road that led to and from Asbury-on-Thames, she became aware of strange movement in the air above her. She looked up, squinting, straining to see what it was. Then she spied a colorful bird in flight—a wonder to behold, like a winged rainbow. The bird circled around them for a few moments, drawing an elliptical shadow on the ground, finally alighting on the stranger's shoulder. It had something shiny around its neck which glittered in the morning sunlight. It hopped closer to the stranger's reddish-golden mane, inserted its beak into it, and whispered in his ear.

A Prologue to The Florist's Tale

My mother, who is of Dutch descent, called me "Tulip" as a child because I was tall and slender and—so she said—beautiful to look at. I had bright orange hair then, which fit her chosen theme rather well—the monarchy of the Netherlands descends from the House of Orange, making me a visual match, or, at least a *rhyme* with the royal color. My sister, Petra, petite and as lively as a newly-hatched chick, was nicknamed Sweet Pea. We had a beautiful garden, filled with the flowers that were my first friends. My mother would often sit under the fig tree with us, serve us dollhouse tea, and tell us stories that she called Tulip Tales.

My given name—Ryland—possessed far less resonance for her than Tulip. She and her parents and siblings, in the last year of World War II—when the Nazi occupiers stole Holland's meagre food supplies and shipped them to Germany—were forced to eat tulip bulbs in order to survive. That's a tricky business, too, because tulip bulbs, if they're not prepared properly, can be poisonous. So, at best, a tulip bulb will taste like a mealy potato; at worst, it will make you sick; if there is nothing else to eat, not having a tulip bulb could kill you.

Sometimes flowers are more than symbols. They can be power-players in their own right, deciding matters of Life and Death. In the 17th-century, Amsterdam was the locus of Tulipomania, a craze that turned a nation of merchants into a nation of degenerate gamblers. Over a period of a few years, fortunes were made and lost on inflated bulb futures. This happened because a botanical virus caused genetic mutations in some of the bulbs, resulting in haphazardly occurring rarities—tiger-striped, multi-colored, one-of-a-kind, freak tulips. Ordinary citizens borrowed and stole, and risked the little that they possessed, just to purchase a single rare bulb. Prices rose hourly and outpaced any realistic evaluation of what was being bought and sold. Flowers had become a form of currency, rather than objects of beauty. A human virus—Greed—had caused mutations in Europe's psyche, resulting in wide-spread financial devastation when the tulip market crashed and the craze ended. Passion for tulips made many a grown man cry, and obsession brought some unfortunate few to suicide. Roses and violets had never done that. No flower had.

To atone for the Devil's work done by tulips in the past, an over-looked storage sack of ordinary bulbs had saved my mother and her family from starvation in 1944, as did many other such stores of bulbs across the Netherlands. No flower had ever done that either.

Flowers—their vivid colors, their beguiling scents, their elaborate Latin names—are a significant part of who I am, owing my life as I do to a woman who owes hers to a sack of tulip bulbs. Beyond my natural partiality to my flower-inspired namesake—actually a *nicknamesake*—I confess to my love for *all* flowers, without prejudice, but with a single exception. A gladiola will always make me think of Death holding hands with the Devil.

For use at funerals, the gladiola is the florists' friend. They "hold up" well—as if death-resistant—which makes me uncomfortable. It's the root of my distaste for them. There's something demonic about a floral arrangement competing with a deceased person to determine which of them can stay fresh longer. Flowers—at least at funerals—*should* wilt, and they should do so as obviously as possible, for all to see. There could be a useful lesson in that for the bereaved. Sadly, people don't go to funerals to learn things, do they?

The tulip, of all flowers, is closest to my heart— I can only hear the name of that flower as it sounded in my mother's voice. They are the most versatile in their colors, the most ambitious in their thrust heavenward; all they do is extreme, yet simply and modestly executed. Their blooms enjoy the briefest of life spans, so they must make their time with us count. The tulip's motto, and my own as well, is *Sed fugit interea, fugit inreparabile tempus*—truthful, insightful words penned by the great Roman poet, Virgil, during the reign of Augustus Caesar—*Fast flies, meanwhile, the irretrievable hour.* When one fully understands the full implication of the word *meanwhile* in that observation, the first true step towards Nirvana has been taken.

Flowers bring man much pleasure and a glimpse of our long-lost Eden—alas, if only Eve had picked a nice red tulip for Adam instead of an apple. The tulip makes a spectacular entrance, but visits briefly. It's a reminder to us to appreciate the happiness we're given before the inevitable wilting.

My childhood, and the childhood moniker, Tulip, straggle on the road I travel. I'm Ryland now, or just plain Ry. I'm still tall and slender and—my mother and some flatterers like to say—beautiful to look at, but my orange hair has *autumnized* into a receding and thinning dark auburn. When I dream that I'm looking in a mirror, my reflection in the dream glass is a smoothly polished monolith of Baltic amber in which a fly is trapped. My soul is the fly. Looking out at the world, all appears in a golden haze. Hold jars of honey before each of your eyes, like spectacles, if you want to see what the fly in the amber in the reflection in the mirror in my dream sees.

The season of my wilting will soon be upon me. I can sense it coming, especially on breezy, cool afternoons. Preparing for it, I've become an astute observer. I've noted that a tulip achieves the zenith of its beauty just as it begins to droop in a graceful downward arc, and a petal—or two—have dropped to the table.

Sitting with me under our fig tree, my mother was peeling apples for a pie. She said, "Your little sister asked me to make my special Dutch pea soup tonight, and I said I would if you approved."

"Will it be so thick that the spoon can stand up in it?"

"Only if you eat it while it's hot. If you leave the spoon standing too long like you did the last time, his feet will get cold, and he'll run away and jump in the sink to get warm in the soapy water."

"If I put a tulip in the soup, would that stand up like the spoon?"

"It would grow so tall in the soup it would bang its head on the ceiling and get knocked out. But, that's silly—tulips don't belong in soup—they're not food," she said. A sad look stole over her face, and she looked as if she might begin to cry. After a silent moment, she stood up, gathered her things, and took my hand. "Now come inside, sweetie. If you do your homework, clean your room, pick up Sweet Pea's toys in the den, take out the garbage, bring all the trash cans out to the curb and make sure the covers aren't loose, rake the lawn, pull up the weeds—if you see any—water the grass and the vegetable garden, pick up the figs that fell from the tree before the dog gets to them and makes himself sick, bring the dirty laundry basket down to the cellar, take your bath, clean your nails and ears, lay out your school clothes for tomorrow, polish your shoes, wash your hands, and take care of anything else you happen to remember that I forgot, I will reward you with a nice Tulip Tale at bedtime."

"Okay!" I said, and then she laughed and laughed and laughed. She laughed so much that—this time—she really did start to cry.

I'll always remember her list of prerequisites for a Tulip Tale, because—according to my recollection and my established reputation—I failed to perform *any* of them, including the homework. In all fairness to me, she had deliberately listed everything I was least likely to do. In all fairness to her—despite my shortcomings—I got the pea soup, the Tulip Tale, and a goodnight kiss as a bonus. Such is the life of a tall, slender, possibly beautiful, one-time tulip-boy.

TEMPUS FUGIT

Do you recognize this man? He is being sought for questioning in connection with the June kidnapping of an English bulldog answering to the name Doctor Watson. Any information will be treated in strict confidence.

— NYPD

LONG ISLAND TRAINS

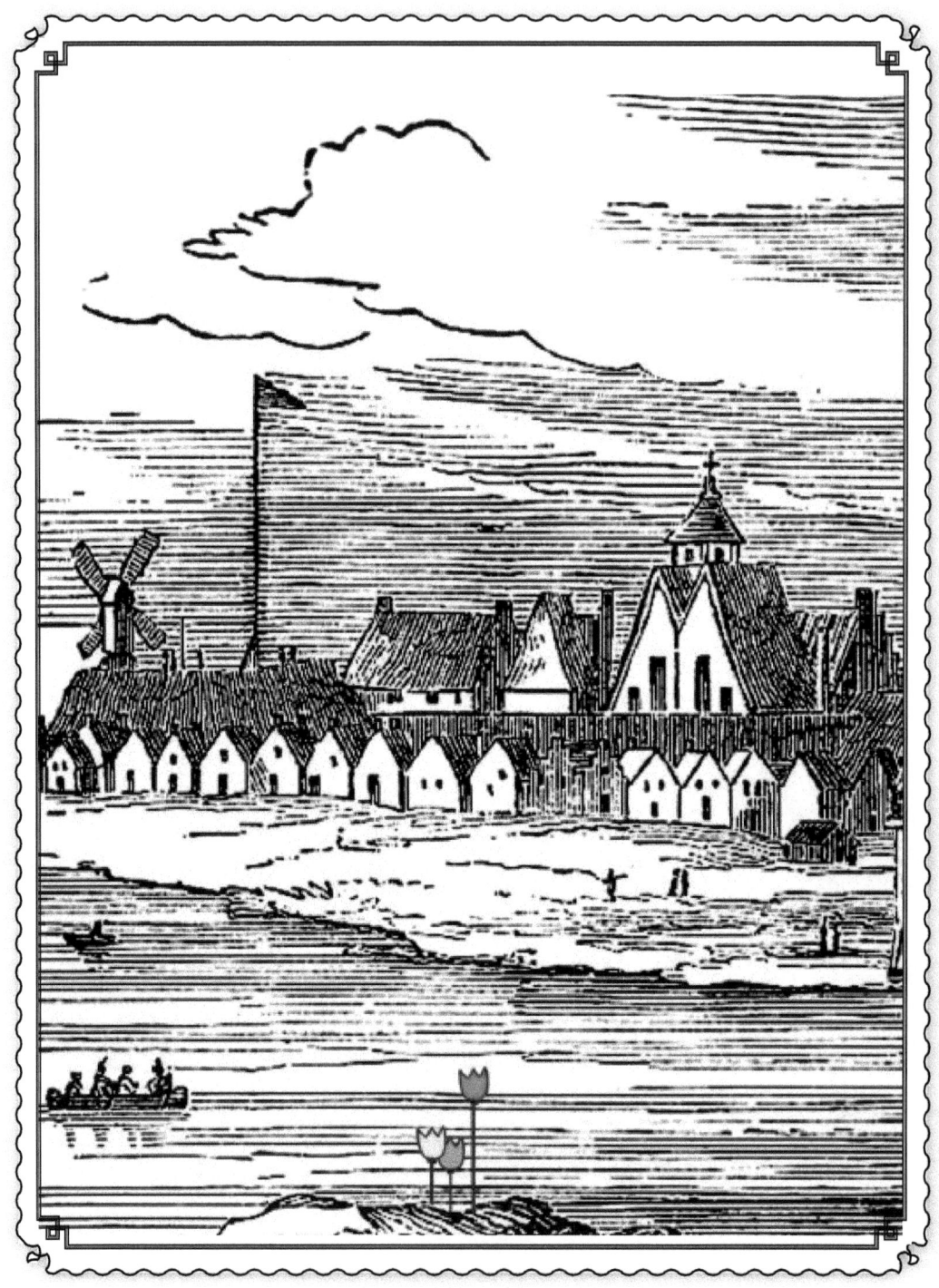

The Florist's Tale

The Tale of a Tall Tulip

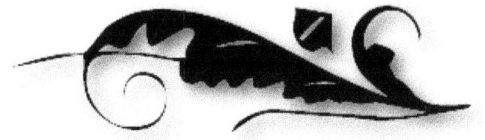

It was around the year 1640 when a ship arrived in Nieuw Amsterdam carrying a wooden crate addressed to Henrik-Jan Knickerbocker. When he got the huge crate home and pried it open, he found what appeared to be a sack of onions inside, carefully wrapped in many layers of protective materials. He knew at once that the contents were not onions. He was a Dutchman, well-educated, and knew a flower bulb when he saw one. Knickerbocker also knew that cousins back in Holland had lost all they possessed in the disastrous Tulipomania craze which had swept Europe a few years earlier. A letter that accompanied the crate explained all. His cousins implored him to accept restitution of a small family debt with this shipment. He was also asked to take a portion of the bulbs with a similar request to another colonist—wealthy Jonas Bronck—a Dane who lived north of the settlement, on a very large farm on the mainland, named for its owner, and known to all as De Broncks.

So, it came about that Knickerbocker—with his eldest son, Pieter—set out with a horse and wagon on a journey to a part of the New World they had not yet seen, even though it was a scant 14 miles distant from their town.

There were some dangers inherent in the journey, but they carried firearms with them as well some items to trade with any natives they might encounter, knowing very well that the red man would have no interest in tulip bulbs, no matter how rare or exotic they might be—or once *were*—to the Europeans. Their journey was further protected by the presence of other traffic along the rough road that connected the relatively safe Dutch settlement to places north of it. Scarce as other wayfarers might be, they were lucky not to be completely alone and found themselves traveling with a motley company heading in the same direction as they were.

One in that group was an elderly, talkative man named Maarten Swaans, who was, coincidentally, employed as a dairyman at Jonas Bronck's farm.

Upon reaching the ferry crossing at the northern tip of the island, they were obligated to respect the ferryman's schedule at the cost of an hour of delay. One and all lit their pipes and commenced gossiping to pass the time.

During this hiatus, Swaans pointed out a small clearing beside the waterway, dominated by a very large tree. "This is where Peter Minuit bought this island from the natives back in 1626," he informed the Knickerbockers as they strolled along the water's edge. There was no mistaking the reverence in his voice as he invoked a notorious event that would forever hold a place of honor in the pantheon of Dutch mercantilism. The purchase had been made from the unsophisticated natives for a shamefully low price, a bargain favoring the purchasers that could easily make amends for 1,000 additional epidemics of Tulipomania. The magnificent sheltered harbor—which held no significance beyond visual splendor to the landbound natives—was worth millions of guilders in international trade to the settlers.

Knickerbocker was overcome with awe to unexpectedly find himself at this historic site. There was a lump in his throat as he excused himself and ran back to his wagon. A moment later he returned with what appeared to be—to Swaans' unsuspecting eye—a common onion. "With thanks to our Lord and in honor of this miraculous place," said Knickerbocker, falling to his knees. Swaans turned away in embarrassment, assuming, good-naturedly, that the man before him was just a harmless lunatic or religious fanatic. Swaans—a

Dutchman himself—knew his countrymen to be equally tolerant of both, and drew little distinction between the two. He had no idea at all that Knickerbocker had just buried a valuable tulip bulb eight inches down in the damp earth.

It was the first tulip, in fact, to be planted on American soil.

Later, an extraordinarily tall and exquisite tulip shot up in the shadow of the huge tree's canopy. It grew in a place that would—years later—come to be known by the unlikely name of Spuyten Duyvil, which meant, in Dutch, "In spite of the Devil." The tree that stood guard over the first tulip was known as The Tulip Tree for 300 years until it was severely damaged by a storm in 1938. An engraved marker commemorates the spot today.

While their wagon was ferried across the waterway, Knickerbocker, in a gentle voice—without the slightest hint of regret—commented to his son, "How ironic our lives are, Pieter. Only three years ago, while still in its sack, that tulip bulb was worth more than a thousand times the price Minuit paid for the island on which we live. I could have bought your mother De Broncks for her birthday!"

Standing on the shore of Spuyten Duyvil, the famous Tulip Tree, photographed in 1913.

The Whitman Carriage on *The Brown Fox*. Built 1878. Restored 1951.

The Roosevelt Carriage on *The Brown Fox*. Built 1878-79. Restored 1952.

WINNER OF THE F.I.R.R. AWARD
ROBOTIC TOILET ATTENDANT OF THE YEAR

HERCULE POIROT

A paragon of discretion, Monsieur Poirot unravels many
perplexing mysteries, but he never reveals a lady's age
or a gentleman's *dimensions privées*

A Prologue to The Rabbi's Interview

ne of the Yeshiva students impulsively rose to his feet and spoke with urgency: "But wait just a moment, *Rebbe*, if you will be so good. The theory you put forth is either illogical or mathematically flawed. A *Mitndrinnen Gornisht Ort* that is composed of 20% nitrogen and other gases and 90% of bagel holes adds up to 110%!"

Shocked silence ensued. In a moment, his face reddening, the student regretted his outburst. He realized that it was extremely disrespectful to correct a pious elderly person in front of his fellow Yeshiva students, no matter how far-fetched and unbelievable his beliefs were. Actually, they were supposed to be humoring the venerable old man. The student thought, *If only there was a bagel hole nearby that was big enough to swallow me!*

Meanwhile, the ancient rabbi, whose shoulders had long ago atrophied into a catatonic shrug, could shrug not one millimeter further in response to the question, so he merely bobbed his head up and down and made a combination facial expression and hand gesture that customarily accompanied a shrug when properly enacted by younger, less arthritic, shruggers.

Shruggingly—this combination of *grudgingly* and *shrugging* was a unique malapropism created by Rabbi Scholnik for his personal use—he admitted, while smiling knowingly, his gold tooth glinting in the light of truth—that there was no established scientific method for measuring the volume of a mass of bagel holes, as such a mass was, first of all, a variable composed of variables, and secondly, a single bagel hole could only be evaluated in relation to the missing—now eaten—bagel that spawned it. There was not a scholar to be found who could summon the energy to dispute the ironclad logic of this explanation or make a single chip in the stone of senility it was carved in.

"Irregardless," the rabbi concluded, using another non-existent word that older Jewish men were so inexplicably fond of, "the *Mitndrin-nen Gornisht Ort* is like the space between Mars and Jupiter, which is not materially different than the space between Jupiter and Saturn, or the space between two fat people on the subway that your *tuches* won't fit between. It's just more space or less space, more or less. *More* space, not *different* space. Outer space, inner space, who-knows-where space. What does it matter?"

At this point, the withered rabbi looked up to discover that the conductor was standing next to him. "What can I do for you now? I gave the ticket already. You punched it already. And look—here, where you punched it—there's a hole. Do you know what this hole signifies?"

The conductor shook his head. "I'm not here about the ticket," he said, "or about holes. I came over to you to ask a question."

"*No questions.* I give lectures, not answers."

"It's not *my* question, Rabbi. There are four men in another carriage who want to interview you. They asked me to come and..."

"Interview me? For what do they want an interview?"

"Excuse me, but didn't you just say '*No questions*' to me?"

"What *you* said just now—'*Didn't you just say No questions?*'—happens to be a question. And when I said to you '*No questions*' I meant I won't *answer* questions, not I won't *ask* them. So now I am asking, what do four men who I never heard of, who I never laid eyes on, who I don't know from His Holiness, the Pope, want to interview me about?"

"Your life, I imagine."

"My life? *Oy,* some interview that will be—too bad I'm not talking! Tell me—which do I look like I had when I was your age, young man? A life that was all raisins and almonds, or a life that was some kasha with a scrap of meat, or a life that was a boiled shoe?"

"I'd guess a scrap of meat, with maybe one boiled shoelace on the side."

"This is true, you're very smart. And now, after all these years, my life is a nice piece of roasted chicken, a baked sweet potato, a piece of strudel, a glass of tea. On my way to Here, I saw many things, I learned many things. Now I have my Yeshiva students, and the students have questions. When I don't have the answers, I shrug. When I shrug, I'm in pain. You maybe heard of *lockjaw*? Shrugging pain is a new disease afflicting elderly Jewish men— they should call it *lockjew*. My life now is a piece of roasted chicken and an advanced case of lockjew. The scrap of meat and the one boiled shoelace— in my old age—are starting to look like they weren't so terrible after all."

What the rabbi was telling the conductor was not a complete exaggeration. One day, several years earlier, he had come home from his lecture at the Yeshiva, looking very haggard. He collapsed into a chair at the kitchen table and said to his sister, "They asked, I shrugged. Questions, questions, questions. I shrugged and I shrugged. I shrugged my *kishkas* out. Look at me— from all the shrugging, I'm two inches shorter than I was when I walked out the door this morning. *Oy vey*, my neck! Chop my head off, Esther, *please!*"

Chattering, she scurried back and forth between the refrigerator and the stove. "I'll make a new man of you with something tasty, like always."

"No food, *please!* My shoulders are hanging from my earlobes like a pair of earrings. God knows where my stomach is, maybe it's on the moon. "

"Let me cook you up something, Isaac. Aren't you hungry?"

"Don't ask me anything. No questions, *please!* God forbid, I might give a shrug. Leave me alone, just let me die."

Since he didn't know up from down, he decided to split the difference and lie on his bed. Staring at the ceiling in his bedroom, he swore he would answer no further questions, not even for the promise of money. Not having answers was painful, and the resulting shrugs made it much worse. At his advanced age, uncertainty mixed with interrogation was an unhealthy combination. It was psychological torture.

Now he had to deal with the crisis on the train. The rabbi, despite his state of decrepitude, still enjoyed attention, which made rejecting four willing attention-payers a serious matter—quadruple opportunities did not come along very often. Rejecting intellectual suitors, shunning the spotlight, was not in his nature. It brought him almost as much pain as shrugging.

He cleared his throat and extended his hands as if he were deciding an important matter for the Talmud or parting the Red Sea. "First your friends send you here to ask—will I let them interview me," the rabbi said to the conductor. "So, that's already *one* question. Then—if I agree—right away they'll run in and ask, 'How are you, Rabbi?' That makes *two* questions, and we didn't start the interview yet. Do I look like I could survive a thousand questions from four bored nobodies who think they're too good to play cards like everyone else does? So, let me think—maybe there's another way." He called to one of the Yeshiva students. "Moishe, can you look in my satchel and find a copy of my old bagel interview so I can give it to the nice train man? And wipe your hands before you put them in there."

Within moments the boy was back with a manila folder, which he placed in the rabbi's arthritic, wrinkled hands. The rabbi passed it to the conductor. "Whoever is asking, give them this to read. It's an old interview, maybe it's from ten years ago, the last time I remember answering questions."

"The last time you answered questions was ten years ago?"

"When did I say that? I said the last time I *remembered* answering questions was ten years ago. The last time I answered questions was, maybe, twenty years ago. Maybe it was more. How should I know?"

The little student leaned and over and whispered urgently to the old man.

"*What?*" The rabbi cupped his hand to his ear. "You know I hear nothing with nothing. What is it you want, little one? Speak up so I can hear."

The boy's face reddened, and he spoke louder. "I have to go to the toilet."

"The toilet, *keyn einhoreh?* Oy, what do you have to do? *Aleph* or *bais?*"

"Aleph," the boy replied shyly.

"Okay, you know where it is, but be careful. Don't talk to the electric man in there, and don't let that *goy* sneak any looks at your little *pretsl*."

"Okay, I won't let him."

"And don't get your *tzitzit* stuck in your zipper like last time."

The little boy ran off and the old rabbi turned back to the conductor. "Mister, what kind of *meshugeh* toilets have we got on this train? Inside, there's a television where there should be a mirror, and on the screen is a man with a dyed moustache who talks with a *feygeledich* French accent the whole time you are trying to do your business. You're making a *pish* and he's asking, 'Would you like to try the cologne, or shaving *parfum?* My little grey cells tell me you need to use the comb for only *une* dollar, or the *petite* toothpaste pack for the same price. *Oui, oui,* it's very cheap, *mon ami!*' Then there are two hands coming out of the wall and pointing at who-knows-what, and six glass windows, like in the Horn and Hardart, but instead of sandwiches and baked apples, there's Alka-Seltzer and Pepto-Bismol for sale inside. Meanwhile, the electric *yenta*, who claims to be the world's greatest detective, is looking for clues where he shouldn't be looking—he's some busybody, that one—and who knows what those hands of his are doing when they aren't tearing squares of toilet paper for you. Do you think I didn't catch him sneaking a peek at my ancient *schmekel* when I was doing my business? He knew I saw him, too—so then he asks—as if all I need is more questions, and in a toilet, yet—'What do they do with the part they cut off? Do they just throw it away, or do they bronze it like they do with the shoes?'"

The conductor had to suppress a laugh. "I'm sorry, but it's meant to be amusing."

"Amusing? How could that be? Once, in Warsaw, I heard a corpse pass wind and that was funnier."

"It defies analysis. You go *wee-wee* and he goes *oui, oui,* that's the sum of it, Rabbi. It's just a form of entertainment."

The conductor now tried to extricate himself from the rabbi's conversational clutches. He said, "Well, thank you again, rabbi—on behalf of the gentlemen in the next carriage who sent me—I'm sure this interview will be more than enough information for them. I'll deliver it right away."

He was about to leave, but the rabbi grabbed his sleeve and pulled him back. He pointed to little Moishe, who was now returning from his adventure in the toilet. He summoned the boy to come over again. As he approached, the boy held up his hands and wiggled them, as if to demonstrate that he had washed them.

"*Nu?* You went in the *meshugah* toilet and made a *pish?*"

"Yes, *elter-zayde*. The man in the mirror was very nice to me. He reminded me to wash my hands and gave me a little towel to dry them. Then he asked me where I was going."

"And what did you answer?"

"I said I was going to be with God—in one hundred and twenty years."

The rabbi cackled and put his arms around the boy affectionately. He turned to the conductor and said, "Take a look at this soon-to-be bar-mitzvah boy—you could never guess how clever he is, *keyn einhoreh!* He spends his entire day, from sunrise to sunset, bending over his books. God forbid he should become a hunchback or ruin his eyes from all the studying he does!" He pinched the boy's cheek and sent him back to his schoolmates. "I'll tell you a little secret—but only because you didn't ask me. That little one I just showed to you is my great-grandson."

Suddenly, without the slightest warning, the rabbi was stamping on the floor of the carriage with all his might. *Boom! Boom! Boom!* Leaning forward as best he could, the decrepit old man began shouting in the direction of his feet. "Did you hear that, Adolf? That was my great-grandson just now! Here we are in the land of milk and honey and kosher hot dogs, with streets paved from gold, and with talking toilets that say *thank you* when you have a bowel movement! That's right, even our shit brings them joy here! And, look at us, we go on shitting, and we go on breathing, so we must still be alive, right? *Ha-ha-ha!* How do you like *that*, Hitler? I hope that's okay with you! If not, *ir kenen brenen in genem.* The Devil should spit in your eye and kick you in the balls when you go to wipe your face."

The conductor was completely stupefied. The rabbi had turned very red and was cackling and slapping his knees gleefully. The Yeshiva students did not react at all. They didn't even turn around. They just continued throwing pickles at each other. Apparently, they had seen this performance before. After a moment or two, the rabbi regained his composure and sat upright. The conductor, at a loss for words, fanned the old man with the manila folder while he waited for his wheezing to subside. Meanwhile, the rabbi smoothed his beard out over his shirt, as if he was tucking himself in for the night.

"Yes," the rabbi said, having collected what remained of his wits, "my little great-grandson, *meyn sheyn kleyn eyngl.* I would eat him alive this very minute, but I had already a nice tongue sandwich and a few pickles and a little potato salad. As you can see for yourself, the little old rabbi has left the boiled shoelace behind him—very far behind—back in a *shtetl* they wiped from the earth—it's an empty hole now, a *nisht-shtetl*—a *Mitndrinnen Gornisht Ort-Shtetlach*—from which I, Isaac Scholnik, came into the world, maybe it was ninety years ago, the year that Vodnik's cow died. I can barely remember it. So, don't ask me anything about it. I probably already told you that I don't answer questions."

"So, Rabbi Scholnik, if all I asked you was whether or not you wanted mustard for your tongue sandwich, would you answer that?"

The rabbi tilted his head to one side, defiantly folded his arms over his chest, shrugged with his eyebrows and lips, but said nothing.

BAGEL BAKERS CONCLAVE
KRAKOW 1875

The Rabbi's Interview

The Theory of Bagel Relativity

[This article originally appeared in the *Jewish Gourmet & Garment Inquirer*]

Banish all stereotypes of the grotesque bagel-craving lunatic of the sepia-tinted past—there is a colorful *new* generation of bagel-eaters on the scene. The bagel-lover of our time is hale, hearty, and hungry—a virtual Eating Everyman. Step up and meet Dick. Also meet Jane. Also see Spot run—especially when a bit of bagel falls to the floor. See Dick and Jane eating bagels and lox with a nice *schmear* of mayonnaise. Dick and Jane and Spot are devout Mormons. They "just *love* bagels" and don't mind saying so during their frequent cellphone calls.

In a recent visit to a Manhattan bagel shop, we encountered Caucasian ba-gel-eaters, African-American bagel-eaters, Middle-Eastern bagel-eaters, matched Latino and Latina bagel-eaters, Asian-American bagel-eaters, Euro-trash bagel-eaters, bagel-eaters named Corky and Muffy and Juanita and Jamal and Gian Marco. From far, from wide, the new bagel-eaters keep coming—the blond, the blue-eyed, the proudly uncircumcised—shrug-ging off years of reticence, and demanding today's bread of choice, sweep-ing their formerly-favored fads—English muffins, croissants and their like—into oblivion's moldy bread-bin. Even the common slice of toast has been relegated to an unmarked grave in the high-glycemic graveyard.

Babies are given teething rings made to look like bagels; rumors circulate that Baked by Melissa will produce a line of assorted thimble-sized bagels; crime reporters expose budding Arab terrorists who claim to have learned to eat bagels while smiling as part of their comprehensive infiltration train-ing.

Rabbi Isaac Scholnik addresses many readers' concerns—culinary, social, religious, mystical, mundane—about the common bagel in all its varieties. The questions most commonly asked of him are answered, and they run the gamut from a little of this to a little of that and back again. One might call this the "everything bagel" of bagel inquiries.

The good rabbi proposes that the bagel has never held a more prominent position in the public eye than it does today. "When gluten-free licorice bagels with a low-sodium tofu *schmear* appear on menus, it is time to take a probing look at what is happening," he stated before our interview began. "With gentiles running to the bagel stores like there will be no tomorrow, perhaps it is time to ask ourselves how we Jews woke up one Sunday morning and found ourselves waiting at the end of the line behind them."

Bagels, he asserts, also play an important role in cosmology and mysticism, although he readily admits that for most bagel-eaters, the consumption of a bagel is—in his terminology—just a "*nosh*." There are others, however, for whom the bagel is not merely food, it is a metaphysical question in the form of food. Rabbi Scholnik is among those *others* and he will make a persuasive case for why you should be one, too.

In the rabbi's words: "A large part of the bagel is non-bagel in nature. What are we to make of this missing matter? And where—in our vast universe—are the holes from all the old bagels?"

AN INTERVIEW WITH RABBI SCHOLNIK

— *Dear Rabbi, why are bagels so fat?*

Take a look at who is eating bagels, and you'll have your answer. People today are quite fat, and history tells us that where there are oversized people, there is oversized food. In the middle of this country there are people so fat—*chazzers*, really—it is hard to believe what you are seeing is real.

But, the real reason that bagels are increasing in girth is that—for the most part—they are no longer boiled. To be a real bagel, a bagel must be boiled. If the ring of dough is not boiled in a kettle before baking, it is—for lack of a better term—a *nisht*-bagel and it will most likely be a fat one. To save time and labor, (which means to save money) *nisht*-bagels are steamed instead of boiled; they are steamed in a machine that becomes the oven that bakes them as soon as the steaming is over. This also saves steps (from the rolling table to the kettle to the oven), and to understand saving steps, you must study the phenomenon known as the mother-in-law. *Nisht*-bagels, like mothers-in-law, do not move from one place to another, they do not take steps (why should they? they have you for that) and the more they sit, not taking steps, complaining, making comments, the fatter they get. And the less appealing.

To the ignorant, bigger bagels are better bagels. They don't know that bagels should have a thin, hard crust, that—when you take a bite into them—they should make a slight crunch sound, not a *whoosh* like an old sofa when your fat mother-in-law sits down on it. You should have to jerk your head back from the neck—just a little—to take a bite from the bagel. Let the ignorant go on thinking that the bigger bagels are better. The ignorant don't know they don't know. Now that's what I call a blessing!

Surprisingly, though, *nisht*-bagels are in some ways practical for certain people—mainly the elderly. Firstly, the elderly have long ago lost their memories and have no recollection of the real boiled-then-baked bagels of yesteryear. They say they do, but they don't; they like to reflect on the past, for them, everything was better years ago, but what do they really remember? *Nisht, nisht,* and more *nisht*. Secondly, the elderly have no teeth with which to take a bite from a crusty bagel. Thirdly, most older people would not survive the necessary jerks of the head required without risking serious neck injury or a dizzy spell. My great-grandfather—he should rest in peace—once took a bite of a bagel at the breakfast table, and when he put the bagel down to take a sip of tea, his dentures followed to the plate as well, still deeply impaled in the bite mark, a terrible sight for a child to behold. At a tender age, I had no idea there was such a thing as false teeth, and I ran from the room in terror. My mother explained it all to me, but still, I had nightmares. Later, when he died and I tried to recall his beneficent smile, I could only conjure images of his false teeth clenching the bagel-of-life from beyond the grave. But I digress.

Big, puffy bagels with the consistency of mattress stuffing are also good for making sandwiches—that typically American meal, which we first encountered on Ellis Island. The fat, airy bagel has taken the place of bread as a more filling option. And, I must admit, the bigger it looks, the better it sells. A sandwich that looks like it wouldn't fit in the mouth of a horse, is easily compacted with a little squeeze of the fingers, for there is no substance in the steamed-to-death dough. One good pinch and the whole bagel is flatter than *matzoh*. Hence the mile-high *nisht*-bagel has gone to war with the mile-long hero. May the fattest person—who doesn't know any better—win the sandwich of his dreams.

— What is a water bagel?

While walking with me on the Lower East Side years ago, my grandson saw a sign in a bakery window that said in neon letters "WATER BAGEL" and he was confused. He asked me if the water bagel was an aquatic roll caught by fishermen with the lox already in it. No, I told him. It was a bagel that was boiled—as it should be—before it was baked. Then he wanted to know what a bagel that hadn't been boiled was. "Nothing," I told him, "that's what. *Gornisht*. Believe me, the hole is the tastiest part."

— Rabbi, from matzoh we have matzoh-meal pancakes, and matzoh-brei and matzoh-ball soup. Is there also bagel-brei, and bagel-ball soup, and so on?

No, thank God. Maybe the goyim make donut-meal pancakes, donut-brei, and donut-ball soup. You'd have to ask one of them.

— Are thirteen bagels unlucky?

This is not just one question. Look carefully, and you will find three or four questions lurking here. Maybe there are thirteen questions—even worse luck! To answer, one must first grapple with the concept of luck—a fearful prospect. One wrong move could prove ruinous. Just dare to suggest there is no such thing as luck and right out the window goes the profitable

Wednesday night bingo game at the *shul*. Then, one must decide—assuming that there is such a thing as luck—if it could apply to a food item, such as a bagel or a *kreplach*, and by extension to the possessor or maker or eater of the food item. And finally—probably toughest of all to tackle—one must play the role of numerologist, to determine if the number thirteen (or any number, for that matter) will alter the questionable luck of the inanimate food item favorably or not. A related question is also of interest—"Lucky for who?"—and I can partly respond to it by saying that to be asked if thirteen bagels are lucky is not lucky for the rabbi who gets asked about it.

Imagine the appetizing counter of your delicatessen and think to yourself: is *this* lucky? is *that* unlucky? what about the *kishka*? the *kasha varnishkes*? the chopped liver? how about a half-pound of nice sliced Nova? maybe a couple of pickles? six? seven? thirteen? The refrigerated case has turned into a minefield. What if the ultimate success of your wish for your *mees-kayt* daughter to marry a doctor—nurtured by you for years—depended on whether or not you manage to buy the correct lucky number of *latkes*?

Out there, somewhere, there is someone who ate the thirteenth bagel and one hour later won a ten-million-dollar lottery. Out there, also, is someone who choked to death on just such a bagel. Are these events God's Will or Coincidence? No doctor, no matter how crazy, will say that someone choked to death from Coincidence. He might write down Natural Causes, but if he is Jewish, he is thinking this was surely God's Will. The man who wins the ten-million-dollar lottery is also thinking this is surely God's Will. After all, who ever won a lottery through Coincidence?

Now we come to the curious case of the man who eats the thirteenth bagel and—while he is eating—sees in the newspaper that he has won the ten-million-dollar lottery. He gets so excited that he chokes to death on the bagel. God's Will compounded by God's Will is the very definition of Coincidence! Here, then, is Rabbi Scholnik's Equation of Luck:

> God's Will Squared Equals Coincidence
> expressed as follows
> $$GW^2 = C$$

Hopefully, this answers all your questions about the thirteenth bagel. The next time you buy bagels, you can avoid the thirteenth bagel—if you feel you must—by buying just eleven instead of twelve. The baker will think you are a *shmoiger*, and it won't be by Coincidence. Or God's Will.

— *Learned Rabbi, should you give the thirteenth bagel to the poor?*

Here we are, back to the thirteenth bagel from which there is no escape. Let me begin by saying, this question is not so much about whether or not to give the free bagel away, but what constitutes the "poor" and whether giving away something that you got for free constitutes "giving."

The second part is easier to respond to. Anytime you *give* something, you *give* it. It makes no difference whether it cost you something or not. If giving something should happen to be a sacrifice, however, the *mitzvah* is larger than it would be than if it wasn't a sacrifice.

Here are some illustrations of this. Let us say you are dying for a knish. You buy one from a vendor. One minute later, you see a beggar who is starving, and you give him the knish. This is a *mitzvah*. If you don't have any money to buy another knish for yourself, it is a bigger *mitzvah*. If the knish you gave away is the last knish on earth, you have hit the *mitzvah* jackpot in the knish category. You can't squeeze more *mitzvah* out of a knish than this. In another scenario, you go to the bakery and buy twelve bagels. The baker, as always, gives you thirteen bagels. The thirteenth bagel is a gift, it cost you nothing, except you had to endure the baker's miserable expression as he ceremoniously put the thirteenth bagel in the bag as if it were one of his kidneys. You feel very generous. When you go outside you see a beggar. "Would you like a bagel?" you ask. "Nah!" he says. "I just ate a knish."

You are walking home, and you feel like a *putz*. What just happened? You bought twelve bagels—which you needed like a hole in your head—just so you could get one free bagel. Then you couldn't even give it away. A beggar, no less, wouldn't even take it from your hand. That *schnorrer*, the baker, got the *mitzvah*, not you. He gave something away. He made a big *megillah* sacrifice of two cents, so it was a very small *mitzvah*, but you spent almost ten dollars on a dozen bagels—many of which you didn't need—

and in your dealings with the beggar you got a *nisht-mitzvah*. So far, the baker is winning. A *mitzvah* trophy will soon be in the bakery window.

The baker is closing down the bakery for the night. He is thinking about how poor he is. He reflects, "This is natural, isn't it? Everyone thinks they are poor. There are very rich people who think this." Nevertheless, he is a little resentful when he recalls the customers with enough money to splurge on twelve bagels who he has to supplement with a thirteenth bagel because the Gentiles do that with their powdered donuts. "Ridiculous!" he thinks. In his mind, he can see the smug faces of the customers who are sucking his blood with their free bagels.

He makes up his mind to bend the rules. From now, he will institute a new policy. "If you buy thirteen bagels, you get the fourteenth bagel for free." He knows quite well that elderly, superstitious customers from the old country won't ask for thirteen bagels. It will be a war in their souls to risk the dreaded unlucky number just to get something free. He covers his mouth and giggles. But in God's eyes, a fourteenth bagel bandied about with malicious intentions can never be a *mitzvah*, not even if you give away a trillion of them. The baker is in grave spiritual danger; God could smite a baker's oven for such a shenanigan.

— *My mother says that a garlic bagel wards off the evil eye. Is it true?*

Yes. It is not as effective as saying the phrase "*Keyn einhoreh!*" and spitting three times, but if you have terrible garlic breath when making that utterance, it might lend extra protection. It certainly couldn't hurt. If fear that a gypsy will put a curse on your child keeps you awake at night, you can make a necklace of garlic bagels and put it around the child's neck. For an infant, you can make a mobile from a few and hang it above their crib.

— *Do other bagel types have specific uses or attributes?*

And how! It is awkward to address such peculiarities in the context of the lowly bagel, but I understand that the rainbow bagel is used by some persons for attracting members of the same sex. So, the secret is "out" as those rainbow bagel-eaters like to say!

Recently I noticed that the local priest was buying a lot of these rainbow bagels, and I asked the baker on Rivington Street about it. He gave a shrug at first, then an earful... maybe there were *two* earfuls! I can now write a book about what people who are not being fruitful and multiplying are doing instead with their extra free time.

A few warnings about these bagels. First, don't ask the baker about them, or you will soon have a headache. Second, be careful how the rainbow bagel is handled. In these communities—along with the many other colorful peculiarities I won't bring up—there is a secret code system for their proper display. I think eating with the left hand is for attracting people who like meat, and the right hand is for people who prefer dairy. Also, there are certain implications if a bagel is cut or uncut and which half is the top and which is the bottom. Use caution, or you run the risk of sending a false signal and may wake up in a strange room, bagel-cuffed to a rainbow radiator.

The rainbow bagel is occasionally referred to—rather humorously—as the *feygeleh-bageleh*. At the Stage Deli, olive cream cheese on a rainbow bagel appears on the sandwich menu as "The Judy Garland." If you want to know more about rainbow bagels, you should write to the Pope.

There are other bagel varieties to be found which are associated with specific communities. The most well-known is the green bagel for Irish people on St. Patrick's Day. I will only say, regarding this variety, it is not a pretty sight when someone has had too much to drink—a routine occurrence on this holiday—to see green bagel, pink lox, and who knows what else, splattered all over a person with a bloody nose who is urinating between two cars. *Feh!*

— What are the latest bagel shapes on the market?

Of those that come immediately to mind, there is the flagel (flat), the squagel (square), the bowl-shaped spraygel (soup filled), the ball-shaped boccibagel (Italian sun-dried tomato and mozzarella bagel with three holes), and the newly-introduced Holy Communion wafer-bagel, the praygel.

— What is the backstory of the bagel and the schmear?

The story of the Polish bagel from Krakow and the little *schmear* from Philadelphia is a love story like no other. Not even Abelard and Heloise can rival it. It should be a children's book, and then a children's movie. Already we have Bucky Bagel on television on Sunday morning. Before you turn around there will be Shelly Schmear and Larry Lox dancing around with him. I cannot explain to you why this type of comedic misfortune is prone to befall the beleaguered Jews. Can you imagine turning on the television and seeing a leg of lamb dancing an Irish jig with a jar of mint jelly? Probably not.

So, you want to know about cream cheese and how it ended up on the bagel? One taste and you'll have your answer. As they say in Yiddish, it was *bashert*—fated.

Theirs is a true May-December romance. The bagel hails from Poland, and it is centuries old. Cream Cheese (which is the maiden name of the *Schmear*) is much younger; it first appeared in the mid-19th century with the fancy-schmancy name of Philadelphia, later to be mass-marketed by Kraft after the first World War.

Such cheese was light, delicious, easily spreadable, and it held up well in the primitive electric refrigeration of those long-gone days. Who brokered the marriage to the Bagel Family from Krakow I cannot tell you, but certainly it was an inspired moment in the history of matchmaking, which was once a leading Jewish industry.

Eastern European Jewry was, historically, quite fond of cured and smoked fish, so it was only a matter of time before the lox jumped into the bed with the bagel and the *schmear* for the Sunday morning *ménage à table* we love so well. Add a nice thin slice of red onion and maybe a few capers, and you are—as they say—in business. But you must be lucky enough to live near a good delicatessen, with a real artist at the lox counter, to fully enjoy such luxury. Pre-packaged lox has probably been frozen at some point, as is most restaurant lox, and will surely have an unappealing gummy texture. It will also be sliced as thick as the sole of your shoe. Restaurants serve this inedible lox piled a mile high like a corned beef sandwich. Such disgraceful lox is also to be found ground up and mixed with cream cheese, sold to gullible gentiles as "Lox Spread."

For such sins of the fish-flesh, I, Rabbi Scholnik, give the rating of Triple-F: "*Feh, Feh, Feh!*" How bad is that? For comparison: pickled pig's feet are awarded one extra *Feh!* and arsenic two extra.

— *What is a bagel without lox?*

About five dollars cheaper.

— *Are today's bagels still Jewish or are they now non-sectarian?*

I make no claim to speak for other religions, but as something of an expert on Judaism, I can state with great authority that there is no such thing as food that is Jewish. Kosher, yes; Jewish, no. For one thing, we allow the animals we eat to walk around on *Shabbat* and do whatever comes naturally to them. We don't force our cow to sit on her *tuches* when she hears the *shofar* blowing inside the *shul* on Friday night, do we? If a chicken feels an egg coming, we just shrug and we don't throw the egg away, either. Don't we turn a blind eye to the big fish who are eating the little fish on the day of rest? Furthermore, we don't circumcise our animals, we don't pinch their cheeks, and we don't force them to undergo a bar-mitzvah if—God willing—they should live to thirteen.

Different rules apply in other religions. Buddhists, for example, have sacred cows, and they believe in reincarnation, which—if there is any truth to it (which of course there isn't, as any imbecile could tell you)—makes it possible for your mother-in-law to come back as a salmon and end-up as a slice of lox on your great-grandchild's bagel. *Oy*, what a thought *that* is!

Thanks to Lenders and their ilk, with their new step-saving dough-steamers, their flash-freezers, their polyethylene packaging, all of which have robbed the bagel of its character—they even pre-slice them, so you don't have to cut, you don't have to chew, you don't have to taste—the *nisht-*bagel has been popularized to the extent that it is not seen as belonging to any particular community or religion. It's not Polish, it's not Jewish, it's not from the planet Earth, and quite frequently today, it's not even good to eat. Utah, a state heavily afflicted with Mormons, consumes more than 22 million bagels a year. Imagine eating that many bagels without allowing yourself a little glass of tea to wash them down!

— *Is the cartoon character, Bucky Bagel, Jewish?*

Bucky Bagel is a carbuncle on the advancing foot of humanity.

— *Does the Everything Bagel hold a special place in the family of bagels?*

The Everything Bagel is the most important of all bagel varieties because the word *everything* imparts a metaphysical context that no other bagel can claim. But first, I would like to tell you the fascinating story of how the Everything Bagel came to be.

Our old friend the baker—who you might remember from the "Thirteen Bagels Scandal" which we discussed earlier—was opening his new bakery on Rivington Street. His old bakery had burned down when God—angered by the baker's nefarious bagel hooliganism—smote his oven. Luckily, the baker had insurance. Luckily the baker's wife didn't turn into a pillar of poppy seeds. All was not lost. Not only that, the baker gained a greater awareness of his weakness of character. To repent, to avoid all temptation, he decided to once again change the rules. From now, to thwart the Devil's love of the number thirteen, he decided, he would sell no more than eleven bagels to a customer. Some business might be lost, but he wouldn't have to give anything away. This was a good compromise, and one that would displease few—although his wife was convinced her husband had lost his mind. "They're all calling you The Bagel Nazi," she scolded, to which he replied, flicking his fingers at her, "Sticks. Stones. *A deigeh hob ich?* I should worry?"

To attract more customers, and to offset any income lost due to his "Eleven-Only Policy," the baker expanded the range of his products to include a variety of enticing new bagel flavors. He was, before long, doing very nice business with plain, salt, onion, garlic, poppy, sesame, sunflower, and caraway bagels. Up to the number eleven, his only desire was to please his customers and God, and to keep his wife as far from the bakery as possible. Every day he swept the oven clean of all the burned seeds and flavor bits that had fallen from the bagels during their baking and threw them away. While doing this one day he heard a long-forgotten voice calling to him from the depths of the oven. "Don't waste food, Shmuel!" the voice moaned, with a breath both hot and onion-y. "There are people in Asia eating wood!" He was sure he recognized his paternal grandmother's ancient, crackly voice, and he remembered those very words (and the agonizing pinch on the fleshy part of his arm that went along with them) from his childhood in Flatbush. "Bubbie!" he called into the hot, empty oven. "Before you go, please, what's the recipe for your potato and parsnip *latkes* that you never wrote down?"

Meanwhile, the baker's hysterical wife was running like the wind to the rabbi. "Oy, Rabbi, what a *brokh!*" she cried, pulling her hair and rocking her head to and fro in despair. "My husband is talking to his dead grandmother in the bakery oven! Even here, three blocks away, I can smell his beard burning!"

The rabbi, fearing a *dybbuk* might be loose in the bakery, came running with a hastily assembled *minyan* of ten old Jewish men and the rusty, medieval instruments of exorcism under his arm—just in case. The terrified group of decrepit old men hobbled as fast as they could behind the rabbi's flapping coattails all the way to Rivington Street, wheezing like a ten-octave squeezebox, with no idea what they might come up against. "The crazy Bagel Nazi has finally flipped his *kugel*," was all that the rabbi had told them. When they got there, the baker was sitting inside, whistling a tune and calmly wiping soot from his eyeglasses with a piece of cheesecloth. To the *shvitzing*, traumatized rabbi, he said with the utmost respect, "Can I help you with anything less than twelve bagels?" The baker's wife fainted dead away on the spot.

There is no escaping one's true nature. The baker was a *schnorrer* to the core, always thinking of clever ways to squeeze something from nothing. So, it was only a matter of time before he came upon the idea, with his dead grandmother's heated prodding, to use the wasted bits of this and that from the oven floor to make a new kind of bagel. This, Bubbie's baked-in-the grave whisper told him on another of her oven visitations, stinking of garlic and burned poppy seeds, he should name the "Everything Bagel." She was less forthcoming with the *latke* recipe, and he never managed to get it, no matter how much he pleaded into the bowels of the oven.

So, this is how the most popular bagel (after the generic plain bagel) in the history of the world was invented. Before a week had passed there was an enormous line to enter the Eleven-Only Bagel Bakery to buy the widely-discussed Everything Bagel. And before a full month had passed, the Everything Bagel was the Everywhere Bagel, in all the city's bagel bakeries. Eventually, the furor died down and life continued much as before. But millions of assorted seeds and grains of salt, and bits of onion and garlic were saved and put to good use. The Everything Bagel gave life more variety, made living seem better, sweeter, somehow—even if only just a little bit. The baker did not take advantage of his connection to the other world. He maintained his limited sales policy of eleven bagels per customer and—except for occasional problems with his nervous wife—led a peaceful, blessed existence. After a few years, the baker went deaf and could no longer hear his Bubbie croaking in the gullet of the oven. But neither could he hear his wife nagging him, so the good, the bad, and the ugly all balanced out.

One could say that all ended well, except for one loose end: the people in Asia who—according to Bubbie—were eating wood. But without more specific details, after almost 70 years, Asia being such a large place, that loose end was a cold case, sadly unsolvable, even by those with the most humanitarian intentions and relief funds to spare.

So now that the origin of the singular Everything Bagel has been established with this interesting series of events, we take a closer look at the metaphysical aspects of something that declares itself to be Everything while at its very center is a hole symbolizing Nothing.

More than any other bagel type, the Everything Bagel intrigues the mind of the scholar. There is a delicate balance between what is and what isn't, of that which we see and that which we imagine, that which we experience, and that which we cannot comprehend. Just as no bagel could really be Everything in the strictest sense, the hole of the bagel cannot really be Nothing. Something is there that perhaps only God can know of. Is the hole the soul of the bagel? Is the part the eater holds just the flesh, to be consumed, digested, and eventually molded to buttocks and thighs as stored fat? The Everything Bagel is the ultimate symbol of the mystical nature of all bagels, which share in common one essential thing—a hole. Even the lowliest *nisht*-bagel in Utah has *that*. Therefore, the real question, the most challenging of all, addresses the part of the bagel that is not there. In other words—the unknown. Let me introduce the lowly—possibly holy—bagel hole.

— *Rabbi, my son is asking: after he eats a bagel, what happens to the hole?*

This is a question which no person has the definitive answer to. There can be many answers, and all of them can be correct. Who is to say they are not?

In the realm of physics, we have string theory, parallel universes, alternate universes, multiple dimensions, and who knows what else. A theoretical physicist, such as the brilliant Stephen Hawking, could give us a colorful explanation for what happens to bagel holes when they are freed of their breadly-bindings. He could clarify, theoretically, for instance, if the hole escapes when the bagel circle is broken by a bite, or if the hole remains attached to the bagel until the entire circle is consumed or destroyed. Then, *mitndrinnen*, the mathematicians—such as those *mishugenah* Chudnovsky Brothers with their homemade supercomputer made from old bicycle parts—show up to determine if the circle of the hole in the bagel, which they are measuring with a piece of string, is subject to the laws of *pi*. As if that would help in any meaningful way!

— *Rabbi, perhaps, as you have with bagels, you can also enlighten us about donuts?*

I don't answer questions about donuts. If you want answers about donuts, please write to The Pope. His address is very simple. Just write this on the envelope:

```
Pope
c/o The Vatican
```

There's no need to write down *Rome* or *Italy*. The Pope has his own country, unlike me, who must make do with a little office in the back of the *shul*, with a water-damaged ceiling and a noisy radiator.

Put a stamp on the envelope if you want to. I admit I don't bother with the postage. Report me to the police if you want to, I'm not worried. The Pope never pays for anything, and, with all his talking, he never says anything I want to hear, so why should I pay to ask him a question? And do you think our postal workers would dare to trifle with the Pope's holy mail? They are so busy falling all over themselves when they see the magic name, *Pope*, they don't bother to check to see if there is a stamp on the envelope or not—they run right into the bathroom to see if their underpants are clean.

Ask the Pope what he thinks happens to the holes from donuts. Isn't that why he's called *His Hole-iness*? See what he has to say. My prediction? *Bupkis*.

— *Rabbi, is the plight of world Bagelry as dire as traditionalists claim it is?*

Who can say for certain? This much I can tell you—one day, I was shopping for something to *nosh* on, and I came across a very strange food item. I said to myself, "What kind of cockamamie eclairs are these without chocolate on them?" Then I looked closer. They were *bagel* eclairs with the cream cheese already inside them. What can I say? My heart sank all the way to China. Once they take the hole away from the bagel, and no one is making a protest, only God knows what they will they take away next. I suggest you hold on to the little button at the top of your *yarmulke*—if it's still there!

A Sex Stop

Nobody Gets Off At This Stop

[Five cigarettes and one Viagra tablet (each), and fifty minutes later.]

—Oh, honey, make me want to call you Daddy.
—Why don't you *make* me want to make you want to call me Daddy.

Pause.

[A few seconds later.]

—Make *me* want to make *you* want to make me want to call you Daddy.
—Make me want to make you want to make me want to make you want to call me Daddy.
—Make me want to make you want to make me want to make you want to make me want to call you Daddy.
—Make me want to make you want to make me want to make you want to make me want to make you want to call me Daddy.
—What the fuck...? You put too many "make me-s" in there!
—Make me make you ... *infinity!*

Strategic pause.

[Another helping of Viagra (each), six cigarettes (each), two aspirin (each), and another fifty minutes later.]

—Can we get on with this?
—Make me want to.
—Call me Daddy first.
—You first.
—No, you.
—Make me.
—Make me make you.
—Make me make you make me make you.

Hiatus.

[Two Viagra (each), five cigarettes (each), and 45 minutes later.]

—Makememakeyoumakememakeyou... Oh boy, this is very boring!
—Childish ...
—Boring ...
—Childish ...
—Boring. Boring, boring, boring, boring, boooooooring!

Intermission.

[Two shots of vodka (each), four cigarettes (each), a small serving of crystal meth (each), one Viagra (each), two lines of cocaine (each) and 30 minutes later.]

—What's next?
—You were going to call me Daddy.
—You were going to make me want to.
—I wasn't.
—I want you to make me want to, otherwise forget it.
—Make me want to forget it.
—Not going to happen. Ten dollars on it.

—Who says?
—I say. I say it won't happen. Twenty dollars on it.
—I say it will.
—It won't. Thirty dollars on it.
—Will.
—Won't.
—Stubborn stubborn stubborn stubborn...
—You're stubborn.
—I am not. You are.
—No, you.
—Who was stubborn first? You.
—Only after you were stubborn.
— - - - - - -
—Did you hear me?
— - - - - - -
—Daddy? Daddy?
— - - - - - -
—Daddy, wake up! Please wake up! Daddy! Daddy! Oh my God, Daaaaad-ee!
— - - - - -

Not much later.

—Nine-One-One. What is your emergency?

America's most revered poet, Walt Whitman, poses in a reflective mood for an ectoplasmograph, while looking at tea in *The Brown Fox's* historic dining carriage.

Teatime for the Disembarked

A Ghostly Prologue featuring Mrs. Lincoln and Mr. Whitman

They had actually never met before, even though they both had resided in Washington City at the same time—during the terrible, tumultuous war years—and their paths had crossed tangentially numerous times. Walt Whitman, during the 16th Presidentiad, would often see the President riding past in his *barouche* on Pennsylvania Avenue. Mrs. Lincoln had once been riding with her husband and, upon spotting the bearded poet strolling on the street nearby, called him to her husband's attention. "That's Mr. Whitman," she said. "Quite the accomplished poet, I understand. He was pointed out to me at the Veteran's Hospital, where he volunteers as a nurse for both Union and Confederate cases. His writing is admired by Mr. Longfellow, Mr. Thoreau, and other important writers, and he appears to have a healthy appeal to the intellectuals among the voters. Perhaps we ought to invite him to the White House for tea or dinner."

"As you wish, my dear. I leave it in your hands." The President tipped his hat to Mr. Whitman, who returned the gesture. In life, the Lincolns and Whitman never saw each other again.

Afterlife etiquette demands that one—or both—parties in an unexpected post-mortem encounter address the obvious, even if they had done so with each other on a previous occasion. Someone is obligated by courtesy to acknowledge that physical death has occurred, regardless of what pretenses are being engaged in at the moment. Even if you are carrying your guillotined head around in a basket, even if you are dripping ectoplasm and vaporizing with every movement you make, you must still acknowledge—verbally—

that you are genuinely dead. Naturally, there are graceful, discrete ways to do that without offending. A writer, who publishes under the delightful pseudonym Emily Posthumous Post, has a nice list of suggested methods in her book *Manners Are Not Dead (Even if We Are)*.

As Emily so correctly points out, "There are far too many deceased persons pretending to be alive to afford the Afterlife the trappings and trimmings of a respectable address—which it certainly deserves, being a *permanent* address, irrevocable, with no exceptions—despite its lack of an official ZIP code or desirable *Arrondissement* number. Even the game of Monopoly, designed for living players though it may be, has its respectable real estate tracts—its Boardwalk, its Park Place, and its Illinois Avenue. Why should the precincts of death have less appeal than those found in a board game?

"The growing numbers of offenders engaging in PTA—Pretending To Be Alive—ruin all that is enviable about not being alive for everyone who isn't. One must *always* be a team player, even if your entire team has crossed the Jordan or sailed the Styx. Posterity demands nothing less than the very best we dead can muster from Beyond.

She opines thusly in a later chapter, "One spends an entire lifetime thinking that life is the only way to go, but when it finally comes time to *really* go, the only truly *respectable* way to go is to just *go*—period—plain and simple. Just go, be gone, and stay gone."

Dead psychiatrists and researchers agree. Dr. Vladimir Pokovsky of the Siberian Institute of Dead Soviet Heroes wrote: "In the mindset of the living, death is something to be avoided as long as possible, procrastinated over like a visit to the dentist. Therefore, the state of being dead has the potential to invoke a sensation of regret so potent, susceptible deceased individuals might contemplate suicide as if it were still a viable option for obtaining relief. Chance encounters with old acquaintances in the Afterlife (in shopping malls or on buses, for example) could trigger such episodes, bringing them on without warning, much like random epileptic seizures. It would appear, from statistical analysis, that these post-mortem encounters occur with the same frequency in death as they do in life. Such episodes make death—which *should* be a time for repose and order—both messy and calamitous. No one wants that. When you are alive, you will always *eventually* be dead. When you are dead, the paradigm of *eventuality* is forfeited; there are no detours. The best anyone can say about it is that you won't—no matter what transpires—find yourself any deader."

The required acknowledgment that one's life is a thing of the past does not have to be, by necessity, an elaborate procedure to carry out successfully, and any motivated decedent can master it. Even a dead three-year-old can be taught to do it properly. There are just too many wandering souls for fanfare to be feasible at every encounter that occurs.

Death acknowledgments can take the simplest of forms—as quick and painless, for example, as a man tipping his hat (if he died wearing one) and saying, "How lovely to see you, Mathilde. I had no idea you were dead." Or, if one wanted to prolong the encounter, "How's being dead been treating you, Walter?" or, leaving options for afternoon stroll open-ended, "Fancy that, Grace, here we are—dead—but we're neighbors all over again! How quaint!" These are forms of proper Afterlife etiquette, but, predictably, for every appropriate method used when confronting the issue in practice, there are two that are highly inappropriate.

It is considered extremely bad form, for example, upon entering a space of any sort, to immediately announce one's prior demise to a room full of dead people in a provocative, attention-craving manner. You cannot make an entrance and shout for all present to hear, "Hey, look at me, everyone, am I not absolutely one-hundred-percent dead?" People who address their state of NLB—No-Longer-Being—from the far side of a room, or the opposite end of a train carriage, commit OBM—Obituary by Megaphone. This is simply not done by decedents of former good breeding. No one wants to have their face rubbed in someone else's ashes.

An extremely egregious example was offered by Senator Joseph Mc-Carthy, who cleverly engineered an escape from Hell by filibustering his watch-guard into a coma. He made a run for freedom in his still-smoldering undershorts, screaming "Better Dead than Red, that's what I am!" in the most uncouth, blatant manner imaginable, shouting it in the face of every floater-by he encountered. The Devil was rip-roaring mad about the escape—stammering, sputtering, and blowing gaskets the way Vesuvius blows boulders and sulfur. He summoned a feral gang of minions to help him apprehend the Senator. Together, they proceeded to gear-up and pursue him with their pitchforks and halberds like a posse out of a John Ford western, careening from one end of the Afterworld to the other. They finally succeeded in cornering him with the help of some dead prostitutes and dragged him back to Hell for judication. The Devil himself presided over the case—and in the worst mood imaginable.

Facing the prisoner—who was sitting to his left in the witness box, still wearing his singed boxer shorts and dabbing at his tears with a scrap of an anti-communist leaflet—the Devil was thoroughly disgusted and made no attempt to conceal it. "Have you no sense of decency, sir, at long last?" he demanded of the former Senator, who responded by pleading the Fifth. The Devil smashed him in the face with his gavel for insolence, breaking his nose and jaw, and knocking out two of his favorite teeth. "Fifth my fucking foot!" the Devil roared. "The only 'Fifth Pleading' you'll be doing is 'Let me out of here!' when I consign you to the Fifth Circle of Hell."

As a punishment for breach of contract with the Devil—a serious criminal offense in Hell known as a First-Degree Breach Death—the Devil had him jailed (what he actually said, mockingly, was "en-Car-thy-rated") at the Sartre Motel (rated at minus three stars), locked in a cheesy, roach-infested room with Josef Stalin and Patricia Highsmith as roommates, and there the trio remains, frothing at the mouths like rabid dogs, perpetually short a fourth for a distracting game of bridge or Mahjong. The seedy Sarte address was notorious for its nausea-inducing wallpaper, see-through drapes, and shag rugs, in addition to its award-winning hospitality torture, worse than the most disreputable dump in Sodom or Gomorrah. The night tables contained Bibles with all the pornographic parts ripped out. The writing desk was filled with reams of *The Sartre Motel, Hell* engraved stationery, but there wasn't a pencil or pen to be found anywhere. The door handle of the mini-bar was rigged to give powerful electric shocks. So was the cold-water faucet. Lucky for the occupants, they were no longer among the living, because the very worst that can happen to anyone in Hell—*ever*—is having a reason to dial 911. Imagine being so banged up when you're already dead that you need an ambulance.

Requiescat in pace, thought the Devil sardonically, as he cracked the waste-pipe of their toilet, ripped out their phone, pocketed the remote control for the television, and swallowed their room key.

"If he wants that key," the Devil told Lilith in bed that night, "he can send his lackey, Roy Cohn, to go scrounge around for it in my shit."

Neither of them had counted on a post-mortem encounter, but it was a wonderful surprise for both that it came about without planning. Now they found themselves passing a shard of eternity in each other's company, having failed to do so in the White House when the Lincolns and Mr. Whitman were still *des personnes vivantes*, as the First Lady liked to phrase it. It had always been her intention to have Mr. Whitman to the Executive Mansion for tea, but in those calamitous days, it was hard to plan anything around the exigencies of an ongoing war. Then, when the war ended, only a short time later, at Ford's Theater...

Here, on *The Brown Fox*, they discovered each other—America's One-Time First Soldier of Arts and Letters and the One-Time First Lady General of the Union Army—death mask to death mask, after so many years—more than one hundred, in fact—with the long-delayed tea party and its *accoutrements* arrayed about them. In truth, these were the dirty dishes of the just-ended Elevenses that had been served to the passengers at their seats. The train staff had collected them and left them temporarily on some unlaid tables in the empty

dining car in preparation for a clean-up. Mrs. Lincoln and Mr. Whitman had seated themselves at one such table and took scant notice
that they were attending a party that was ostensibly over. The larger
party containing this smaller party had ended for them a century earlier, so nothing seemed amiss to either. It was all part of a continuing
entropic process that they no longer noticed, like a persistent ringing
noise in their ears they had learned to live with.

The *F.I.R.R. Brown Fox* chugged over the iron ribbon of the *Paumanok Line*, carrying them blithely along, even though they were
going nowhere and drinking nothing. The teapot was empty, as was
most of the serving ware. The late-arriving guests—one full century
late!—for this impromptu *tête-à-tête* swirled spoons in their china
cups as if there was something in them that wanted mixing. The
cups, betraying their emptiness with hollow clinks when placed in
their saucers, were, nevertheless, lifted again and again to smiling, pallid lips. Sprouting from the hands that held the delicate
handles, elongated, ectoplasmic pinky fingers pointed outward,
most elegantly, in opposite directions—his to the North, hers to
the South, as the train forged ahead, heading East towards Montauk, with the past tumult of their lives left behind them—not in
the receding West, unspooling behind the train's caboose, but in a
different dimension entirely.

Mr. Whitman had tucked a corner of a napkin into his shirt collar,
allowing it to dangle down over his belly. As delicately as he could
manage it, he lifted the bottom-most corner of the napkin to dab at
his mouth, his mustache, and his beard. There was nothing for him
to dab at, but he dabbed as earnestly as he could. He had often heard
it said in Washington City that Mrs. Lincoln was quite keen on good
manners—as was befitting a lady of her station from the State of Kentucky. Mr. Whitman, on the other hand, hailed from Long Island and
grew up in Brooklyn—from substantially baser stock, working-class
people—and he understood that he needed to be at his gentlemanly
best or risk Mrs. Lincoln's disapproval. Old habits die hard, as was
often said. This was never truer than when the old habits that were
dying hard were the habits of dead persons.

No one saw them. They barely saw each other. But they were—in some sense that would be unfathomable to the minds of living persons—together as they *might* have been if the previously wished-for tea party had occurred one hundred years sooner. The dirty cups and plates, the crusts of bread, the smears of butter, the discarded toothpicks, the orange peels, and cherry pits—none of it mattered, nor was any of it even noticed. The only thing they counted as missing was Mr. Lincoln, and neither his wife nor the poet wanted to be the one to comment on it. Had the president, too, been a transitory presence at this private *fête*, none of the three guests would have found anything amiss.

"In Life, future Happiness is expressed in the language of Hopefulness," Mrs. Lincoln observed, leading up elegantly to the Acknowledgement of Death required by etiquette, "whereas, in Death, future Happiness can only be expressed in the language of Nostalgia. Now that we are dead"—here the second shoe finally fell, much to Whitman's relief— "I feel naught but the greatest nostalgia for the delightful tea conversation we *might* have had those many years ago."

"Yes," Mr. Whitman said, "it *is* rather strange to have nostalgic sentiments for things that *didn't* happen. It's like experiencing Regret with the bittersweet juice of Sadness wrung out of it."

"You are ever the poet, Mr. Whitman," she said admiringly. "Mr. Lincoln and I never had the opportunity to support the arts as we would have wished to if the war had not shifted our focus from beauty to ugliness. America has taken you, nevertheless, to its bosom and raised you high, for which I feel very gratified."

"Each year—in the years when I was still physically able—I gave a 'Lincoln Lecture' in Manhattan, in which I reminisced about your husband and the war years. People never lost interest in him."

"Nor should they. It is bad enough that they have lost interest in the presidency itself. And lost respect for what it meant and what it yet might be. How else could one account for the bizarre creature that currently inhabits my former home? It walks through the rooms my children played in, it touches everything with adulterous and greedy hands and it finds value in nothing. Oh, Mr. Whitman, the horrors one suffers at the mere sight of that grotesque, ill-favored hair and the scowling, florid face! And the infantile hands fluttering at its wrists like parakeets while it spits venom! What an unfortunate looking creature it is! *Quel comportement malheureux et désagréable!*"

She shuddered suddenly, causing a few precious drops of vaporous ectoplasm to float away from her vaguely-defined perimeter. After briefly sparkling in the sunlight that streamed from the dining car's windows, the droplets evaporated.

"*Après les Lincolns, le déluge,*" she sighed whilst watching fractions of herself disappear.

Bowing his head as he spoke, he said, "I cite a phrase taken from our Chinese brethren—some say it is a curse, others a blessing—which is, 'May you live in interesting times.' So it has been for us, Mrs. Lincoln."

"Mr. Whitman, there is no doubt that we have lived in interesting times. And now, like it or not, we find ourselves dead in interesting times as well."

Mrs. Emily Posthumous Post, DP (Deceased Person) has many notable acquaintances in the Afterworld and is a vibrant non-living, non-breathing storehouse of knowledge about Life Post-Operational. She was famously interviewed by a well-known journalist, Joe Franklin, DP, who coaxed her to share highlights of her encounters with well-known shades. "Who," he asked, "were your favorite DPs? If you had an A-list, who would be on it?"

"I've always enjoyed Helen Keller very much," Mrs. Post said without any hesitation. "She was a great inspiration in life, and she was better prepared than most for Afterlife, where she continues to philosophize with no hint of regret or longing. Amazingly, Helen had no idea she was even dead until her fingers stumbled upon an announcement in the *Con-*

necticut Braille Gazette a week later. 'I barely notice the difference,' she confided in me long ago. 'Everything is still shapeless, colorless, quiet, but I no longer feel the isolation that once haunted me. I am much more like everyone else now that everyone around me lives in a void, too.'

"Who else would you like to share your thoughts about?" Franklin asked while wading through miles of coffee-stained scribblings.

"Well, President Teddy Roosevelt is certainly high on my list. A genuine bull-in-a-china-shop, as they say, but his is a china shop where everything has already been broken. He still likes his guns and shooting things, even if the only things to hunt are already dead. The advantage he has now is that he can shoot the same elephant over and over and has no need to apologize. He has a privately-owned dead elephant that's been trained to fall down whenever it hears a rifle being fired. And—my-oh-my—does Rough-and-Ready-Teddy love to laugh and guffaw and slap his knees! He has a loud, coarse lion's roar of a laugh and big horse teeth, like another Roosevelt—I refer to Eleanor, of course—although I think Teddy is the prettier of the two. Another woman, who I adore for her spunk, is Carolina Otero, otherwise known as La Belle Otero."

"Come sit up here with me," Franklin said, taking Mrs. Post by the hand and helping her mount a slippery hillock of rotting memorabilia. They sat down next to each other near a small mound of mold at the top. "Now, tell me about Otero," he said.

"She was a famous courtesan of the *Belle Époque*. In addition to her American conquests, such as Joseph Kennedy, Sr. and William K. Vanderbilt, her pillow book included Alfonso XIII of Spain, Edward, Prince of Wales, future King of England, Leopold II of Belgium, Prince Albert of Monaco, Kaiser Wilhelm, Nicholas I of Montenegro, Tsar Nicholas II of Russia, and many others. She has a sketchbook containing drawings of all the royal penises, and each 'member' has a little *crêpe papier* crown pasted on its 'head.' The title of the book is 'My Collected Crowned Heads of Europe.' Most amusing."

"I can imagine. Well, I certainly wouldn't hesitate to have her on my show," Franklin said. "Anyone else you'd care to tell us about?"

"There are others, but most of the interesting DP's are in Hell, Mr. Franklin, and I tend to avoid the place, if at all possible."

"Any regrets?"

"Some few."

"Such as...?"

"I'm *dead*, Mr. Franklin. It's impolitic, however, to complain about it. I am a staunch opponent of openly expressed, morbid regret, as you would know if you had actually taken the trouble *read* my book instead of merely *pretending* to, as is your wont. That said, I am still happy to be here. I had no idea you were ever alive to begin with, Mr. Franklin, so your invitation quite took me by surprise. And, I must say, I love what you've done with this place. It's a bit disorganized, but it's truly a monument to the fate of all sentimental mementos—an expansive valley of rot and decay stretching as far back as the Gate of Life itself."

The carriage door opened. "It's past time for us to lay these tables," a voice said. "We're very close to the first lunch seating, so we'd better get a move on."

Mrs. Lincoln and Mr. Whitman looked up to see a pair of young men, the age of university students, both dressed in white busboy uniforms, proceeding to clear the tables and lay fresh linens on them. They began in the center, close to where the First Lady and First Poet had located themselves and worked towards opposite ends of the dining car.

Their party props—cups and saucers and other tea *accoutrements*—were being taken away. Mr. Whitman suddenly recalled the napkin he had tucked into his collar earlier and quickly pulled it loose. He tossed it to the table where it was snatched away by one of the busboys the moment it landed. Both Mrs. Lincoln and Mr. Whitman smiled at the efficiency that was wiping away all trace of their long-awaited meeting. He actually winked at her, which caused what there still was to experience of the presidential widow to turn a shade of ecto-pink.

The train rocked and swayed and rumbled. She remembered the railroad journey to Washington City for her husband's first Inauguration—the train had been festooned with bunting in red and white and blue, it had been greeted by cheering, boisterous crowds and brass bands and speeches given by local dignitaries. Fireworks and confetti burst from the heavens. And her precious son, her little Willie—lost to her so cruelly—sitting across from her in their elegant carriage, reading to his father from a book almost too large for him to hold. *My dear, dear, darling Willie,* she thought.

She hadn't been present on the funeral train back to Springfield. She was too grief-stricken to board that iron hearse, draped in black ribbon and crepe and many other trappings of mourning, which bore not only her husband, but also her disinterred Willie, poetically tracing the route of the Inauguration train in reverse. It was a mirror train, two sides of the same lives, stories moving in opposite directions. It was hard to get her mind around the myriad events of four years duration that had caused time itself to splinter in two trajectories on a single train line.

A curious thing was happening. Both Mrs. Lincoln and Mr. Whitman had been worn down by the passage of Aftertime near to the thinness of paper. Neither of them had much more substance remaining to them than would their memoirs scribbled on onion skin and held to the sunlight. In these final stages of existence, they were *there* and they were *not there,* both states at the same time, flickering like candles in a draft. Each of them could see through the other to the extent that they could both perceive—as if their vision was penetrating a finely woven veil—what was happening on the opposite ends of the dining car. Neither of the deceased could recall ever having intentionally studied a living person through the lens of another person's dissipating remains. This was, for both of them, very strange. It had the potential to get stranger.

In her case, Mrs. Lincoln could vaguely make out a young man dressing the mahogany tables a few table rows behind Mr. Whitman's aura. He was smoothing the newly-laid tablecloths, arranging small vases of flowers, and carefully placing the silverware, napkins, and glasses at each setting. Periodically, he would step back to view his work from a more critical angle, then return to make minor adjustments. There was something childlike, almost playful, about the way he went about his work. He seemed to be dancing as he moved around the tables. Mrs. Lincoln heard—or imagined she heard—the boy whistling a familiar waltz tune.

Opposite her, Mr. Whitman, while stroking his beard thoughtfully, was pleasantly fixated on the other young man, visible to his scrutiny just beyond Mrs. Lincoln's transparent form. That young man was doing the same as his colleague—getting the dining car ready for the lunch guests. To the poet's eyes, this fellow seemed a bit older, worldlier, perhaps more sexually ripened, than the smaller boy, whose care-free whistling had reached the poet's ears as well.

The younger boy's deft movements as he snapped the folds out of the linens and polished the glassware to a sparkling shine were beginning to hypnotize Mrs. Lincoln. She hummed the tune the boy was whistling—its exact title was playing hide-and-seek with her memory— the wisps of melody slowly gathered themselves into a nameless symphony of remembrance, and she found herself dreaming of days gone by, of balls given for ambassadors and senators and congressmen in the White House, and country dances in Kentucky, and later, in Illinois where she met and married Mr. Lincoln and she had given him their four sons. She was dancing in one of the gowns Mrs. Keckley had sewn for her, a creation of beads and sequins and taffeta, cleverly adapted from a Parisian magazine—she had a clear memory of pointing at the lovely dress and saying *this one* to Mrs. Keckley *but I think done in white*. It had been amply modified for her, of course, as she was of a different, more buxom, American stock than her heavily-corseted French counterparts. Her susceptibility to crippling headaches prohibited the use of such pain-inducing whalebone devices. Free of the restrictions inflicted by corseting, in that sparkling, white taffeta gown, the envy of every woman present, she was dancing waltz after waltz, and the musicians were pouring music into the ballroom as though they were filling it to the brim with champagne. Meanwhile, a war was raging on the other side of the Potomac. Its dirty, corpse-infested waters had invaded the White House and sickened two of her sons with typhoid, although they seemed to be rallying. She had no idea, dancing and jesting and flirting in her Kentucky manner with this senator and that senator, that one of her sons, her precious Willy, was slowly succumbing in an upstairs sickroom. She danced while his fever increased and his life leaked away, and by the time anyone had a chance to notice that he had taken a very unexpected turn for the worse and...

She stopped waltzing and looked again at the boy setting the tables at the far end of the carriage. He could easily have been her Willy if he were but a few years younger. Then, as if a restraint had snapped, an unwelcome urge to fly past Mr. Whitman's tremulous aura and embrace the young man began to overwhelm her, a powerful desire to bounce him on her knee and feel his cheek against her bosom and sing a silly song to him, as she had done with all her darlings before the presidency and the war and the parade of deaths had marched through the life of Mary Todd Lincoln.

Perhaps because she viewed the cheerful, unspoiled young man through the faint remains of the wordsmith who hovered between them like waxed paper, she was able to form words around the futility she felt so deeply. Death had exiled her to a foreign land where remedies existed which could have saved three of her children from their juvenile deaths. If only, she thought, the society in which she had lived her life had been focused on science and progress instead of slavery and warfare, the story of the Lincolns of Springfield would have been quite different.

Opposite her, Mr. Whitman found himself wandering in an arcade of erotic remembrances. Watching the young man as he prepared his tables with such athletic vigor had conjured tantalizing images of his life's memorable loves—Peter Doyle first of all, a trolley conductor he had met in his younger days, before the war, with whom he had an enduring relationship of many years—and William Duckett, a boarder, with whom he shared an autumnal romance in his final years. They, and others, were mostly lost to him now, alive in poems for others to read, but fading from the paths of memory where he was accustomed to wander around, and—on his luckiest days—bump into some of them. Seeing them now through the soul of Mrs. Lincoln, a woman who had lost—**one by one, and each too soon**—every person she had ever loved, only intensified the bittersweet taste of separation. If only, he thought, the society in which he and his beautiful men had lived their lives had been focused on love and brotherhood instead of repression, strife, and enmity, the story of Walt Whitman and his many loves might have been quite different.

Saddened as he was, he understood that such emotional indulgences would only distort the unique nature of his visit with Mrs. Lincoln and render it less memorable. Decisively, he summoned both himself and her out of their individual reveries and aimed for a change of mood. He said, "My dear Mrs. Lincoln, as we may or may not have the chance to meet again, death being such a capricious and inconvenient state to find oneself in, I'd like to take the liberty to inquire about something that I've wondered on for many years. I hope you won't mind if I solicit your opinion about..."

"Don't, Mr. Whitman," she said with a weary sigh and a discrete roll of her eyes. "Just *don't*."

William Duckett
and Walt Whitman

Mary Lincoln and her
young son, Willie

John Wilkes Booth (left) with Satan at Ford's Theater.

Mary Todd Lincoln, former First Lady of the United States, graciously poses for an ectoplasmograph, while wafting through our restored carriages.
~ *Courtesy of F.I.R.R. Publicity* ~

Mary Todd Lincoln's Film Review

Mrs. Lincoln Has Scant Praise for Mr. Spielberg's Bio-Pic

However, she waxes rhapsodic over Mr. Zapruder's earlier film work

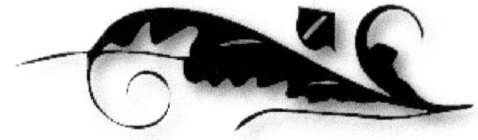

For more than a hundred years, overly-imaginative historians and traffickers in shabby anecdotes have portrayed me as a woman who is not in full possession of her faculties. The American people have long-believed—that is to say, they have long been *led* to believe—that I am not a reliable diarist. Nevertheless, despite the considerable derision I have endured in my lifetime and, pursuant to that, in my deathtime, I feel strongly motivated to risk the remnants of my moth-eaten reputation to speak my mind at last—and plainly, too. I will be blunt. Very blunt indeed.

Listen America, listen one and all—my beloved husband, my Dear Abraham, was *not* gay. He was not even moderately cheerful. The fact is, he was thoroughly committed to ending the most tragic of all wars, no simple matter by any means. He had neither the time nor the energy to be gay. If there were balls in the White House, they were mine. I held those balls—so blame me, Mary Todd Lincoln. Point your finger at me if you must make accusations of gaiety. I continued the great tradition of bringing marital value to the White House, a tradition which can be traced back to First Lady Dolly Madison, my dearest companion in the Afterlife. Just a week ago, we two floated down Pennsylvania Avenue, arm in arm, and when Mrs. Madison and I passed the gates of the White House, we looked at each other and sighed deeply. "Who would ever have imagined, Mrs. Lincoln," she said, tragic overtones tinting her confidences, "that it would come to *this*." I had not the heart to answer her. I, too, sighed from the grave.

Note you, too, Brother and Sister Americans, the truly deplorable *current* state of the State—merely for comparative purposes—and the somber Lincoln Years will shine brighter than does the Sun. Mrs. Donald Trump, the present First Lady of Our Nation Under God, is not likely to speak a complete, coherent sentence about any serious subject during her husband's term of office—which is probably all for the best anyway—and thus she is fated to be remembered by history only for her most meaningful utterance thus far—the words "I do."

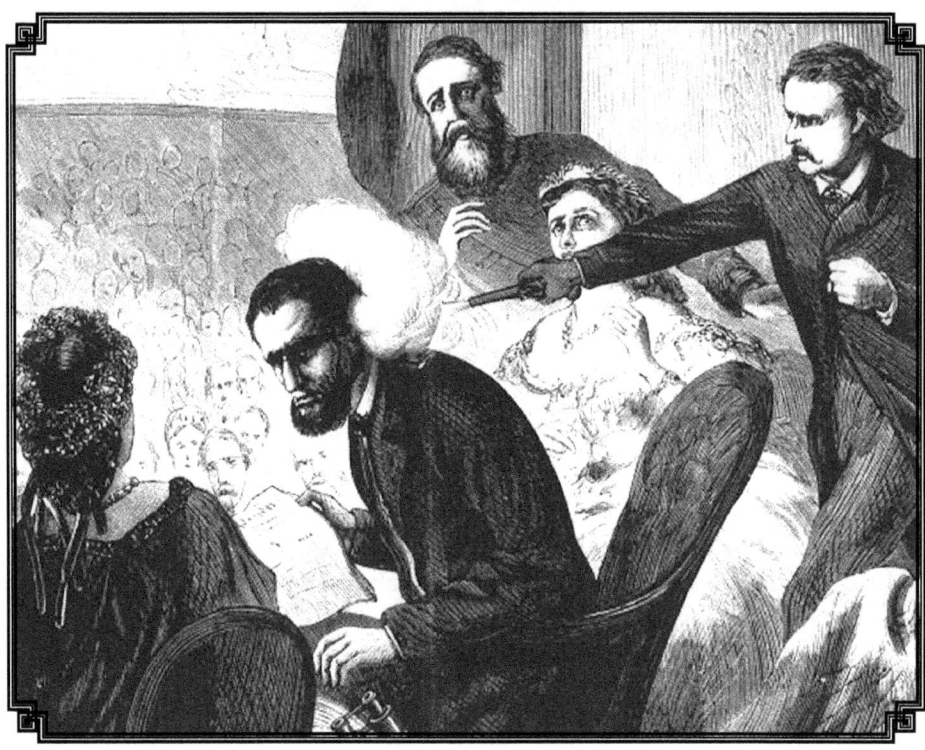

At the opposite end of history's telescope, a giantess of largesse, in contrast, is Mrs. John F. Kennedy Onassis—like myself, a victim of service to Our Nation, who also, from the vantage point of a few inches distance, witnessed her husband being blown to pieces in the seat beside her—mine in Mr. Ford's Theatre, and hers in Mr. Ford's motor vehicle, coincidentally called a Ford Lincoln. She shared my affinity for the history of the White House (or, more likely, purloined it), and strove to preserve and protect its artifacts for the benefit of Posterity.

Further, on the subject of myself and the years of my service to Our Great Nation, there is something I must finally clarify—if only because people have been badgering me about it for years beyond counting. Despite all that went awry—*yes, yes, yes, yes!*—the show was not bad at all (uncharacteristically, my Abe was heartily slapping his knees at the wealth of clever dialogue—at least he did so until a certain point in the evening), and may the Lord forgive *mon cher publique* for asking such an insensitive question of a poor widow. But, while we touch upon it—since it seems we always *must*—to be perfectly clear about this oft-discussed matter, when I refer to the "show," I refer solely to Mr. Charles Taylor's play *Our American Cousin*, not to Mr. Spielberg's seriously flawed bio-pic, *Lincoln*. I will have more to say on *that* anon!

Although it risks further tarnish to my unfairly compromised reputation, I take this opportunity to confess a secret desire, one harbored in my bosom for many years— someday I should like to learn exactly how *Our American Cousin* ended (by that I mean, how it  ended on nights when an assassination didn't bring the curtain down in *actus interruptus*). Never have I mustered the nerve to inquire about that sensitive matter for fear of being derided—a pity, too, because it is perfectly reasonable for the intelligent theatergoer to wonder if Mr. Asa Trenchard finally proposes to Mistress Mary, or if Mrs. Mountchessington's wish will come true instead. Perhaps, if Mr. Spielberg had the wit to make his film of *that* amusing comedy, he might have pleased me more, and come closer to achieving the professional success he desires. At the very least, I'd know what transpires in Scene II of Act III without having to stoop to inquire.

And now, America Dearest, I come to my chief personal objections to this misinformed film. I have lived the most torturous years of my lifetime breathing stinking cigar smoke in those dingy, cavernous

rooms. I paced those creaking floorboards many a long night, worrying over my sickly children, my dyspeptic husband, and the rising price of strawberries. In all fairness, young Mr. Spielberg's film really should have been called *The Lincolns*. If the Truth be told, with such a simple gesture, he would have come far nearer cinematic Truth!

As is known to all, on April 14, 1865, during Act III of *Our American Cousin*, a great tragedy occurred in a murderous re-write from the pen of Mr. John Wilkes Booth. Yet, perversely, Mr. Spielberg glosses over the highly dramatic events at Mr. Ford's Theatre! Quite disrespectful of him, I say, to cut my most dramatic and sumptuously-costumed scene into little more than a cameo appearance by the soon-to-be widow. This is *precisely* where a great film-maker like Mr. Zapruder proves his merit. Now, *there* was a true artist and director—the George Cukor of Assassination Widows! Please be sure to take note, Mr. Steven Spielberg, of what Mr. Zapruder's film did for Mrs. John F. Kennedy Onassis—to date, it has had more viewings than *My Fair Lady* and *The Sound of Music* combined.

Not that Mr. Spielberg troubles himself to show the audience much of it, Mr. Lincoln and I had no choice but to give the appearance of being well-adjusted to our lives of chaos and calamity. For my acting chores alone, I should have been awarded Oscars on a weekly basis.

Admittedly, I emerged from the debacle at Mr. Ford's Theatre in considerably better condition than my husband, but one needs to appreciate that the President and I were the brave, unheralded First Veterans of the Great Civil War. We just didn't march, nor did we blow bugles and play drums, not even in our private quarters. I have always abhorred loud noises, dirty clothes, and muddy boots, and Mr. Lincoln's digestion was no match for Union Army cuisine.

Do not listen to Confederate rumor-mongers—those years in the White House were not all baubles, balls, and barbecues. Believe me, beloved American people, I *suffered*. It was ironic, even tragic, that later on, I had to sue our government for a widow's pension, despite my recurrent headaches and numerous travails. Were there real justice in America, the Treasurer himself would have fallen to his knees before me and implored me to take that meager $3,000 per annum. I had to sew all my savings into the seams of my dresses, so convinced was I that our drunken President Johnson (a *bona fide* dyed in-the-wool dipsomaniac if ever I've seen one—and being from Kentucky, the Bourbon State, I certainly have seen my share), along with his equally besotted Congress, would file an appeal to have all the pension money returned to the government. Then, my one surviving son, Mr. Robert Lincoln, had me institutionalized for daring to complain about it. Sharper than a serpent's tooth, that surely was, as King Lear was wont to decry in performances of Mr. Shakespeare's drama of the same name. Even the Devil would treat his mother better.

The Civil War ruined life in the White House for me, for Mr. Lincoln, for the First Children, for everyone. The liberated First Ser-

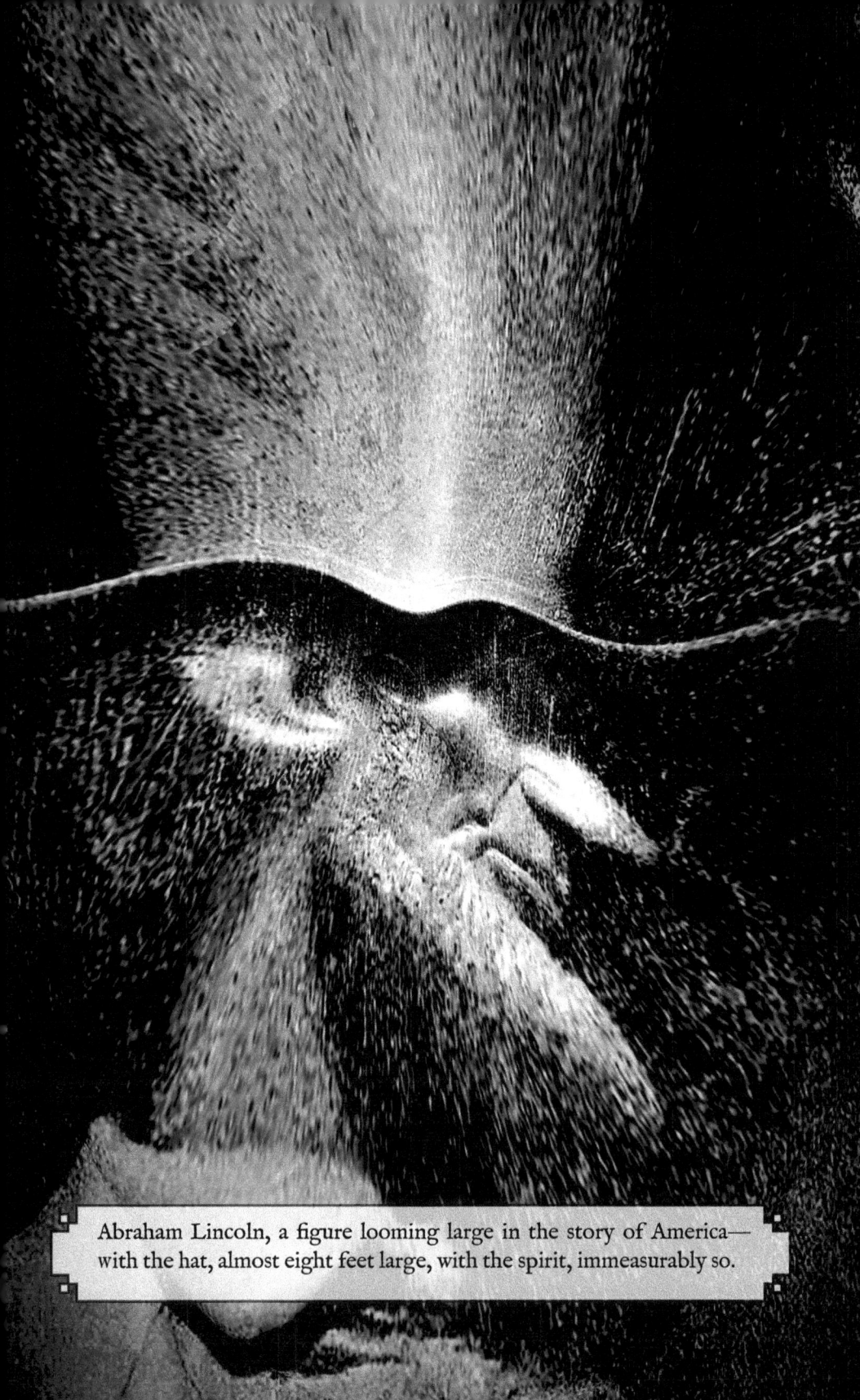

Abraham Lincoln, a figure looming large in the story of America—with the hat, almost eight feet large, with the spirit, immeasurably so.

vants never got to enjoy their freedom. We didn't even have a tele-phone to cry our late-night miseries into. Mr. Spielberg showed you none of that!

I never got to enjoy anything. I never got to finish anything. The only reason something did not intervene, as it inevitably did, to cur-tail my enjoyment (scant as it was) of Mr. Spielberg's *Lincoln,* is that I am already quite dead, and being dead is not a state of "being" that can be interrupted when something more irritating or inconvenient just happens along.

So, I take up the mantle of Mrs. Honest Abe, as my spouse did his of Honest Abe, and I'll just state it one last time for Posterity and the sake of Truth—life with President Lincoln was tough and he was not the merest bit gay. I never saw him smile, not even once.

A Fugue in Phone Major

Seating for Four,

1. Going to Israel headache

Yes, I've just come back.

From Israel. And I'm very, very depressed. I think I'm suffering from a serious case of BFISD, Back-From-Israel-Stress Disorder.

You're going to Israel, too? When?

My uncle is going to Israel then.

We go to Israel a few times a year. There's almost always someone in this crazy family going to Israel, or someone coming back from Israel, or someone talking about going to Israel, making their going-to-Israel plans until you want to jump out the window from it. Israel, Israel, Israel, Israel. The only way to get away from the talk about Israel is to get on a plane and go there. To tell the truth, I'm just as bad as the rest of them with my Israel this, Israel that... It's not like I'm not non-stop Israel just like the rest of them.

No, it's mainly to Israel.

I'll be going back to Israel in a few months.

Yes, as I said, I just returned from Israel, you're right, but I'm going back very soon.

Why not? I've been to Israel many, many

2. I literally went headache

And then she literally went why not? I mean Iris goes like yeah actually she's got her nerve and then I went but she has every right to complain because he actually went behind her back you know he went to Coney Island on Friday night which is where Sabina went and that's where she ran into Freddy and Dillon and they literally went on the Cyclone which is like when Sabina saw them and she called Ella and she went they just went on the Cyclone together those fags and Ella goes no way what are you talking about they're not fags and Sabina goes like they sure act like fags and I was like you know you're literally crazy and she's like I'm not crazy I saw them like literally ten minutes ago — whatever — I mean there's something really gay-like with those two I mean like — you know — like whether they're actually fags or not — like what guys go on rides together? Whatever. Who cares anyway? Literally — why are we even like bothering to talk about them? I mean like that's what Roberta would say actually and I mean you know actually she did say that when we went to the boardwalk and she went who knows what the actual deal is with those guys they

Conversation for Eight

3. I said, *What?* headache

I said, *What?*

After that she told me Tyrell came home drunk as hell. He slugged her and gave her a black eye. — I said, *What?*

Next, she says, he started throwing things. He smashed the glass in her new breakfront and broke some of her grandmothers dishes. — I said, *What?*

That's right, she said. You don't know the half of it. You don't know the quarter of it. You don't know nothing about it. But if you want to know, I will tell you, girl. That bum has stolen my check every month for the last six months. — I said, *What?*

Girl, she said, that good-for-nothing devil took all my jewelry and brought it to the pawnbroker to get some drinking money. They went and told him, that shit's fake, mister, so he brought it back and threw it

4. Got another call headache

You're breaking up, dude. What? Oh listen — never mind — I'm getting another call, man. I'll call you later when I have some talking space and we can pick it up then. Awesome, man. Okay. Keep it real. Later, dude.

Oh hi, Mark. Thanks for returning my call. No no no nothing major. I was cooking and I basically had some down time. I was doing a major burger selfie, a good time to talk on speaker. And listen, dude, that was truly the best burger ever. I wish you had been on the phone to share the experience with me. I laid down some cheddar and some Indian spice ketchup with some finely chopped white onion and some finely chopped sweet gherkin. Awesome, man. Totally awesome. I mean I really went all out because I bought a

329

times. Let me see... Israel, how many times...? Maybe twenty. If I looked at my passport I could tell you exactly because I always insist on getting Israeli immigration guys to stamp the Israel stamp in it. So, when is *your* trip?

The one to Eretz Yisrael.

Oh, terrific. Israel is nice at that time of year. I've never been to Israel in that month, but I hear it's terrific then. Imagine, twenty trips, maybe more, to Israel, and still I've never been to Israel in April. A lot of tourists then, though, I've heard. It's actually very non-Jewish in April because of Easter. I've been to Israel in January, in February, in March, and so on down the line. Israel is great in those months, too. But... hey... it's Israel... What could be bad in Eretz Yisrael?

Besides so many Israelis in Eretz Yisrael, what could be bad?

Okay, besides all those Palestinians in Eretz Yisrael, what else could be bad?

Yes, yes, but besides the gassy Israeli food, and all the non-Jewish tourists, what else is there for a person to complain about? Israel is like a little foretaste of Heaven.

No, I said *foretaste*, not *foreskin*. I've never tasted foreskin, thank God. They say it's like old chewing gum that has no flavor left in it. Oh well, Israel is not a place that's famous for its foreskin. Even the Palestinians throw that part away. If you want falafel in your mouth, that's a different story.

I agree. I just had lunch, too. You know, on another note, more compatible with digestion, my Marty always makes a little joke about Eretz Yisrael. He says, "I can't believe this place Is-Real." Get it?

are literally out of control I mean like for real and I went yeah they kind of are — literally — and she went yeah — blah blah blah blah — yeah yeah yeah — right — maybe they're not fags but they're kinda gay-ish anyhow — so what? I mean like right? They are for sure on the ish-spectrum gay-wise.

Then — out of nowhere — I suddenly have to go. So I went to Roberta — let's go to the hot dog concession so I can go — so we went. Then ten minutes later on the boardwalk right before the freakin' fireworks are starting when we're now already like fifty miles away from the concession — Roberta is like oh now I have to go and I went we just went to the hot dog toilets — why didn't you go when I went? And she's like literally in tears and she's bawling she didn't have to go when I went — so I go okay — let's go and then we went and missed the freakin' fireworks because she had to go when she could have went when I went before.

So while she is going along comes Freddy and Dillon and they're holding hands big time right on the freakin' boardwalk and I mean I'm like where's fucking Roberta to see this shit going down — what a time to pick to go. She's missing *everything*. Dillon goes hey did you see those freakin' fireworks they were like genuinely awesome — totally excellent. Then Roberta comes out of the bathroom and she's like totally oblivious to these two fagging-up the whole boardwalk with their hand-holding and shit and she's like how were the fireworks guys? So Freddy goes totally awesome — these were some righteous fireworks — very cool indeed. And then his faggy boyfriend says yes — *indeed*.

What the fuck? Like who says things like *indeed*? Are they for real or what? I don't understand why they don't just stay at home if in my face. He said, next time I take something of yours, bitch, I'm goin' to come for the worthwhile shit. And I said, what worthwhile shit? There ain't none in this house. This is the house of fucking nothing worthwhile. The shit you just threw at me is the shit you bought for me and at that point he cracked me in the mouth and ran out the house. — I said, *What?*

That's right, she told me, he ran out and I got on my knees and prayed.

She goes on and tells me, I prayed and prayed and prayed. Dear Brother Jesus, dear Mother Mary, let him get hit by a fucking truck, let him fall on the subway tracks and get himself diced-up real good like a can of crushed tomatoes, let someone blow his brains out of his ugly head with a 45 automatic, give that lousy mother a bullet for every time he slapped me or one of my kids.

But it did no good at all, girl, she said, as I am sure you coulda guessed, 'cause in a few hours, back he comes, only now he's got a scrawny Chinese bitch with him, and he's fixin' to fuck her right in my bed! — I said, *Whaaaaaaaaaaaaaaaaaaat?*

She says, don't you go thinking you didn't hear me right. That's the truth of what happened. He brings this slanty-eyed cunt into my house and she's lookin' around and saying things like Ugh, ugh, so dirty here, rike pigsty, ugh, ugh. I said to her, listen bitch, what are you doing uptown anyhow? Why ain't you down on Mott Street with the other scrawny-assed, can't-speakee-no-fucking-English bitches? Why don't you go back home, if trash like you even *has* a residence Oh, she says, you very ugry mean rady, I go way now. I told her, there's the door, get your no-meat-on-it ass out

package of special brioche hamburger buns which are like six dollars for six buns, so like essentially a dollar for a hamburger bun, but it's so seriously worth it because the bread really does make the sandwich like they say and I guess there's a lot of truth in that for damn sure. So I put the bun in the toaster oven and after I got it browned real nice and all I basically slathered it with garlic butter and some fresh chopped parsley. I literally must have suffered a budget breakdown because I bought a bag of those chips that are made with truffle oil — you know — the really expensive ones and some kale and heirloom tomatoes to finish my burger masterpiece. I also went for some Ben & Jerry's — two pints — because I couldn't decide between Chunky Monkey and Cherry Garcia. I had a Stewart's Root Beer with a little scoop of Cherry Garcia in it with the burger so it was like a Cherry Chocolate Sarsaparilla float and then I had some Chunky Monkey for dessert. So where were you last night when I called? Oh really? Fantastic. Excellent. At Wendy's? You had the fish sandwich — not the burger? Oh that's right, yeah yeah yeah, I remember now — you don't do red meat. Oh? Oh — it's *non-kosher* red meat that you don't do... Hey, dude, I think I have another call coming in. I'd better get this. Can I call you back later? Yeah — sure thing, man. How about Friday night? Oh — that's right — Friday night is like your Sherbot or whatever they call it. I totally get it. Okay, another time then. Later, dude.

Oh, hi Billy. Are you like returning my call? No no no, basically it wasn't anything important. I called you while I was cooking — making a totally awesome burger. Listen dude that was the most excellent burger I ever had. I slapped some cheddar cheese on it and some spice ketchup with chopped white onion and chopped gherkins. I truly

Yeah, I know it's not really so funny. That's my Marty for you. But he's great to travel with, he's fun even if the weather is bad, which it never is in Israel. I mean Israel is known for its good weather and its falafel.

I didn't know Israel had a rainy season but I enjoy Israel no matter what. I'm sure I'd like Israel in April, too, but like I said, I've never been there in April. I was once in Israel in March and I came back on March 31st, so I was *almost* in Israel on April 1st, which is April Fool's Day, but of course, not in Israel, and I wasn't in Israel in April, having just left. There are enough Israeli holidays in Israel, they don't need non-Jewish Israeli holidays like April Fool's Day, or holidays for groundhogs and office secretaries.

I bet you didn't know that Marty and I got married in Eretz Yisrael. We go to Israel for our anniversary every year and I'm planning to go to Israel to give birth to my daughter.

Five years ago, and then we had to come back right after the wedding to close on our condo. Two weeks later we went back to Israel and had our honeymoon there. Isn't that funny? We had our wedding in Israel and our honeymoon in Israel, two weeks apart, but one was in the north of Israel and one was in the south of Israel. It was an Eretz Yisrael whirlwind, let me tell you.

A tree? In Israel? Me too! My grandmother had a tree planted in my name in Israel when I was born. I visit the tree every time I go to Israel, and now it's grown very large and I can pick grapefruits off it and bring them home with me as gifts. I have some nice Israeli grapefruits for you, from the very heart of Israel, if you want to come and get them, from my grandmother's grapefruit tree, may she rest in peace.

they want to say things like *indeed* — I mean like that kind of a verbiage makes everyone uncomfortable about gay guys like apparently they must be — right? I mean why do they have to act all gay and talk gay and dress gay and be hanging with other gays laughing at everything and being happy to be gay? It's really annoying — you know what I'm trying to say? Get a sense of propulsion with the gay this gay that — it's all *ha ha ha ha* — look at us we're gay — look we're holding hands — oh and the fireworks were *soooooo* gay — yes *indeed* — they were righteous gay fireworks and what the fuck else.

Anyway — who cares? — they're like literally not on my radar. I just talk about them because they were there and literally saying things like *indeed* which I never heard anyone else say — not even bigger fags than those two say stuff like *indeed* or at least I never heard them actually say it. *Indeed!* What the fuck — right? Am I the crazy one? Whatever. Finally those two take off tiptoeing through the tulips and I went to Roberta — wow did you see *that* and she goes what's to see — so what? Big deal about them anyway.

So then we decided to walk down to the arcade and I went to her are you sure you won't have to go again because we're here now and if you have to go just go now because I don't want to go to the arcade and then have to go back so you can go for the zillionth trillioneth time. No she says with some majorly uncool attitude — I just went a minute ago. If you're so worried about someone going — go yourself bitch. And I go what do you mean? I know how to go if I want to go and I don't need you tell me when to go or not go. And she's like actually getting mad at me I mean like literally very irritated and so I went to her I hate it when you get like this so if you want to go on acting like all o' my home and take this drunken asshole along with you and then you can both go fuckee suckee in Hell. But she left and he stayed, and he started beating on me. He broke a leg off the dining room table and hit me all over with it. — I said, *Whaaat?*

That wasn't the end of this by a long shot, she says. Oh no, no, no, no, she says. There's more. A lot more. He was just getting warmed up, Binky.

She goes on to tell me that her daughter, Shampale, the older one, heard the shit going down and came out of her bedroom, and Tyrell commenced beating on her, too. She says to me, he hit her with the same table leg and knocked her *other* tooth out, then he ran into the bathroom where Modess was in the bathtub, and he forced her head under the bubbles and tried to drown her. — I said, *Whaaat?*

She says she ran out into the hallway and started screaming for help. Tyrell's gone crazy, he's killing everyone! Get the cops! Someone call them motherfuckers!

Now she started to cry. I tell you, I felt sorry as hell for her. I wanted to reach into my phone and give her a long, long hug.

She said, Binky, what am I going to do? They're gonna let him out in a day or two and he'll come back, sober and all, and sayin' how sorry he is. What am I going to do?

I said, there's only one thing you can do, Vaneesha, and I don't think you're going to like hearing it. But honestly, honey, I think it is high time that you consider getting yourself a new nigger.

She said, you think so, Binky? And I told-

went all the way because I needed to do right by a package of brioche buns I splurged on which are like six dollars for six buns so like a dollar for what could be your basic hamburger bun for each hamburger but it's actually totally worthwhile because.... Oh shit — who could this be? Billy, I think I have another call coming in. I'd better get this. I'll call you back later. Yeah sure thing, man. Call me when you can. Cool. Yeah, cool. Later, dude.

Hello? Who the fuck is this? A free credit card? What the fuck? Don't you realize that — number one, it's dinner time — and number two, this phone is for *important* calls, for *emergencies* and urgent business matters and other *necessary* shit? It's not a reverse public soap box. It's not *911* for morons whose emergency is that they're assholes instead of persons. It's private as in *private*. Do you even *know* what private is, jackoff? Fuck you and don't ever... Shit, who's this calling now? Yeah, goodbye asshole and don't call with your telemarketing crap again. I'm a busy person. Goodbye, and fuck you for calling.

Oh, hi Bob. Thanks for getting back to me. No no no, fuck no dude, it wasn't anything important. I called you while I was doing a burger. Let me tell you, my man, that was the best freakin' burger ever of all fucking time, no question. Totally excellent bigtime. Man oh man I pulled out all the stops. A burger made by a prince for a prince. I dropped some cheddar on it and some spice ketchup and some chopped onion and some chopped pickle. I splurged majorly on those brioche buns which are like six dollars for six buns so like a dollar essentially for each hamburger bun and then I bought a bag of those truffle oil chips... Hey, Bob, I think I have another call coming in. Can I call you back later? Okay next week is good, dude.

Yes, of course she's buried in Israel. Where else would we put her?

She was almost ninety. I visit her grave whenever I go to Israel. It's near the grapefruit tree. So, I visit the grave and I visit the grapefruits, but actually I visit the grapefruits first, so I can put a nice Israeli grapefruit on her grave. Because of her there's a living thing commemorating me in Israel. Where in Israel is your tree?

Oh, I've been there. That's a very nice part of Israel. It's funny how many parts there are to Israel. Israel is like Brooklyn, all different parts, but it's all Brooklyn anyway, just like Israel is Israel, no matter how many different parts of Israel it is.

No, I could *never* live there. I like to go to Israel, and I like to discuss it, but I've never given any serious thought to living in Israel. Except for the falafel, I don't think I'd like Israel much as a place to live... It just feels too Jewish to me. I don't know, I guess I think it's a bit too self-involved.

Going to Israel for the zillionth time, I'm just sayin'...

snotty and everything and like giving major attitude you can go find Freddy and Dillon and get bitchy with them since you seem to be so interested in their total faggy-ness — yes *indeed* you can for all I care any time you want to get faggy with *those* two be my freakin' guest — you can knock yourself out with those two. *In-fucking-deed!*

Then along comes Ella and she's got Dillon and Freddy with her and she's all lovey-dovey with Dillon and poor freakin' Freddy's all rejected-looking walking behind them by himself. So Dillon somehow has his arm around Ella when five minutes ago he was saying *indeed* and I mean literally on the Cyclone with his boyfriend Freddy going *whoo hoo!* and *ha ha ha ha!* like two assholes and now he's ready to get Ella pregnant with his fag baby while Freddy is all like pushed away on the side and looking majorly suicidal and all.

Wow these people sure are confused. But you know — who cares? — right? That's their thing. It's on *them*. As far as I'm concerned they're just extra shit to talk and text about and I bet they're saying the same shit about me and probably about you too bitch.

Like whatever, right?

her that I never would have said it if I didn't think it. What do you think? D'you think I shoulda kept my mouth shut?

Hello?

Hello?

Rhonda?

Shit. Motherfuckin' battery's dead.

I said, What ???

Or whenever. Later bro. *Ciao*.

Oh, hi Don. Whassup, dude? Oh, right – *I* called *you*. I totally forgot, man. No no no, it wasn't anything super-major or anything. I called you while I was making my special Wednesday burger. So where were *you* when I called? Oh really? You're like the tenth person in a row in the last five minutes who had a burger last night. That's freakin' *weird*. Oh shit, man... I have another call coming in. I'd better get it. It could be something important.

So there I am,
cookin' another
freakin' burger ...

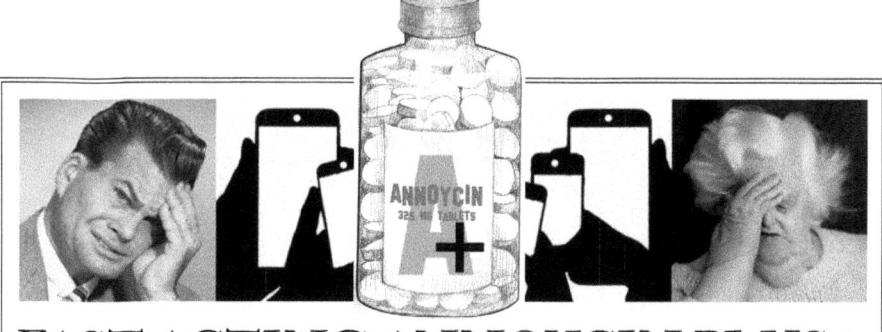

A Prologue to the Acting Conductor's Tale

On entering the dining carriage, it was immediately obvious to Carl that things were not sufficiently ready for the guests to be seated. He approached the two busboys in charge of setting up and asked them to hurry the preparations. "Also, guys," he said, "I'd like you to spray some air-freshener around this carriage because there's a vague, weird smell in here, like a one-hundred-year-old dead mouse. I've heard people say this train is haunted, but it shouldn't smell haunted. Not at these prices."

He went over to the kitchen service window and rapped lightly on the frame with his knuckles. Niall McDougan-Gonzalez, the chef, appeared immediately.

"It's now or never, Mr. Chef," Carl said, holding his opened pocket watch up to the service window. "Curtain's about to go up on lunch, so if you give me the menus and the seating chart, I'll get things organized and send your guests down here in five to ten minutes."

"Don't we have a *maître d'hôtel* to do all of that?" Niall asked.

The conductor laughed. "Where do you think you are, Maxim's? I'm the *maître d'* of the dining room *and* the conductor *and* anything else the railroad office wants me to be. This is all just make-believe, a chugging-along fairytale, and I play almost all the parts."

"Not the Chef's part, and the food is real," Niall replied defensively. "I should know—I've been slaving over this menu for hours and planning it for months."

He came out through the kitchen door and stood across from Carl, ready to shake hands. Carl introduced himself, and wished the chef the best of luck, adding, "I don't think punching tickets is going to lead to an offer for me to play Hamlet but like the genuine trouper I am—since you're a real chef and I'm a fake conductor—I'll do all I can to keep the spotlight focused on you. It's a shame that you've lost a third of your matinee audience because the Yeshiva people in the Roosevelt Carriage won't be joining us. Seems a real waste."

"Yes, that's a major screw-up for me."

"Not as much as kosherizing your kitchen would be," Carl said. "I understand you have your *own* guests today. You're the cousin of one of the passengers in the Whitman Carriage—the curly-haired blond guy with the nose off a Greek coin—aren't you?"

"I am. He is. We are." Niall hadn't expected this. "How did you know?"

"He's been telling the story of his parents' wedding and other family anecdotes, and I happened to overhear a few choice bits and pieces—you know—about your mothers being twins and so on. There's some sort of story-telling contest going on down there, and they're yakking up a storm—your cousin, his pals, a strange foreign guy, and a veiled lady in mourning." Suddenly Carl looked worried. He glanced at the seating chart that Niall had just handed him. "That's five in that group, and all the tables are for four. How am I going to work this?"

"Not to worry," the chef said. "Put them at two 'fours' on opposite sides of the aisle and add three more hungry storytellers to make up the eight. Keep the bereaved lady with Ryland, my business partner—he's the one with the auburn hair. If she's in mourning, he's the best choice to keep her company. Divvy up Cousin Scotch and the others amongst the newcomers, and make sure the new people are closest to the aisle. That way, if the newbies want to tell stories, they'll be in the center of the group, rather than all the way on the sidelines, against the windows."

"You certainly have a talent for organizing this sort of thing, don't you?"

"I have a catering business. I think I know how to do a seating plan."

"Put them *here*?" Carl pointed to a spot on the chart. "Or *here*?"

"Put them closest to the kitchen, so I can visit with them if I get a free moment." Niall was about to return to his kitchen when he had another thought. "Anyone important on the train today?" he asked.

"Me," Carl said without hesitation. "Maybe you."

"Oh, so you're a famous make-believe railroad conductor-*maître d'hôtel*-singer-dancer-actor-model-waiter, *etcetera* with a special emphasis on *etcetera*? Have I seen you in anything?"

"You're seeing me today, featured in multiple roles in *The Tale of The Brown Fox and Its Journey of a Thousand-and-One Fables*. That seems '*etcetera*' enough, don't you think?"

"No complaints. Just curious, that's all. What was the greatest role you've played?"

"The Devil. If not the greatest, certainly the most memorable."

"Goethe? Virgil? Dante? Irving? Twain?"

"Unscripted. At a Halloween party. It's quite a story."

The Acting Conductor's Tale

Be Careful Who You Wish For

Upon arrival at the threshold of a Halloween party, if one is ambushed by departing guests warning them to proceed no further, it might be worth pausing to consider one's next move. An alternate argument makes a good case against such hesitation—departures that circumvent arrivals are generally viewed as faint-hearted gestures designed by, and for, cowards. They're life experienced through the wrong end of a telescope. On Halloween, a notorious reality-bending, ante-upping annual happening, a telescope is—possibly—a kaleidoscope wearing a telescope's costume. What's life experienced through the wrong end of a kaleidoscope likely to resemble? What's the funhouse you've never been inside of like on the inside? What does the fun-fearing, would-be entrant, miss at a Fun-You-Might-Have-Had Funhouse?

"I'd turn around, if I were you," the vampire costumed as Count Dracula said. His companion, a vampiress in the elaborate guise of Countess Dracula, bobbed her head up and down in agreement. Mr. and Mrs. were holding hands so tightly, their fingernails were

on the verge of drawing blood. They looked very much in love. Both displayed prominent bite marks—proudly worn love trophies—in the region of their carotid arteries and there were some additional embellishments on offer—fresh-looking speckles of husband-and-wife blood on their collars and chins.

The couple was done up to the old-world nines, outstanding specimens of red-blooded blue-bloods of the vampire nobility.

"Why would I turn around?" I asked with my customary blend of sarcasm and skepticism, "Is there something behind me?"

"Take my advice, man, this party is sixty-percent bad news first and seventy-percent even worse news second. Some wiseguy dropped a tab of industrial strength acid the size of the Sunday Times in the punch, and everyone in there is on a bad trip to Hell."

"Lucky for me, I've dressed appropriately," I replied indicating my satanic regalia which consisted of nothing more than a mask and a black motorcycle jacket. "If Satan can't handle a party in Hell, who can?"

"I warned you," he said.

"I did too," the Countess added. She held up two fingers. "We *double* warned you."

A third vampire, who I hadn't previously noticed, stepped out from behind the Count and Countess—their teenage son, more than likely. Young Dracula held up three fingers and said, "Triple."

I found myself wondering if—like a nested Russian *matryoshka* doll—a still smaller fourth vampire was about to manifest itself from behind the third, this one displaying four baby fingers while sucking on the remaining thumb and raising the warning level up to "Quadruple." It didn't happen. The Draculas left off at a worrisome triple alarum, which might have been dire enough to scare off some potential guests—but certainly *not* this inspired version of Satan.

I said, "If anything bad happens, I'll send a telegram to your castle in Transylvania, and give you all the details."

Countess Dracula made a regal, dismissive gesture with her hand

and said, "Never mind about that. Just send the telegram if anything *good* happens."

They disappeared into the night. I disappeared into the party.

T hen the fun began. It started on the fire escape. I had taken a seat out there to escape the loud music and the increasing heat in the loft. I wasn't the only one out there, but everyone had spread themselves out a bit, so there was a lot of space around me. That didn't last very long. It was going to be a night of *matryoshka* dolls, but not the familiar kind that get successively smaller as each doll is opened. Each of these dolls had a kernel of evil nested within it. And within that kernel was another doll, and another, and another, each more insidious than the doll before it, until...

I t was only two days later, just after dinner, that the call came. An unfamiliar voice, with no preamble whatsoever, launched into an icy tirade. "I have been cleaning up your crap for the last two days, making good on dozens of lousy deals you scored in my name. Have you any idea how many calamities I've had to organize, how many killings I've had to subcontract? Or do you think I go around killing people myself, throwing them out windows and down stairs, choking them on popcorn, electrocuting them in bathtubs? Which brings me to my next subject—how do you want to go? Because at this moment very little would please me more than to do away with you next. The only thing that's stopping me is that you managed to walk off with my bag, and I want to get it back. Then I'll decide what to do with you. Get ready, because I'm coming over at midnight."

"How do you have my address? And this number, how did you get it?"

"One of my potential customers—who you so rudely borrowed for your own amusement—was happy to tell it to me with their dying breath."

Suddenly there was an ominous stillness. I knew for a certainty that Satan had just hung up on me. Something just tells you. You don't need a click. He would be knocking on my door in a little more than three hours, and I had run out of milk for coffee.

What clothing do you change into when you're expecting a visit from Satan? If you asked your mother, she'd advise you to wear clean underwear. She'd say, *clean underwear is not just for getting hit by cars*. Beyond that, is there a dress code for this type of visit? Should I adjust the lighting? Conceal a weapon?

By default, I decided upon a carving knife. It wasn't my self-protection tool of choice (that would have been a one-way ticket to Rio de Janeiro). I slipped a sharp blade from the knife block in the kitchen and slid it under a cushion on one of the club chairs. I went back into the kitchen and looked around for something to offer him. All I could find was a snack bag of wasabi peas. At least they were hot. Maybe he'd like them. While I was in the kitchen, I slipped a clove of garlic into my pants pocket. Insurance.

I realized how little I actually knew about Satan. Perhaps I could use the time before the sound of the impending three knocks on the door to bone-up on the satanic. I went to my computer and googled him. After some dry surfing around, I came across this juicy bit on a website called *The Biblical Apologist*:

We have learned that when Satan was cast to the earth, he took with him fully one-third of the hosts of heaven. Think of it! One out of every three children of God who existed in pre-mortality, sided with Satan against God and were cast to earth, never to obtain a physical body. Let's look at it another way. It has been estimated that between twenty and thirty billion people have inhabited this earth since the beginning of time, although no one can know for sure, short of revelation. Of course, this doesn't include all those yet to be born.

But let's be really conservative. Say there were a total of 21 billion people who were originally slated to come to earth. Of these, seven billion were cast out of heaven to earth, never to obtain a physical body, leaving fourteen billion souls

who would be allowed to progress into their second estate. Currently, there are seven billion people on the earth. Given this scenario, there are seven billion evil spirits here also, who want nothing more than to destroy and make miserable (like themselves) those who kept their first estate. That's one evil spirit for each person in mortality. Do you think Satan would have so much equanimity as to assign only one of his minions per soul? If you do, think again.

Consider this: Who does Satan hate the most? If you answered Christians, you'd be correct. If you answered those who follow Jesus Christ, Satan's dreaded enemy, you'd again be correct. So, do you really think Satan would assign, say, one of his followers to an aborigine in the Outback of Australia and just one to you, a follower of Christ? Or do you think he might pull off, oh, a hundred of his best fellows from the Outback and reassign them to you? If you said, "Yes," you'd likely be correct.

If only I was an aborigine or had enough time to grow a rabbi's beard, I thought, *I might stand a chance.* My thoughts raced. I remembered that Arthur Billheimer, my Jewish next-door neighbor, was away in California until the end of November and that he had a very large, ostentatious *mezuzah* on his door. *He won't mind,* I thought. *A mezuzah, a postage stamp, a cup of sugar—what's the difference between friendly neighbors?* Using a screwdriver, I pried the *mezuzah* loose and glued it to my own door frame. Then I put the screwdriver under the cushion of the *other* club chair—the chair facing the one that concealed the carving knife. More insurance.

How did it come to this? As I recall, I was sitting on the fire escape, wearing a black leather jacket and a dime-store Devil mask. My first customer was Marie Antoinette. She had a little difficulty, her wig being so high—and, chemically speaking, she being even higher—climbing out the window of the loft and keeping her balance, but she managed it and, after smoothing her elaborate gown and adjusting her Harlem Bling diamond necklace, she swept over to the iron steps where I was seated.

"So, it's true," she said in an off-putting, trust-fund-baby manner. Her New York accent and her cigarette did not jive well with her costume. "They said you were out here. So, what I want to know is—are you just slumming tonight like everyone else, or are you here conducting business?"

"That depends on the business."

"I have a proposition, and I'd like to know your rates."

"That depends on the business that I would be doing for you."

"How much to get rid of someone?"

"Again, that depends on the business particulars."

"Do it however you like, Grandpa Satan. How much?"

"I need more information to give you an accurate quote. Who is the proposed 'rid-ee' and why do you want to get rid of them?"

"My husband. He's cheating on me." She threw her mostly-smoked cigarette off the fire escape into the street. Someone from down below yelled *Hey!* She shrugged and lit another. "I came to this party to enjoy myself, so I don't want to haggle. I'll send him over and you can size him up. He's dressed as King Neptune. I'll come back later and we can iron out details, negotiate, whatever. If you offer me a good deal, I'll throw in this fabulous fake diamond necklace. Maybe you can use it to seduce a nun. Or a cardinal."

"They said you were out here," King Neptune said when he arrived a few minutes later holding his trident in one hand and eating suspicious-looking sushi with the other. "What kind of rates do you charge? Or is it a *one-soul-fits-all* deal?"

"That depends on the business."

"How much to get rid of someone?"

"That depends on the business."

"I don't care how you do it, as long as it's done very soon. How much?"

"Can you give me specifics?"

"Sure. I have some serious trouble with a chic I've been screwing. She's got herself pregnant and refuses to get an abortion. She's threatening to ruin my marriage."

"Who are we getting rid of? The girlfriend or the baby?"

"Is it the same price for either? Or is there a box discount, like two for one, or the second at half-off?"

I said, "It's Halloween, so everything is theoretical unless proven otherwise."

"I'll send her over and you can size her up. She's dressed completely in red, like the whore that she is. If you give me decent terms on the deal, I'll throw in this trident as a bonus. You can use it as a spare pitchfork."

A few minutes later Little Red Riding Hood was standing in front of me. "How much will you charge me?" she asked.

"That depends on the business."

"Does it have to be *my* soul on the contract, or can it be my baby's soul? Do you care which? Do I get better terms for a completely stain-free soul?"

"We can discuss the fine print later. What is it you want me for?"

"Get rid of my boyfriend's wife. She's in my way, that rich cunt. And if the terms are right, I'd also like to get rid of my boss. He's a rotten, thieving, sex-harassing bastard. And he's a lawyer, too. If you give me a good deal, I'll throw in this wicker basket. It could come in handy if you want to gather poisonous mushrooms on your way to grandmother's house—if you have a grandmother—or someone else's grandmother if you don't."

"I'd like to see your boss. You know, check him out. Can you send him over?"

"Yeah, he's dressed as a pirate, with an eye patch."

Blackbeard had his own request. "My law partner," he said. "He's skimming."

"I'll have a look. Send him over."

"He's dressed as Donald Duck."

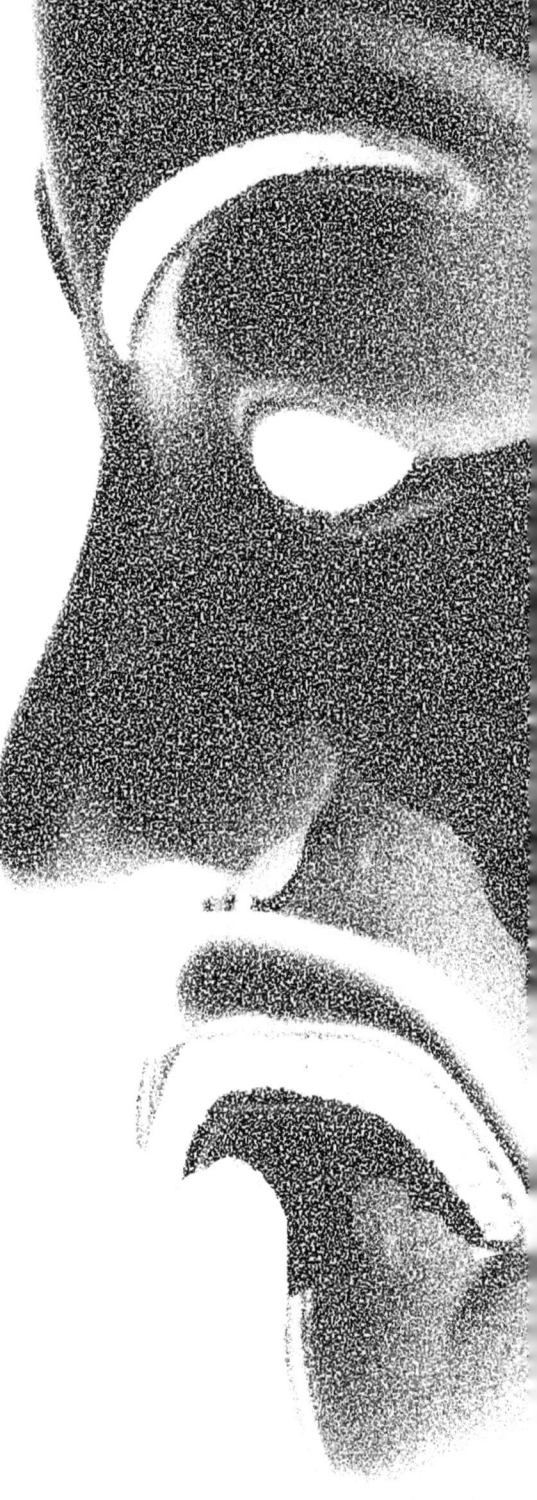

It wasn't long before the duck waddled over. "*Quack quack quack,* look over my shoulder and don't be obvious. Do you see the lady dressed as Marie Antoinette in the big wig?"

"Clear as day."

"That fucking bitch you're looking at is my step-daughter. I'm managing her gazillion dollar trust fund. If I get rid of her, the money's mine—and better yet, if you let me keep my soul, there's a piece of that action dog-eared for you."

That made two souls (or one soul and a large offer of cash) on the table for one chain-smoking faux-French monarch. Both Bluebeard the Pirate and Little Red Riding Hood were ready to sign over deeds to their souls for the same "rid" (that term is so much less violent-sounding than "hit")—and, in addition, there were pending trans-actions for "rids" on King Neptune, Red Riding Hood, and Donald Duck—what a bonanza if one could keep it all straight without a pencil and a pad or a secretary—*and it was only going to get worse.*

The complications became intolerable when—beyond all the hag-gling and counter-offers—the applicants each demanded that Satan provide an alibi for them during his execution of their "rid." This was clearly going to be a logistical impossibility—every target being fitted for cement shoes was needed alive and well to supply an alibi for one—and sometimes two—of the other scheduled victims. On the plus side, Satan would have no worries about returned merchan-dise or dissatisfied customers—it appeared that the entire roster of clients would be dressed in either white sheets with eyeholes or belt-less striped pajamas when the last of the evil dominoes had fallen. In any case, a little buyer's remorse never killed anyone, especially if they were already dead.

When arrangements with the Queen of France, King Nep-tune, Little Red Riding Hood, Blackbeard the Pirate, and Donald Duck had all been finalized, the deadly quintet evaporated into the crowd of acid-affected guests. I began to look forward to enjoying myself. I began to forget that I was Satan.

Across the street, in a similar industrial building, a similar fire-escape was similarly festooned with similarly costumed revelers. Their diaphanous capes and gowns rose and fell in the chilly October gusts of wind. Their jewels and crowns glittered in the light of the street lamps. From where I sat, the people opposite me looked like moths and fireflies clinging to a metal trellis. Up and down Wooster Street there were other parties in progress. It was actually possible, on such a night, to crash any party at will, since all and sundry were incognito for the night. Just wandering around, if you had a yen for *samosas* and *gulab jamun* you could crash an Indian party by seeking out a preponderance of bejeweled Maharajahs and Maharanis chattering like flocks of exotic birds while smoking just outside. *Scungilli* and *zeppole*? Look for zoot-suits, violin cases, and teased hair. Kegs of beer? Sniff around for excessive odors of urine and vomit. Gluten-free? Walk behind trendy, emaciated people talking on cellphones and see where they go for their kicks.

ust when you've retired your dance card for the evening, they throw something like a group of crazed, WASPy kiddies at you. Enter the contingency of Little People. Nothing politically incorrect intended, but this troupe was a genuine microcosm of the murderous gang led by Queen Marie Antoinette. There were only three little persons in the entourage—Dick, Jane, and Sally—right out of your pre-school storybook. Short pants, gingham dresses, pink socks, blue socks, hair ribbons, Buster-Browns, Mary-Janes, clean underpants, the works. They insisted that they were the real Dick, Jane, and baby Sally, and that the *Doppelgängers* in the storybooks we remembered from our childhoods were the fakes. As proof, they claim to have consulted the world's most esteemed expert on phonies, Holden Caulfield, and had their book versions declared one hundred percent horseshit. "Ask him yourself," Jane said, between licks on her lollipop. "He's right over there." She pointed to a rather suicidal-looking fellow carrying a suitcase and wearing a red hunting

cap. He was over at the punch bowl, filling up.

Once the trio learned that Satan was on the fire-escape, *Modern-Day Fun with Dick and Jane* began in earnest.

Jane said, "Jane wants to see Dick dead."

Dick said, "See Sally die. Die, die, die Sally!"

Sally said, "Sally is happy. See Sally jump up and down. Jane is dead. Sally is not dead. Sally is jumping up. Jane is lying down."

Jane said, "See Dick go to fucking Hell. Go, Dick, go!"

Despite their diminutive stature and their kid-die-costumes, all three were in their late thirties, heavy smokers of the hard stuff—Camels, Luckys, and Ay Gringo Cigars—and boozing it up with the best of the Big Guys. Possibly due to their smaller stature, the drugs in the punch had an exaggerated effect on them. Whatever the cause, they became increasingly belligerent and were unwilling to take *No* for an answer no matter how vehemently I rejected their requests. They accused me of size-ism and mini-phobia. "We insist," Dick demanded, "that you take care of Francis, the Good Humor Man. He killed our dog, Spot, and we want him dead."

"Why would the Good Humor Man kill your dog?" I asked.

Baby Sally had already begun to cry. Jane put her arm around her little sister and said, "We told him over and over again, 'See Spot run,' but he just wouldn't listen. Then he hit Spot with his ice cream truck. Mother said that Francis the Good Humor Man is a drunk because he gets chicken-pecked by Mrs. Good Humor Man. Let's get rid of her, too."

"Yes," I said, completely exasperated. "Let's."

Finally, the inevitable knocks, straight from Satan's very own knuckles, sounded. Once. Twice. Thrice. My pulse was like thunder in my ears as I walked to the door, which I had been avoiding so much as glancing at since hanging the borrowed *mezuzah* three hours earlier. I resisted using the peephole for a preview and just swept the door open as wide as it could go.

His Satanic Majesty stood on my threshold, wearing the same mask I had worn to the party. Had I been wearing mine, too (I had already tossed it into a garbage can on my way home from the party) you could easily have mistaken either of us for either of us.

He extended his hand toward me, but not to shake mine. Using a handkerchief to avoid actually touching it, he held out Arthur Billheimer's purloined *mezuzah*.

"Yours? Sort of, right? Sorry to bring bad news—well, not *that* sorry, actually—this *thing* fell off your door frame," he said. "On my second knock. Fell right to the ground. Hit me, in fact, on the foot. Allow me to share some sound household advice with you. I've always found that it pays—in the long run—to use better quality glue on these emergency do-it-yourself projects. For affixing *mezuzahs*, I recommend a kosher product called CrazyJew® which you can also use—if you're bald—to anchor a yarmulke on a breezy day. By the way, as a rule, I don't bend down to pick fallen objects up for people. But it seems you went to a lot of trouble over this sorry bit of Judaica—tainted as it is by a recent criminal act—so I made an exception."

He pushed past me and opened the nearest window to the entryway. Then he returned to the center of the room and removed the knife and the screwdriver from their places of concealment beneath the chair cushions. After

See Sally shop !

throwing both of my weapons out the window along with the *mezuzah* and the handkerchief, he shut it, returned to the chairs, and sat down. He took his shoes off as if to indicate he wasn't going to be leaving any time soon. The scent of Gold Toe powder filled the room.

What ugly feet, I thought. Five little appendages of fungus on each foot had apparently become infected with a case of toenails. *Ugh!*

"You wouldn't happen to have a spare apple lying around here, would you?" he asked.

"I beg your forgiveness, but as a struggling, out-of-work actor, I have nothing to offer. Certainly nothing *extra*. As you can see for your Majestic Dark Self, all I possess is the bare minimum."

"But you do have my bag, don't you? Identity theft wasn't satisfying enough for you, was it?"

"I didn't *steal* anything. It was Halloween, and I was playing a role. I'm sure there were hundreds of Devils-in-the-Bud that night."

"None busier than you, though. Perhaps I should get you to write a modern-day business plan for me. Meanwhile, though... my bag?"

"It was just a simple mix-up. I have it for you. What about mine?"

He scoffed. "*Your* bag? Do you really imagine I would return it to you after all the trouble you've caused me? Well, that's nervy, isn't it? Anyway, there was nothing more than a book of monologues in that bag, and some crumpled, dirty gym clothes. If you insist on knowing, I threw it all away except for the smelly jock-strap."

"Why would you keep *that*?"

"I didn't. I sent it to the Saint Ignatius Seminary in a package tied with a blue ribbon and a bow. I'm sure the professors and the students are fighting over it as we speak if they haven't already ripped it to shreds."

"Surely you're putting me on," I said, more than a little horrified by the image he had conjured.

"No, as a matter of fact, I'm not joking at all," he answered. "I'm as serious as the Titanic, Hiroshima, September 11ᵗʰ, and an isolated island of lepers combined. For an actor, your attitude comes across to my pointy ears as exceedingly ungrateful. My advice is—don't be a snob. You should be basking in the unexpected adulation. Think of your jockstrap as a portfolio grouping featuring some of your best parts. Think of the joy it's bringing to the perfect audience."

"I'll try."

"That's the spirit," he said cheerfully, slapping his knee for emphasis. He stood up abruptly. "My bag," he said. "If you don't mind."

I wasn't especially eager to leave him alone while I got his bag from the linen closet in the bedroom, not knowing what mischief he might get up to in my absence. On the other hand, anything was preferable to having him follow me into the bedroom, so I took a chance on leaving him on his own. When I got back, though, I was a little surprised to discover he was putting his shoes back on.

"Did you look inside it?" he asked while tying his laces.

"Yes—but in my defense, until I looked, I had no idea the bag was someone else's. Those bags are exactly alike."

"So, what did you see inside it?"

"Nothing. Nothing at all. It was—*is*—completely empty."

"Allow me to shed some light on this," the Prince of Darkness said as he stood erect, having finished with his shoelaces. "First of all, those bags are *nothing* alike. You may think they're identical, but I assure you, they are most definitely not. Secondly—my bag is *not* empty. On the contrary, my bag is quite full—perhaps too full. It's ridiculous and presumptuous for you to think otherwise. It's probably for the best that you *think* you didn't see anything in there, because what there is to see would be very hard to forget if you did see it, and, in any case, you would never be able to understand what you saw if you saw it. Thirdly—consider yourself lucky that you're on the outside of the bag looking in, not on the inside looking out."

He headed towards the door. "I'll show myself out now," he said.

"Well, thank you, Your Satanic Majesty, for being so understanding about our misunderstanding."

"Wait and see how the rest of your life turns out," came his parting words, "before you rush to thank me."

THE BROWN FOX
LUNCH
MENU

New York — THE PAUMANOK EXPRESS — Montauk

Chef de cuisine
Niall McDougan-Gonzalez
Winner, Prix de Montpellier

F X
IRONCLAD — RAILROAD

Seatings promptly
at 12:15 and 1:45

Hampton Greens
East of Manhattan Clam Chowder
South of New England Clam Chowder
Shrimp & Sea-Robin Cocktail

Pride of Orient Point Lobster Tail
Lobster Stew with Corn & New Potatoes
Local Waters Atlantic Swordfish
Oyster Bay Sunken Treasure Chest
Paumanok Duckling & Rhubard Compote
Leg of North Fork Ranged Lamb
Tagliatelle with Clams & Blackfish Filets

Coffee / Tea

Dessert Cart

Paumanok Iced Tea
Mixed Berry Lemonade
Apple Cider Sangria
Paumanok Wine Selections

New York ▬▬▬ THE PAUMANOK EXPRESS ▬▬▬ Montauk

F☒X
IRONCLAD RAILROAD

A Prologue to a Trio of Tales at Table

The Dining Car is Now Open

T he Professor was having some difficulty deciding between two Honorary Nightcap titles for the beveragizing ceremony. The two possibilities remaining were the names of single-syllable Norwegian drinks—*Punsch* and *Glogg*. After excessive deliberation—as if this was actually an issue worthy of serious consideration—he finally settled on *Punsch* because—as he had determined with an exaggerated degree of authority—*Glogg* sounded too much like a name for a troll in a Norwegian fable.

Lady Asta followed by selecting the most feminine name on offer—*Blush*. She was hardly the blushing type but it was the name they all knew she would choose the moment it was proposed. That left the three remaining new lunch companions, all of them fresh to the storytelling escapades in progress on *The Brown Fox*. The additional tablemates were given honorary titles, too, primarily so they wouldn't be disinclined to participate in the storytelling at table. Mildred Del Lago, an embarrassingly sexy older woman, was dubbed with an amusing flapper-era name—*Hooch*. Her companion, a lawyer by species—and *sleazy* by genus—became *Schnapps*. Lastly, the lucky journalist was gifted with a supremely enviable Runyonesque name—*Suds*.

The New Nightcaps were fully assembled at two adjacent tables—Scotch, Ry, Soda, Punsch, Blush, Hooch, Schnapps, and Suds. For the sake of fair play, they informed the conductor his newly bestowed honorary title would be *Brew*. Then, left with the still-unassigned name of *Glogg*, they sent a note to Chef Niall McDougan-Gonzalez in the kitchen and informed him of his sudden investiture with a name most befitting a Norwegian troll—at least that's how it was characterized by the sole Norwegian in their assembly.

"Here's to the World of Storytelling," Professor Punsch said, standing at his place and lifting his glass to his seven lunch companions. All touched glasses and took their first sip of a very pleasing wine choice. So ended the extremely silly—but undeniably enjoyable—Nightcap Beveragizing Ceremony—a fanciful, team-building form of clubhouse baptism, something like an intellectual hazing ritual with no serious hazards possible and no long-term commitments implied.

"I suppose I'll have to go first to show you how it's done," Professor Punsch announced, sitting down now, but continuing to take the lead as was his custom. None of the newcomers objected to being denied the opportunity to be first in the tale-spinning spotlight. "To avoid redundancy, let me ask our three new companions what sort of stories they want to regale us with."

As sometimes happens, coincidences occur that can be entertaining and disconcerting at the same time. Scotch, Ry, Soda, Lady Asta, and the Professor, led by the conductor, were heading to the dining car, which required passage through the Roosevelt Carriage wherein the ancient, withered Rabbi Scholnik was holding court with his students. Everyone—students and passersby alike—fell silent as the lunch expedition traversed the Yeshiva carriage, an adventure positively reeking of pastrami and other delicatessen specialties, to the next one, the Grant Carriage. There, the moment she entered, Lady Asta set her eyes upon someone she knew.

"Millie! Millie!" she cried out. "Over *here*, my darling! It's me, Asta!"

"Are you kidding us? Is that Egg Cream Millie?" Scotch asked, seizing Lady Asta's elbow to prevent her from dashing off.

"No, *that* Millie was Mildred *Bathbaum*, my dead sister-in-law, who made that cockamamie egg cream. This one is Mildred Del Lago, a very old friend, who is, coincidentally, related to the other one." She dropped her voice to a confiding whisper. "This one is crazy, too."

"Asta! So soon?" Mildred Del Lago cried out. She was referring, they all understood, to the fact that Lady Asta's son, Thom Fulton, had just died and was traveling with her in a shoebox. The two women hugged, careful not to cause any disarray in each other's makeup or garments. Lady Asta proceeded to explain about the shoebox and the planned ash disbursement. Her friend was eager to join them. "Merv will want to be there, too." She signaled to a tall, stooped man with very thick glasses and a bulbous lower lip that protruded from his face like an awning. He was introduced as Mervyn J. Schlissel, Esquire.

Bubbling with excitement, Lady Asta gave her friend's sleeve a girlish tug. "Millie, dear, you simply won't believe what I'm about to tell you. Do you recall the twin ladies we've seen shopping in Saks all these many years, the ones we call the Mirror Girls? This gentleman—and the chef who is preparing our lunch today—are their sons!"

Mildred Del Lago's exquisitely manicured hands flew to her cheeks in disbelief. The supersized Bulgari gold nuggets that comprised her bracelets made loud, clunky noises like slavery chains. Meanwhile, Lady Asta continued to tie up other loose ends with her running narrative. "Gentlemen, this dear lady, my old friend Mildred Del Lago, is actually the first cousin of my sister-in-law, Millie Bathbaum, who I spoke about earlier. She's related to Millie and Maury by blood, while I'm only related to them by marriage, so if one of us has the 'crazy' gene, it's *her*, not me. It so happens that we all met, including Big Merv who you see looming over us here, when my sister-in-law was being prosecuted and he was representing her."

The Professor was very intrigued by this twist. "Prosecuted for what?"

"The charges were all dropped eventually," Lady Asta replied, looking a little embarrassed, "but there was some concern on the part of the district attorney that my sister-in-law was poisoning Maury."

The lawyer added, "They called it Munchausen by Proxy Syndrome."

"Yes," Mildred said. "I remember her calling me in hysterics and telling me that she might be going to prison for munching on pretzels. She had gotten it all mixed up, of course. But being mixed up was nothing new for her. She practically invented it."

"Millie, Millie, Millie," Lady Asta said, unable to resist a nostalgic smile. "She was always one slice of bread short of a sandwich, the poor thing. I'll never forget the time, when Maury was still not much more than an infant, that her husband—my brother-in-law, Irving—came home from work and found his apartment filled with neighbors and strangers. People were backed-up into the hallway and down the staircase. He panicked like any normal father would have under the circumstances. At first, he thought something tragic had occurred. Shaking from head to foot like a cholera victim, he shouted, 'What's all this? Is everyone okay? Did something happen?' A neighbor grabbed him to prevent him from collapsing on the linoleum. 'Calm down, Irv,' someone said. 'Everything is fine. Just go look in the baby's room.' He rushed to the door of the nursery, and there was Millie inside—along with a dozen curiosity seekers—a garrulous mob milling around Maury's crib, everyone talking and gesticulating at once.

"The baby's crib stood against a wall that had been covered in streaks of stinking excrement. 'Look what your son the artist did!' she announced to her husband proudly. Irv's blood pressure must have soared from zero to two hundred in a single instant. 'What did he do? Arrange for us to get evicted?' She was highly offended. 'You haven't even looked, Irv. Can't you see he's drawn a mural with a little piece of ca-ca? Here's Adam and Eve and here's the apple, and here's the Devil with little horns. See, the long squiggly smear is the Serpent. We should take a picture. Do you have film for the new Polaroid?'

"Hearing that, he completely lost control of himself and turned on the crowd. 'Out, out, out, out, out!' he shouted. 'Everyone that doesn't have a soapy rag in their hand can get the hell out!' Then, to Millie, he said. 'Clearly, that child must have dropped you on your head.'

"Years later, she still lamented that Irving had refused to take a picture of Maury's first masterpiece. You'd think her child had created the Sistine Chapel out of diaper turds."

W hen the Professor inquired about the types of story the new guests wanted to contribute, Hooch perked up at once. "Since you find them so entertaining, I'll tell a story about my cousin Mildred and her crazy son."

Ry said, "We've already had a Mildred and Maury tale from Lady Asta Blush, so your story would be like a sequel—*Mildred and Morris II*, or *Revenge of the Bathbaums.*"

Soda was equally impressed. "Our first sequel—and so soon, too! If we stay on this train long enough, we'll have enough of Mildred and Maury to make up a franchise."

"Yes," said Hooch. "And what a franchise Mildred and Maury would be!"

Her lawyer companion, Mervyn J. Schlissel, Esq., now dubbed Schnapps, snorted contemptuously, pushing his glasses back up his nose three times in quick succession as if that would anchor them there three times longer. "A franchise of abject stupidity is closer to how I'd describe anything connected with those fourteen-carat nuts," he said dismissively, shaking his head. "But, if a franchise ever actually materialized, I certainly could handle any legal issues that would arise therefrom. There's always some monster lurking between the lines of those franchise deals."

"Oh, *you!* You just see demons everywhere, especially the profitable ones," Hooch scoffed, waving him off impatiently. "It's *sooo* boring, dear. *'Arise therefrom!'* How'd you dream up that doozy of a phrase? Save it for when we get where we're going." She turned to the others. "Our dear Schnapps is on his way to the Fire Island Pines to serve his standard Loudmouth Jewish Lawyer Subpoena on a nefarious food store entrepreneur, a fellow who's been on the lam for months."

"That's right," the lawyer said, making it clear that being labeled a loudmouth Jewish lawyer presented no problem for him. He was actually proud of the implications and would have printed similar words on his business card if he could have done it without being censured by his professional colleagues. Despite the fact that other attorneys might have been offended, he was convinced many potential clients would find themselves hypnotized by that phraseology. Seekers of legal representation had always appeared more than eager to be represented by loud, fast-talking, pushy lawyers, especially if they had Jewish-sounding last names.

For example, "Attorney Abraham J. Lipschitz" (the ubiquitous "J." in the middle of the sandwich was always there to hammer home the Jewishness), in his opinion, was an unbeatable lawyers' moniker. The name Lipschitz subliminally hinted at three indispensable requirements for superior lawyering: a cultural knack for assigning guilt with a mere glance, a facility with machine-gun vocal theatrics, and an ability to produce an unlimited supply of bullshit at the drop of a hat. Lipschitz said it all. It was litigation music, a tune you couldn't get out of your head. The addition of an Irish and/or WASP name—or two or three—on the marquee was helpful, too. McInnes, Pearce, White & Lipschitz was as perfect a front as anyone could wish for. Anyone denying that Lipschitz was the name that sealed the deal was committing perjury.

"And it's not your usual 'slip and fall' type of litigation this time," he explained gleefully to the other Nightcaps. "It's more like 'bite and barf' when you study the evidence. We allege that a shithole establishment served a dead rodent to my client, fried in a donut. Imagine Topo Gigio encased in a greasy *zeppole*, covered in powdered sugar, and you're not even close to what my client endured. The responsible food concession owner, a jerk named Max Hypantts, has been hiding out on Fire Island ever since, trying to avoid legal proceedings."

"But now old demon-hunting Uncle Schnapps is on the case!" Hooch said, pinching her man's cheek affectionately. "You'd think he was running after Osama bin Laden. Look out Mr. Hypantts. Here we come!"

Lady Asta turned her head to Scotch and discretely rolled her eyes.

heir newest member, Artie Williamson, now dubbed Suds, was the only member of the group, other than Professor Punsch, who was not journeying further than Sayville. He explained that he was traveling to the little hamlet to research a story on the discovery of a relic of early radio history. "The place I'm going to was once known as the Devil's Tower. It's nothing more than a ruin now, but a small stash of evidence was recently discovered there by a local woman."

"Surely you mean the Devil's *Castle*," said Scotch. "That's the place our Professor Punsch is heading for, if I'm not mistaken."

"No, these are two different places. The Devil's Castle is a house on Macon Drive which still exists. That's where the Reverend Major Jealous Divine, otherwise known as God, had his shindigs on Sundays—a hotbed of controversy after World War One until his arrest and the infamous court case that resulted in the voodoo death of Judge Smith. I have a story for you about a completely *different* structure named for the Devil. Serious intrigue and espionage went down at the site of a 500-foot tall wireless tower, erected by the German government in Sayville, in 1912."

"What kind of evidence was found?" Schnapps asked.

"A young woman, a long-time local resident, was intrigued by the fact that no one, not even town officials, could direct her to the precise location of such an important historic site. In fact, there were residents who were unaware that anything at all had happened years earlier. An important page of local history had seemingly disappeared into a black hole. So, she decided to go on a personal expedition to identify the location of the infamous Devil's Tower. After a great deal of wandering around in undeveloped areas of Sayville, using satellite imagery and GPS, she unearthed some concrete piers and a bunch of old radio tubes and wireless components that were stamped by the German manufacturer, Telefunken. That's all that remained of a site that allegedly launched America's involvement in the first World War. Without a doubt, it's the location of the first hostile action the United States took against Germany in that conflict. That part is well-documented in newspaper and government records. It's indisputable."

"And now it's just an assortment of busted tubes?"

"A *small* assortment. In an ordinary cardboard box. In a young lady's Sayville garage, keeping company with a lawn mower, a garden hose, and other artifacts of modern-day suburbia. Once, though, the Devil's Tower, which cost millions to build—when millions were *billions*—was the crowning glory of early communication science, the most important wireless transmitter in the world, and a crude precursor of today's internet."

"The Devil sure had his work cut out for him in Sayville way back in the day—castles, towers, and maybe some deviled eggs, too," Soda commented. "Now it's just a place for families, ferries, and fairies."

"As long as the Devil doesn't decide to pay a return visit while I'm going about my business there," the Professor said, inexplicably beaming from ear to ear. "I think I should regale you with a fun story about the Devil while we enjoy our wine, since the spotlight is on him anyway—at least for the moment. And also, as an expert on fables and tales, I should pay some homage to the Devil for being the lead player in the world's very first story—the story of the Garden of Eden and the Fall of Man."

Lady Asta Blush said, "Excuse me, Professor darling, but if I am not mistaken, the first story of all is the story of the Creation."

"Nonsense!" he scoffed. "All that 'let there be *this*' and 'then there was *that*' is just window-dressing for the drama to come a few pages later. The Bible is all set and costume design in the beginning. Isn't 'Let there be light' the very first lighting cue? The action starts *after* all that preparatory flub-a-dub is dispensed with. The curtain goes up in the Garden of Eden, when the Serpent slithers onstage. That's when storytelling kicks off for real."

"So, you're going to tell us the story of Adam and Eve and the Serpent?" Ry asked. "I think we know that one, don't we, guys?"

Professor Punsch took this jibe badly and felt compelled to score some points in return. He said, "First of all, none of you snarky wiseguys knows how that story *really* ends because it still hasn't ended. Don't think for a moment that Man fell once and isn't still falling. Secondly, I have no intention of telling that story as *you* know it, because it's corrupted by inaccuracy, and it maligns the Devil most unfairly. Lastly, it shows Eve in a rather unfavorable light, which is equally unfair, because—as we all are quite aware—the vast majority of villains in history are men, not women. It would be much more enjoyable for everyone if I delve into my grab bag for an entertaining story about the modern-day Devil—a sophisticated Devil for a sophisticated audience, as told in a sophisticated manner by a sophisticated authority on fables.

"I'll tell a contemporary Devil tale, too," said Schnapps. "The true story of the Devil's Commission on the Assassination of President John F. Kennedy. Let's call it 'The Devil Does Dallas.'"

"So, first we'll have my introductory tale while we enjoy our wine and cocktails," said the Professor, "then the Kennedy Assassination story after the appetizers, then the Devil's Tower story after our main course, and, last, a continuation of the Adventures of Mildred and Maury for a humorous dessert. We may need another bottle or two of this wine."

"I'll attend to the wine, but be sure to speak up," a voice said. Looking up, they saw Glogg, in his chef's hat, peeping out of the louvered kitchen window. He winked at his cousin and twirled his half-Mexican mustache. To all, he said, "Feed me and I'll feed you. I'll be auditing you in the kitchen, and I don't want to miss a word."

Professor Punsch cleared his throat and began, "Listen well, my seven curious companions—and invisible auditors, wherever you are hiding—for I'm ready to reveal all I know about the Devil's Daughter's Doll's Diary . . . ."

A Trio of Tales—The Professor's Second Tale

The Devil's Daughter's Doll's Diary

Lhe Devil's daughter, to be perfectly truthful, looks—more or less—like an ordinary little girl looks and the Devil's daughter's little doll, to be perfectly truthful about *that*, looks—more or less—about as ordinary as the Devil's daughter looks. The Devil's daughter's doll's diary looks very much like the book you *would* be holding might look right now if you were reading this story in bed instead of listening to me tell it to you at lunch. More or less.

If there is a certain amount of po-faced homeliness—what one might call the hum and the drum—in what I'm about to tell you, it can be traced back to the Devil Himself—*i.e.*, blame *him*—for no creature or being or entity in existence (or nonexistence) is as thoroughly ordinary as is the Devil. There is absolutely nothing more boring and nothing more banal than Evil, and Evil—as is well-known—is the Devil's meat and the Devil's potatoes. The truth is, the Devil just wants to have fun and feel satiated. When he gets tired of mischief, and he is fully sated by his meat and potatoes, it's his great pleasure to yawn first and belch afterward, right in God's face.

It so happens that this very same yawning, belching, evil-loving Devil has a daughter (adopted), who has a doll (adopted), who keeps a diary (adapted). Are you dying to know what's in the diary? Who isn't?

Many years ago, I had the opportunity to meet the Devil. Lucky for me, it was on his day off, so he wasn't shopping or doing business. Otherwise, I'd likely be going to Hell sometime further down the timeline. As it turned out, we became moderately friendly and had a nice chat—nothing more. I, being a devout Catholic, have fully confessed my innocent dealings with the Evil One, so I pray my final appointment will be with Saint Peter and not Old Scratch. But nothing is certain. Until the ink dries, you can never be fully sure which book your name is written in.

Sitting in the park one lovely afternoon, I saw the most hideous-looking dog in existence being walked by the most ordinary-looking man in existence. The dog had so much personality, and the man so little, it was possible to believe that the bulldog was doing the walking, and the man was at the wrong end of the leash. It turned out that this pair, tethered to each other by a long chain, was the real, bible-certified seal-of-disapproval Devil and his grotesque mascot, taking a leisurely stroll. The dog seemed interested in being admired for his ugliness and the Devil, out of pride, I suppose, allowed his dog to drool on my shoes and sniff them with his snorting bulldog snout.

"What's his name?" I asked, looking up from my shoes to the stranger's pale, unreadable eyes. I had no idea who stood before me, and I was only attempting to be polite. The mollycoddling came later.

He smiled and petted his slobbering pet. "Dognapped," he said. At once, having heard its name intoned, the dog raised its bulbous head and widened its eyes. He panted anxiously—more drooling ensued—obviously hoping for a treat. The man put his hand into a pocket of his trench coat and produced a dead mouse which he dangled from two fingers by its tail. The dog lunged for it and yanked it from his hand.

I said, "No judgments, neighbor, but am I supposed to infer from his name that you've stolen your dog from its proper owner?"

The stranger nodded affirmatively and signaled for me to move over to make room for him to sit next to me, which I did; meanwhile, the dog was chewing its prize underneath our bench. It was at this point that the Devil extended his hand—his left hand to be precise—and introduced himself.

"I am The Devil," he said. "No doubt you've heard of me."

Should I have said, "I'm glad to meet you" or "Nice to finally make your acquaintance" or something to that effect? Etiquette manuals don't cover this type of encounter. Lacking guidance, I said, "How would you like me to address you? Satan? Lucifer?"

"You can call me 'The' for brevity or 'T' if you prefer it, as some of my other Wednesday afternoon acquaintances do."

"So, *Devil* is your family name and *The* is your Christian name?"

"*Christian* name? *Oy gevalt!*" He found my gaffe extremely amusing. "Let's not belabor the point, friend. Don't call me anything if that's what suits you. I can just as easily be the Big Nothing as the Supreme Negator." He shrugged. "Today is my day off—Wednesday, the Devil's Sabbath—so you're perfectly safe to enjoy a nice conversation with the greatest *raconteur* of all time. Pick a topic— any topic at all—and I'll help you discuss it to death."

We conversed about many things that day. Most interesting to me was the Devil's long-term project to shrink the size of the human penis. It was hard to imagine anyone maintaining interest in *anything* for millenniums, but genitalia, as it happens, is a unique subject with unique rules. Members of our species manage to maintain an unflagging, lifelong interest in the size and other attributes of the genitalia of both sexes, often valuing them more highly than the brain. If objects of such ungainliness remain fascinating for a human lifetime, why not for the Devil's lifetime? It was a matter of scale in time—as well as flesh—for him.

He clarified the issue for me: "The current problem is the continent of Africa with its abundance of large endowments. I've been working for the last four centuries to integrate the Black African with the smaller White Caucasian. To succeed in that would advance my project considerably. That integration, by my standards, would be a very useful shortcut—the pun is unintentional—but it hasn't been easy."

"I'm a little confused," I said. "Isn't the integration of the races a *good* thing? Aren't you advancing a *good* cause just to alter a portion of human anatomy for your own amusement?"

"There's some truth there, but you take into account only the small picture. You overlook the fact that I'm in this for eternity. All of *you*"—here he gestured at me and the other people around us, all of us enjoying the afternoon outdoors—"are fly-by-nights... fireflies... gnats...." He flicked his fingers to stress the insignificance of humanity. "Look at it this way—first I introduced the black race to the American continent as slaves; then came the Civil War; then came the KKK and all the lynching; then came the race riots; then came O. J. Simpson; then came Tawana Brawley and Reverend Sharpton. And so on and so on. The road to the reduced penis via integration has provided a lot of sideshow amusement for me. Throughout all of that, I never whipped anyone. I never fired a cannon or a rifle. I never burned a cross. And for that matter—while we are on the subject of things I *didn't* do—I never *made* anyone eat an apple. I only ate one myself and said 'Yum yum yum!' That's *all* it took. Truth to tell, I haven't been bored for a moment since the dawn of man and I don't see that changing. Entertaining the Devil is what man does best."

Some weeks later, I was seated on the same bench when the Devil and his bulldog came by again. This time, he was holding the hand of a young girl with a wan, vacuous look about her. She wore old-fashioned pantaloons and a gingham dress and shiny patent leather shoes. She looked like a Victorian daguerreotype come to life. Partially, anyway.

"What's her name?" I asked. "Or, shall I guess? Is it 'Kidnapped?'"

"*Kidnopted*, if you will. I call her Kiddie for short, and so can you."

"How old are you, Kiddie?"

She stared at me with blank, unblinking eyes. The Devil just laughed.

"She's shy," he said. "But be careful. She bites worse than the dog."

"What's that you have there, Kiddie?" I asked. She was clutching a rag doll to her breast. The doll was costumed very similarly: gingham dress, pantaloons, etc., and its lacquered coat button eyes were as expressionless as Kiddie's were. "Is that Little Miss Dollnapped you're hugging?"

"Like father, like daughter," the Devil chuckled. "We call her new little baby Dollie. My granddaughter—in a manner of speaking."

"Don't tell me Dollie bites, too."

"Not yet that I'm aware of," he said, once again taking the seat next to mine. He gave Kiddie some quarters from a ragged change purse and sent her off to buy ice cream from a nearby vendor. He also fed another disgusting treat to the bulldog, who seized it and hid under our bench, noisily chomping on it with audible relish.

"How's the Penis Project coming along?" I inquired. I didn't think it would be advantageous to ignore the Devil's personal interests, no matter how revolting or incomprehensible. Eugenics of the Penis was not the worst possible choice of topics, all things considered.

"Small progress," he sighed. "Very small. Disappointing and unsatisfactory. To tell the truth—which I only do on Wednesdays—the rate of shrinkage this calendar year, by my best estimation, is approximately .000000042 millimeters. I've adjusted the completion date for the project accordingly to 5,019 A.D. So, it appears—like it or not—I've still got a lot of shriveling and shrink-dinking ahead of me."

Some weeks later, I was seated once again on the same bench when little Kiddie came strolling by. Neither the Devil nor Dognapped was along for this jaunt, but one thing was new: Kiddie pushed a small baby carriage in front of her. She came over and sat beside me, swinging her feet back and forth because she was too short for them to reach the ground.

"Where's your Daddy today?" I asked after an uncomfortably long silence.

"In Hell," she answered.

Those were the only two words I ever heard Kiddie say. Within moments of speaking, she had slid off the bench and run off. She was soon skipping down a pathway into the depths of the park, abandoning the baby carriage next to me.

At first, I didn't think much of it, but after an hour had passed, I began to feel anxious. What if, I wondered, there were toxic chemicals or explosives in the carriage? What if it concealed a kidnapped baby? Or a cache of stolen money and jewels? I could possibly be held responsible for a crime... arrested... tried... convicted!

I jumped up and looked. To my great relief, I discovered that the carriage was occupied by Dollie with her jet-black button eyes taped over with duct tape, indicating—I think—that she was sleeping. Clutched to her bosom was a small book, which I presumed was a diary. That guess was prompted by the pose, one universally accepted as the standard way a child would hold their secret diary. I really couldn't be sure what the book was, because the front of it was pressed against Dollie's gingham dress, but I was absolutely certain it wasn't a bible.

Another two hours passed. I had read the newspaper from cover to cover no less than three times. The sun was gradually sinking behind the office buildings near the park. Shadows were lengthening all around me. Still, there was no sign of the Devil and Dognapped, nor had little, creepy Kiddie come back for Dollie and Dollie's diary. It didn't help that passersby slowed down as they went past me, trying to sneak a peak in the carriage. The few that managed to get a satisfactory glimpse were horrified to behold a rag doll with tape over its eyes tucked inside. The looks of astonishment aimed at me by these busybodies had me cringing with embarrassment all afternoon.

I was much more concerned about Kiddie's absence after five-thirty had come and gone. Ultimately, anxiety mixed with curiosity overcame my reticence and fear of devilish reprisals. I pulled the book out of Dollie's flimsy grasp and fled the park with it, walking briskly and purposefully, like a criminal might when attempting to flee the scene of a crime unnoticed. That book, I reflected, while breaking out in a sweat, was the only thing I had ever stolen in my life.

My nervous exhaustion had reached such a peak that I had to lie down when I got home. I fell asleep, unintentionally, clutching the book to my chest, much as Dollie had. When I woke, it was around midnight. The first thing I did was switch on the reading lamp at my bedside. I turned the book over.

The title on the front was *Sayville Tales, a Book of Travelers' Tales.*

I opened it to the last entry and—to my complete horror—read the following:

> "The Devil's daughter, to be perfectly truthful, looks—more or less—like an ordinary little girl looks and the Devil's daughter's little doll, to be perfectly truthful about *that*, looks—more or less—about as ordinary as the Devil's daughter looks. The Devil's daughter's doll's diary looks like the book you *would* be holding might look right now if you were reading this story in bed instead of listening to me tell it to you at lunch. More or less..."

My first stop the next morning was Heavenly Saints Church. I dashed up the steps two at a time and headed for the nearest available confessional. Inside, enveloped in the shadowy silence, I roughly pulled the curtain closed, nearly ripping it in the process, and I tried to collect myself. My heart was pounding. My breathing was ragged from the onslaught of an anxiety attack.

After a respectful moment of silence, from behind the grille, a soothing voice spoke to me. "How can I help, my son? I am here for you."

"Forgive me, Father, for I am out of breath."

"Excuse me?"

"Sorry... Forgive me, Father, for I have sinned."

"When was your last confession?"

"Tuesday."

"Two days ago? How have you managed to sin again so soon, my son?" I heard a barely audible, quasi-judgmental gasp issue from the other side of the grille. "Not Number Four, Heaven forbid..."

"I stole something," I interrupted. I proceeded to tell him the whole devilish story. From time to time he emitted a compassionate sigh, but there was also a strange scraping sound nagging for attention, as if he, or someone nearby, was filing their nails with an emery board. I had only gotten to the part about Dollie and the baby carriage when I heard what was unmistakably the sound of an unrestrained yawn. This was followed by a lengthy, disturbing silence.

"Father? Father? Are you awake?"

"Of course, my son. I wouldn't miss a word of this for anything," the voice said from the shadows that huddled behind the grille. His words were immediately superseded by an extremely prodigious belch.

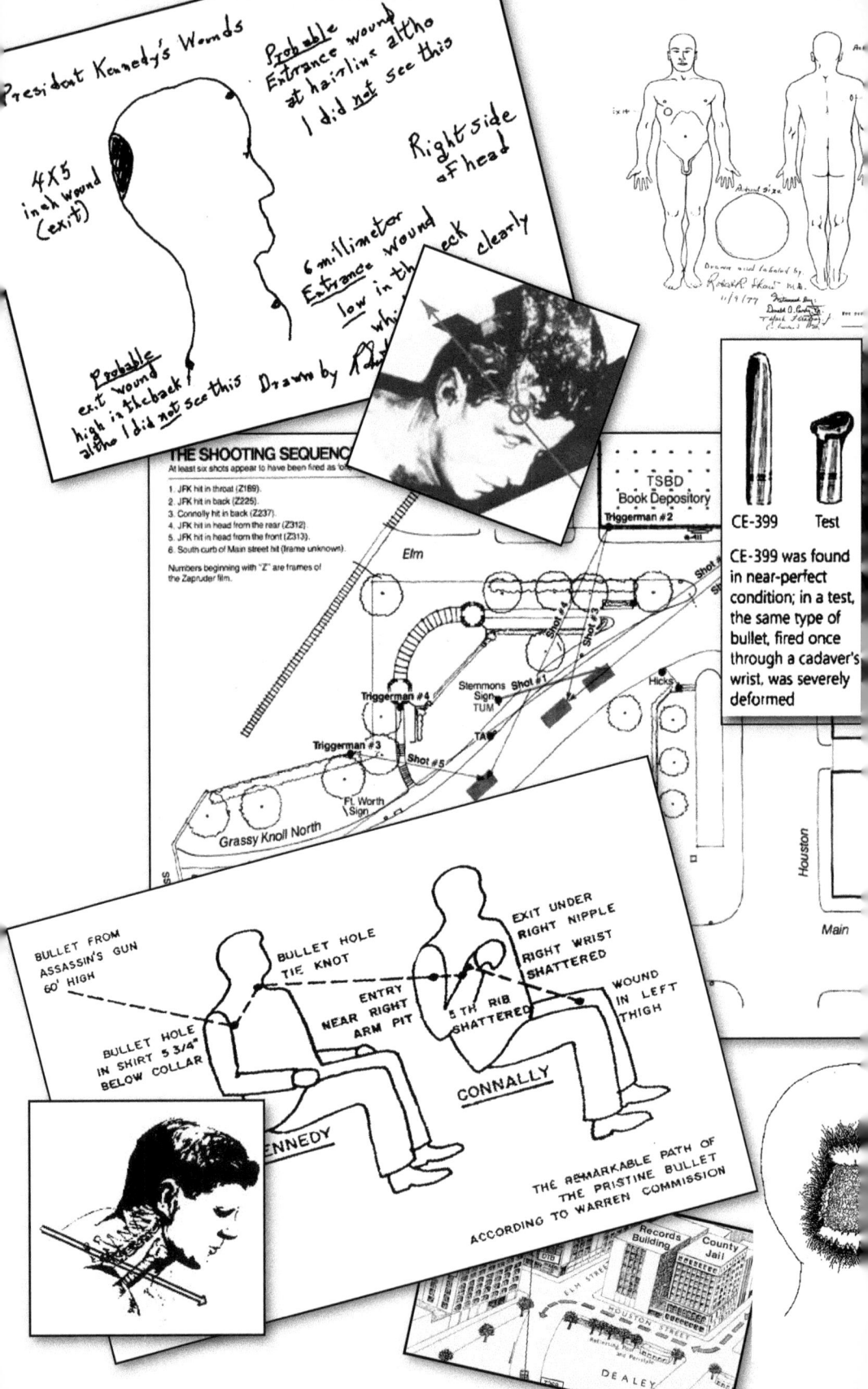

President Kennedy's Wounds

Probable Entrance wound at hairline altho I did not see this

Right side of head

4X5 inch wound (exit)

6 millimeter Entrance wound low in the neck which ... clearly

Probable exit wound high in the back altho I did not see this

Drawn by R...

Drawn and labeled by Robert F. Karnei M.D. 11/9/77

THE SHOOTING SEQUENCE

At least six shots appear to have been fired as follows:

1. JFK hit in throat (Z189).
2. JFK hit in back (Z225).
3. Connally hit in back (Z237).
4. JFK hit in head from the rear (Z312).
5. JFK hit in head from the front (Z313).
6. South curb of Main street hit (frame unknown).

Numbers beginning with "Z" are frames of the Zapruder film.

Elm

TSBD Book Depository

Triggerman #2

Shot #4
Shot #3
Shot #1
Shot #5

Triggerman #4

Stemmons Sign TUM

Triggerman #3

TA

Ft. Worth Sign

Grassy Knoll North

Hicks

Houston

Main

CE-399   Test

CE-399 was found in near-perfect condition; in a test, the same type of bullet, fired once through a cadaver's wrist, was severely deformed

BULLET FROM ASSASSIN'S GUN 60' HIGH

BULLET HOLE TIE KNOT

EXIT UNDER RIGHT NIPPLE

RIGHT WRIST SHATTERED

ENTRY NEAR RIGHT ARM PIT

5TH RIB SHATTERED

WOUND IN LEFT THIGH

BULLET HOLE IN SHIRT 5 3/4" BELOW COLLAR

KENNEDY

CONNALLY

THE REMARKABLE PATH OF THE PRISTINE BULLET ACCORDING TO WARREN COMMISSION

Records Building

County Jail

ELM STREET

HOUSTON STREET

DEALEY

A Trio of Tales—The Man-of-Law's Tale

Things That Never Happened

on the Grassy Knoll While Justice Warren Played Golf

ccording to the infamous Magic Bullet Theory, on November 22, 1963, a rifle bullet fired from a sixth-floor window of the Texas School Book Depository in Dallas, Texas, passed through President Kennedy's neck and Governor Connally's chest and wrist and then embedded itself in the Governor's thigh. The bullet, while doing all this, made several physics-defying turns in its trajectory and passed through fifteen layers of clothing, seven layers of skin, and fifteen inches of body tissue. It hit a necktie knot, separated four inches of rib, and shattered a radius bone. Later, the bullet was found on a gurney that had borne Governor Connally at Parkland Memorial Hospital. The bullet found on the gurney, CE399, was singularly pristine considering all of all the *magical* things it had done that day. That only served to make it *more* magical.

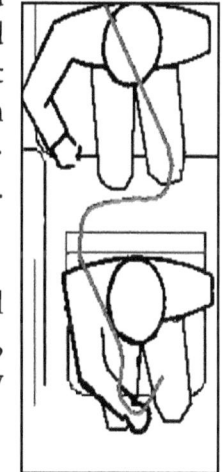

In discussing this during an unaudited, informal session, Special Agent Robert Wilcox, a consultant, stood before the men gathered in the investigatory commission chambers and proposed the following:

"According to my understanding of the testimony and evidence, it appears to me that this 'single bullet' was able to achieve what is clearly impossible. Undoubtedly, some of you agree with my incredulity about this. If we intend to give this theory our support—to endorse it, as it were—I believe we are duty-bound to enhance it with enough technological details to divert attention away from its ample implausibility. If not, our report may be ridiculed, to say the least, and we—for all our efforts in this matter—may even be accused of dissembling—possibly fraud. On the other hand, if we handle this *correctly*, the press and the public will assume that they simply don't understand the science governing the evidence. Then, since no one wants to appear ignorant—and here I refer especially to reporters, newspaper editors, radio hosts, and political commentators—they will *defend* our decision as if they actually see merit in it. In other words, they will do our job for us. Maybe better than we can."

"What sort of enhancements, in your opinion, would help us get that done?"

"That's open to debate, I'm sure, and—in due course—I expect various solutions will present themselves to choose among. But, I can give an example, if it would help clarify the point I'm trying to make." He cleared his throat and reflected for a moment before resuming. "Suppose we say that the bullet—after passing through JFK's neck and the Governor's chest and hand and thigh, and—after jumping over the kitchen sink—entered a time machine, went back about a hundred years and traveled to Ford's Theater in Washington, and upon arrival, makes a few sharp turns, goes up to the balcony, and strikes Abraham Lincoln in the back of his head."

The entire room had burst into laughter before the speaker had gotten to the part where the bullet fell into Mrs. Lincoln's purse. Some of the investigators began to applaud and cheer. Luckily, it was a closed meeting, because the prevailing atmosphere of frivolity did not reflect the serious nature of the gathering. This was, after all, an investigatory body convened by order of the President of the United States, Lyndon Baines Johnson, to investigate the assassination of his predecessor, John Fitzgerald Kennedy.

Supreme Court Chief Justice Earl Warren was presiding at the President's request. He struck his gavel and demanded silence. "We can't allow that in our recorded minutes, or anything like it. Obviously, it's completely ridiculous, even if it is amusing and very imaginative. Everyone knows that there's no such thing as a time machine that works. Even the one at Area Fifty-One never worked."

"It doesn't work because it's an alien beauty parlor chair, not a time machine," someone interjected, quite out of turn.

He struck the gavel again. "Gentlemen, *please*, no more outbursts. Let us not get sidetracked just because we're bored. That bit of vaudeville has cost me ten minutes of my golf game."

Representative Gerald Ford—hopefully joking, but it was hard to tell with the deadpan delivery—said, "I think we need to stick to believable scenarios. Let's drop the silly Lincoln angle, even if it does lend plausibility to everything else by being so outlandish."

"So, the bullet in question—number two or three, I forget which—comes from behind the vehicle, from above?" asked Hale Boggs. "It goes over one hundred yards, and then through JFK's neck and throat, Connally's back, Connally's chest, Connally's wrist, Connally's thigh, and ends up on the gurney at Parkland?"

"Works for me," Allen Dulles said. "Show of hands?"

"Wait. Who drops the bullet on the gurney at Parkland?"

"Governor Connally, presumably."

"But why?"

"Let's leave the retrieved bullet out. Then we won't have to explain it or establish its authenticity."

"But, we have 36 volumes to fill. How are we supposed to accomplish that if we keep cutting things out?"

"We can put out 26 volumes instead of 36 volumes. What's ten volumes of gibberish more or less? No one is going to read anything but the abstracts anyway. Only an insane person would actually read something like this—fringe trolls, people of no consequence whatsoever, and they can be dismissed like *this*." The investigator flicked his fingers as though he were sending a crumb into orbit.

"Look," Dulles said, clearly showing his frustration. "Let's be honest with ourselves about at least *one* thing today. We're shoveling out USDA Choice Grade-A bullshit here. We can do it in one of two ways. One way is with a floodgate to control the *quantity* of bullshit that's being squeezed out of our sluice. The other way involves the *quality* of the bullshit. We can 'quality control' how far the shit stink stretches. Do we want to harvest it for the American market only, or do we want troublemakers in Moscow to be walking around, sniffing the incoming breezes and wondering what died in the walls of the Capitol Building? Do we want Castro calling Khrushchev on his hot-line and saying, 'Comrade Nikita, have you smelled this *apestando mierda malvada*? The stink is so bad, the fish are swimming here from America and jumping up onto my beaches to get away from it.' So, gentlemen, which is it going to be—quantity or quality, or in what proportions should we mix our recipe?"

"Let Lyndon decide."

"No, we can't. He wants to stay upwind of the stench and doesn't want to live in the shadow of the shit mountain. We're on our own."

"The way I see it, the real problem is the kid."

"Yeah, the kid."

"That's right—that kid is going to clog-up our plumbing, mark my words. This investigation is a *show* and one of the cardinal rules of theater, handed down to us by W. C. Fields—a showman's showman—is that you *never* appear on stage with animals or kids."

"Yeah, he's almost believable in his dumb ass 'aw shucks golly gee willikers' way. Maybe more than just *almost*."

"Yeah, believable *and* he saw the shooter. That's a rotten combination."

"Well, we say he didn't see *anyone*, and we're grownups and he's just a kid in short pants. There *was* no second shooter, remember?"

"He says he saw the shooter? How much do you want to bet he can be persuaded he *didn't* see the shooter?"

"What would it take?" Justice Warren asked.

"Yogi Berra's catcher's mitt...?" Dulles suggested.

"Signed?"

"We can get Lyndon to sign Yogi's name. That'll give him a laugh. He hates those fuckin' Kennedys, and that'll give him a gratifying long-distance whiff of this shit-pile He won't come any closer than that, but he'll wet his pants with glee."

"You think it could work?"

"Leave it to me," Mr. Hoover said. "I've been at this for almost forty years and I haven't destroyed the country yet."

"Tomorrow is another day, Scarlett," suggested one of the younger consultants. A few of the others chuckled and whispered.

The FBI director was not nearly as amused as his colleagues. "Watch out, or you may discover the next person I'm investigating is you."

"Suit yourself, Mr. Director," came the reply. "Go ahead, investigate whatever tickles your fancy—or fantasy. Just don't expect me to drop my pants to facilitate your investigation like some others have."

This time, no one in the room laughed. At least not aloud

After a weekend of golf and grandkids, the informal discussions resumed. This time, a more serious, businesslike atmosphere prevailed, but only because it was Monday morning. By Thursday afternoon, the hearings would be completely chaotic all over again.

"Who's got the checklist?" Justice Warren asked.

"Me," Allen Dulles replied.

"What are we up to? Was it the snack room?"

"Yes, the snack room. We have four people who say they saw Oswald in the snack room when the assassination was going down."

"We have fifty impaneled witnesses who say they *didn't* see him in the snack room."

"So what? They weren't *in* the snack room. That's why they didn't see him in there."

"Let's not think in the negative. This actually helps us," Dulles said. "The fact that they aren't claiming to have been in the snack room absolves them from any snack room credibility issues. Fifty people who *didn't* see something trumps four who *did* any day of the week in my book. Anyway, who's going to believe some guy who's taking a break over a guy who's trying to do an honest day's work? Those snack room ballbusters are just a bunch of malingerers. Trust me, we've got the snack room covered. Next?"

"The limousine. The bullet hole in the front windshield."

"I thought we flew the limousine to Detroit to have the glass replaced. Didn't we get it back before anyone noticed it?"

"Sensational work done out there by our Detroit boys, you'd never know a pigeon had ever shit on that windshield when they got done with it," Hoover said. "I had my chauffeur drive the limousine from the airport to the Secret Service garage after making a personal inspection of the workmanship. We're all good on the windshield angle."

"Great. Let's move on. What about the wounds?"

"What wounds?"

"What do you mean *what wounds*? Are you suggesting we claim Kennedy succumbed to a case of chicken pox?"

"No, what I mean is that we lost his brain. No one knows where it got itself to. So, there's no internal wound to discuss, and the back of the skull—I mean a really whopping, substantial piece of it—which was cleanly blown off by a rifle blast—flew out of the Lincoln and got lost in the grass at Dealey Plaza. Someone probably took it home as a souvenir ashtray. Meanwhile, the Admiralty's surgical team stitched his scalp together around some padding, and Kennedy looked fresh as a daisy when he was photographed at Bethesda. The photos show what looks like a very convincing rear-entry wound."

"Moving him to Bethesda was a stroke of genius," Hoover acknowledged, tilting his chair back and lacing his fingers behind his head in a display of satisfaction. "What about the pain-in-the-ass Jewish guy, with his goddam home movie? Have we managed to clean that disaster up yet?"

"Well, it's cost us a fortune, but we managed to coordinate our theory of the bullets and their trajectories with the frames of his film, so we emerge with a cohesive narrative. We can definitively point to any frame and make our case about what was happening at each moment in a way that supports our conclusions. Of course, if it wasn't for that meddlesome bastard, we could have said whatever we wanted from the get-go and saved ourselves a lot of time and effort. That train should never have been allowed to get out of the station. All things considered, though, we neutralized the Cecil B. Zapruder film of the Kennedy bar-mitzvah to the point where it makes some

#P2340323

P2340323/WC

Photo file: Exhibit P2340323. Warren Commission

Date: November 22, 1963. Time: Appx 12:30 p.m.
Location: "The Grassy Knoll" / Dealey Plaza, Dallas, Texas.
Provenance: Federal Bureau of Investigation.

REDACTED

Identified from left to right:

1. Clarence "Lumpy" Rutherford (#22340323-a)
2. Edward "Eddie" Haskell (#22340323-b)
3. Wallace "Wally" Cleaver (#22340323-c)
4. Theodore "Beaver" Cleaver a/k/a "The Beav" (#22340323-d)

small contributions here and there and causes no significant damage."

"Which brings us back to the kid," Justice Warren sighed. He looked genuinely worried concerning this point. "Our wild card."

"Yeah, if anyone can turn this work of art into a fiasco, it's that fucking kid."

"What's his name again? The Chipmunk? The Groundhog?"

"No, it's the *Beaver*, otherwise known as *The Beav*, or just plain *Beaver*," Dulles said, consulting his witness list. "No explanation. His parents might be insane. Why don't we claim he's got rabies and have him quarantined until Lyndon's out of office?"

"It would be better to use that kid to our advantage, to bolster our theory," Warren opined. "Let's spend some energy on that, in case the catcher's mitt ploy bombs on us. Mr. Wilcox, Mr. Henderson, why don't you two sub-committee that option and drum up some way to get the little Beav to play ball with us, mitt or no mitt. We're adjourned, and I'm off to the golf course. No use us all being here if we're not paying attention to what the witnesses are telling us, right?"

"You know," Hoover muttered as he lovingly gathered his files to his breast, and then, one by one—as if tucking his precious babies into their beds—put them into his briefcase, "if that kid actually *looks* like a beaver—the animal kind, that is—our problem is solved. Who cares what a kid says if he's not cute? It's a known fact that Americans hate anyone that's ugly."

"Well, that would have to include you among the despised," a voice said. "And, what's more, you're even uglier on the inside."

Fuming, the F.B.I. director lurched to his feet and whirled around to see who the speaker was, but no one else remained in the room.

Good morning, Justice Warren. My, that's a lovely black gown you're wearing today.

I can't swear on the Bible, guys. Dad doesn't let us swear. Anyhow, I am too confused to tell a hunk of lies.

That night the FBI Director was sitting up in bed, next to his assistant, Mr. Tolson. They were watching the Jack Paar Show and eating Lady Godiva chocolate truffles.

"One thing that confuses me," Hoover said during a commercial break, "is why Allen Dulles has been allowed to serve on the Commission. Kennedy blamed him for the Bay of Pigs and fired him. He *can't* be unbiased."

Tolson swiped a smudge of chocolate off of Hoover's upper lip with his pinky, which he then licked clean. "I have no idea why he's been allowed to weigh in but let me remind you that the Kennedys—*both* brothers—are rumored to have been planning to fire *you*. Which means both of *us*. If JFK wasn't dead, we might be sitting on a bench at the Lincoln Memorial, feeding breadcrumbs to the ducks."

"Whether or not there's any truth in that, the fact is that I'm not *officially* on the Commission. My name will never appear as such. I'm just consulting because Lyndon asked me to keep my eye on those guys. I'm mole-ing for him because he doesn't trust them, and why should he? I've never seen such a group of devious and downright stupid people in the same room. Gerald Ford? How'd he ever get into politics? And that creepy Arlen Spector, the one who dreamt up the magic bullet business after eating tainted pastrami and too many pickles and matzo balls. He's living proof of just how sneaky the Jewish mind can be."

"Surely not sneakier than yours," Tolson said,

I really had to pee so I went behind the picket fence and hid from the creepy cop with the rifle and did it in a bottle.

The main thing I remember is that Eddie made me drop my hot dog on the grass.

pinching Hoover's cheek. "I *should* keep my mouth shut, but I think it's time to share my worst fears with you, Hoove. This assassination nightmare has already poisoned the water supply of the entire country, and there's nothing that can be done about it now. Lyndon's belief that an investigatory commission can fix something like this is naive and arrogant—especially when the investigation is as obviously rigged as this one is. JFK's unlived years in office would have brought about many positive changes for America, whether you and I like them or not, and there's nothing that can be done about *that*, either. We can't stuff his brain back in his head, can we? The Commission, on the other hand, stands at the crossroads. If it knowingly produces a manifesto that gives credence to single shooters and magic bullets and other such fairy-tale nonsense, the Presidency could degenerate into anything in the years to come. Life is all about entropy and decay, only mitigated by the rare appearances of unicorns like Lincoln and Kennedy. The two of us will be long dead, most definitely, but the Warren Commission, as things stand now, guarantees that a day will come when America has a President so foul, so unworthy of respect, he should be banned from sitting on the same toilet that JFK took his daily crap on."

"My sweet Cassandra, you have such a colorful mind," said Hoover. "I have another matter—a rather large one—that I could use your assistance with."

"Not tonight, dear," Tolson said, pulling his blanket up to the tip of his nose. "I have a magic headache."

I said, "Hey, Eddie, leggo my arm. It's only a bunch of goofy guys with firecrackers," and he shook me and said, "Get with it, Lumpy, someone just blew the Prez's head off."

ust when it seemed that every question raised by the Zapruder film had been satisfactorily answered, new information of the most unlikely nature emerged through other testimony. A little boy had seen a gunman fire a rifle at the motorcade from behind a picket fence on the Grassy Knoll.

This extremely inconvenient news disrupted the commission's agreed-upon strategy. Previous witnesses provided *refutable* testimony about the Grassy Knoll—any one of them might have consumed a beer or two that day, or been previously convicted of jaywalking, or needed to wear glasses or a hearing aid, or been older than 55. Now, along came the exception, the deal-breaker, the headache-maker—a lovable little boy with a cute name, who had gone behind the picket fence on the Grassy Knoll to make pee-pee. He had done his business in an empty coke bottle, so you couldn't even charge him with a minor misdemeanor as a diversionary tactic. The Devil himself wouldn't be able to taint the cutesy-pootsy, law-abiding Beaver. He was stain resistant.

he Grassy Knoll wasn't the first place Theodore Beaver Cleaver had strutted across the stage of America's consciousness. His family home, in Mayfield, was one of the princi-

pal battlefields of the mid-century Toilet Wars. Not many people are aware of the toilet conflicts because they took place behind closed doors—as is appropriate for toilet controversies in puritanical times—but, without a doubt, the wars and their outcomes were instrumental, for better or worse, in bringing greater verisimilitude to the lives of the American people. The two principal battles took place only a few years apart. The first was the Tank Battle, and the other, following only three years later, was the Battle of the Bowl in Cabin One.

In the weeks preceding October 4, 1957—the premiere date of the first episode of Beaver's television series, *Leave it to Beaver*—censors and producers found themselves locking horns over the visibility of the toilet tank in Wally and the Beaver's *en-suite* bathroom. The episode "Captain Jack" was intended to be the first episode of the series to air, but it had to be delayed due to the outbreak of the conflict. In that premiere episode, Beaver and Wally purchase a baby alligator as a pet and hide it from their parents by putting it in their toilet tank. The censorship office found this problematic—no toilet had *ever* been seen on a television screen previously. It was permissible to have scenes in bathrooms as long as no bodily function was hinted at. Shaving and primping, as examples, were considered acceptable bathroom activities; also, the routine washing of hands, if clearly unrelated to blood or toilet effluvia. Bathing and showering were not allowed unless you did them fully clothed—so, it was okay to shove a drunk in a cold shower or drown your overdressed wife in the bathtub. In the case of the alligator episode, toilet liquid was visible, and showing the toilet tank was considered one step away from showing the horrors of the actual bowl, which the producers and cameramen already understood they had to avoid—and did.

Inevitably, a compromise was reached. In the revised edit, only a side-angle view, in a medium shot, of the very top of the tank was shown, and its appearance was made as brief as possible. The lid, too, was hastily glimpsed. The tank could have passed for any innocuous water receptacle except for the fact that it was located in a bathroom. As finally approved, the satisfied censors felt that only a viewer with a "dirty mind" would recognize this object as part of a toilet. Nevertheless, the toilet floodgates had been opened at last.

Jack Ruby, assisted by incompetent police, persuade Lee Harvey Oswald to plead the Fifth Amendment.

Three years later, Toilet War II broke out with the appearance of Alfred Hitchcock's 1960 masterpiece, *Psycho*. Here censors found much more to cause them displeasure—the violent shower scene and near-nudity in particular, but also the gruesome murder of the detective, the cross-dressing, and the hints of homosexuality. As a warm-up, Hitchcock decided to show his surprise victim disposing of incriminating evidence, in the form of a torn piece of paper, in the toilet before she faced the fateful carving knife in the shower. Since such a plumbing device had never been seen in a motion picture, the director was gambling that the mere sight of it looming over them on a movie screen would be a sure-fire way to set the audience's nerves on edge. The flushing of the toilet, which provoked much nervous laughter, was the cherry on top of the *Psycho* bowl.

The censors were completely appalled by everything they saw. The battle over Hitchcock's flushing commode became the Gettysburg of the Toilet Wars. After losing strategic ground for years, the censorship office was determined to make a last stand. In any event, the censors—even if they would never admit it (or realize it)—were not *really* attempting to protect the American public from filth, humanly produced or otherwise. The censors' *real* agenda was to exercise control over what the American public *thought*. The *sine qua non* of the Cold War years was mind control. Classic examples of that are *The Manchurian Candidate* of 1962 and the *Warren Commission Report* of 1964, both equally fictional. These were followed by the numerous army LSD experiments of that decade of underhanded busywork. Unwitting soldiers were poisoned and driven mad. Entire years passed when the only truths in evidence were those written *between* the lines. We live now in the detritus of fifty years of lies.

As respects the toilet at the Bates Motel, several mitigating factors turned things around for Mr. Hitchcock. Firstly, the Beaver's toilet tank had already created a precedent. In a manner of speaking, his kiddie-crapper had laid the groundwork for a long-overdue *Freedom of Elimination Act*. And, too, Hitchcock was a stalwart opponent, employing a battery of tricks on the enemy censors to get his way—which he did—losing only a few insignificant frames of film in the process. The accepted final edit of *Psycho* was like a Declaration of Independence for bladders and bowels in the hands of film *auteurs*. Within fifty years, movies were fifty percent gunfire and explosions, and fifty percent fart jokes. Entertainment would never be the same.

More importantly, only six years after the First Toilet War in Mayfield, all of America—thanks to the Warren Commission—was flushed down the proverbial toilet—and with the door wide open for all to see, hear, and smell. Government would never be the same either.

The Grassy Knoll had become the *MacGuffin* of the assassination "story" as told by the Commission. The so-called *MacGuffin* was another of Hitchcock's narrative tropes, used in many of his films. A *MacGuffin* was the diamond necklace in the heist caper, it was the coded document in the spy story, it was the *thing* everyone was after but which didn't *really* matter to the story—in *Psycho,* the *MacGuffin* was the stolen $40,000 wrapped in a newspaper. Why did this happen? Because every intelligent American who hadn't buried their ostrich head in the sand already *knew* there was a conspiracy behind the murder of JFK. Nothing about the Grassy Knoll—neither those on it nor events that transpired there—would change that fact. No one ever expected that the Warren Commission would expose the real conspirators of November 22. What Americans wanted—and it was a reasonable, heartfelt desire—was for the government to stop telling lies. To admit the conspirators existed. The Beaver, therefore, could have *saved* America, if someone would have let him. President Johnson's and his minions—the apostles of the Warren Commission, together with their phalanx of lawyers, investigators, and advisors—had a different outcome in mind.

The commissioners continued to meet in Washington to iron out problems arising from the testimony and strategize. In fact, they only left Washington once, to fly as a group to Dallas to interview the man who had murdered Lee Harvey Oswald.

Passengers on the F.I.R.R. Paumanok Express on the evening of November 22, 1963. One of the few times in history that all of America was on the same page. Photo courtesy of F.I.R.R. Publicity Department.

Jack Ruby, while claiming to have information, refused to share it while he was still incarcerated in Texas. He repeatedly begged the commissioners to bring him to Washington, where he promised to cooperate further, but they refused, claiming there were too many legal hurdles and that they had no means to offer him protection. In the end, Ruby gave them no evidence of worth, which was the very definition of success for the commissioners. They decided to end their interview, gambling that he would not get more talkative *after* they published their report. Then cancer silenced Ruby for good. As in *good riddance.*

Meanwhile, Allen Dulles was championing a meeting with the Cleaver family while the Commission team was still in the vicinity of Mayfield. He wanted to put the Beaver matter to bed along with the Ruby matter. To this end, he had brought along Yogi Berra's catcher's mitt (signed by LBJ, who found this ploy uproariously funny), and had contracted the services of a schoolmarmish actress to play the part of a child psychologist. As he explained to Justice Warren and the others over lunch in a steak house, "I don't want that kid's father anywhere near the examination, watching to see if we're going to strong-arm his kid or bamboozle him into saying this or that. The less Daddy knows, the better for us."

"How does *she* fit in, then? Is her involvement supposed to guarantee to the parents that he'll be petted like a good little beaver?"

"Precisely," Dulles said. He took a sip of his cocktail and then added, "If I had my way, I'd pull a 'Hoover.' I'd get the father soused and pack him off to a whorehouse where we could get some usable insurance photos, but I did some investigating, and he's not the type for that. Maybe we can find someone to take him on a tour of Dallas churches while we give his kid a good working over."

"What about the kid's brother, and the other two that were with him, the dimwit and the sociopath? Are we going to examine them, too?"

"Yes, unfortunately," said Dulles. "Camouflage."

"What did *they* see?"

"They saw JFK shot by Oswald from the Book Depository, like my fucking Aunt Tillie and everyone else. That's all there was to see."

His feet did not reach the floor, so he swung them back and forth, occasionally kicking Gerald Ford in the process. Ford said nothing. Since he was the least intimidating-looking of their group and bore the strongest resemblance to the boy's father, they decided to let him ask the questions. Mr. Dulles sat a bit further off, holding the box with the catcher's mitt on his lap. Miss Marks, the actress playing the psychologist, sat primly next to the Beaver.

"So, Mr. Cleaver," Ford began. Beaver registered a strong reaction to that, causing Ford to stop at once. "What's wrong, young man?"

"I'm not Mr. Cleaver. That's my father. He's outside that door," the boy answered, pointing.

"You're Mr. Cleaver, too, Theodore," Miss Marks said reassuringly.

"You look just like my teacher. She's pretty, too."

"Thank you so much, sweet thing. Would you like some chocolate while we talk, Mr. Cleaver?"

"Mom says not to take candy from strangers. So I can't have any."

"Let's continue, Theodore," said Mr. Ford. "Are you now, or have you have ever been, a member of the Communist Party?"

"Well, I did go to a birthday party once," he answered. The room burst into laughter. Warren slammed his gavel down so hard that Beaver jumped off his chair. "Wow," he said, covering his ears with his little pink hands, "that was just how they do it on Perry Mason!"

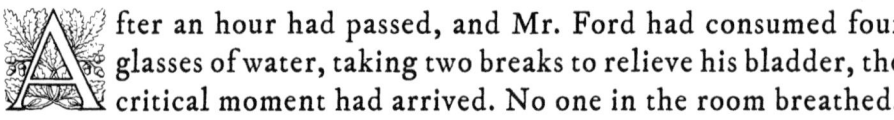fter an hour had passed, and Mr. Ford had consumed four glasses of water, taking two breaks to relieve his bladder, the critical moment had arrived. No one in the room breathed.

"Then the policeman lowered the rifle and said to me 'What are you doing back here, dumb kid? Why don't you go watch the President ride by like everyone else is doing?' The other policeman came over to me, the one who needed a shave, and gave me a shove—just a little one—and he said, 'Scram, kid!' real mean-like."

"What did you do?"

"I hid behind the parked cars and made *number one* in the bottle." He cast a glance over at Miss Marks, hoping against hope that she hadn't heard what he just said. His face was very red. She smiled at him approvingly and then, feeling encouraged, he continued. "Then the first policeman stuck his rifle through the fence and shot a bullet at the President and killed him." Beaver looked from face to face eagerly, very proud that he had seen something so important and hoping for approval despite his confession about *number one-ing*. To the chagrin of the adults at the table, he was beaming from ear to ear.

Dulles cleared his throat and indicated to Ford that he was going to take over at this point. Ford was relieved. He switched places with

Dulles, who was going to be the new target of Beaver's constant kicks. Miss Marks, who had not been completely briefed about the situation, intuitively sensed that things were on the verge of taking a dark turn. It was obvious, even to her, a complete outsider, that the investigators were not getting what they wanted, and were becoming overtly hostile. She was quite surprised, therefore, by the devious tactics that followed.

"Did you know, Theodore," Dulles began softly, "that Justice Warren, the man sitting over there, was at a barbecue when the President died? And did you know that he had a dream that night that he was playing golf that day, and that he made a hole-in-one on the golf course?"

"That's real funny," Beaver said. "'Cause the policeman I saw that day shot his rifle at the people in the President's car and he made a big hole in one, too. It was on the television."

Everyone in the room was stunned. What the boy was saying, in a completely convoluted way—and most unhelpfully to their mission—was that a policeman had made a big hole in one president.

The Beaver, after hours of questions, was eating his third chocolate bar. Chocolate was smeared all over his lips, chin, and hands. On his lap, he was tightly holding a gift box containing a catcher's mitt that had once belonged to Yogi Berra. And Yogi had signed it! He couldn't wait to get back outside to show his treasure to his brother, his parents, and his chums in Mayfield. If only these creepy old men would finish asking him stuff. He already had told them all about the dream he had when he fell asleep on the grass.

"So, when the policeman fired the rifle, you woke up?"

"First I ran back to Wally and Lumpy and Eddie, and we ran away, and *then* I woke up."

"Dreams can be very funny," said Mr. Dulles. "Yogi knew you had a dream that he gave you his catcher's mitt, and he decided to make your dream come true. Have you had any other dreams that you want us to look into? We just want to help you, if we can."

He looked worried suddenly and tightened his grip on the box. "I'm not dreaming now, am I?"

"No, we're all here for real. You've been kicking me under the table all day. My leg is practically broken. Would you like me to kick you back so you can see that you're awake?"

Miss Marks shot Mr. Dulles an angry glance and Justice Warren slammed his gavel down. "That's enough, Mr. Dulles." He turned his attention to the witness. "I am very sorry, and so is Miss Marks, and everyone else here, that you had such a terrible dream about those policemen. I hope you never dream about them again."

"I'm going to try very hard not to. I sure hope I forget about them."

"I knew I could count on you, little soldier," Justice Warren said, and he mussed Beaver's hair, before patting him on his rump and sending him on his way.

utside the Dallas Civic Courthouse, where the examination had taken place, the Beaver, Wally, Lumpy, and Eddie were standing on the steps, waiting for Mr. and Mrs. Cleaver to join them.

"What makes you so special, Squirt?" Eddie said to the Beaver while poking him repeatedly in his pudgy belly. "How come you get to walk away from this with the giftware, and us guys get nothing?"

"That's 'cause I have big, big dreams," boasted the Beaver. "and I'm the court's smallest soldier, and you're just big creepy Eddie."

"Which of you is Mr. Cleaver?" someone asked. They turned to see a man in his late thirties, holding a pad and pen. Even though the Beaver was not supposed to talk to strangers, he could not resist the temptation to use his new moniker. Standing on his toes, he said, "I am Mr. Cleaver, whom you are now presently addressing."

"I'm Jerry Reinstein from the *Sacramento Bee*—that's a newspaper in California—and I heard that you'd be here today, so I came all the way here to meet you. Can I shake your hand?"

"You certainly may, Mr. Jerrystein," he replied, handing the cardboard box to his brother to hold. "How can you let me help you?"

"I was just wondering what you told them in there."

"Oh, *that*," he said, shrugging. "I told them about a dream I had."

"Can you tell me, too?"

"Sure. I fell asleep on the grass on the day the president got himself shot, 'cause I was tired from the long train ride I had from Mayfield the night before. In the dream, I had to pee real bad and so I went behind the fence on the Grassy Hole. There were two creepy policemen hanging out there and one of them shot at the car through the fence."

At this moment, Ward Cleaver came down the steps of the courthouse and introduced himself to the reporter.

"You should be very proud of your son, Mr. Cleaver," he said.

"I don't have a son," Beaver said to the reporter.

The two men smiled and winked at each other. Mr. Reinstein knelt down to meet the Beaver eye-to-eye. "Tell me, Mr. Cleaver... in this dream you had, did you find out the policemen's names, or see their badges, or find out what police force they came from?"

"Oh, certainly," he replied. He took his father's hand because he wanted to be sure Ward was witnessing how good his memory was, and how responsibly he was answering questions. He really *was* Mr. Cleaver, and he wanted his father, the original Mr. Cleaver, to notice it.

He said, massaging his chin in imitation of one of his father's typical mannerisms, "Funny, the old guys didn't ask me about any of that inside, but in the dream I had, one of the policemen had a badge that said he was Officer T. Murdoch, and his number was *26749* and his hat said *Dallas* and the patch on his shirt said *6th Precinct*. Then I dreamed that the other one, the one who needed a shave, was Officer J. Clancy...."

Mr. Reinstein scribbled furiously, barely able to keep up with him.

Ward Cleaver was extremely proud of the Beaver. At first, because of the traumatic incident his sons witnessed in Dallas, he was sorry he had allowed his wife to talk him into permitting the trip to visit Wally at college. Unexpectedly, though, the assassination and the subpoena had elevated his youngster to a new level of maturity, and now that he was claiming his encounter with the murderous policemen was just a dream, there didn't seem to be any reason for fatherly concern. Certainly, decades later, his Theodore would have great stories to tell his own children about his adventures in Texas. The thought of that made Ward smile.

While driving back from Dallas, Ward and June Cleaver had taken the Beaver to the Alamo in San Antonio. The movie, also called *The Alamo*, made a few years earlier, was one of their son's favorites. Wally remained at school. Clarence and Eddie took a train back to Mayfield. The adventure to Dallas to see the President's motorcade and to visit Wally at school was, for better or worse, finally over.

As soon as the Cleavers returned home and settled in, Ward began making trips to the Mayfield Library to look through the newspapers. He was particularly interested in the *Sacramento Bee* because he was hoping that the reporter who had interviewed his son, Mr. Reinstein, had gone on to write an article about the Beaver's Texas adventures.

Finally, Ward actually did find something in the *Sacramento Bee*. It was a small article about Gerald Reinstein, one of the Bee's star journalists, and a father of three, who had been killed in a freak car accident on the Stemmons Freeway, not far from Dealey Plaza. He had died instantly, a day after his chat with the Beaver on the steps of the Dallas Civic Courthouse.

Ward never mentioned the article to his wife or his son, and he never stepped foot in the Mayfield Library again.

Epilogue: If John Fitzgerald Kennedy had not been felled on November 22, 1963, he would have kept his promise to end the war in Vietnam within a few months—his intention to do so has often been cited as one of the motivations behind his assassination.

The new President, Lyndon B. Johnson, wasted no time in reversing that policy by signing NSAM273, a National Security Agency memorandum, on November 26, 1963, four days after JFK's death, and thereby committing the nation to continued involvement in Vietnam. Within five years, Arlen Spector's magic bullet had claimed 30,000 American lives (and one president) and LBJ's approval rating had plummeted from 70% to below 40%. Meanwhile, the Beaver attempted to enlist in the Marines but was told that—due to his fame—he would have to remain stateside. His death or maiming in combat would have been a public relations nightmare for the armed forces and for President Johnson.

Fate intervened to reward LBJ with a richly-deserved royal screwing. A rumor began, inflated by powerful anti-war sentiment, that the Beaver—a beloved American figure of lily-white purity—had been killed in Vietnam. The story became an enduring urban legend, persisting for over twenty years, certainly outlasting both LBJ *and* the Vietnam War. There wasn't a word of truth in it. The same could be said about another of Johnson's great legacies—the 26 volume Warren Commission Report.

The Beaver is discovered alive and well twenty years after his falsely reported death in Vietnam. He tells the media "I was just a patsy."

Shouldn't the Devil's Tower point downward, to Hell?

A Trio of Tales—The Journalist's Tale

Sayville Spies and Whispers

nce someone told you that they called it The Devil's Tower, you couldn't see it any other way. One glance up towards the sky, and there it always was—although its full visibility depended on where in town you were standing when you looked (just outside the barbershop was the best place)—pointing heavenward like a giant horn that had sprouted from the Devil's brow. It was big and more than a little intimidating, despite having been built, in large part, by local Sayville residents, crafted by friendly American hands.

The men who came and went through the gate in the fence that ran around it were all business and no play and spoke businesslike German that had nothing playful to the ear about it. That made it seem even more like an ironwork appendage of an alien nation, a transplanted bit of foreign soil concocted from girders and struts and bolts, an inviolate embassy of a foreign power. But whose? Kaiser Wilhelm's? Or the Devil's? With war raging in Europe, how did an outsider get a toe-hold—or was that a horn-hold?—on neutral American soil anyhow?

he tower only *looked* like it was joining the Town of Sayville to Heaven. Inquisitive children asked, in their cute, innocent way, *Shouldn't the Devil's Tower point downward, to Hell?* And then Mommy—or whoever was the official Arbiter of Storytelling in the household—would reply that the Devil liked to build his towers upright to fool people and to annoy saints, angels, and Heavenly Hosts. And then the child would ask, *Mommy, what's a Host?* And Mommy would say, *Ask in Sunday School if you want to know that. I'm busy. And don't say the word Hell again or I'll wash your mouth out with soap.* And the child would say, *You can't, you're too busy.*

It goes without saying that no household Arbiter of Storytelling worthy of the title would simply tell a child that there was no such thing as the Devil. It wouldn't occur to them. It was antithetical to the storytelling universe, a realm that had traditionally harbored among its denizens a variety of similar unsavory characters, including Bogeymen, Hobgoblins, Gnomes, Trolls, and others of their ilk.

Storytelling is a way of exerting control, as is demonstrated by these two examples from the practical handbook *One Thousand Uses for Sausage.* In Chapter 6, you (the omniscient parent) are urged to tell your little boy one of two stories about sausages. If you want him to eat a sausage, you tell him the first story (#221)—the sausage will put hair on his chest. [Subliminal translation: *It will make a man out of you*]. If you *don't* want him to eat a sausage (assume, for instance, you want them all for yourself) you tell him the *other* sausage story (#222)— the sausage will stunt your growth. [Subliminal translation: *It will turn you into a freak and everyone will laugh at you*]. The child buys whichever story you tell, and the sausage's fate is sealed.

This explains how the original transmission tower in Sayville, built as part of an impressive German communications network—an operation so vast, very few understood its reach and its implications—later attained legendary status as The Devil's Tower. Kaiser Wilhelm told Woodrow Wilson a story. *Mein kleiner Funkturm,* my little radio tower, the Kaiser said, will put metaphoric hair *auf deiner Brust, Herr Präsident,* which will be *sehr gut* for your image. The tower was anything but *kleine,* and the promised hair never sprouted. But, President Wilson was determined to keep America out of World War One if he possibly could, so he bought the Kaiser's bratwurst and bit his tongue.

Things were bound to get more complicated as the war in Europe dragged on and America remained steadfast in its neutrality. The British succeeded in cutting the underwater transatlantic telegraph cables in April of 1915, preventing Berlin from communicating directly with its operatives and financial backers on the American continent. In order to keep the Kaiser happy and continue to stay neutral, President Wilson, ever eager to appear the gentleman—sporting chest hair or not—agreed to allow the Telefunken Transmission Station in Sayville to remain active, but under the supervision of the United States Navy. No coded messages would be allowed. The Kaiser and his war ministers had a good laugh over that decision. The German wireless technicians went to the Kensington Hotel in Sayville and got drunk. They danced with local girls, called them "Kleines süßes Fräulein," and even managed to cop a few feels.

The edict forbidding the transmission of coded messages, necessitated by America's position of neutrality, was the most unfortunate decision of all. The United States government had just given Germany permission to play some of the oldest tricks in the war manual. No evil genius would be needed and nothing new had to be invented. All it would take was one clueless naval officer to make all the subterfuge in the world operate like a well-oiled machine.

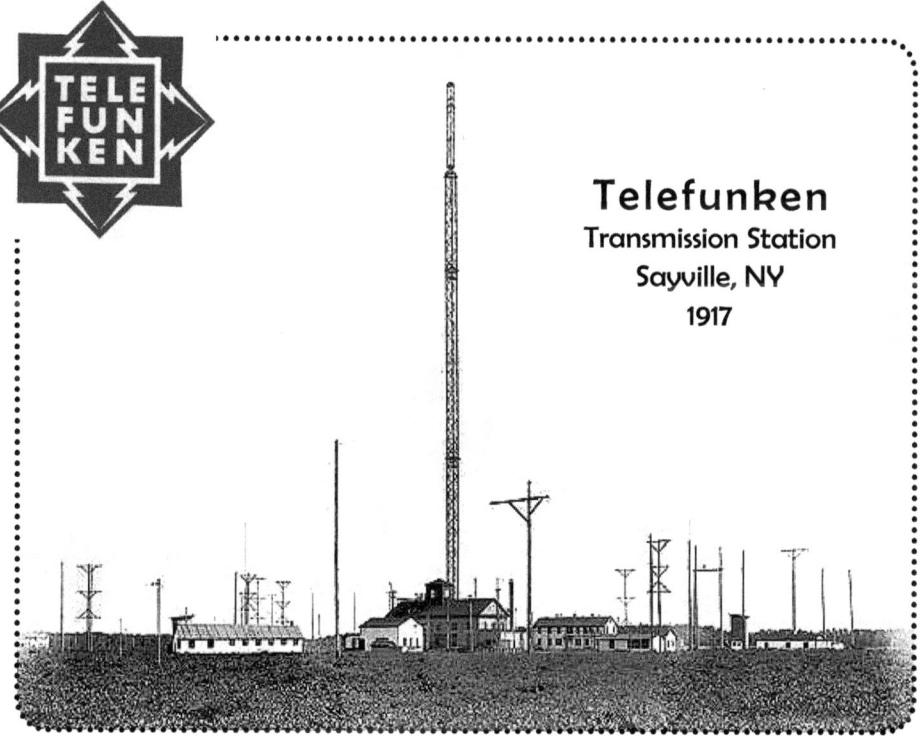

TELE FUN KEN

Telefunken
Transmission Station
Sayville, NY
1917

At this juncture in international affairs, the Telefunken Tower should have been under the *scrutiny* of the United States Navy, not its *supervision*. The so-called "supervision" quickly devolved into an ongoing beerfest in the social room of the Kensington Hotel. As things turned out, the tower pointing heavenward in the Sayville landscape proved to be Kaiser Wilhelm's way of giving Woodrow Wilson and the citizens of America a proverbial 500-foot-long finger.

The story of The Devil's Tower had its beginning in 1911 when the Stollwerck brothers, German businessmen who owned a chocolate factory in New York City, purchased seventy-nine acres of land bordering the railroad tracks in Sayville. The local residents were understandably excited to have a new business development in town, one that could provide them with needed jobs. Everyone rolled up their sleeves and got ready to start making candy bars. But the much-anticipated chocolate factory never materialized.

It wasn't long before oystermen working on the Great South Bay observed a large tower rising like an iron beanstalk on shore. By the end of December 1911, it had reached a height of 300 feet. The news quickly spread that the German communications enterprise, Telefunken, was building a massive wireless transmitter, a broadcast station, a power plant, and a barracks for their workers. Local draftsmen were invited to compete for the design and construction contracts. The F.I.R.R. trains brought more and more workers and building materials to Sayville Station every day. According to local newspapers, the corresponding Telefunken transmitting station in Nauen, Germany, just outside Berlin, could boast of a broadcasting tower that was 640 feet tall, making it—after the Eiffel tower—the second tallest structure in Europe. The radio *Golem* of Nauen was affectionately called *Onkel Günther*.

The quiet hamlet of Sayville, where nothing much had ever happened previously, was apparently destined to be part of something much larger and more important than the harvesting of oysters. Decades before the internet came into being, German technology had established an efficient worldwide communications network, the first of its kind. Sayville was chosen by Germany to be a critical cog in this machinery.

Transmissions, totally unmonitored, began. The important news stories of the day, financial reports from Wall Street, vital diplomatic communications—all these, and more, were transmitted astonishing distances every evening at 9:15 pm.

The German technicians, residing in a barracks at the station behind a tall iron fence, operated in isolation and secrecy. There was nothing to be concerned or suspicious about until August of 1914 when World War I broke out in Europe. Afterward, it took a long time for sentiments in Sayville to change, but as the war intensified, and reports of the destruction filtered back to America, the locals began to feel increasingly uncomfortable about the foreigners in their backyard. No more work was being offered to the locals, and they were, ostensibly, locked out of the town's biggest mystery by fences, gates, and language. Many in town were not supportive of America's position of neutrality in the war, but everyone—those for entering the war, as well as those opposed to it—lived in the shadow of the tower that whispered to the Kaiser while they slept whether they liked it or not.

Less than a year later, when Britain cut Germany's transatlantic cables, it transformed, by default, Sayville's wireless station into the most crucial asset in the German communication network—a piece of essential war machinery built by American hands and standing on American soil—in short, a big problem. To maintain a position of neutrality from this point forward, with Britain carefully observing America's counter-maneuvers, it was necessary for the United States Navy to send censors to monitor what was being broadcast from Long Island. Two officers were assigned to review the transmissions—Lieutenant Francis Cogswell and Second-Class Seaman Daniel Cozzens. The legend of The Devil's Tower was about to spring into being.

At about this time, Francis Hoag, editor of the *Suffolk County News* was informed that a friend of his, Daniel White, wanted to see him. Mr. White, a young justice of the peace, was a resident of the Kensington Hotel in Sayville. What he wanted to share with Hoag were his observations about a Kensington *habitué* also named Daniel—Second-Class Seaman Daniel Cozzens.

Telefunken Wireless Tower, Sayville, NY

"This navy fellow, Cozzens, is either a dope or a dupe, or I'm a monkey's uncle," White told Hoag. "Trust me, Frank, something fishy is afoot in Sayville. First of all, from what I've been able to learn and observe, the Navy has its two men stationed in town to monitor messages going out of the big tower. I know those transmissions are picked up by our own stations at the Brooklyn Navy Yard and Fire Island and verified as harmless—at least I hope they are—but Cozzens' job is to review the messages *before* they're sent, not after it's too late to close the barn door. I can't see how he could possibly be fulfilling those duties. To begin with, he's being wined and dined on a daily basis by the Krauts from the tower, and it looks to me like he's more than chummy with these wireless guys. They buy drinks for him, get him drunk, sometimes late at night, and as a result, he doesn't make an appearance until nearly noon the next day and even then, he has plenty of time to go zipping pell-mell in fancy automobiles and play tennis with the girls around town."

GET LUCY

"Interesting," said Hoag, sure something substantive was coming from Mr. White in the next few moments. He lit a cigar and waited.

"A few days ago, I was in the Kensington dining room, eating right next to Cozzens. Logically, Lieutenant Cogswell *should* have been on duty at the wireless station in his absence. I'll wager he wasn't because of what happened next. Suddenly, one of the Krauts comes running in with a piece of paper and a pen in his hand. It was the big, hairy technician—Gustave Reuther is his name, I think. He says 'Danny, it's my sister's birthday tomorrow and I just now remember this so late. I want to send a message to my father, so he can get her a present quick for me. Can you initial so I can send to Onkel Günther?' Cozzens had to hold the permission form up to the light to read it, which gave me a chance to read it, too, right over his shoulder. It said, 'GET LUCY NICE SURPRISE GIFT' and a few other words I don't remember.

THE EVENING OBSERVER.

OFFICIAL PAPER OF THE CITY — VOL. LXXXVI. — DUNKIRK, N. Y., FRIDAY, MAY 7, 1915 — NO. 13 — OFFICIAL PAPER OF THE CITY

LUSITANIA TORPEDOED

MAMMOTH CUNARDER SUNK ON IRISH COAST

Latest Reports Say All Her 1400 Passengers Were Taken Off In Safety By Small Boats.

WERE WARNED BEFORE THEY LEFT NEW YORK

Queen of the Fleet Was Struck at 2:33 This Afternoon—Frantic Wireless Calls Were Sent Out For Assistance.

London, May 7—The steamer Lusitania, filled with passengers, many of whom were Americans, was either torpedoed or blown up by an infernal machine, while off Old Head of Kinsale at 2:33 this afternoon. The latest reports received here indicate that all the passengers were saved.

Driving of the Lusitania was the foreign fate of the war in fact so far as concerned commerce was concerned. The captain received them at frequency but all agree that the log later began calling for help by her wireless at 2:33. The first to pick her up was the wireless station at Lanfoord. The appeal was urgent. "We have a big list quite badly," flashed through the air and immediately orders were sent to the nearest points to get every available craft to the point.

GREAT GUNS ARE SHELLING LINE

Paris Reports Enormous Amount of Artillery Being Brought Up by Germans.

WILL TRY TO BLOW BRITISH OUT OF YPRES

City of Turnow is Reported Captured by the Austrians—Berlin Claims to Have Reinforced Hill 60 After Terrific Contest with the British.

By W.M. PHILIP SIMMS (United Press Staff Correspondent) Paris, May 7—The Germans are bringing an enormous amount of dismal artillery into action at every point of the battle line. It is plain their present staff has doubled its strength since trained to reinforced armies the strong allied positions are reduced, and that they are pushing against of their heavy guns to bring them to a new contest against them.

CHINA AND JAPAN FIX DIFFERENCES

Chinese Government Makes Concessions Which Are Acceptable to Mikado.

JAPAN WITHDRAWS OBNOXIOUS DEMAND

Agrees Not to Insist That She Have Her Advisers in Political, Financial and Military Affairs of China.

Pekin May 7—The Chinese government has sent a new reply to Japan which is expected to avert a serious crisis, while the reply is as yet unknown officials say that in effect it is an acceptable, under pressure, of the allied diplomatic demands. It is reported in diplomatic circles here that President Yuan Shi Kai and his advisers, after an all-night conference, decided that it would be suicidal to attempt to oppose the Japanese demands in time of stress.

GET LUCY NICE SURPRISE GIFT

W. McDOWELL

I didn't think much of it at the time, but when I saw the newspapers the next day..."

"My God," exclaimed Hoag, so shocked he jumped to his feet and slapped his forehead. "*Get Lucy....*"

"Yes, that's what it said. *Get Lucy.*"

"So, you're telling me two guys in the dining room of the Kensington managed to sink the Lusitania and drown over a thousand people with what amounts to little more than a birthday greeting?"

"That's right, Frank, that's exactly what I'm thinking and exactly what I'm saying. If Lieutenant Cogswell was at the station covering for Cozzens—as he should have been—Reuther could have had him approve the message on the spot instead of running into town to find Cozzens. Supposedly, we're neutral in this war, yet somehow more than a thousand passengers—among them a hundred Americans—and Cunard's flagship ocean liner, are all at the bottom of the sea. I was a few feet away—this far"— he demonstrated a distance of roughly 24 inches with his hands— "eating roast beef and mashed potatoes when those execution orders were initialed by a blithering idiot on behalf of the United States Navy. In a manner of speaking, the U-boat shot its deadly torpedo from the dinner table right next to me."

The editor strode decisively to the open door of his office and spoke to the secretary working outside. "Jeannie, please have some coffee and a few sandwiches sent in here for myself and Mr. White and cancel my appointments for the rest of the day." Closing the door for privacy, he returned to his seat and continued. "You should know that I can't investigate this personally. No one on our staff can. We're all too well known at the Kensington. We'd be showing our cards just by dropping in for a beer. But, I know the editor-in-chief

The Suffolk County News.

No. 49. Francis Heag, Publisher. SAYVILLE, N. Y. SUBSCRIPTION, $1.50 PER YEAR. Single Copies, 5 Cents

UM ON TO BERLIN

Germany Sent President.

EMS IMMINENT

Must Cease Submarine chant or Freight Vessels Will Sever All Relations—Loophole Left Settlement.

on will wait at least the week for Germany's virtual ultimatum, the intention of the severe diplomatic relations the Berlin government res up present methods—submarines against right carrying vessels submarine policy with humanity and inter-

me limit was set here on, the president is the opinion that there would be a reasonable to Germany for a definite forthcoming within the step accomplishes relations with all this will be taken. Court Von Bernstorff's his passports, and at Berlin would some hence.

rman consuls and consular be dismissed and consular representatives recalled in case diplomatic relations severed was diplomatic, that a rupture would be no consuls.

leader of the Democrats in the senate, said in an addressing he added that no officer of congress was called not expect that any

ote have been sent to in Washington for

PRESIDENT WILSON.

United States Never Will Fight For Own Interest, He Says.

Photo by American Press Association.
President Woodrow Wilson, telling the Daughters of the American Revolution at Washington, declared that when America "begins human rights she will never fight for little to her own high tradition, America will never fight merely for herself."

RUSSIAN SOLDIERS TO FIGHT IN FRANCE

Great Force of Czar's Men Land at Marseilles.

A strong force of Russian troops has been disembarked at Marseilles, France. They are to fight beside the allied soldiers in France.

The arrival of the Russian troops is regarded in Paris as an event of great importance and of significance from both a military and political standpoint. It represents realization of hopes aroused early in the war by reports that large bodies of Russians were coming.

SEWER CONTRACT LET

Ocean Beach Improvement Will Require Four Months

VANDERBILT LANDS DRAINED

Wealthy Property Owners Co-operate with the Town Authorities to Eliminate the Mosquito Nuisance—Cast Stone.

EXCITING BOWLING MATCH

Sayville Defeats Patchogue in a Close Contest.

ALEXANDER MAIR.

Republican State Committeeman Died Tuesday Morning

AFTER SERIOUS OPERATION

A Native of Scotland Who for More Than 25 Years Has Been Active and Prominent Here—His Funeral Yesterday Was Largely Attended.

EASTER SERVICES

Musical and Other Programmes in Sayville Churches.

LOOKS

Detachment Out

BROUGHT

at the *New York Tribune.* Maybe I can interest him in this—it may be a size too big for us, anyway—and he can arrange for one of his reporters to check into the Kensington as a guest. I think I know just the guy for the job, too. He's young, maybe about thirty, suave, and well-dressed, and he has a Harvard accent. He could easily manage to get friendly with your idiot seaman, and since he's on the staff of the *Trib*, he knows what needs doing and how to get it done. If there's a scoop here, he'll get it for sure."

"I'll help any way I can... background info, and so on. But let's not lose sight of one important thing. That damned tower should have been dismantled as soon as war broke out overseas, not left in use for the Kaiser to play God with. It looks like we may be needing all the iron in that 450-foot monster to build ourselves some tanks, be-cause—if things like this continue to happen—our days of neutral-ity are numbered."

While nodding in agreement, Hoag suddenly remembered a detail that had confused him. "I meant to ask you earlier," he said, "about a name you mentioned. Who is *Onkel Günther?*"

"Oh, right. I'm told that's what the Krauts call their tower in Ber-lin. Apparently, the Devil has more than one tower."

"What's ours called?"

"Who knows? Maybe they call "him" *Schatzi* or *Cousin Adolf* or maybe just plain *Satan*. Whatever he's called, we should neutralize him before he has a chance to make more trouble."

n a day of cottage hunting for a suitable rental property, Charles Pincus-Whitney III, the incognito reporter sent to Sayville by the *New York Tribune,* and his new friend, Seaman Daniel Cozzens, failed to find any cottage worth serious consideration. It was late in the rental season, and very little that was tempting remained on the market. They visited four or five cot-tages, found them to be run-down or ill-equipped, and gave up for the day. They planned to renew their search on the following after-noon. Meanwhile, they retired to the Kensington Hotel to dine to-gether. At once, the reporter spotted Lieutenant Cogswell—who he recognized from a photo—seated on the opposite side of the dining room. Clearly, neither of the navy men were monitoring activities at the wireless station. He said nothing, of course. He was content to observe and let Cozzens do most of the talking.

"Since tomorrow is Sunday, I think I can convince a couple of local girls to come scouting with us, and we can persuade them to make us a nice picnic lunch. It's going to be a beautiful day."

"When exactly are you on duty?" the reporter asked casually. "Do you go to the station later tonight?"

"Whenever," Cozzens replied casually. "There's a big time differ-ence between here and Berlin, so the station is most active late in the evening, and in any case, the Germans won't pull a fast one on us. We're all pals. No one is saying it, but we're just out here to create the *appearance* of watchfulness for the benefit of the Brits. There's no espionage going on in this boring town. Believe me, these Ger-mans are just a bunch of lonely, out-of-shape, middle-aged guys who are really desperate for the ladies. And me?—I'm the gatekeeper to the girls in this town. So, if they screw me, they screw themselves."

"If they *don't* screw you, aren't they actually screwing the Kaiser?"

The seaman burst into laughter. "Let them. Who cares? Do you think the Kaiser needs *me* to get himself laid? That's a laugh!"

Pincus-Whitney joined in the laughter. *Oh brother*, he thought, *what a story this is going to make! He won't be laughing so hard when this fiasco makes its merry way into the headlines.*

"Why is it," Cozzens continued, suddenly more serious, "that ev-eryone in this country thinks you're stupid if you're blond? I'm get-ting good value from those Germans and I'm a lot smarter than you and most other people think. First of all, as Navy jobs go, you can't beat this one. And secondly, those guys are teaching me German, which means—if war with Germany is in the cards—I'll be in a good position for a translator's job, or something equally safe. *This* 'dumb' blond has a few things figured out." He held out his glass to signal to the waitress that he wanted another beer.

"Hey, I'm blond, too, you know," Pincus-Whitney said.

"Yeah, but look at yourself. Look at your seersucker suit and straw boater and cane. You're Harvard blue-blood blond and I'm Indiana hayseed blond. There's a big difference."

"Not to a torpedo."

"There are no torpedoes in Sayville. That explains why you and I are here... planning picnics."

It most certainly does not, the reporter thought, while watching the waitress replacing Cozzens' empty glass with a fresh, foaming lager.

Three days later, Pincus-Whitney stopped back in the *Suffolk County News* office to personally thank Francis Hoag for the tip to a great story. Hoag wanted details, but the reporter told him to be patient—the story had some unusual legal ramifications and security risks attached to it. "For example," he explained, "I seriously doubt that the *Tribune*'s attorneys will permit us to write *anything* about 'Lucy' or make a connection with the sinking of the Lusitania. For one thing, to print that supposition—which is what it essentially is—would expose the government to endless litigation from the survivors and the families of victims. Then there are the national security issues. Delicacy is required. We want the Navy to have an honorable way to respond, so we can't make them look incompetent. 'Innocently unaware of the necessity for greater vigilance' is just about as tough a charge as the powers-that-be will allow me to throw at them."

Hoag sat back and considered the situation from this entirely new perspective. "I can see the pressure that's going to be brought on us. Are we going to tell them what we know *before* we go to press?"

"We rarely do that," the reporter replied firmly. "But this time, national security requires us to work with them to downplay the seriousness of the damage, even if it means going to press *after* they've fixed the problem. And, if we so much as dare to mention Lucy, Woodrow Wilson will have a stroke. Cozzens—a decent guy, despite his *naïveté*—is going to take a lot of the blame, although, in my opinion, Cogswell is the bigger jackass for not putting Cozzens on a much-needed leash."

When the story appeared in the *New York Tribune* sometime later, it had been considerably watered-down, just as Pincus-Whitney predicted in Hoag's office. It succeeded in making Cozzens a victim of his own youthful high spirits which the evil German radio workers had seized-upon and taken advantage of. This gave the United States Navy enough latitude to respond to the situation without seeming lax, but also without the severity a more threatening situation would have demanded. Cozzens was reassigned, not court-martialed, and censorship was increased. The most significant invention the Navy came up with was a story—completely fictitious, but ingeniously detailed—in which Cozzens was intentionally injured by the Germans and put out of commission two weeks prior to May 7. This enabled them, should the "Lucy" message come to light, to deny Cozzens' (i.e., the Navy's) knowledge or involvement. Should it ever be revealed, the Navy could simply say that neither Cozzens nor Cogswell had been shown the message. Of course, the Germans still had the initialed copy—Daniel White had witnessed Cozzens signing-off on it—but the Germans wouldn't dare offer it in evidence, and if they did, the Navy would counter that revelation by saying the Germans had forged Cozzens' signature.

The story that emerged after the Navy's counter-investigation is a near-breathtaking fictional masterpiece. It begins with a rather tepid acknowledgment of culpability in Sayville and then proceeds to distract the reader from it by vilifying the Germans at the wireless station without offering concrete evidence of any wrongdoing. Cozzens graduates—in this telling, which is both false *and* a factual muddle—from a lax censor to a victim of attempted murder.

Four More Men Rushed to Tower to Prevent Break in Censorship; Seaman Leaving Tower; Believes He Was Purposely Shocked to Loosen Censorship Net
Sayville, June 8

— Direct wireless communication between this country and Berlin, Germany, by means of the wireless plant, has suddenly taken on a new and rigid supervision by the United States Government. Instead of the former complaisant censorship exercised by one officer and one enlisted man detailed by the Navy Department, there are now three officers and two enlisted men on duty at the wireless plant, under orders from Washington. Those familiar with the way things have been going at the tall wireless tower here assert the change is due to the definite realization by the Government that there were times when there was no actual censorship and when any kind of a message might have been flashed across the sea from here without the United States Navy representatives, supposedly in charge, knowing anything at all about it.

One story which is being circulated in Sayville centers around the circumstances of the accident to Second-Class Seaman Daniel Cozzens at the wireless plant on April 27. Cozzens is one of the Navy's wireless experts and he has been at the plant under Lieutenant Francis Cogswell, the two being in charge of the censoring. On April 27 Cozzens was knocked unconscious and rendered unfit for duty for nearly two weeks by electric shock received as he was about to climb the tower. Some Sayville residents have been told by Cozzens that the wireless operators who sent the message that caused the shock knew he was about to climb the wireless tower to take a picture of the new tower, then in course of construction. Some of the intimates of Cozzens assert that he made a formal report to his superiors about the matter and requested that he be transferred because of the way in which he was injured. Whether or not this report and this request were actually made, local Sayville authorities have no means of knowing.

The two additional officers who are now here as censors with Lieutenant Cogswell are Lieutenant Charles R. Clark and H. H. McCormack. Their assignment here followed a visit paid to the wireless station about two weeks ago by Captain Bullard, U.S.N. They began their duties yesterday, and with them came two enlisted men to relieve Cozzens. It is planned that one of the three officers will be on duty every hour of the day and night at the plant. Formerly, when Lieutenant Cogswell and Cozzens were the censoring board, the lieutenant lived in the village, and there were many hours when no representative of the United States was at the plant.

Cozzens Tells How He Received the Injury
— Cozzens, when he arranged to take a photograph of the new tower,

on April 26, concluded that the best place from which to make his picture would be a point half way up the old tower. "I went into the dining room of the station," Cozzens said today in telling of the accident which followed his attempt to climb the old tower, "where three of the engineers connected with the station, Ludwig Batterman, Gustave Reuther, and a man named Sesolovsky, were still seated at the table eating their luncheon. "I told them I would like to take a photograph of the new tower from the old mast, and Batterman told me to go ahead, and, in fact, advised me as to the best way of taking the picture. Leaving the three engineers still in the dining room," the young radio operator continued, "I went to my own rooms to put on an old uniform before climbing the tower, which is covered with grease, and then with my camera, walked to the structure, which is a great iron tripod, and which is at all times insulated from the ground. No sooner had I grasped one of the iron crosspieces, however, when I sustained a terrific shock, which rendered me unconscious for fully six hours, and inflicted burns on my hands and feet which still cause me much pain and annoyance. When I recovered, I learned that after I had left the dining room Sesolovsky had turned on the power in the old tower, to test it, and naturally when I placed my hand upon it I grounded the current, with the result that I was shocked into insensibility. Had any unneutral message been sent while I was unconscious it would have been picked up by the various stations at Fire Island, the Brooklyn Navy Yard, Philadelphia, and many others, and we would have learned of it at once. Furthermore, as soon as I was injured, Lieutenant Cogswell was notified and at once hurried to the station.

SECRETARY OF NAVY DANIELS DENIES CHANGE IN CENSORSHIP
— Secretary of the Navy Daniels denied today that there had been any change in the system of censorship at the Sayville wireless station, or that it had been made more rigid than hitherto. The Navy Department put the Sayville station under censorship shortly after the outbreak of the war in Europe, because of complaints that it had been used improperly in the transmission of German military communications. Mr. Daniels said today that the station had been variously in the charge of one officer, two officers and sometimes three. He was under the impression that there was one officer there now. Changes that have been made in the detail from time to time, Mr. Daniels said, were merely in the course of routine and were for the purpose of giving the officers a rest from their duties. He said they had no other significance. Secretary Daniels was asked also if there had been any report regarding trouble Seaman Cozzens had had at the Sayville plant. He said that he had heard nothing about it. In what appears to be a well-orchestrated and well-timed media blitz, a story about the night adventures of Mr. Cozzens suddenly appeared in the *Tribune* newspaper. Cozzens was relieved of his responsibilities and the censorship at the station was increased.

he original cargo manifest of the RMS Lusitania, yet another official document brimming with falsehoods, declared its hold transported a large shipment of butter and cheese—perishable food products which could not survive the voyage without considerable spoilage. This was of little concern at the time of sailing because those enumerated food products were, in reality, disguised armaments that the Americans were smuggling to Great Britain. The passengers were unfortunate props in this charade. As documentation revealed decades later, President Wilson's stance of neutrality was nothing more than a false front that enabled him to dangle his feet on both sides of the fence—secretly lending American support to the Allied war effort. For all their polite diplomacy, at the end of the day, Woody and Willy were just two kids cheating at chess. So, the worst The Devil's Tower *might* have been guilty of is helping to sink The Devil's Ship.

here was another story, as hazy and intangible as cigar smoke generated by a roomful of saboteurs. A name, briefly glimpsed on a wisp of yellow paper, a name surrounded by a few innocuous words—GET LUCY NICE SURPRISE GIFT—a name? a coincidence? a directive? Whatever else it might have been, here was the first of the dominoes to tumble in a series of dominoes that fell one after another for years.

Editor Francis Hoag occasionally wondered, years later—*who was she?* Who was the shadowy Lucy who figured so fleetingly in the history of World War I? She *could* have been the *süße kleine Schwester* of Gustave Reuther, a sweet German lass, who had her purely innocent birthday party on May 7, 1915, while 1,129 persons drowned. No one ever looked for Fraulein Lucy Reuther, which guaranteed to a certainty that she would never be found. The real Lucy, if not a young miss with a long braid that no one troubled to seek out, could just as easily been a reference to the duplicitous RMS Lusitania, lying prone in the muddy depths of the Celtic Sea with her payload of deadly explosives still clasped to her bosom.

Beyond the scope of White's musings, many years after his passing, the wreck of the Lusitania was sold for $2,400 to entrepreneurs. Soon enough, abundant handfuls of rifle shells were brought to the surface by nautical expeditionists. The ammunition they found might never have seen daylight

... She was still as ill-defined and ungraspable as the smoke that wafted around the clutter in Hoag's messy office ...

previously, having spent its clandestine life in crates which finally rotted and spilled their contents into the sea, like confessions poured into a priest's ear.

"My understanding," said William F. Flynn, chief of the U.S. Secret Service, "from interviews with radio experts, is that you've invented a contraption that can precisely record wireless transmissions for later replay—like cylinders of Caruso singing opera arias—the dots, the dashes, the whole damn show."

He was meeting with Charles Apgar, an amateur radio enthusiast, in mid-1915 because Woodrow Wilson was increasingly worried about Sayville.

"True—I've fitted the electronics of a headphone to a home-made recording head on an Edison cylinder machine. It's crude, but it works."

"My reason for requesting this meeting is to explore how your invention can help the United States as respects possible espionage on Long Island."

"*Possible* espionage? Regretfully, it's my belief that we're now well beyond what's *possible*, Mr. Flynn. Our Navy picks up the Sayville transmissions and diligently compares them to their approved versions, finding no deviations because the subterfuge is not occurring *within* the messages. It's happening, most insidiously, in the *method* of transmission." He held out a strip of paper on which he had inscribed a message in Morse code. "This message was sent three days ago. At the cost of a dollar per word, it says, 'Myra has diphtheria,' along with other harmless trivia. But, if you listen to the transmission I've *recorded* and use it to transcribe what *actually* went out, you'll discover two places where an extra dot has been added to a letter. So, for example, instead of [.---] for the letter *P*, what you have is [.---..], with an extra dot that looks like it could be a simple slip of the hand, which it isn't—not with this frequency. More craftily, there are seven places in the message where extra spaces have been added between letters."

"And this all means... what?"

"It means that cryptography has reached a previously unknown degree of invisibility. It means the Devil is at work in Sayville. It means that Myra may or may not have diphtheria, but the extra dot in the *P* of *diphtheria* and the extra spaces deliberately placed in key positions of the message signify—to a U-boat captain—the exact latitude and longitude of an Allied supply ship."

"We still have to prove this. And we must—absolutely—break the code."

"Every wireless operator has a discoverable and recognizable sending style—like a fingerprint," Apgar said. "It's a highly individualized pattern known in telegraphy as a *fist*. If you know the quirks of the operator's personal *fist*, you can identify him by listening for it on my cylinders. If two or more of the operators have the identical *fist*—if they share the habit of sending the letter *P* and the letter *F* with an extra dot, for example— then that's your proof you have a nest of spies in Sayville. The first step to breaking the code is here, in my hand, Mr. Flynn." He held out an Edison cylinder. "This is a sound recording of a message sent from Sayville that begins with the words 'GET LUCY NICE SURPRISE GIFT.' The *P* in SUR-PRISE and the *F* in GIFT each have an audible extra dot as captured by my recording. Since we have good reason to believe this message was responsible for the sinking of the Lusitania on the following day, it follows, logically, that the extra spaces placed between the letters are code for the latitude and longitude of the target. We know where the ship was struck, so, essentially, we've *already* decoded the message. All we have to do is work backward—using all the aberrations we hear on the cylinder—to unlock the workings of the code."

"Who was she?" Frank Hoag asked Daniel White in 1917. White had stopped by the news office to visit on his way to the battlefront in Europe. Newly enlisted and in uniform, he was there to offer Hoag's newspaper his services as a foreign correspondent for the duration of the war.

Much had changed since 1915. The Telefunken Germans—Ludwig Batterman, Gustave Reuther, and Udo Sesolovsky—had been summarily ejected from the fence-enclosed radio station by the U. S. Navy after the infamous "Zimmerman Telegram" was decoded and war with Germany was declared. They had not even been allowed to gather their belongings. All they had were the clothes on their backs and the change in their pockets. The three radio men were last observed later that day, still wearing their wireless uniforms, boarding the last train out of Sayville. Lieutenant Cogswell had been reassigned and so had Seaman Cozzens. Cozzens was back on the USS Arkansas—at least according to the Sayville girls who wrote love letters to him. There was no one left behind who had any information about the mysterious Lucy. She was still as ill-defined and ungraspable as the cigar smoke that wafted around the clutter in Hoag's messy office. The two old friends were, once more, face to face, but this time they were saying their goodbyes over cups of black coffee and feeling a bit somber.

Hoag said, "Now that our efforts to avoid getting drawn into this war have proven a resounding failure—just as we privately felt they would all along—Fräulein Lucy is the only loose end for me. She still haunts me. What began here as '*our*' tower—an object of significant pride not so long ago in this town—was transformed into 'The Devil's Tower' on Lucy's birthday. I can trace all the foreboding back to the day you, my friend, strolled into this office to tell me about her. So, who—or what—was she really, Danny? A girl with pigtails? An ocean liner? Or, was she just something you *think* you saw on a flimsy piece of paper after eating bad oysters? Do you think we'll ever know?"

"I'm certain of this much," replied the justice of the peace before pausing to produce a large, vacuous smoke ring to illustrate the extent of his uncertainty. A faint, circular puff of *zero* was suspended in the air between them. Through that hazy porthole, he continued to voice his reflections on the matter of Lucy. "We were *fated* to be drawn into this war, and those of us—myself included—that *may* have the misfortune to die fighting, are simply those who are fated to die fighting. Lucy, like every one of us, is an instrument of Fate. So, it matters very little, when all is said and done, whether she's a person or a thing or something purely conceptual. Who knows the truth? Maybe Lucy is nothing more or less sinister than an adorable nickname for Lucifer...."

Once I built a railroad, I made it run
Made it race against time
Once I built a railroad, now it's done
Brother, can you spare a dime?

Translations of chalk markings in Universal Hobo Road Lingo, top row:
Thieves in vicinity / Cop lives here / Vicious dog / House has alarm / Free doctor

Translations, bottom row:
Man with gun lives here / Kind lady lives here / Good place to catch train / Be quiet

Into each life some rain must fall.

The Missing Passenger's Prologue & Tale

They Say Rain

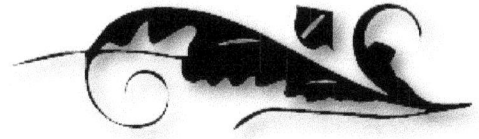

An empty seat on *The Brown Fox* has its story, too. The invisible passenger in the Whitman Carriage—the one who *isn't* sitting in the seat opposite Mrs. Asta Bathbaum, is known to the Story Auditor as Mister X. Being a "Void" (an unused ticket)—a stocking-puppet with the hand yanked out of it—Mister X has, within these pages, been renamed *Ecksie* in an attempt to humanize him a bit for better story deployment. Maybe this is how the story Ecksie *didn't* tell the Professor and his cronies on *The Brown Fox* was supposed to go.

Ecksie was in the habit of joining a mixed group of his pals at a small tea salon called Jane's Veranda on Friday nights. Jane was ordinary, her veranda was a dreary store-front, and the tea she served the customers was tea. Somehow—and this was the sort of weird thing that happened quite often in New York at one questionable location or another—people got the idea that the thing to do when there was nothing to do on Friday night was to patronize Jane's store-front on Greenwich Avenue and buy a cup of her tea. Jane was so good at being inadvertently successful, after a year or so, she no longer bothered to go to Jane's Veranda herself. She became a ghostly legend in the tea business. No one knew where she was and no one cared. As long as Jane's sister, Vera, opened the Veranda door and sold Jane's tea in her place, customers continued to go there. Rather than call the place Vera's Veranda, they rechristened it The Verasanda. That, at least, made it sound more like it was a destination for classy people, or like a clandestine nightclub in Ibiza or Morocco. It didn't sound like it served Lipton's.

On occasion, a random customer might be overheard saying, "Remind me—why do we come to this dump?" and someone else would venture, "In case Miss Edie shows up."

Miss Edie was a fortune-teller right out of the pages of a Damon Runyon story, arriving at the scene—occasionally—on Friday nights, in a flurry of noisy-looking fabrics and ready-to-rip shopping bags brimming with old newspapers and unfinished knitting. Turbaned, heavily made-up, reeking of Jean Naté, she would enter through a back door—no one besides Vera and Miss Edie even knew where the other side of that back door was—and she would proceed to force customers to change their seats if they happened to be situated in her location of choice or were blocking her view—view of *what* no one could figure out. Perhaps she meant her view of the future.

The first thing she would do after sitting down and sorting herself out was call out "Next?" as if there had been a previous customer to be superseded by a new one. Beyond her unabashed rudeness, what separated her from all other fortune-tellers was the veracity of her readings. Where some fortune-tellers, foreseeing that you would be hit by a bus, would trim the barb on the deadly stinger and say, "It would be best if you were careful crossing the street," Miss Edie would tell the customer—without the slightest hesitation—"You'd better stay indoors for the next three days, or by Wednesday you're going to be ketchup on asphalt." Her fortune-telling diplomacy style was to throw diplomacy out the window and go for broke. This was marvelous for the customer who had a tall, dark stranger awaiting them for a lifetime of romance. It wasn't so good if they had a tall, dark stranger awaiting them for a lifetime of infidelity, humiliation, and battery, but it could, potentially, save the love lottery loser a lot of inconvenience and pain later on.

In most cases, your risk with fortune-tellers was the ignominy of gambling foolishly with your money. With Miss Edie, who only charged an untorn fiver with all its corners intact, the gamble was with your peace-of-mind. Once heard, Miss Edie's prophesies were impossible to dismiss. Thus, quite understandably, many patrons of

The Verasanda kept their distance and remained only "potential" customers. For others, watching her massacres from the safety of the sidelines, from the highest tiers of the oracle's prediction stadium, was riveting spectator sport. Then there were the risk-takers, who faced Miss Eddie fearlessly, fiver in hand, willing to wrestle with the alligators she might toss at them.

Ecksie—the Void—was not a risk taker. He had succeeded in dodging Miss Edie's tongue on numerous occasions, and he was intending to continue with this policy. His friends, on the other hand, thought it would be entertaining to watch him squirm, and so they urged him in Miss Edie's direction whenever they were all present at once.

"Listen," Ecksie would say, "I've already nearly died eight times. I'm living my ninth life like a mangy cat, and I'm not going near that woman, even she wants to pay *me* instead of the other way around."

"How did you almost die eight times? You're only 35 years old."

"First of all, I've never had cancer, so I am—at the very *least*—a *bona fide* Junior League Cancer Survivor. That's one escape from death right there. Then there's all the accidents and illnesses, a real hotchpotch of calamity, from severe hepatitis to flowerpots falling from balconies. Enough has happened already to convince me that I don't want to know what else might happen. My will is written, my decision is made, and that's that."

His friends were very persistent. They worked him over and called him a coward and a poor sport. Finally, they managed to break his resistance down and he agreed to hand a four-cornered fiver to Miss Edie and get his palm read. "For *your* entertainment only," he said.

The first thing Miss Edie did, though, was send him away. "You've touched far too many hands today," she said. Go into the loo and wash them, and just let them air dry. I want to read the real you."

About this she was entirely correct. He had been to a reception earlier in the day and shaken the hands of dozens of complete strangers. So, he did as she asked and came back, waving his hands at his sides to get them dry. He sat down at Miss Edie's table and extended his right hand to her. She glanced at it quickly, without touching it or even leaning forward.

"You have a very loud clock in your bedroom. It's annoying."

"It's a pendulum clock. I'm used to it."

"It's annoying."

"How do *you* know about it?"

She sighed. "You just told me." She glanced, once again, from afar, at his palm. "You're about to take a trip."

"That's right. On Wednesday."

"On a train."

"That's right."

"Don't keep saying that," she said. "And, *don't.*"

"Don't what?"

"*Don't* say 'that's right' again, and *don't* take the train."

"Why not? Is something going to happen?"

Her lips tightened into a fine line. No one had ever seen Miss Edie flinch from the prediction of a bad outcome, even if the outcome was as dire as death. If the subject of the reading was going to win a million-dollar lottery or get struck by lightning, it was all in a day's work for Miss Edie. Without as much as blinking, she'd tell someone—even her own mother, "I hope you're wearing clean underwear because you're going to die of a fatal aneurysm in six minutes, and there isn't enough time for you to change into something fresh."

This was precisely the sort of torment Ecksie had wanted to avoid. Now he *had* to know what was going to happen on that train. "Tell me," he demanded, retracting his hand. "I want to know."

"Rain must fall," she said.

No one breathed. Eighteen cups of tea were gradually losing their heat, but no one moved.

"Into each life," Miss Edie said in a strangely tragic voice, "some rain must fall."

"Miss Edie," he said, regaining some of his composure, "you're quoting Longfellow, not the Oracle of Delphi. Explain yourself, or I'll tear a corner off this fiver and ruin your day."

"You've repeatedly survived death and destruction. You know it and I know it. Now, at long last, the spirits around you say that some rain will fall."

"So, I should cancel my train trip because it's going to rain?"

"They say rain, but it won't rain real rain. Trust me."

"The train will crash or derail?"

"The train will be fine."

"So, there won't be a guy going postal with a gun?"

"That already happened," she said. "A long time ago. No, there won't be any guy going postal."

"Well, what is it, then?" he demanded. "Out with it!"

Her hesitation had nothing to do with uncertainty. The only thing holding her back was her reluctance to predict something that might not seem—to some people—readily acceptable. After turning over the range of possible reactions in her mind, she came to a final decision. She sat back and said with her usual conviction, "You know how some fortune-tellers like to say 'You will go on a long journey' when they do a reading? Well, I could say the same to you. Only your long journey might be a bit longer than just Wednesday."

"Terrific," he said, throwing his hands in the air. "Am I allowed to know where I'll be going? If it's okay with you, I'd like to check the weather reports so I can be sure to pack the right clothes."

"When rain is about to fall, it's not a good time for jokes. An umbrella wouldn't hurt, though. It's a good thing to bring anywhere. And maybe a sweater with buttons—another sensible choice. Wear comfortable shoes. And bring some Dramamine. Anyway, I can't say where you're going because I don't know the lingo. You can ask someone on the way. In the meantime, I repeat, if you get on that train on Wednesday, rain *will* fall, and you *will* be abducted by aliens."

The entire room burst into laughter.

Ecksie was furious. "One of you assholes paid her to do this to me!"

"Most certainly not! Miss Edie takes no bribes!" she protested vehemently. She was as indignant as Ecksie was angry. She deftly pulled the fiver from underneath Ecksie's teacup, where he had stowed it. The bill was pristine—as she required—guaranteeing that her karma wouldn't be soiled by money that had undergone abuse. "This is all I take for my truth. Just remember what I told you." She pointed upwards, her eyes following her fingertip heavenward. "They say rain."

Miss Edie's seemingly absurd prophesy immediately—although only temporarily—took the intimidating edge out of her brutally truthful readings. Anyone in The Verasanda who had harbored the slightest reluctance to pay her fee of a nice, clean fiver, got over it at once and lined up for a reading of their own. The silliness was just too much fun to pass up.

Miss Edie understood the basis for her sudden popularity only too well—it was somewhat demeaning—but she made more money that night than she ever had previously, and no matter what horrid predictions she made, the customers—much to their detriment—laughed them off as nonsense.

his spur line of narrative explains the vacant seat directly opposite Mrs. Asta Bathbaum on *The Brown Fox* as she had occasion to observe it while on her way to Sayville with her son's ashes in a Thom McAn shoebox. The conductor onboard was unexpectedly one ticket-punch short of a full carriage. The Professor was irritated to find himself inconveniently made one tale short of his intended quota. Ecksie—our Mister X—neither knew nor cared about outcomes that sprang from his non-appearance.

The preceding six pages relate the story Mister X *would have* told as part of the Professor's masterfully engineered day of auto-entertainment. It was recounted here for the sake of thoroughness, as well as to demonstrate the following twisted, Möbius strip of storytelling logic—The story Mister X *didn't* tell on the train because he never got on it was actually an excuse for why he hadn't boarded the train to tell his story in the first place.

Not only did he leave his fellow passengers in the dark concerning some matters of importance—while managing, albeit unintentionally, to throw *The Brown Fox's* hospitality tabulations out of whack—he never even *attempted* to go to Sayville to deliver his lecture at the Annual Science Fiction Writers Convention.

Overheard on the way to the toilet
A Cellphone  ctet

1. Back to Israel

Just as they say at the end of every Seder, "Next year in Jerusalem," I should say to you, "Next month in Israel."

-

I'll try to plan it with you when I get back from the Hamptons.

-

How funny, I'm on the train right now.

-

I sure am. Let's both stand up so we can see where we are. Oh, hi Shanna! Here I am, honey, way down here! Can you see me? Wave to me.

-

-

-

-

I'd really love to, Shanna, but there are at least three more very important calls I have to make before we arrive.

-

-

2. Me too!

-

-

-

It would be wonderful if we can arrange for a get-together when we're both there.

-

I'm actually heading for the Hamptons myself.

-

What? Me too! Are you on the Brown Fox train in the cellphone isolation carriage?

-

-

This is just *too* funny. We've both been here all this time and neither of us had a clue. What a shame, we could have had a nice lunch together. Why don't you move down to where I am? There's room for you here. We can catch up in person.

-

-

Okay, I understand. Anyway, what more could we have to talk about for today, right? I think we've covered Eretz Yisrael and just about everything else. Bye, Zora, honey!

3. Unh huh!

Unh huh.
I knew it.
So, the story continues.
It will never end, will it?
Unh huh. No shit!
Unh huh.
Oh, no, don't tell me... !!!
Unh huh.
Unh huh.
Unh huh.
Unh huh.
No way.
You're killing me. No way.
Unh huh.
Oh yeah?
Really?
Oh no! Really?
What a hoot!
Hell no.
You're kidding, right?
Unh huh.
Unh huh.
Oh my God. Let me guess...
She did?
He did?
She did?
He did *what*?
She did, too?
They did?
I did not!
Wow!
Unh huh.
Unh huh.
Yeah. Right.
Unh huh.
Unh huh..
Unh unh.
She said what?
Now there's a nerve for you!
She'll be hearing from me!

4. Public sob story

SOB ssssssssssssssssssssssssssssssssssss
sssss - wiss - sssssssssssssssssssssssss - wiss
- ssssssssssssssssssssssssssssss COUGH
ssssssss BROKE UP WITH ME ssssssssss
SNIFFLE SNIFFLE ssssssssssssssssss
- wiss - wiss - sssssssssssssssssssssssss
sssssssssssssssssssssssssssssssssssssssss
ss COUGH sssss COUGH SNIFFLE
SOB SOB SOB COUGH ssssssssss
ssssssssssssssssssssssss - wiss - wiss -
ssssssssssssssss SNIFFLE SNIFFLE
sssssssssssssss CALLED ME A CUNT
ssssssssss - wiss - sssssssssssssssssssss
- sssssssssssssssssssssssssssssssssss - sssss
sssss COUGH COUGH COUGH
ssssssssss CALLED ME A TRAMP
AND A LIAR ssssssssssssssssssssss
sssssssssssssss - wiss - wiss - sssssssssss
- wiss - sssssssssssssssssssss SNIFFLE
SNIFFLE SOB SOB SOB SOB SOB
SOB sssssssssssssssss - wiss - wiss - ssss
ssssssssssssssssssssssssssssssss COUGH
sssss COUGH SNIFFLE SOB SOB SOB
COUGH ssssssssssssssssssssssssssss
sssss - wiss - wiss - sssssssssssssssssss
ssssssss - shh - SOB SOB SOB SOB SOB
SOB sssssssssssssssssssssssssssssss - SOB
SOB SOB SOB SOB SOB SOB SOB
ssssssssssssssss COUGH sssss COUGH
SNIFFLE ssssssssssssssssss PACKED
HIS STUFF AND LEFT ssssssssssss
sssssssssssssssss - wiss - wiss - ssssssssss
ssssssssssssssssssssssssssssssssss SNIF-
FLE SNIFFLE SNIFFLE SNIFFLE
SNIFFLE ssssssssssssssssssssss - wiss
- sssssssssssssss wiss - sssssssssssssssss
- ssssssssssssssssssssssssss HIS
MOTHER CALLED MY MOTHER
ssssssssss COUGH COUGH COUGH
ssssssssssssssss SNIFFLE SNIFFLE
sssssssssssss - wiss - wiss - sssssssssss
sssssssssssss COUGH sssss COUGH
SNIFFLE SOB SOB SOB ssssssssss
SUING MY WHOLE FAMILY FOR
FRAUD sssssss - ssss - wiss - wiss - ssssss
ssssssssssssssssss - wiss - SOB SOB
SOB SOB SOB SOB sssssssssssssssss
sssssssss SOB SOB SOB SOB SOB SOB
SOB SOB SOB ssssssssssssss COUGH
sssss COUGH SNIFFLE SOB sssssssssss
sssssssssssssssssssssss

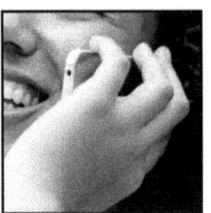

5. Sooooooo sick

The people on this train have been talking on their cells non-stop since minute one and now I have a headache, Nina, like the worst I can remember, maybe the worst of all time. I feel *sooooooooo* sick. The conductor gave me Annoycin tablets and said they would help, but I don't like to take strange new medications.

Harmless? Are you sure?

So, you've taken this stuff? And it's safe? And you're sure it's gluten-free? How do you take it? With water?

You're kidding! In my ears? One in each? I'm ready to try anything at this point. Here goes. Pray for me.

What? Nina? Are you there? I can't hear you. Nina? Nina? I don't know if you can hear me, but I feel better already.

6. Breaking up

What? I can't hear you.

You're breaking up.

I said, breaking up.

BREAAAKING UPPP !!!

Oh, you heard that?

No?

How about now?

Maybe your battery is weak.

Wait, we're going through a tunnel.

A tunnel, I said.

A TUUUNELLL !!!

We're out now.

What?

You're breaking up again.

What was that?

You're what?

Going through a tunnel?

How funny is that! I just came out of a tunnel.

What?

Another tunnel?

7. Non-Jew ham

I certainly wouldn't dream of accepting another invitation from them. The place was wall-to-wall non-Jews.

In the center of the table they had a turkey and a ham. You could tell from the way they presented it that they wanted you to be sure to notice the ham looming over the turkey. It was like 'Look at us, look at us, we're non-Jews serving Jews a big *trayf* ham.' Just leave it to non-Jews to hammer it over your head that they're non-Jews and using a giant ham to do it. Believe me, that ham was right in your face. My cousin Charlene got a six-carat diamond engagement ring, and even that wasn't shoved in my face as much as that giant ham was. And do you think the non-Jews even went for the ham? Not at all. They massacred the turkey. In ten minutes it was a pile of gristle and bones, and there was the ham, barely touched. You could almost hear them laughing at you. "Be sure to leave some ham for the Jews. Get them doggy bags so they can take some home."

And do I need to describe the white icing on that nauseatingly sweet *goyische* birthday cake?

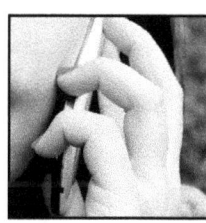

8. Burgered-out

... while I was doing a burger. Let me tell you, my man, that was the best freakin' burger ever of all fucking time, no question. And I thought I was all burgered-out. Totally excellent big-time. Man oh man, I pulled out all the stops. I threw some cheddar on it and some spicy ketchup and some chopped onion ...

Sure I can wait. Go ahead.

Rick? Rick?

Oh, you're back. I thought I lost you. Where was I? Oh yeah, I was telling you about the buns I bought for the burger. I splurged majorly on those brioche buns which are like six dollars for six buns so like a dollar essentially for each hamburger bun and then I bought a bag of those truffle oil chips... Hey, Rick, I think I have another call coming in.

No, I can't do tomorrow. I actually have a job interview lined up.

They describe it as a work-from-home telemarketing thing. Yeah, but why spend time talking about it when they haven't started paying me to talk?

A Printer's Devil was hired to set type for *The Author's Tale*, as it could only be expressed in print by employing Latin filler text—known as *Lorem ipsum* in the printing industry. A note, in the author's distinctive handwriting, was discovered right here, on the railroad tracks near Page 441 The note was sent to more than twenty of the author's closest associates for interpretation last January. To date (six months later) however, the publishers have not received a single reply to the inquiry. The man seen in this photograph is believed to be the author. He is considered missing at this time. Note that even the road signs have turned their backs to the figure, here seen trudging off to an uncertain future and an unknown destination.

THE AUTHOR'S TALE

LOREM IPSUM DOLOR

 ipsum dolor sit amet, consectetur adipiscing elit, sed do eiusmod tempor incididunt ut labore et dolore magna aliqua. Ut enim ad minim veniam, quis nostrud exercitation ullamco laboris nisi ut aliquip ex ea commodo consequat. Duis aute irure dolor in reprehenderit in voluptate velit esse cillum dolore eu fugiat nulla pariatur. Excepteur sint occaecat cupidatat non proident, sunt in culpa qui officia deserunt mollit anim id est laborum. Lorem ipsum dolor sit amet, consectetur adipiscing elit, sed do eiusmod tempor incididunt ut labore et dolore magna aliqua.

Ut enim ad minim veniam, quis nostrud exercitation ullamco laboris nisi ut aliquip ex ea commodo consequat. Duis aute irure dolor in reprehenderit in voluptate velit esse cillum dolore eu fugiat nulla pariatur. Excepteur sint occaecat cupidatat non proident, sunt in culpa qui officia deserunt mollit anim id est laborum. Lorem ipsum dolor sit amet, consectetur adipiscing elit, sed do eiusmod tempor incididunt ut labore et dolore magna aliqua. Ut enim ad minim veniam, quis nostrud exercitation ullamco laboris nisi ut aliquip ex ea commodo consequat.

Duis aute irure dolor in reprehenderit in voluptate velit esse cillum dolore eu fugiat nulla pariatur. Excepteur sint occaecat cupidatat non proident, sunt in culpa qui officia deserunt mollit anim id est laborum. Lorem ipsum dolor sit amet, consectetur adipiscing elit, sed do eiusmod . . .

BE PREPARED !

Lady Hooch's Aborted Tale

Little Maury Goes to Summer Camp

ousin Millie Bathbaum became a very young member of the Morrisania Widows Mahjong Club when—with no warning at all—Irv died after only ten years of marriage. Little Morris was just eight and a very difficult child, even if Millie would never admit it to anyone. She was also raising Irv's two sons from his previous marriage, Miles and Bernie, but they were quite a bit older and much less needy than Maury. Desperate for money, her only option was to return to work in the garment district as a bookkeeper. In those rough times, to economize, she habitually bought clothing from the "Irregular" bins, even when she could afford better. As a result, no undergarment had ever touched little Maury's *tuches* and other private business areas that wasn't stamped "Irregular" on the waistband, or worse, on rare occasions, directly on the peenie sack. Lucky for Maury the ink didn't rub off on him. No, the next worst thing happened instead—at summer camp.

A year after Irv died of a reaction to a penicillin shot right in her own living room, Millie sent little Maury to a sleepaway camp in the Catskills. As any good Jewish mother would, she sent him well-stocked with clean underwear, all of it marked with the humiliating insignia of the indigent. Disaster struck when laundry bags got mixed up and it was discovered by some of the nastier campers that all of Maury's clothes were stamped "Irregular." Kids being cruel, that became his nickname, and people were still calling him "Irregy" and "Bargain Butt" when he was going through High School at the age of—

[*Here an interruption caused Mildred Del Lago's story to be unexpectedly aborted...*]

The Engineer's Incident Report

Sayville in Three Minutes

Just as the conductor finished announcing their upcoming arrival at Sayville and the availability of connections to Fire Island ferries, *The Brown Fox* inexplicably slowed to a quiet halt. In place of the pervasive vibration emanating from the locomotive, an ominous stillness filtered through the carriages, while simultaneously, through the darkening windows, the passengers began to notice purple smoke swirling up from the train's undercarriage.

The following is excerpted from the Engineer's Incident Report:

LOCATION
Fifty yards beyond Signal #322, 3 minutes prior to the scheduled arrival time at Sayville Station.

SITUATION
Poor visibility / Object(s) on track at 300 yards
Something that looks like—as far as I can make out in all this smoke or fog or whatever it is—either a cow on the tracks ahead, or someone holding a picture of a cow. Not sure what it is.

ACTION TAKEN
Safety regulations in the Engineers Manual mandate complete stop of engine, followed by investigation by train personnel when there is any possibility of danger to persons, animals, or...

Deus ex Machina

It was Bang! after Bang! after Bang! And then, for the sake of variety, Boom! There is nothing like an invasion of robots to create a symphony of unexplainable noises, both perplexing and painful to hear, worse than imprisonment in an automobile factory without the benefit of earplugs. Doors flew open and slammed shut, the robots' heads scraped against the ceilings, smashing light bulbs in the hanging fixtures, causing shards of glass to rain down everywhere. Their eyes—they had three each—squealed when they rotated from side to side. And as to their voices—the more they left unsaid, the better.

The only respite the passengers had from the terror was when the robots conferred amongst themselves and stopped looking around for potential lab rats in the seats. The leader seemed to be the tallest one. He—or It—was tallest because he had what looked like a radar tower on top of his head. The head was itself a true work of design restraint—a plain, rectangular box made of a metallic material with very few features to distinguish it. There was a triangular-shaped mouth-like area that was sealed but might unseal itself without warning to be a weapons-grade pie-hole or just a loudspeaker. There was no nose. Above the absent proboscis, there were three apertures that were definitely the eyes. Independently, the lenses inside the openings roved from person to person. They might have been taking pictures or transmitting images to a Mother Ship. They also consulted with Radar Robot as they progressed up the aisle. Pincer-like hands were concealed in the inner reaches of the arms but emerged when an object of interest presented itself. The object would be caught in the pincers, lifted to the three eyes and turned to different viewing angles. Rudely, the objects were not returned to their owners. They were dropped on the floor unceremoniously and sometimes crushed underfoot by the next curiosity-seeking monster in the parade. There was also an amorphous grab bag being dragged along by the smallest robot—possibly a child robot or a trainee—in which objects of interest were tossed for later examination. There was no way to figure out why some things held more interest to the invaders than others. Poor Thom McAn, much to Mrs. Bathbaum's grief, ended up in Robot Junior's bag. The nun's rosary didn't, but it was crushed underfoot, and the loose rosary beads rolled off in every direction, causing one of the robots to slip. The upended robot fell in the aisle and lay there, inert, until Radar Robot dragged it into the next carriage. Several of the robots and the baby robot remained behind to continue their pilfering. Bang! Bang! Boom!

Soda's typesetting manual was selected for inclusion in the grab bag, along with Mildred Del Lago's Louis Vuitton signature pocketbook. That was the object of greatest interest to the robots. They all took turns looking inside it, removing objects for closer examination. The large collection of credit cards—about thirty in all—were a big source of fascination. The robots got in a tussle over them, but they dropped more of them than they stole. The baby robot opened what was, presumably, his mouth—it was like the hopper of a dumbwaiter—and quickly popped in a stick of Mildred's lipstick. The hopper slammed shut immediately afterward with a clang.

The passengers watched the proceedings in fascination and horror, while green and purple smoke swirled outside the windows of *The Brown Fox*.

"What the fuck are these things?" Ry whispered to Scotch, hoping the plundering robots were out of hearing range—if they could hear at all.

"Pizarro, Cortés, and Columbus," whispered Scotch in reply. "We're the native Indians, and we're all about to get the clap."

"I certainly hope I'm going to get credit for wearing clean underwear to this disaster," Soda said after wracking his brain for something positive to say. "Could one of you tell my mother for me, if you make it out of this and I don't?"

"Clean underpants only matter if you get hit by a car," Ry said. "Flying saucers don't count. It stands to reason that space aliens have a completely different concept of *shmutz* than our mothers do."

Meanwhile, Scotch turned his attention to the Professor, who had yet to comment in any way about the unfolding calamity. "Got any ideas? Any defensive weapons stockpiled in that carpetbag?"

The Professor didn't respond. He sat motionless, arms crossed over his chest, looking extremely displeased. Ears reddening, eyes tightly squeezed shut, he seemed quite ready to explode.

"And what's with all the purple smoke outside?" Ry asked.

"That's actually not purple," Soda observed, unable to stop himself. "I'd place it somewhere between mauve and pale violet."

"Mauve," said Mildred Del Lago. "I have a cocktail dress the same color. Am I right, Asta darling? That smoke is mauve."

"Definitely mauve, Millie," Lady Asta said. "I've always loved that old mauve dress. I remember that you wore it to Rochelle's wedding. And to Monica's a few years later. In fact, I once had a dream about you, and in the dream—I know you're going to think this is ridiculous—in the dream, you were wearing that same mauve dress."

Mildred Del Lago threw her head back and laughed girlishly. Putting her arm around her old friend, she said, "I remember you telling me about that dream. So many years ago! As I recall, it went something like this: I was in my mauve dress, sitting in a parterre box at the opera. You arrived late, long after the curtain went up—very discretely, of course—and you were wearing the identical mauve dress."

"I think that smoke might be better described as a lilac or a periwinkle," Scotch interrupted pointedly. The mental image of two women wearing the same dress had completely set his nerves on edge. He added, "Almost, but not quite, heliotrope, I'd say." Then he turned to Soda and said, "I hope you realize that you're entirely to blame for this nonsensical conversation. I really wish you'd learn to keep your quirky artistic opinions to yourself."

"Plum," said Ry. "I hope that helps clarify this mess we're in."

Mr. Schlissel pushed his glasses up the slope of his nose for the thousandth time that day. He stood up and leaned over his companions to get a better look through the window. His protruding bottom lip made a wet smear on the glass while he peered around. "Optimistically speaking—which is a something of a stretch under these circumstance, I admit—if this interruption is temporary, I wonder if we'll make it to Sayville in time for the last ferry. I'd hate to be stranded there after all this inconvenience and terrorization. If it's not temporary, we may get an unexpected chance to visit Millie Bathbaum in outer space."

"Not that I need the money," Lady Asta said to the lawyer offhandedly, "I'm just wondering aloud here—do we have a case against the railroad for this? If I wasn't sitting next to you, it wouldn't have occurred to me, but just being near you makes me think of litigation and punitive damages."

"I think this falls under *force majeure*," he said, stroking his chin. "Otherwise, there might be some actionable claim of liability for 'bait and switch' fraud regarding the excursion, the destination, and so on and so forth."

The old Rabbi was dangling from Radar Robot's hand, suspended roughly eight feet off the ground. He hadn't been this far above sea-level since he visited a fifth-floor dentist on the Grand Concourse to have his tooth cleaned, but that was a few years earlier, and of course, he couldn't remember exactly when. Terrified, he kept his eyes squeezed shut. As an added precaution, he covered them with his beard, holding it over them like a large handkerchief with his left hand, while with his right hand he kept a firm grip on his black beaver hat. At the same time, his feet scrabbled in the air, looking for purchase on something solid. Finally, the robot roughly dumped the squirming rabbi in an empty seat, where he continued to tremble and mumble prayers until, after a few minutes, he began to calm down. That was when he became aware of a strange, guttural sound nearby. Curious, he cautiously lifted a tuft of his beard and uncovered one of his eyes. There was, of all things, a nun in the seat next to him, fast asleep and snoring loudly, only inches from his nose. Her dour face, flat and white as an unkneaded wad of pizza dough, was so close that the rabbi could see himself reflected in each lens of her rimless glasses. To make matters even more bizarre, she suddenly emitted a somnambulistic moan that seemed incongruously sexual in nature. He, in turn, emitted a long-suffering sigh, then mumbled a single word to summarize the latest twist of fate—*"Mitndrinnen"*—after which, still curled up like a fetus, he put his beard back over his eyes.

As for the nun, she was in the throes of a wonderful dream, and she had no incentive to wake up before it had a chance to play itself out. At this point in the narrative, the Bishop, accompanied by Holy Emissaries, was just about to arrive at the Abbey of Saint Pollye Loquaicius to investigate charges of rampant lust. The dreaming nun was ready to bet a year's worth of floor scrubbing and freezer defrosting that the Abbess was going to be excommunicated, expelled, and, thusly impoverished, would fall victim to Satan's perverse sexual machinations which could lead anywhere—even to a liaison with Wigbert, the laughing, lovesick donkey. At least she hoped so. Her dream was in its fifth reel, and she couldn't wait to discover how it all turned out. The *dénouement* was something of a foregone conclusion, though, because all the nun's dreams ended in much the same manner. Everyone always went to Hell—except her. She took great comfort from that. It was unlikely that this dream would be an exception to this well-established pattern.

Another robot entered the carriage carrying a cracked television screen and two severed mechanical arms. Those of the passengers who had already visited the Men's Toilet had seen enough while there to recognize what remained of Monsieur Hercule Poirot. The elegant garnet cuff links and Masonic ring were sufficient forensic evidence to identify the corpse, as was the meticulous manicure. The robot dumped the broken pieces of the detective on the floor and conferred with his colleagues, utilizing a series of irritating squeaking noises. Meanwhile, the damaged television screen emitted static and showed sporadic images of the Belgian detective's face, running through his complete repertoire of programmed facial expressions in quick succession, which made him look as if he was experiencing a looped series of orgasms. His accompanying vocalizations were an indecipherable combination of French, English, Frenglish, and Microsoft Modern Robotic. The two arms, lying in the aisle, were anything but inert. The right one—the one wearing the Masonic ring—was dragging itself towards Radar Robot's leg by limping on its fingertips. After arriving at its destination, the hand alternated between knocking urgently on the robot's leg to get its attention and pointing purposefully at the nearby Professor. The other arm—the left one—was in the process of crawling up the Professor's trousers, hand-hold by hand-hold, seemingly headed for his crotch.

"That just about does it!" the Professor shouted unexpectedly. He bolted to his feet and tried to yank the spasmodic hand off his trousers, but it resisted by digging its nails into the double-knit fabric and wouldn't budge. First, the Professor retrieved a fork from his carpetbag and stabbed the hand repeatedly, but when that effort failed to get it loose, he flicked open a cigarette lighter and burned the pinky finger. That did the trick. The arm fell to the floor and flopped around like a netted salmon. The Professor then stomped on the wriggling fingers with all his might, and a metallic crunch was heard, accompanied by a voice from the loudspeakers on the edges of the television screen that cried out, "My oh *Dieu*, I am for done" or something to that effect.

"I've had all I can take of these intrusive assholes!" the Professor roared, thoroughly exasperated. "An entire day's work come to naught because of this clanking pile of junkyard shit!"

The Professor's sudden transformation was rather shocking for his new acquaintances to behold. He had turned an unhealthy shade of crimson, and his eyes had narrowed with such malice, they resembled deadly gun slits on a bunker more than they did windows of the soul.

A few decisive steps brought him to within inches of the gang of robots. That they towered above him didn't seem to intimidate him in the least. With uncharacteristic aggression and a degree of force that surprised everyone who was watching, he shoved the first robot quite roughly. It tumbled backward and fell against the three full-size robots and the one half-robot looming behind it. Then all five fell to the ground in a heap. Something gave. There was a definite aural indication that something vital had broken. Sparks and squeaks came from the pile and some emergency lights were flashing inside the rubble. Poirot's right arm had managed to take cover in there as well. Its fingers were gathering nearby pieces of broken robot around itself for protection and camouflage.

The collapse of the robots made such a racket, it jolted the nun right out of her dream. Upon sitting upright and opening her eyes she discovered, only inches away from the tip of her nose, what appeared to be a curled-up child with a woolly, gray sweater pulled over its face, wearing a hat five sizes too large for its head. She was quite disoriented and had no idea that the child was actually the crumpled-up rabbi. "Oh, merciful Mother Mary," she whimpered, "please don't tell me I've missed my stop! Where in Heaven's name are we?"

From under his beard, the rabbi replied, "In Hell.'

Hearing that unwelcome news, the nun lapsed back into unconsciousness—only this time she wasn't asleep. She was either in a coma or dead of shock. She certainly wasn't snoring or dreaming about a donkey named Wigbert.

"Get up and get going!" the Professor shouted at the mess at his feet, kicking it for emphasis. The pieces of metal began to move. Noisily, the parts reassembled themselves into a single robot with ten arms. The abundance of arms to assist helped to speed the process considerably. The teamwork involved was impressive. One of the limbs held what was left of Poirot, the others just dangled. The giant robot then stood, inert, waiting for instructions. After a pause, it emitted a little squeak. Another pause. Then the robot began to babble.

"You are *not* excused, and, no, you may *not* take the old man with you," the Professor interrupted, addressing what was, presumably, one or several ears located somewhere within the tangles of metal.

He then turned his attention to the astounded passengers. "Ladies and gentlemen, it has been a pleasure," he announced. "Excuse me while I escort this intrusive pile of bargain-basement hardware back to its vehicle."

"Don't forget your pocketbook, Professor," said Mildred Del Lago, handing him his carpetbag. "And thank you for a wonderful afternoon, and, especially, thank you for saving us."

"Wait and see how the rest of your life turns out," he replied, "before you rush to thank me."

With that, he shouted "March, fool!" to the reassembled robot—if that's what it was—and walked out of most of the passenger's lives forever, leaving behind him only the smoke and shadows of stories—spoken and inspired—as keepsakes of a memorable day. Not one of the ten arms at the robot's disposal (actually nine, because one was holding Poirot) even bothered to wave goodbye.

The sound of an imaginary beating drum faded from hearing—the metaphoric circus had come into town at one end of Main Street and exited at the other with barely a sneeze, featuring far too many fluttering leaflets and not enough laughs—its thrills, spills, and chills vanishing over the curve of the horizon, and in its smoldering wake, a rubble heap, a carpet of peanut shells, watermelon rinds, and denuded corncobs, was all that remained. The unexpected and unexplainable confluence of unicorns and donkeys and foxes and hounds and bakers and owls and spiders and mice and tulips and tapestries and bagels and vampires and donuts and loansharks and losers and a whole wide world of what-not, what-for, and whatever, the glimpses of the sheer fecundity of happenstance's possibilities, mingled with the glorious and deplorable parade of lives and life—in itself resembling a roll of vividly imagined wallpaper imprinted with a design that never repeated itself even once—had suddenly out-spooled itself to a rough-edged end, leaving the passengers with blank expressions and storytelling whiplash.

The calliope had tooted its last. After a day of noise, one could hear the unsettling sound of dust settling. Not a substantive sound was heard for a long time, but it was a foregone conclusion that the first to break ranks would be the lawyer—doctors and morticians always had the last word, lawyers the first. Finally, Mr. Schlissel fulfilled his fellow travelers' expectations when he turned to Mildred Del Lago and fell back on an old-but-reliable tension-breaker. "So, Mrs. Lincoln," Mr. Schlissel said, with an obviously strained show of jocularity. "In spite of all *that*, how was the show?"

Perfectly in keeping with this day of unbridled craziness, it so happened that the real (that is to say, the *formerly* real) Mrs. Lincoln was floating near enough to overhear what he said. She was—to say the least—*not* amused in the least. In fact, she was so thoroughly *unamused* that she permitted herself the unladylike license to kick Mr. Schlissel in the shin. He never felt a thing, but *she* felt better, which is no small accomplishment in the Afterlife.

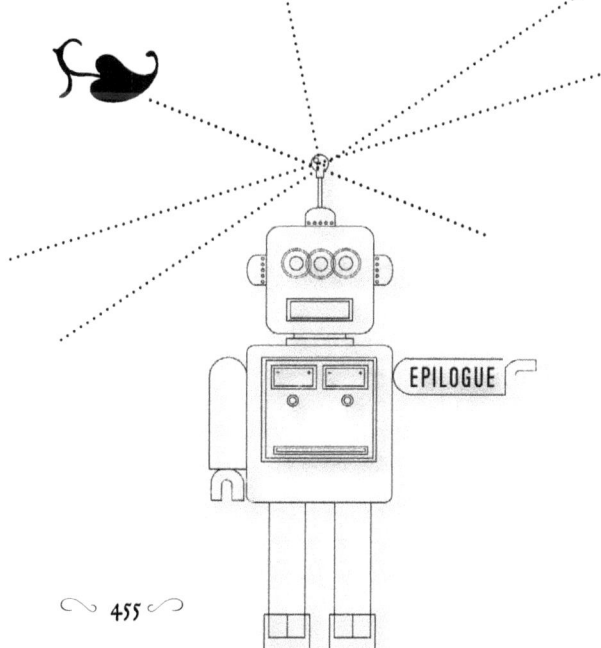

EPILOGUE

Zwölf Boxkämpfer Jagen Victor Quer Über Den Großen Sylter Deich

Zwölf Boxkämpfer jagen Viktor quer über den großen Sylter Deich

Zwölf Boxkämpfer jagen Viktor quer über den großen Sylter Deich

Zwölf Boxkämpfer jagen Viktor quer über den großen Sylter Deich

Zwölf Boxkämpfer jagen Viktor quer über den großen Sylter Deich

Zwölf Boxkämpfer jagen Viktor quer über den großen Sylter Deich

Zwölf Boxkämpfer jagen Viktor quer über den großen Sylter Deich

Zwölf Boxkämpfer jagen Viktor quer über den großen Sylter Deich

Zwölf Boxkämpfer jagen Viktor quer über den großen Sylter Deich

Zwölf Boxkämpfer jagen Viktor quer über den großen Sylter Deich

Zwölf Boxkämpfer jagen Viktor quer über den großen Sylter Deich

Zwölf Boxkämpfer jagen Viktor quer über den großen Sylter

Zwölf Boxkämpfer jagen Viktor quer über den großen Sy

Zwölf Boxkämpfer jagen Viktor quer über den großen

Zwölf Boxkämpfer jagen Viktor quer über den groß

Zwölf Boxkämpfer jagen Viktor quer über den gr

Zwölf Boxkämpfer jagen Viktor quer über den

Zwölf Boxkämpfer jagen Viktor quer über de

Zwölf Boxkämpfer jagen Viktor quer über

Zwölf Boxkämpfer jagen Viktor quer über

Zwölf Boxkämpfer jagen Viktor qu

A Pangrammatic Epilogue, translated from German

Twelve Boxers Chase Victor Across the Great Dike at Sylt

As told by Dr. Théoden Dramstad, a Professor of Folkloric Studies at Tromsø University, to passengers on the Hamburg-Frankfurt Boxkämpfer Express Zug

nce Victor was sure—as Oktoberfest drew near enough to tinge the breezes with the scent of lagerbier, and length-ening shadows rippled upon the awnings of beer gardens all around Sylt—that the time for the 1938 Boxing Festival was soon to follow, he waited with a pounding heart for the annual matches to begin, while thinking of running, running, running, and of little else. Festive folk-dance melodies, cranked out by the out-of-tune *oom-pah-pah* band from the Rathskeller, announced the upcoming re-opening of the Dike, reaching the most cauliflowered ear in the furthest boxing gymnasium on the island of Sylt. From the first note of that warning, Victor knew he would once again be running across the top of the Dike, chased by twelve champion Boxers, culled from the local division of the Schutzstaffel, ac-companied by their vicious Dobermans and Pit Bulls. At a time of the year when others of his kind were happily gathering and eating acorns, walnuts, and chestnuts, the brown Jewish Squirrel would be running for the amusement of the well-fed Damen und Herren of the district, citi-zens of pure Aryan blood, one and all—red-cheeked and laughing and robust. The SS, the police, and the boxing contestants were impeccably turned-out in their uniforms and boots. The Townsfolk, including the Bürgermeister and his Frau, were dressed most colorfully in their leder-hosen, dirndls, and ball-heaped bollenhuts.... *(the story is to be continued af-ter Mittagessen is served in the Speisewagen)*

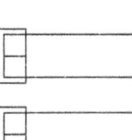

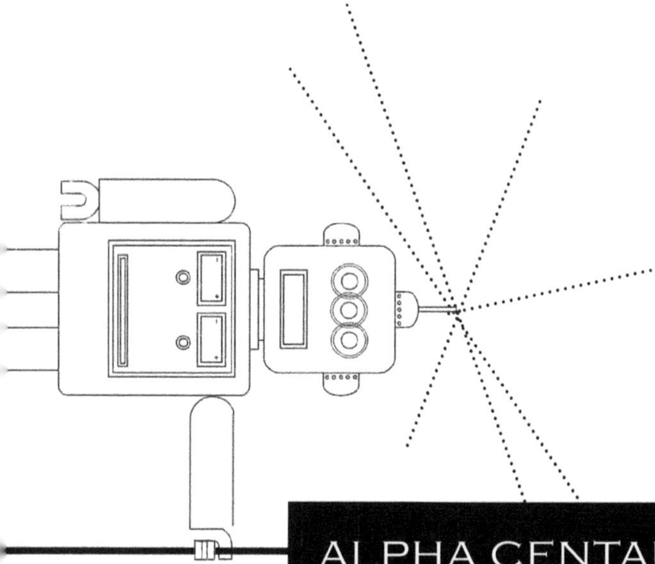

ALPHA CENTAURI TALES

Lightning Source UK Ltd.
Milton Keynes UK
UKHW020628071019
351149UK00013B/1028/P